The lady knows what she wants,
but the scoundrel knows
what she desires...

P9-DOF-808

LINDA HOWARD

"If you read a good book—get this"

"Tell me, Lady Philippa . . ."

"In your study of anatomy, did you ever learn the name of the place between the nose and the lip?"

She resisted the urge to lean toward him, to force him to touch her. She answered on a whisper. "The philtrum."

"Clever girl. The Romans believed it was the most erotic place on the body." As he spoke, he ran his finger along the curve of her lip, a temptation more than a touch, barely there. "They believed it was the mark of the god of love."

She inhaled, low and shallow. "I did not know that."

He leaned down, closer, his hand falling away. "I'd be willing to wager that there are any number of things about the human body that you do not know."

He was so close . . . his words more breath than sound, the feel of them against her ear, then her cheek, sending a riot of sensation through her. "I would like to learn," she said.

"This is your first lesson . . ."

She wanted him to teach her everything.

"Do not tempt the lion," he said, the words brushing across her lips, parting them with their touch. "For he most certainly will bite."

SARAH MacLEAN

One Good Earl Deserves a Lover

THE SECOND RULE OF SCOUNDRELS

AVON

An Imprint of HarperCollinsPublishers

This book is a work of fiction. The characters, incidents, and dialogue are drawn from the author's imagination and are not to be construed as real. Any resemblance to actual events or persons, living or dead, is entirely coincidental.

AVON BOOKS
An Imprint of HarperCollins*Publishers*
10 East 53rd Street
New York, New York 10022-5299

Copyright © 2013 by Sarah Trabucchi
ISBN 978-0-06-206853-8
www.avonromance.com

First Avon Books mass market printing: February 2013

Avon Trademark Reg. U.S. Pat. Off. and in Other Countries, Marca Registrada, Hecho en U.S.A.
HarperCollins® is a registered trademark of HarperCollins Publishers.

Printed in the U.S.A.

10 9 8 7 6 5 4 3 2 1

For girls who wear glasses

Cross

London
Early Spring 1824

There were benefits to being the second son.

Indeed, if there was one truth in society it was this: Rake, rogue, or scoundrel—an heir required reformation. He could wreak his havoc, sow his wild oats, and scandalize society with his youthful indiscretions, but his future was cast in stone by the finest of masons: He would eventually find himself shackled to his title, his land, and his estate—a prisoner of peerage alongside his brethren in the House of Lords.

No, freedom was not for heirs, but for spares. And Jasper Arlesey, the second son of Earl Harlow, knew it. He also knew, with the keen understanding of a criminal narrowly escaping the gallows, that—despite having to forgo heredity title, estate, and fortune—he was the luckiest man on Earth to have been born seventeen months to the day *after* Owen Elwood Arthur Arlesey, eldest child, first son, Viscount Baine and heir to the earldom.

On Baine lay the heavy weight of respectability and responsibility that came with being heir. On Baine rested the

hopes and dreams of a long line of Lords Harlow. It was
Baine who was required to live up to the expectations of
those around him—parents . . . peers . . . servants . . . all.

And flawless, proper, boring Baine lived up to every one
of those expectations.

Thankfully.

Which was why that evening, *Baine* had chaperoned their
younger sister at her first visit to Almack's. Yes, Jasper had
originally agreed to the task, promising Lavinia that he
wouldn't dare miss such an important evening in her young
life. But his promises were more whisper than word—
everyone knew that—and so it had been Baine who had
done the chaperoning. Living up to expectations, as ever.

Jasper, instead, had been busy winning a fortune at one
of London's wickedest gaming hells . . . then celebrating by
doing precisely the kind of thing errant younger sons were
wont to do. In the bed of a beautiful woman.

Baine wasn't the only one who lived up to expectations.

One side of Jasper's mouth kicked up in a private smile as
he recalled the pleasure he'd found in excess that evening,
then faded at the twinge of regret he'd felt as he'd climbed
from warm sheets and willing arms.

He popped the latch on the rear entrance to the Arlesey
House kitchens and crept inside. The room was dark and quiet
in the pale grey light of a bitterly cold March morning, dark
enough to hide his disheveled clothes, half-tied cravat, and the
love bite peeking out from beneath his loosened collar.

As the door closed behind him, a startled kitchen maid
looked up from where she crouched, half-inside the hearth,
stoking the flames in preparation for the arrival of the cook.
She stood, one hand to her lovely, blossoming breast. "My
lord! You gave me a fright!"

Jasper tossed her a wicked grin before offering a bow
that would make a courtier proud. "Apologies, darling," he
drawled, adoring the blush that flared high on her cheeks,
forgiving him.

He leaned past her, brushing close enough to hear the breath catch in her throat, to see the wild pulse at her neck, snatching a hard biscuit from the plate she'd prepared for the rest of the kitchen staff, lingering a touch longer than was required, loving the way she trembled in anticipation.

He wouldn't touch her, of course; he'd learned long ago that the staff was off-limits.

But it didn't stop him from loving her just a little.

From loving all women—all shapes, all sizes, all walks of life. Their soft skin and softer curves, the way they gasped and giggled and sighed, the way the wealthy ones played their coy games, and the less fortunate ones looked at him, stars in their eyes, eager for his attention.

Women were, without a doubt, the Lord's finest creation. And, at twenty-three, he had plans for a lifetime of worshipping them.

He crunched into the sweet biscuit and winked at her. "You won't tell anyone you saw me, will you?"

Her eyes went wide, and she shook her head instantly. "N—no, sir. My lord, sir."

Yes, there were definite benefits to being the second son.

With another wink and another stolen biscuit, Jasper snuck from the kitchens into the back hallway that led to the servants' stairs.

"Where have you been?"

Cloaked in black, Stine, his father's man of affairs, materialized from the shadows, accusation and something much worse on his long, pale face. Jasper's heart raced from the surprise though he'd be damned if he'd admit it. He did not answer to Stine. It was bad enough that he was required to answer to Stine's employer.

Jasper's father.

The man whose expectations for his youngest son were lower than all others' combined.

The son in question rocked back on his heels and grinned with practiced affectation. "Stern," he drawled, enjoying the way the older man's posture stiffened at the misnomer. "It's rather early for haunting, isn't it?"

"Not too early for you."

Jasper smiled, a cat with a canary. "How right you are. Late, instead. I have had a night, and I would prefer you not ruin . . . the afterglow." He clapped the other man on the shoulder and pushed past him.

"Your father is looking for you."

He did not look back. "I'm sure he is. I'm also sure it can wait."

"I don't think it can, Lord Baine."

It took a moment to hear the words. To hear the title. To understand its meaning. He turned, horror and disbelief coursing through him. When he spoke, the words were young and broken, barely a whisper. "What did you call me?"

Stine's gaze narrowed barely. Fleetingly. Later, it would be that nearly imperceptible movement over cold, black eyes that Jasper would remember.

His voice rose, furious. "I asked you a question."

"He called you Baine."

Jasper spun to face his father, Earl Harlow, tall and strong and unbending even now. Even in this moment. Even as his legacy crumbled around him, and he faced his life's disappointment.

Now heir.

Jasper fought for breath, then for words.

His father found them first.

"It should have been you."

Chapter One

*Avenues for investigation have become severely
limited, as has time.*

*In the name of proper enquiry, I have made
adjustments to my research.*

~~Secret~~ Serious adjustments.

The Scientific Journal of Lady Philippa Marbury
March 21, 1831; fifteen days prior to her wedding

Seven years later

The lady was mad.

He would have realized it five minutes earlier if he hadn't
been half-asleep, shocked as hell to find a young, blond, bespectacled female seated at his desk, reading his ledger.

He might have realized it three minutes earlier if she
hadn't announced, all certainty, that he'd miscalculated
column F, ensuring that his understanding of her madness
was preempted by shock at her pluck and admiration for her
mathematical skill. Or perhaps the reverse.

And he most definitely would have realized that the
woman was utterly insane sixty seconds earlier if he hadn't
been rather desperately attempting to clothe himself. For

long moments, his shirt had appeared to lose a rather critical opening, which was a distraction indeed.

Now, however, he was quite awake, had closed the (correctly accounted) ledger, and was fully (if not appropriately) clothed. The universe had righted itself, and rational thought had returned, right around the time she'd explained what it was she wanted.

And there, in the silence that followed her announcement, Cross had understood the truth.

There was no doubt about it: Lady Philippa Marbury, daughter to the Marquess of Needham and Dolby, sister-in-law to the Marquess of Bourne and lady of excellent *ton,* was barking mad.

"I beg your pardon," he said, impressed with his ability to remain civil in the face of her utter insanity. "I am certain I did not hear you correctly."

"Oh, I'm sure you did," the lady said simply, as though commenting on the weather, big blue eyes unsettling and owl-like behind thick spectacles. "I might have given you a shock, but your hearing is quite sound, I should think."

She advanced on him, navigating a path between a half dozen towering stacks of books and a bust of Medusa he'd been meaning to move. The hem of her pale blue skirts brushed against one long serpent's body, and the sound of the fabric rustling against bronze sent a thread of awareness through him.

Wrong.

He was not aware of her. He *would not be* aware of her.

It was too dark in this damned room. He moved to light a lamp a good distance away, near the door. When he looked up from the task, it was to find that she had altered her course.

She came closer, crowding him back toward the heavy mahogany, throwing him off-kilter. For a moment, he considered opening the door just to see if she might charge through, leaving him in the office, alone and free from her.

From what she represented. Able to close the portal firmly behind her, pretend this encounter had never happened, and restart his day.

He knocked into a large abacus, and the rattle of ebony yanked him from his thoughts.

He stopped moving.

She kept coming.

He was one of the most powerful men in Britain, part-owner of London's most notorious gaming hell, easily ten inches taller than she, and rather fearsome when he wanted to be.

She was neither the kind of woman he was conditioned to notice nor the kind of woman who expected to receive his notice. And she was certainly not the kind of woman who rattled his control.

Pull yourself together, man.

"Stop."

She stopped, the word hanging harsh and defensive between them. He did not like it. Did not like what the strangled sound said about the way this strange creature had instantly affected him.

But she didn't see any of that, thank God. Instead, she tilted her head the way a puppy might, curious and eager, and he resisted the temptation to take a good long look at her.

She was not for looking at.

Certainly not for looking at *by him.*

"Shall I repeat myself?" she asked when he said nothing else.

He did not reply. Repetition was unnecessary. Lady Philippa Marbury's request was fairly burned into his memory.

Nevertheless, she lifted one hand, pushed her spectacles back on her nose, and took a deep breath. "I require ruination." The words were as simple and unwavering now as they had been the first time she'd spoken them, devoid of nervousness.

Ruination. He watched the way her lips curved around the syllables, caressing consonants, lingering on vowels, turning the experience of hearing the word into something startlingly akin to its meaning.

It had become quite warm in his office.

"You're mad."

She paused, clearly taken aback by the statement. Good. It was time someone other than he was surprised by the events of the day. Finally, she shook her head. "I don't think so."

"You ought to seriously consider the possibility," he said, edging past her, increasing the space between them—a difficult endeavor in the cluttered office, "as there is no additional rational explanation for why you would be unchaperoned in London's most notorious gaming hell, asking to be ruined."

"It's not as though a chaperone would have been rational," she pointed out. "Indeed, a chaperone would have made this whole scenario impossible."

"Precisely," he said, taking a long step over a stack of newspapers, ignoring the scent of fresh linen and sunlight that curled around her. Around him.

"Indeed, bringing a chaperone to 'London's most notorious gaming hell' would have been rather more mad, don't you think?" She reached out and ran one finger along the massive abacus. "This is beautiful. Do you use it often?"

He was distracted by the play of her long, pale fingers over the black rounds, by the way the tip of her index finger canted slightly to the right. Imperfect.

Why wasn't she wearing gloves? Was there nothing normal about this woman?

"No."

She turned to him, her blue eyes curious. "No, you don't use the abacus? Or no, you don't think that coming with a chaperone would have been mad?"

"Neither. The abacus is unwieldy—"

She pushed one large disc from one side of the frame to the other. "You can get things done more quickly without it?"

"Precisely."

"The same is true of chaperones," she said, serious. "I am much more productive without them."

"I find you much more dangerous without them."

"You think me a danger, Mr. Cross?"

"Cross. No need for the mister. And yes. I think you a danger."

She was not insulted. "To you?" Indeed, she sounded pleased with herself.

"Mainly to yourself, but if your brother-in-law should find you here, I imagine you'd be something of a danger to me, as well." Old friend, business partner, or no, Bourne would have Cross's head if Lady Philippa were discovered here.

She seemed to accept the explanation. "Well then, I shall be quick about it."

"I'd rather you be quick about leaving."

She shook her head, her tone rising just enough to make him aware of it. Of her. "Oh no. I'm afraid that won't do. You see, I have a very clear plan, and I require your assistance."

He had reached his desk, thank God. Lowering himself into the creaking chair, he opened the ledger and pretended to look over the figures there, ignoring the fact that her presence blurred the numbers to unintelligible grey lines. "I am afraid, Lady Philippa, that your plan is not a part of *my* plans. You've come all this way for nothing." He looked up. "How did you come to be here, anyway?"

Her unwavering gaze wavered. "The usual way, I imagine."

"As we've established, the usual way involves a chaperone. And does not involve a gaming hell."

"I walked."

A beat. "You walked."

"Yes."

"Alone."

"In broad daylight." There was an edge of defensiveness in her tone.

"You walked across London—"

"Not very far. Our home is—"

"A half mile up the Thames."

"You needn't say it as though it's Scotland."

"You walked across London in broad daylight to the entrance of The Fallen Angel, where I assume you knocked and waited for entry."

She pursed her lips. He refused to be distracted by the movement. "Yes."

"On a public street."

"In *Mayfair.*"

He ignored the emphasis. "A public street that is home to the most exclusive men's clubs in London." He paused. "Were you seen?"

"I couldn't say."

Mad. "I assume you know that ladies do not do such things?"

A tiny wrinkle appeared between her brows. "It's a silly rule, don't you think? I mean, the female sex has had access to bipedal locomotion since . . . well . . . Eve."

Cross had known many many women in his lifetime. He'd enjoyed their company, their conversation, and their curiosity. But he'd never once met a woman as strange as this one. "Nevertheless, it is 1831. In the present day, females such as you use carriages. And they do not frequent gaming hells."

She smiled. "Well, not *precisely* such as me, as I walked, and here I am. In a gaming hell."

"Who let you in?"

"A man. He appeared eager to do so when I announced myself."

"No doubt he was. Bourne would take pleasure in destroying him if your reputation had suffered."

She considered the words. "I hadn't thought of that. Indeed, I've never had a protector."

He could protect her.

Where had that come from?

No matter. "Lady Philippa, it appears that you require an army of protectors." He returned his attention to the ledger. "Unfortunately, I have neither the time nor inclination to enlist. I trust you can see yourself out."

She advanced, ignoring him. He looked up, surprised. People did not ignore him. "Oh, there's no need to Lady Philippa me, really. Not considering my reason for being here. Please, call me Pippa."

Pippa. It suited her. More so than the fuller, more extravagant version of the name. But he had no intention of calling her such a thing. He had no intention of calling her at all. "Lady Philippa"—he let the name stretch between them purposefully—"it is time for you to leave."

She took another step in his direction, one hand coming to rest on the large globe to the side of his desk. He slid his gaze to the place where her flat palm smothered Britain and resisted the urge to draw cosmic meaning from the gesture.

"I am afraid I cannot leave, Mr. Cross. I require—"

He didn't think he could bear her saying it again. "Ruination. Yes. You've made your purpose clear. As I have similarly made my refusal."

"But . . . you can't refuse."

He returned his attention to the ledger. "I'm afraid I have."

She did not reply, but out of the corner of his eye, he could see her fingers—those strange, improper fingers, trailing the edge of his ebony desk. He waited for them to stop. To still. To go away.

When he looked up, she was staring down at him, blue eyes enormous behind the round lenses of her spectacles, as though she would have waited a lifetime for him to meet her gaze. "I selected you, Mr. Cross. Quite carefully. I have a very specific, very clear, very time-sensitive plan. And it requires a research associate. You, you see, are to be that associate."

A research associate?

He didn't care. *He didn't.*

"What research?"

Damn.

Her hands came together, tightly clasped. "You are quite legendary, sir."

The words sent a chill through him.

"Everyone talks about you. They say you are an expert in the critical aspects of ruination."

He gritted his teeth, hating her words, and feigned disinterest. "Do they?"

She nodded happily and ticked items off on her fingers quickly as she spoke. "Indeed. Gaming, spirits, pugilism, and—" She stopped. "And—"

Her cheeks were awash in red, and he wanted her to consider the rest. To hear its absurdity. To stop this madness. "And . . . ?"

She righted herself, spine straight. He would have wagered everything he had on her not replying.

He would have lost.

"And coitus." The word was soft, and came on a firm exhale, as though she'd finally said what she'd come to say. Which couldn't be possible. Surely he'd misheard her. Surely his body was responding incorrectly to her.

Before he could ask her to repeat herself, she took another breath and continued. "That's the bit at which you are purported to be the most proficient. And, honestly, that's the bit I require."

Only years of playing cards with the most skilled gamers in Europe kept Cross from revealing his shock. He took a good, long look at her.

She did not look like a lunatic.

In fact, she looked rather ordinary—hair an ordinary blond, eyes an ordinary blue, slightly taller than average, but not too tall as to draw attention to herself, dressed in an ordinary frock that revealed a perfectly ordinary expanse of plain, pure skin.

No, there was nothing at all to suggest that Lady Philippa Marbury, daughter of one of the most powerful peers in Britain, was anything other than a perfectly ordinary young woman.

Nothing, that was, until she opened her mouth and said things like, *bipedal locomotion.*

And *coitus.*

She sighed. "You are making this very difficult, you know."

Not knowing quite what to say, he tried for, "I apologize."

Her gaze narrowed slightly behind her spectacles. "I am not certain I believe your contrition, Mr. Cross. If the gossip in ladies' salons across London is to be believed—and I assure you, there is a great deal of it—you are a proper rake."

Lord deliver him from ladies and their flapping tongues. "You should not believe everything you hear in ladies' salons."

"I usually do not, but when one hears as much about a particular gentleman as I have heard about you . . . one tends to believe there is a kernel of truth in the gossip. Where there is smoke, there is flame and all that."

"I cannot imagine what you have heard."

It was a lie. Of course he knew.

She waved one hand. "Well, some of it is utter nonsense. They say, for example, that you can relieve a lady of her clothing without the use of your hands."

"Do they?"

She smiled. "Silly, I know. I definitely do not believe that."

"Why not?"

"In the absence of physical force, an object at rest remains at rest," she explained.

He couldn't resist. "Ladies' clothing is the object at rest in this particular scenario?"

"Yes. And the physical force required to move said object would be your hands."

Did she have any idea what a tempting picture she'd painted with such precise, scientific description? He didn't think so. "I am told they are very talented."

She blinked. "As we have established, I have been told the same. But I assure you, sir, they do not defy the laws of physics."

Oh, how he wanted to prove her wrong.

But she had already moved on. "At any rate. This one's maid's sister, that one's cousin's friend, the other's friend's cousin or maid's cousin . . . women talk, Mr. Cross. And you should be aware that they are not ashamed to reveal details. About you."

He raised a brow. "What kind of details?"

She hesitated, and the blush returned. He resisted the pleasure that coursed through him at the pretty pink wash. Was there anything more tempting than a woman flushed with scandalous thoughts?

"I am told you are the kind of gentleman who has a keen understanding of the . . . mechanics . . . of the act in question." She was utterly, completely matter-of-fact. As though they were discussing the weather.

She had no idea what she was doing. What beast she was tempting. What she did have, however, was courage—the kind that was bound to drive fine, upstanding ladies directly into trouble.

And he knew better than to be a party to it.

He placed both hands on the top of his desk, stood and, for the first time that afternoon, spoke the truth. "I am afraid you were told wrong, Lady Philippa. And it is time for you to leave. I shall do you a service and neglect to tell your brother-in-law that you were here. In fact, I shall forget you were here at all."

She stilled for a long moment, and he realized that her lack of movement was out of character. The woman had not been still since he'd woken to the soft sound of her fingertips sliding over the pages of the ledger. The fact that she was still now unnerved him; he steeled himself for what came next, for some logical defense, some strange turn of phrase that would tempt him more than he was willing to admit.

"I suppose it will be easy for you to forget me."

There was nothing in the tone to suggest that she angled for a compliment or a refusal. Nothing he would have expected from other women. Though he was coming to realize that there was nothing about Lady Philippa Marbury that was at all like other women.

And he was willing to guarantee that it would be impossible to forget her.

"But I'm afraid that I cannot allow it," she pressed on, frustration clear in her tone as he had the impression that she was speaking to herself rather than to him. "I have a great deal of questions, and no one to answer them. And I've only fourteen days to learn."

"What happens in fourteen days?"

Dammit. He didn't care. He shouldn't have asked.

Surprise flashed at the question, and he had the sense that she had forgotten him. She tilted her head again, brow furrowed as though his query was ridiculous. Which, of course, it was.

"I am to be married."

That, he knew. For two seasons, Lady Philippa had been courted by Lord Castleton, a young dandy with little between his ears. But Cross had forgotten her future husband the moment she'd introduced herself, bold, brilliant and not a little bit bizarre.

There was nothing about this woman to indicate that she would make an even-halfway-decent Countess of Castleton.

It's not your problem.

He cleared his throat. "My very best wishes."

"You don't even know who my husband is to be."

"As a matter of fact, I do."

Her brows shot up. "You do? How?"

"Aside from the facts that your brother-in-law is my business partner, and that the double wedding of the final sisters Marbury is the talk of the *ton,* you will find that there are few things that happen at any level of society about which I do not know." He paused. "Lord Castleton is fortunate indeed."

"That's very gracious of you."

He shook his head. "Not grace. Truth."

One side of her mouth twitched. "And me?"

He crossed his arms over his chest. She'd be bored of Castleton within twenty-four hours of their marriage. And then she'd be miserable.

It's not your problem.

"Castleton is a gentleman."

"How diplomatic," she said, spinning the globe and letting her fingers trail across the raised topography on the sphere as it whirled around. "Lord Castleton is indeed that. He is also an earl. And he likes dogs."

"And these are the qualities women seek in husbands these days?"

Hadn't she been about to leave? Why, then, was he still speaking to her?

"They're better than some of the lesser qualities with which husbands might arrive," she offered, and he thought he heard an edge of defensiveness in her tone.

"For example?"

"Infidelity. Tendency toward drink. Interest in bull-baiting."

"Bull-baiting?"

She nodded once, curtly. "A cruel sport. For the bull and the dogs."

"Not a sport at all, I would argue. But more importantly, are you familiar with a great deal of men who enjoy it?"

She pushed her glasses high on the bridge of her nose. "I read quite a bit. There was a very serious discussion of the practice in last week's *News of London.* More men than you would think seem to enjoy its barbarism. Thankfully, not Lord Castleton."

"A veritable prince among men," Cross said, ignoring the

way her gaze narrowed at the sarcasm in his tone. "Imagine my surprise, then, to find his future countess at my bedside this very morning, asking to be ruined."

"I did not know you slept here," she said. "Nor did I expect you to be asleep at one o'clock in the afternoon."

He raised a brow. "I work quite late."

She nodded. "I imagine so. You really should purchase a bed, however." She waved a hand toward his makeshift pallet. "That cannot be comfortable."

She was steering them away from the topic at hand. And he wanted her out of his office. Immediately. "I am not interested, nor should you be, in aiding you in public ruination."

Her gaze snapped to his, shock in her eyes. "I am not requesting public ruination."

Cross liked to think he was a reasoned, intelligent man. He was fascinated by science and widely considered to be a mathematical genius. He could not sit a *vingt-et-un* game without counting cards, and he argued politics and the law with quiet, logical precision.

How was it, then, that he felt so much like an imbecile with this woman?

"Have you not, twice in the last twenty minutes, requested I ruin you?"

"Three times, really." She tilted her head to the side. "Well, the last time, *you* said the word *ruination,* but I think it should count as a request."

Like a *complete* imbecile.

"Three times, then."

She nodded. "Yes. But not *public* ruination. That's altogether different."

He shook his head. "I find myself returning to my original diagnosis, Lady Philippa."

She blinked. "Madness?"

"Precisely."

She was silent for a long moment, and he could see her attempting to find the right words to sway him toward her request. She looked down at his desk, her gaze falling to a pair of heavy silver pendula sitting side by side. She reached out and set them in gentle motion. They watched the heavy weights sway in perfect synchrony for a long moment.

"Why do you have these?" she asked.

"I like the movement." Their predictability. What moved in one direction would eventually move in the other. No questions. No surprises.

"So did Newton," she said, simply, quietly, speaking more to herself than to him. "In fourteen days, I shall marry a man with whom I have little in common. I shall do it because it is what I am expected to do as a lady of society. I shall do it because it is what all of London is waiting for me to do. I shall do it because I don't think there will ever be an opportunity for me to marry someone with whom I have more in common. And most importantly, I shall do it because I have agreed to, and I do not care for dishonesty."

He watched her, wishing he could see her eyes without the shield of thick glass from her spectacles. She swallowed, a ripple of movement along the delicate column of her throat. "Why do you think you will not find someone with whom you have more in common?"

She looked up at him and said simply, "I'm odd."

His brows rose, but he did not speak. He was not certain what one said in response to such an announcement.

She smiled at his hesitation. "You needn't be gentlemanly about it. I'm not a fool. I've been odd my whole life. I should count my blessings that anyone is willing to marry me—and thank heavens that an *earl* wants to marry me. That he's actually *courted* me.

"And, honestly, I'm quite happy with the way the future is shaping up. I shall move to Sussex and never be required to frequent Bond Street or ballrooms again. Lord Castleton has offered to give me space for my hothouse and my experiments, and he's even asked me to help him manage the estate. I think he's happy to have the assistance."

Considering Castleton was a perfectly nice, perfectly un-intelligent man, Cross imagined the earl was celebrating the fact that his brilliant fiancée was willing to run the family estate and save him the complications. "That sounds wonderful. Is he going to give you a pack of hounds as well?"

If she noticed the sarcasm in his words, she did not show it, and he found himself regretting the tone. "I expect so. I'm rather looking forward to it. I like dogs quite a bit." She stopped, tilting her chin to the side, staring up at the ceiling for a moment before saying, "But I am concerned about the rest."

He shouldn't ask. Marriage vows were not a thing to which he'd ever given much thought. He certainly wasn't going to start now. "The rest?"

She nodded. "I feel rather unprepared, honestly. I haven't any idea about the activities that take place *after* the marriage . . . in the evening . . . in the *bed* of the marriage," she added, as though he might not understand.

As though he did not have a very clear vision of this woman in her marriage bed.

"And to be honest, I find the marriage vows rather specious."

His brows rose. "The vows?"

She nodded. "Well, the bit before the vows, to be specific."

"I sense that specificity is of great importance to you."

She smiled, and the office grew warmer. "You see? I knew you would make an excellent research associate." He did not reply, and she filled the silence, reciting deliberately, *"Marriage is not by any to be enterprised, nor taken in hand unadvisedly, lightly, or wantonly."*

He blinked.

"That is from the ceremony," she explained.

It was, without a doubt, the only time someone had quoted

the Book of Common Prayer in his office. Possibly, in the entire building. Ever. "That sounds reasonable."

She nodded. "I agree. But it goes on. Neither is it to be enterprised, nor taken in hand *to satisfy men's carnal lusts and appetites, like brute beasts that have no understanding.*"

He couldn't help himself. "That's in the ceremony?"

"Strange, isn't it? I mean, if I were to refer to carnal lust in conversation over, say, tea, I should be tossed out of the *ton,* but before God and London in St. George's, that's fine." She shook her head. "No matter. You can see why I might be concerned."

"You are overthinking it, Lady Philippa. Lord Castleton may not be the sharpest of wits, but I have no doubt he'll find his way in the marriage bed."

Her brows snapped together. "I do have a doubt."

"You shouldn't."

"I don't think you understand," she said. "It is critical that I know what to expect. That I am prepared for it. Well. Don't you see? This is all wrapped up in the single most important task I shall have as wife."

"Which is?"

"Procreation."

The word—scientific and unemotional—should not have called to him. It should not have conjured long limbs, and soft flesh, and wide, bespectacled eyes. But it did.

He shifted uncomfortably as she went on. "I quite like children, so I'm sure that bit will be fine. But you see, I require the understanding in question. And, since you are purported to be such an expert on the topic, I could not imagine anyone better to assist me in my research."

"The topic of children?"

She sighed her frustration. "The topic of breeding."

He should like to teach her everything he knew about breeding.

"Mr. Cross?"

He cleared his throat. "You don't know me."

She blinked. Apparently the thought had not occurred to her. "Well. I know *of* you. That is enough. You shall make an excellent research associate."

"Research in what?"

"I have done a great deal of reading on the subject, but I would like to better understand it. So that I might happily enter into marriage without any concerns. To be honest, the brute-beast bit is rather unnerving."

"I imagine it is," he said dryly.

And still, she talked, as though he weren't there. "I also understand that for women who are . . . untried . . . sometimes the act in question is not entirely . . . pleasant. In that particular case, the research will help, I should think. In fact, I hypothesize that if I have the benefit of your vast experience, both Castleton and I will have a more enjoyable time of it. We'll have to do it several times before it takes, I'm guessing, so anything you can do to shed light on the activity . . ."

For some reason, it was growing difficult for Cross to hear her. To hear his own thoughts. Surely she hadn't just said . . .

"They're coupled pendula."

What?

He followed the direction of her gaze, to the swaying metal orbs, set in motion in the same direction, now moving in opposition to each other. No matter how precisely they were set along the same path, one of the large weights would ultimately reverse its position. Always.

"They are."

"One impacts the movement of the other," she said, simply.

"That is the theory, yes."

She nodded, watching the silver orbs swing toward each other, and away. Once. Twice. She looked up at him, all seriousness. "If I am to take a vow, I should like to understand all the bits and pieces of it. Carnal lust is no doubt something I should understand. And do you know why marriage might appeal to men as brute beasts?"

A vision flashed, crooked fingertips on flesh, blue eyes blinking up at him, wide with pleasure.

Yes. He absolutely knew. "No."

She nodded once, taking him at his word. "It obviously has something to do with coitus."

Dear God.

She explained. "There's a bull in Coldharbor, where my father's estate is. I am not as green as you think."

"If you think that a bull in a pasture is anything like a human male, you are absolutely as green as I think."

"You see? That is precisely why I require your assistance."

Shit. He'd walked right into her trap. He forced himself not to move. To resist her pull.

"I understand you're very good at it," she continued, unaware of the havoc she was quietly wreaking. Or, perhaps entirely aware. He could no longer tell. Could no longer trust himself. "Is that true?"

"No," he said, instantly. Perhaps it would make her leave.

"I know enough about men to know that they wouldn't admit a lack of faculty in this area, Mr. Cross. Surely you don't expect me to believe that." She laughed, the sound bright and fresh and out of place in this dark room. "As an obvious man of science . . . I should think you would be willing to assist me in my research."

"Your research in the mating habits of bulls?"

Her smile turned amused. "My research in carnal lust and appetites."

There was only one option. Terrifying her into leaving. Insulting her into it. "You're asking me to fuck you?"

Her eyes went wide. "Do you know, I've never heard that word spoken aloud."

And, like that, with her simple, straightforward pronouncement, he felt like vermin. He opened his mouth to apologize.

She beat him to it, speaking as though he were a child. As though they were discussing something utterly ordinary. "I see I wasn't clear. I don't want you to *perform* the act, so to speak. I would simply like you to help me to better understand it."

"Understand it."

"Precisely. Per the vows and the children and the rest." She paused, then added, "A lecture of sorts. In animal husbandry. Of sorts."

"Find someone else. Of another sort."

Her gaze narrowed at his mocking tone. "There is no one else."

"Have you looked?"

"Who do you think would explain the process to me? Certainly not my mother."

"And what of your sisters? Have you asked them?"

"First, I'm not certain that Victoria or Valerie have much interest in or experience with the act itself. And Penelope . . . She turns absurd when asked about anything to do with Bourne. On about love and whatnot." She rolled her eyes. "There's no place for love in research."

His brows rose. "No?"

She looked appalled. "Certainly not. You, however, are a man of science with legendary experience. I'm sure there are plenty of things you are able to clarify. For example, I'm very curious about the male member."

He choked. Then coughed.

When he regained his ability to speak, he said, "I'm sure you are."

"I've seen drawings of course—in anatomical texts—but perhaps you could help with some of the specifics? For example—"

"No." He cut her off before she elaborated with one of her straightforward, scientific questions.

"I am happy to pay you," she announced. "For your services."

A harsh, strangled sound cut through the room. It came from him. "Pay me."

She nodded. "Would, say, twenty-five pounds do?"

"No."

Her brows knit together. "Of course, a person of your— prowess—is worth more. I apologize for the offense. Fifty? I'm afraid I can't go much higher. It's quite a bit of money."

She believed that it was the *amount* of money that made the offer offensive? She didn't understand that he was half a tic from doing it for free. From paying *her* for the chance to show her everything for which she asked.

In all his life, there had never been anything Cross had wanted to do more than throw this strange woman down on his desk and give her precisely that for which she was asking.

Desire was irrelevant. Or perhaps it was the only thing that was relevant. Either way, he could not assist Lady Philippa Marbury.

She was the most dangerous female he'd ever met.

He shook his head and said the only words he trusted himself to say. Short. To the point. "I am afraid I am unable to accommodate your request, Lady Philippa. I suggest you query another. Perhaps your fiancé." He hated the suggestion even as he made it. Bit back the urge to rescind it.

She was quiet for a long moment, blinking up at him from behind her thick spectacles, reminding him that she was untouchable.

He waited for her to redouble her efforts. To come at him again with her straight looks and her forthright words.

Of course, there was nothing predictable about this woman.

"I do wish you'd call me Pippa," she said, and with that, she turned and left.

Chapter Two

$\mathcal{W}$hen Pippa was no more than six or seven, the five daughters Marbury had been paraded about for a musical interlude (as hosts' children often were) like little blond ducks before a gathering of peers at a country house party, the details of which she could no longer remember.

As they exited the room, an older gentleman with laughing eyes had stopped her and asked which instrument she preferred to play. Now, had the gentleman inquired such a thing of Penelope, she would have answered with complete assurance that the pianoforte was her favorite. Had he asked Victoria or Valerie, the twins would have replied in unison that they enjoyed the cello. And Olivia would have won him with her five-year-old smile—coy even then—and told him that she liked horns.

But he'd mistakenly asked Pippa, who had proudly announced that she had little time for music, as she was too busy learning general anatomy. Mistaking the gentleman's quiet shock for interest, she'd then proceeded to lift the skirts of her pinafore and proudly name the bones of her foot and leg.

She got as far as the fibula before her mother had arrived,

shrieking her name against the quiet musical backdrop of society's laughter.

That was the first time Pippa realized that she was odd.

It was also the first time she'd ever been embarrassed. It was a strange emotion—entirely different from all the others, which seemed to fade with time. Once one had eaten, for example, it was difficult to recall the precise characteristics of hunger. Certainly, one remembered wishing one had food, but the keen desire for sustenance was not easily recalled.

Similarly, Pippa was no stranger to irritation—she had four sisters, after all—but she could not exactly remember the way it felt to be utterly, infuriatingly irritated with any one of them. Lord knew there had been days when she could have cheerfully pushed Olivia from a moving carriage, but she couldn't resurrect the emotion now.

She could remember, however, the hot embarrassment that came with the laughter at that country gathering as though it had happened yesterday. As though it had happened moments ago.

But what had *actually* happened moments ago seemed somehow worse than showing half of the *Beau Monde* one's seven-year-old ankles. Being labeled the strangest Marbury from such a young age allowed for one to develop something of a thick skin. It took much more than snickers from behind fans to rouse Pippa's embarrassment.

Apparently, it took a man refusing her request for ruination.

A very tall, clearly intelligent, obviously fascinating man.

She had done her best—laid out her proposal in detail, appealed to him as a man of science—and still, he'd refused.

She hadn't considered that possibility.

She should have, of course. She should have recognized it the moment she stepped inside that glorious office—filled with all manner of interesting things—should have known that her offer would not intrigue him. Mr. Cross was obviously a man of knowledge and experience, and she was the fourth daughter of a double marquess, who could name all the bones in the human body and was therefore somewhat abnormal.

It mattered not a bit that she required a research associate and that she had a mere fourteen days—just 336 dwindling hours—to resolve all her questions regarding her future marriage.

He'd obviously completed plenty of his own experimentation and did not require a research associate.

Not even one who was willing to pay him.

Looking around the large, empty main room of the casino, she supposed she should not have been surprised by that either. After all, a man who owned a casino that dealt in the kind of finances accounted in the large, leather-bound ledger she'd discovered when she'd entered his office was not the kind of man who could be tempted by twenty-five pounds. Or fifty.

That, she should have considered.

It was a pity, really. He'd seemed altogether promising. The most promising option when she'd conceived of the plan, several nights earlier after reading the text of the ceremony to which she would be a party in two weeks' time.

Carnal lust.

Procreation.

It was wrong, was it not, that a woman was made party to such things without any experience? Without even a sound explanation of the items in question? And that was before the priest even came to the bits relating to obedience and servitude.

It was all entirely unsettling.

Even more unsettling when she considered how disappointed she'd been that Mr. Cross had refused her.

She would have liked to have spent more time with his abacus.

Not just the abacus.

Pippa did not believe in lying, either to herself or to others. It was perfectly fine if those around her wanted to hide the truth, but she had found long ago that dishonesty only made for more work in the long run.

So, no, it was not only the abacus that intrigued her.

It was the man himself. When she'd arrived at the club, she'd expected to find the Cross of legend—handsome and clever and charming and able to strip the clothes from any female in his presence in a matter of seconds . . . without the use of his hands.

But she hadn't found that man at all. There was no doubt he was clever, but there hadn't been much charm at all in their interaction, and as for handsome—well, he was very tall, all long limbs and sharp angles, with a mop of finger-combed ginger hair that she would never have imagined he'd have. No, he wasn't handsome. Not classically.

He was interesting. Which was much better.

Or worse, as the case may be.

He was clearly knowledgeable in the areas of physics and geography, and he was good with numbers—she would wager that the lack of scratch paper on his desk pointed to his ability to calculate the ledger in his head. Impressive, considering the sheer quantity of numbers held therein.

And he slept on the floor.

Half-nude.

That part was rather curious.

Pippa liked curious.

But apparently he did not. And that was critical.

She'd gone through a great deal of trouble concocting a plan, however, and she would not let the contrariness of one man—however fascinating—get in her way. She was in a gaming hell, after all. And gaming hells were purported to be filled with men. Surely there was another man who might be more amenable to her request. She was a scientist, and scientists were nothing if not adaptable.

Pippa would, therefore, adapt and do whatever it took to gain the understanding that she required to ensure that she was completely prepared on the evening of her marriage.

Her *marriage*.

She didn't like to say it—she didn't like to even think it—but the Earl of Castleton wasn't exactly the most exciting of potential husbands. Oh, he was fair to look at and titled, which her mother appreciated. And he had a lovely estate.

But he wasn't very smart. Even that was a generous way of putting it. He'd once asked her what part of the pig the sausage came from. She did not want to even consider what he believed the answer to be.

It wasn't that she didn't *want* to marry him. He was no doubt her best option, dull or less than brilliant or otherwise. He knew he lacked intellectual prowess and seemed more than willing—eager, in fact—to have Pippa help him manage his estate and run his house. She was looking forward to it, having read a number of texts on crop rotation, modern irrigation, and animal husbandry.

She would be an excellent wife in that sense.

It was the rest about which she had questions. And she had fourteen days in which to discover the answers.

Was that too much to ask?

Apparently so. She cast a look at the now-closed door to Mr. Cross's rooms, and felt a pang of something not altogether pleasant in her chest. Regret? Discontent? It did not matter. What mattered was, she had to reconsider her plan.

She sighed, and the noise swirled around her, drawing her attention to the enormous, empty room.

She had been so focused on finding her way to Mr. Cross's private offices earlier that she hadn't had an opportunity to explore the casino itself. Like most women in London, she'd heard the gossip about The Fallen Angel—that it was an impressive, scandalous place where ladies did not belong. That it was on the floor of the Angel and not that of Parliament where men forged the future of Britain. That it was the owners of the Angel who wielded London's most insidious power.

Considering the quiet, cavernous room, Pippa conceded that it was certainly an impressive space . . . but the rest of the gossip seemed slightly exaggerated. There wasn't much to say about this place except that it was . . .

Rather dark.

A small row of windows near the ceiling on one side of the room was the only source of light, allowing a few errant rays of sunshine in. Pippa followed one long shaft of light, peppered with slow, swirling particles of dust, to where it struck a heavy oak table several feet away, lighting thick green baize painted in white and yellow letters, numbers, and lines.

She approached, a strange grid of numbers and words printed down the long oval coming into view, and she could not resist reaching down to run her fingers across the fabric, along the markings—hieroglyphs to her—until she brushed up against a row of perfect white dice stacked against one wall of the table.

Lifting a pair, she examined the perfect dimples in them, testing the weight of the little ivory squares in her palm, wondering at the power they held. They seemed innocuous enough—barely worth considering—and yet, men lived and died by their toss. Long ago, her brother-in-law had lost everything on one wager. True, he'd earned it all back, but Pippa wondered at the temptation that made one do something so foolish.

No doubt, there was power in the little white cubes.

She rattled them in her palm, imagining a wager of her own—imagining what it would take to tempt her to game. Her research. An understanding of the secrets of marriage, of married life. Of motherhood. Clear expectations for that too-cloudy future.

Answers. Where she had none.

Information that would ease the tightness in her chest that cloyed every time she considered her marriage.

If she could wager for that . . . she would.

She rotated the dice in her hands, wondering at the wager that would bring revelation before she could establish her fate, however, a thunderous pounding at the door of the club gained her attention with its loud and unceasing racket. She set the dice on the edge of the hazard table and moved toward the noise before realizing that she had nothing to do with the door in question and should, therefore, not open it.

Bang.

Bang bang.

She cast a furtive look about the massive room. Surely *someone* heard the clatter. A maid, a kitchen girl, the be-spectacled gentleman who had facilitated her own entrance?

Bang bang bang.

No one appeared to be in hearing distance.

Perhaps she should fetch Mr. Cross?

The thought gave her pause. Or, rather, the way the thought brought with it a vision of Mr. Cross's disheveled ginger hair standing at haphazard angles before he ran his fingers through it and restored it to right gave her pause. The strange increase of her heartbeat at the thought gave her pause. She wrinkled her nose. She did not care for that increase. It was not altogether comfortable.

Bangbangbangbangbang.

The person at the door seemed to be losing patience. And redoubling commitment.

Clearly, his or her matter was urgent.

Pippa headed for the door, which was masked behind a set of heavy velvet curtains that hung from twenty feet up, solid mahogany standing barely open, shielding a small, dark entryway, quiet and unsettling—a River Styx between the club and the outside world.

She moved through the blackness to the exterior steel door, even larger than its interior partner, closed against the day beyond. In the dim light, she ran her hand along the seam where door met jamb, disliking the way the darkness suggested that someone could reach out and touch her without her ever even knowing he was there. She threw one bolt and another before turning the massive handle built into the door and pulling it open, closing her eyes instinctively against the grey March afternoon that seemed somehow like the brightest summer day after her time in the Angel.

"Well, I'll tell you, I hadn't expected such a pretty greeting."

Pippa opened her eyes at the lecherous words, raising her hand to help her vision adjust to the light.

There were few things she could say with certainty about the man in front of her, classic black hat banded in scarlet silk and tilted to one side, silver-tipped walking stick in one hand, broad-shouldered, and handsomely dressed, but she knew this—he was no gentleman.

In fact, no man, gentle or otherwise, had ever smiled at her the way this man did—as though he were a fox, and she were a hen. As though she were a houseful of hens. As though, if she weren't careful, he would eat her and wander off down St. James's with a feather caught in his wide, smiling teeth.

He fairly oozed reprobate.

Any intelligent woman would run from him, and Pippa was nothing if not intelligent. She stepped backward, returning to the darkness of the Angel.

He followed.

"Yer a much better door-man than the usual lot. They never let me in."

Pippa said the first thing that came to mind. "I am not a door-man."

His ice blue eyes glowed at the words. "You are no kind of man, love. Ol' Digger can see that."

The exterior door closed with a loud bang, and Pippa

started at the noise, backing toward the hell once more. When her back came up against the interior door, she edged through, pushing aside the curtains.

He followed.

"Perhaps you're The Fallen Angel herself, then?"

Pippa shook her head.

It seemed to be the answer he was looking for, his teeth flashing in the dim light of the casino floor. He lowered his voice until it was more rumble than sound. "Would you like to be?"

The question hovered in the fast-closing space between them, distracting her. She might not know this man, but she knew, instinctively, that behind his weathered smile he was a rogue and perhaps a scoundrel, and that he knew much about vice in all forms—knowledge she had been seeking when she'd arrived here not an hour ago, prepared to request it from another man. A man who had shown absolutely no interest in imparting it.

So when this man, wicked and carefree, questioned her, she did as she always did. She answered him truthfully. "As a matter of fact, I do have some questions."

She surprised him. His strange blue eyes widened just barely before narrowing in a wide, jolly grin. He laughed, bright and bold. "Excellent!" he boomed, and reached for her, wrapping one strong arm about her waist and pulling her to him, as though she were a rag doll and he a too-eager child. "I've answers aplenty, pet."

Pippa did not like it, the feeling of being possessed by this too-bold man, and she reached out to brace herself against his chest, her heart pounding even as she realized that she might have said the entirely wrong thing to the entirely wrong person. He thought she wanted to . . .

"My lord," she rushed to stop him. "I did not mean . . ."

"While I'm no lord, moppet, I should certainly like to be *yours*," he laughed, pressing his face into her neck. Pippa struggled against the caress, trying not to inhale. He smelled of perspiration and something sweet. The combination was not pleasant.

She turned her head away, pushing against his chest again, wishing she'd thought this entire thing through slightly more clearly before leaping to converse with this man. He laughed and pulled her closer, promising her more than she'd bargained for with the tightening of his arms and the press of his soft lips against the curve of her shoulder. "C'mon, love, Uncle Digger'll take care of you."

"I am not certain the caring to which you refer is at all unclelike," Pippa pointed out, trying to be as stern as possible as she attempted to extricate herself from his embrace. She looked around wildly; surely there was someone in this massive building who was willing to help her. Where was that someone?

Digger was laughing again. "Yer an exciting one, aren't you?"

Pippa held her head back as far as she could, not wanting to make contact again. "Not at all. In fact, I'm the very opposite of exciting."

"Nonsense. Yer here, aren't you? If that ain't exciting, I don't know what is."

He had a point. But even Pippa knew ceding such a point would start them down an unpleasant path. Instead, she stiffened, and used every ounce of her lady's education.

"Sirrah!" she said firmly, writhing in his arms, eel-like, trying to force his hand. "I must insist you release me!"

"Come on, lovely . . . let's go for a spin. Whatever yer gettin' here . . . I'll double it at my hell."

Double what?

Now was not the time to consider the answer. "As tempting as that offer is—"

"I'll show you a thing or two about temptation, I will."

Oh dear. This wasn't going at all according to plan. She was going to have to scream for help. Screaming was so emotional. Not at all scientific.

But desperate times required . . . well. She took a deep breath, ready to scream as loudly as she could, when the words shot across the quiet room like a bullet.

"Get your hands off her."

Both Pippa and Digger froze at the sound, low and soft and somehow perfectly audible. And vicious. She turned her head, looking over her shoulder at Mr. Cross, tall and trim, that crop of thick ginger hair now perfectly tamed, as though he would have it no other way. He'd also tucked in his shirt and donned a coat in what she assumed was a nod to civility, but it was irrelevant now, as *civil* was about the last word she would use to describe him.

Indeed, she had never seen anyone so furious in her life.

He looked like he might kill something.

Or someone.

Possibly her.

The thought returned her to sense, and she began to struggle again, moving scant inches before Digger's superior strength won the day, and she was hauled to his side like a haunch of prize meat. "No."

Cross's grey gaze settled on the place where Digger's hand sat, wide and possessive against her midriff. "It was not a request. Release the girl."

"She came to me, Cross," Digger said, laughter in his voice. "Led me right into temptation, she did. I believe I'll be keepin' her."

"That is entirely untrue." Pippa instinctively defended herself, struggling against the fox's grip, silently willing Cross to look her in the eye. "You knocked!"

"And you answered, pet."

She scowled and looked to Cross.

He did not meet her gaze. "She does not look as though she is interested in being kept."

"I most certainly am *not*," Pippa agreed.

"Release the lady."

"Always so generous, callin' the Angel's birds ladies."

Pippa stiffened. "I beg your pardon. I *am* a lady."

Digger laughed. "With airs like that, you might fool someone one of these days!"

Irritation flared. She'd had enough of this man. Craning her neck to meet his blue eyes, she said, "I see I made an immense mistake by even conversing with you, Mr.—" She paused, waiting for him to do right and provide his surname. When he didn't, she pressed on. "Mr. Digger. I assure you I am quite thoroughly a lady. Indeed, I am soon to be a *countess.*"

One of his black brows rose. "Is that right?"

She nodded. "Quite. And I don't imagine you'd like to be on the wrong side of an earl's favor, would you?"

Digger smiled, reminding her of a fox once more. "It wouldn't be the first time, moppet. Which earl?"

"Don't answer that," Mr. Cross snapped. "Now, Digger."

The man holding her released her, his touch a slow, unsettling slide against her midsection. The moment she could be free, she hurried to stand next to Mr. Cross, now paying her even less mind, if it was possible. He was advancing on Digger, his words casual, belying the threat that oozed from him with every movement. "Now that's out of the way, perhaps you could explain what in hell you are doing in my hell?"

Digger remained focused on her, more thoughtfully, even as he replied. "Now, now, Cross. You forget yourself. I was simply coming over to give you some information I thought you might appreciate—bein' right neighborly if you ask me."

"We're not neighbors."

"Nevertheless. I've information you'll be wantin'."

"There's no information you have that I could possibly want."

"No? Not even information about your sister?"

Cross stiffened, corded tension tightening the long column of his neck and through the lean muscle of his back, pulling him straighter, taller than before.

Digger pressed on, "I'm guessin' you not only want it . . . you're willin' to pay for it."

The air thickened. She'd always heard the expression and thought it utterly silly. Certainly, air thickened with fog or with smoke . . . she'd even allow for it thickening with the stench of Olivia's perfumes . . . but she'd always considered the very idea of emotion impacting the density of gas rather ridiculous—a silly, clichéd turn of phrase that should be exiled from English.

But this air did thicken, and she found it difficult to draw a deep breath, leaning forward in anticipation.

"Lord knows she ain't comin' to you herself, you fine cheat."

Pippa gasped at the insult. Surely, Mr. Cross would not allow it to stand. But he seemed not to hear the personal slight. "You will not touch my sister."

"It ain't my problem if the ladies are drawn to me," Digger said. "A gentleman doesn't turn 'em away if they're askin' for a minute or two." His eyes slid to Pippa once more. "Ain't that right, Lady Soon-to-be-a-countess?"

"I find it difficult to believe either that ladies are drawn to you or that, in such a case, you would act the part of a gentleman," Pippa retorted.

"Cor! Listen to this one!" Digger laughed, the sound booming around the floor of the hell. "She's a little mink."

Pippa narrowed her gaze. "I believe you are looking for the word *minx*."

"No, I found just the right word. You're a mink. All sharp teeth and"—his lecherous gaze slid over her—"I'm bettin' very soft fur. Tell me, Cross, 'ad a feel yet?"

Pippa did not understand the words' meaning, but when Mr. Cross lunged at Digger, hands like lightning clutching the older man's lapels with wicked force, she had no doubt that she'd been thoroughly insulted. "You will apologize to the lady."

Digger pulled away from the grip without much effort,

straightening his maroon frock coat. "Ah, not yet then, I'm guessin'," he said smartly. "But not long of a wait now, neither. Not yer usual type, I'll say." He bowed low, a teasing gleam in his eye. "My apologies, Lady Soon."

Her teeth clenched at the mocking name.

Mr. Cross spoke, quiet menace in his tone. "Leave this place."

"Don't you want to hear what I came to say?"

His hesitation was so slight . . . a half second . . . less. But Pippa heard it. "No."

One side of Digger's mouth crooked up in a smirk. "You will change your mind. I give you two days." He waited a beat, and Pippa had the distinct impression that there was an invisible knife hovering between these two men, each strong in his own way. She wondered who held the weapon.

Digger drove its point home. "You never could resist family matters."

Mr. Cross lifted his chin defiantly.

Digger tipped his hat to Pippa, using the movement to give her a proper leer. "As for you, Lady . . . this won't be the last time we meet."

"If you know what's best for you, it will be." Mr. Cross's words were cold and unwavering, leaving no room for resistance.

"Nonsense. The lady 'as questions." Digger's blue eyes bored into hers. "I've answers, I do."

Mr. Cross took a step toward them, a low, dark sound rumbling in his throat, catching Digger's attention. He turned his wicked smile on Mr. Cross. "Another reason for you to come see me, then."

Mr. Cross's fury was unmistakable, sending a ripple of something not altogether pleasant through her. "Get out."

Digger did not seem impressed, but he did not tarry. "Two days, Cross."

With an insolent wink for Pippa, he was gone.

They stood in silence for a long moment, watching the thick velvet curtains sway with his exit, listening for the heavy sound of the main door closing behind him before Pippa released the breath she had not known she had been holding.

At the sound, Cross turned on her, grey eyes flashing and furious. "Perhaps you would like to explain how it is that you are still here?"

Chapter Three

"It occurs to me that I should have considered this course of action prior to now. After all . . . if one wishes to understand the inner workings of the goose, one must observe the gander.

The common grey goose (Anser anser) boasts one of the most easy to identify ganders in the entire goose genus. Ganders are larger than females, with broader heads and longer necks, and when they reach sexual maturity, they have a tendency toward aggressive behavior around female geese. Interestingly, males can also display intensely protective behavior toward females, though it's often difficult to distinguish between the two types of conduct."

The Scientific Journal of Lady Philippa Marbury
March 22, 1831; fourteen days prior to her wedding

In the interest of self-preservation, Pippa said the first thing that came to mind. "He knocked."

"And it did not occur to you that one knocking at the door to a gaming hell might not be the kind of person with whom you would wish to become acquainted?"

For someone with a reputation for being charming and

affable, he did not seem to be at all such. "I am not an imbecile, Mr. Cross."

He crossed his arms tightly over his chest. "Speaking the words does not make them so, Lady Philippa."

She considered lifting her skirts and naming all the bones in her foot. Instead, she stayed quiet.

"Remaining silent might well be the first intelligent thing you've done today."

"There was no one else to answer. I waited. Indeed, I was rather surprised that the gentleman was allowed to bang upon the door to his heart's content."

His gaze narrowed on her. "I assure you, such neglect will not occur again. And, for the record, Digger Knight is no gentleman."

"Yes. I gather that now." Her blue eyes narrowed behind thick lenses. "Of course, by the time I realized it . . . he was already in."

"Would you like to explain why his hands were on your person?"

She thought it best not to reply to that. She would not like the situation to be misconstrued.

He pounced on her hesitation. "Did you *ask* for it? Was he your next choice for research partner?"

She hedged, looking to the door, considering escape. "Not . . . precisely."

I do have some questions. He wouldn't like to know she'd said that.

He took a step toward her, blocking her exit. "How, precisely?"

She looked up at him, feeling more guilty than she should. After all, it wasn't as though she'd tossed herself into the man's arms. "Did you proposition him?"

"No!" She did not hesitate. She hadn't. *Exactly.*

He heard the thought as though she'd screamed it. "I'm not certain I believe you. After all, you propositioned me not thirty minutes ago."

"It's not the same, and you know it." *If you'd said yes, I wouldn't be in this situation.*

"No?" He rocked back on his heels.

"No!" She exhaled on a huff of displeasure. "You were part of a plan." *A plan you then thoroughly mucked up.*

His gaze was narrowed on her, as though he could hear her thoughts. "I suppose that makes sense in a strange way." He turned away from her, stalking across the dark floor of the club, tossing back, "I suggest you return home and await your brother-in-law, Lady Philippa; he will no doubt come looking for you when I tell him that you're a complete madwoman."

He could not tell Bourne. Bourne would tell Father, and Father would lock her away in Surrey until the morning of the wedding. Without question. And Pippa would be without the information she required. Without the security knowledge brought. Without the safety of it. She could not allow it.

"No!" she cried across the room.

He turned back, his tone dark. "You are under the mistaken impression that I am interested in doing your bidding, my lady."

She hesitated. "I didn't approach him. There's no harm done. I shall go. Please . . . don't tell Bourne."

She might not have said the words at all for the way he ignored her, his gaze having fallen on the hazard table. On the dice she'd left, forgotten, on its mahogany edge.

She took a step toward him, and his gaze swung to meet hers, powerful and direct. She caught her breath. Stilled. "Your dice?"

She nodded. "Yes."

"You wagered?"

"I had been about to," she said, the words coming quickly. "*When a man doth to Rome come,* so to speak."

He ignored her quip. "With Knight?"

"With myself."

"The terms?"

"I hadn't decided. I thought . . . perhaps—" She stopped herself, the heat of her embarrassment washing through her. "Perhaps I could . . ."

His gaze turned searing. "You could . . . ?"

She looked to the dice. "I could redouble my efforts to garner your assistance."

"With your ruination."

Well. When he put it like that, in this big room, it sounded much more scandalous than before. "Yes."

"And if not that? What? You'd go home and wait to be married like a good girl?"

He made her sound like a child. As though her entire plan were idiotic. Did he not see that it was imperative? That it was *science*? "I hadn't decided," she said, smartly. "But I rather think I would have considered alternate opportunities. It's London in season. There is no shortage of rakes to be found to assist me."

"You're as much trouble as your sister is," he said, flatly.

Confusion flared. "Penelope?"

"The very same."

Impossible. Penelope was proper in every way. She never would have come here unescorted. She shook her head. "Penelope isn't any trouble at all."

One ginger brow cocked in wry disbelief. "I doubt Bourne would agree. Either way, Digger Knight is in no way a viable candidate for such a thing. You would do best to run far and fast should you ever see him again."

"Who is he?"

"No one whom you should have ever encountered." He scowled. Good. Why should she be the only one to be irritated? "You did not roll."

"I did not," she said. "I'm sure you count yourself very lucky indeed for that. After all, what if I had won?"

His eyes darkened. "I would have been a win?"

She nodded. "Of course. You were the research associate of choice. But as I never had a chance to wager, you may count yourself very lucky indeed," she said, lifting her skirts to leave as elegantly as possible.

"I count myself no such thing. I don't believe in luck."

She dropped her skirts. "You run a casino, and you don't believe in luck?"

He half smiled. "It's because I run a casino that I don't believe in it. Especially with dice. There are odds in this game. But the truth, Lady Philippa, is that even odds would have had no bearing on your roll. It is impossible to wager against oneself."

"Nonsense."

He leaned back against the table. "There is no risk in it. If the outcome is what you desire, there is no loss. And if the outcome is not what you desire . . . you may simply renege. With none to hold you accountable, there is no reason to follow through on the results."

She straightened her shoulders. "I would hold *myself* accountable. I told you. I dislike dishonesty."

"And you never lie to yourself?"

"Nor to others."

"That alone proves that you are in no way prepared for that for which you would have wagered."

"You find honesty to be an impediment?"

"A wicked one. The world is full of liars, Lady Philippa. Liars and cheats and every sort of scoundrel."

"Like you?" The retort was out before she could stop it.

He did not seem insulted. "Precisely like me."

"Well then, it's best that I remain honest, to offset your dishonest balance."

He raised a brow. "You do not think that affecting your own secret ruination is dishonest?"

"Not at all."

"Lord Castleton does not expect you to come to his bed a virgin?"

Heat washed over her cheeks. She supposed that she

should have expected the frank words from him, but she'd never had this specific topic raised in conversation before. "I still intend to . . ." She looked away. "To do that. I simply intend to be more knowledgeable about the act."

He raised a brow. "Let me rephrase. Lord Castleton does not expect you to come to your marriage an innocent?"

"We've never discussed it."

"So you've found a loophole."

Her gaze snapped back to his. "I have not."

"Dishonesty by omission remains dishonest."

It was a wonder he had a reputation as a charmer. He didn't seem at all charming. "If he asks, I shan't lie to him."

"It must be lovely to live in black and white."

She shouldn't ask. "What does that mean?"

"Only that in the real world, where girls are not protected from every bit of reality, we are all cloaked in grey, where truth is relative."

"I see now that I was wrong in believing you a scientist. Truth is truth."

One side of his mouth twisted in a wry smile. "Darling, it's nothing close to that."

She hated the way the words rolled off his tongue, utterly certain. This had clearly been a mistake. She'd come in the hopes of gaining experience and knowledge, not a lesson in male superiority.

It was time to leave.

He didn't say anything as she crossed the room, headed for the exit. He didn't speak until she had pushed back the curtains and opened the inner door, suddenly eager to leave.

"If you're going to wager, you should do it honestly."

She froze, one hand holding a heavy length of velvet. Surely she had misunderstood him. She turned her head, looking over her shoulder to where he stood, tall and slim. "I beg your pardon?"

He slowly removed one hand from the pocket of his coat and extended it toward her. For a moment, she thought he was beckoning her.

For a moment, she almost went.

"You've come all this way, Pippa." It was the first time he'd called her by the nickname, and she was struck by its sound on his tongue. The quick repetition of consonants. The way his lips curved around it. Teasing. And something more. Something she could not explain. "You should have a real wager, don't you think?"

He opened his hand, revealing two small, ivory squares.

She met his calculating grey gaze. "I thought you did not believe in luck?"

"I don't," he said. "But I find that I believe less in making a wager with oneself, thereby forcing the outcome to accommodate your adventure—"

"Not adventure," she protested. "Experiment."

"What's the difference?"

He couldn't see? "One is silly. The other is science."

"My mistake. Tell me, where was the science in your potential wager?"

She did not have an answer.

"I'll tell you . . . there was none. Men of science don't wager. They know better. They know that no matter how many times they win, the odds remain against them."

He moved closer, crowding her back into the darkness. He didn't touch her, but strangely, it didn't matter. He was close enough to feel, tall and lean and ever so warm. "But you're going to wager now, Pippa, aren't you?"

He was muddling her brain and making it very difficult to think clearly. She took a deep breath, the scent of sandalwood wrapping around her, distracting her.

She shouldn't say yes.

But somehow, oddly, she found she couldn't say no.

She reached for the dice, where they lay small and white in his broad palm. Touched them, touched *him*—the brush of skin against fingertips sending sensation coursing through her. She paused at the feeling, trying to dissect it. To identify it. *To savor it.* But then he was gone, his hand falling away, leaving her with nothing but the ivory cubes, still warm from his touch.

Just as she was.

Of course, the thought was ridiculous. One did not warm from a fleeting contact. It was the stuff of novels. Something her sisters would sigh over.

He moved, stepping back and extending one arm toward the hazard field. "Are you ready?" His voice was low and soft, somehow private despite the cavernous room.

"Yes."

"As you are gaming in my hell, I shall set the terms."

"That doesn't seem fair."

His gaze did not waver. "When we wager at your tables, my lady, I shall be more than happy to play by your rules."

"I suppose that is logical."

He inclined his head. "I do like a woman with a penchant for logic."

She smiled. "The rules of scoundrels it is, then."

They were at one end of the long table now. "A roll of a seven or an eleven wins on the first roll at the Angel. As you are wagering, I shall allow you to name your price."

She did not have to think. "If I win, you tell me everything I wish to know."

He paused, and she thought for a moment he might change his mind. Instead, he nodded once. "Fair enough. And if you lose . . . you shall return to your home and your life and wait patiently for your marriage. And you will resist approaching another man with this insane proposal."

Her brows knit together in protest. "That's an enormous wager."

He tilted his head. "It is the only way you have a chance at gaining my participation."

Pippa considered the words, calculating the probability

of the roll in her head. "I don't like my odds. I only have a twenty-two and two-tenths chance of winning."

He raised a brow, clearly impressed. *Ha. Not a mutton-head after all.*

"That's where luck comes in," he said.

"That force in which you do not believe?"

He lifted one shoulder in a lanky shrug. "I could be wrong."

"What if I choose not to wager?"

He crossed his arms. "Then you force me to tell Bourne everything."

"You cannot!"

"I can, indeed, my lady. I had planned not to, but the reality is this: You cannot be trusted to keep yourself safe. It falls to those around you to do it for you."

"You could keep me safe by agreeing to my proposal," she pointed out.

He smiled, and the flash of his white teeth sent a very strange sensation spiraling through her—as though she were in a carriage that had taken a turn too quickly. "It's much easier for Bourne to accomplish the task. Besides, I like the idea of his locking you in a tower until your wedding day. It would keep you away from here."

From him. She found she didn't care much for the thought.

She narrowed her gaze on him. "You are making this my only choice."

"You are not the first gamer to feel that way. You won't be the last."

She rattled the dice. "Fine. Anything other than a seven or an eleven, and I shall go home."

"And you shall refrain from propositioning other men," he prompted.

"It was not nearly so salacious as you make it out to be," she said.

"It was salacious enough."

He *had* been nearly naked. That bit had been fantastically salacious. She felt her cheeks warm and nodded once. "Very well. I will refrain from asking any other men to assist in my research."

He seemed satisfied with the vow. "Roll."

She took a deep breath, steeling herself for the moment, her heart pounding as she tossed the ivory dice, watching as one knocked into the curved mahogany bumper at the opposite end, bouncing back to land near its sister on a large, white C—the beginning of the word *Chance*, curling down the table in extravagant script.

Nine.

Chance, indeed.

She had lost.

She put her hands to the cool wood of the table, leaning in, as though she could will one die to keep turning until the game was hers.

She lifted her gaze to her opponent's.

"*Alea iacta est*," he said.

The die is cast. The words Caesar had spoken as he marched to war with Rome. Of course, Caesar's risk had won him an empire; Pippa's had lost her this last, fleeting opportunity for knowledge.

"I lost," she said, not knowing what else to say.

"You did."

"I wanted to win," she added, disappointment coursing through her, harsh and unfamiliar.

"I know." He lifted one hand to her cheek, the movement distracting her from the dice, suddenly making her desperate for something else altogether. She caught her breath at the rushing sensation—a flood of something indescribable in her chest.

His long fingers tempted but didn't touch, leaving a trail of heat where they almost were. "I am collecting, Lady Philippa," he said, softly. *Collecting.* The word was more than the sum of its letters. She was suddenly, keenly aware that he could name his price. That she would pay it.

She met his grey eyes in the dim light. "I only wished to know about marriage."

He tilted his head, one ginger lock falling over his brow. "It's the most common thing in the world. Why does it worry you so?"

Because she didn't understand it.

She kept quiet.

After a long moment, he said, "It is time for you to go home."

She opened her mouth to speak, to try to convince him that the wager had been silly, to convince him to let her stay, but at the precise moment, his hand moved, tracing the column of her neck, the nearly-there touch an undelivered promise. Her plea was lost in a strange, consuming desire for contact. She caught her breath, resisting the urge to move toward him.

"Pippa," he whispered, and there was a hint of something there in the name . . . something she could not place. She was having trouble thinking at all. He was so close. Too close and somehow not close enough.

"Go home, darling," he said, his fingers finally, *finally* settling, featherlight, on the place where her pulse pounded. Somehow giving her everything and nothing she wanted all at once. She leaned into the caress without thought, wanting more. Wanting to refuse.

He removed his hand instantly—before she could revel in the brush of his fingers—and for a mad, fleeting moment, she considered reaching for him and returning his touch to her person.

How fascinating.

How terrifying.

She took a deep breath and stepped back. A foot, two. Five, as he crossed his arms in a tightly controlled movement she was coming to identify as specific to him. "This is not the place for you."

And as she watched him, feeling an unsettling, nearly irresistible pull to remain in the club, she realized that this place was far more than she had bargained.

Chapter Four

"The roses have sprouted—two perfect pink buds, right off the stalk of a red bush, as hypothesized. I would be deeply proud of the accomplishment if I had not failed so thoroughly in avenues of non-botanical research.

It seems I've a keener understanding of horticulture than humans.

Unfortunately, this is not a surprising discovery."

The Scientific Journal of Lady Philippa Marbury
March 23, 1831; thirteen days prior to her wedding

"Really, Pippa"—Olivia Marbury sighed from the doorway of the Dolby House orangery—"one would think that you would have something better to do than fiddle about with your plants. After all, we're to be married in twelve days."

"Thirteen," Pippa corrected, not looking up from where she cataloged that morning's floral observations. She knew better than to explain to Olivia that her work on the roses was far more interesting and relevant to science than *fiddling about*.

Olivia didn't know science from sailing.

"Today doesn't count!" The second—or first—bride in what was purported to be "the double wedding of the century" (at least, by their mother) replied, the excitement in her voice impossible to miss. "It's practically over!"

Pippa resisted the urge to correct her younger sister, supposing that if one were looking forward to the event in question, today would not, in fact, count. But as Pippa remained uncertain and anxious when it came to the event in question, today did indeed count. Very much.

There were fourteen hours and—she looked to a nearby clock—forty-three minutes left of today, March the twenty-third, and Pippa had no intention of relinquishing the twelfth-to-the-last day of her premarital life before she'd used every single minute of it.

Olivia was now on the opposite side of Pippa's worktable, leaning well over the surface, a wide smile on her pretty face. "Do you notice anything different about me, today?"

Pippa set down her pen and looked at her sister. "You mean, aside from the fact that you're about to sprawl into a pile of soil?"

Olivia's perfect nose wrinkled in distaste, and she straightened. "Yes."

Pippa pushed her spectacles up on her nose, considering her sister's twinkling eyes, secret smile, and generally lovely appearance. She did not notice anything different. "New coiffe?"

Olivia smirked. "No."

"New dress?"

The smirk became a smile. "For a scientist, you're not very observant, you know." Olivia draped one hand across her collarbone, and Pippa saw it. The enormous, glittering ruby. Her eyes went wide, and Olivia laughed. "Ah-ha! Now you notice!"

She thrust the hand in question toward Pippa, who had to lean back to avoid being hit with the jewel. "Isn't it gorgeous?"

Pippa leaned over to assess the jewel. "It is." She looked up. "It's enormous."

Olivia grinned. "My future husband adores me."

"Your future husband spoils you."

Olivia waved away the words. "You say that like I don't deserve to be spoiled."

Pippa laughed. "Poor Tottenham. He hasn't any idea what he's getting himself into."

Olivia cut her a dry look. "Nonsense. He knows precisely what he's getting himself into. And he loves it." She returned her attention. "It's so beautiful and *red*."

Pippa nodded. "That's the chromium."

"The what?"

"Chromium. It is an additive in the crystal that turns it red. If it were anything else added . . . it wouldn't be a ruby. It would be a sapphire." Olivia blinked, and Pippa continued, "It's a common misconception that all sapphires are blue, but that's not the case. They can be any color . . . green or yellow or pink, even. It depends on the additive. But they're all called sapphires. It's only if they're red that they're called something else. Rubies. Because of the chromium."

She stopped, recognizing the blank stare on Olivia's face. It was the same stare that appeared on most people's faces when Pippa talked too much.

Not everyone's, though.

Not Mr. Cross's.

He'd seemed interested in her. Even as he called her mad. Right up until the moment he cast her out of his club. And his life. Without telling her anything she wished to know.

Olivia looked back to the ring. "Well, my ruby is red. And lovely."

"It is." Pippa agreed. "When did you receive it?"

A small, private smile flashed across Olivia's pretty face. "Tottenham gave it to me last night after the theater."

"And mother didn't mention it at breakfast? I'm shocked."

Olivia grinned. "Mother wasn't there when he did it."

There was a twinge of something in the words—an awareness that Pippa almost didn't notice. That she might not have noticed if not for Olivia's knowing blue gaze. "Where was she?"

"I imagine she was looking for me." There was a long pause, in which Pippa knew she should draw meaning. "She was not with us."

Pippa leaned in, across the table. "Where were you?"

Olivia grinned. "I shouldn't tell."

"Were you *alone*?" Pippa gasped, "With the viscount?"

Olivia's laugh was bright and airy. "Really, Pippa . . . you needn't sound like a shocked chaperone." She lowered her voice. "I was . . . not for long. Just long enough for him to give me the ring . . . and for me to thank him."

"Thank him how?"

Olivia smiled. "You can imagine."

"I really can't." The truth.

"Surely, you've had a reason or two to *thank* Castleton."

Except she hadn't. Well, she had certainly said the words, *thank you,* to her betrothed, but she'd never had cause to be alone with him while doing so. And she was certain that he'd never imagined giving her such a lavish present as the Viscount Tottenham had bestowed upon Olivia. "How, precisely, did you thank him, Olivia?"

"We were at the theater, Pippa," Olivia said, all superiority. "We couldn't do very much. It was just a few kisses."

Kisses.

In the plural.

Pippa jerked at the words, knocking over her inkpot, sending a pool of blackness across the tabletop toward a young potted lemon tree, and Olivia leapt back with a squeal. "Don't get it on my dress!"

Pippa righted the inkwell and mopped at the liquid with a nearby rag, desperate for more information. "You've been"—she glanced at the door of the orangery to assure herself that they were alone—"kissing Tottenham?"

Olivia stepped backward. "Of course I have. I cannot very well marry the man without knowing that we have a kind of . . . compatibility."

Pippa blinked. "Compatibility?" She looked to her research journal, lying open on the table, filled with notes on roses and dahlias and geese and human anatomy. She'd trade all of it for a few sound pages of notes from Olivia's experience.

"Yes. Surely you've wondered what it would be like—physically—with Castleton . . . once you are married?"

Wonder was a rather bland word for how Pippa felt about the physical nature of her relationship with Castleton. "Of course."

"Well, there you have it," Olivia said.

Except Pippa didn't have it. Not at all. She resisted the urge to blurt just such a thing out, casting about for another way to discuss Olivia's experience without making it seem as though she were desperate for knowledge. Which, of course, she was. "And you . . . like the kissing?"

Olivia nodded enthusiastically. "Oh, yes. He's very good at it. I was surprised at first by his enthusiasm—"

In that moment, Pippa loathed the English language and all its euphemisms. "Enthusiasm?"

Olivia laughed. "In only the very best way . . . I'd kissed a few boys before—" *She had?* "—but I was a bit surprised by his . . ." She trailed off, waving her bejeweled hand in the air as if the gesture held all relevant meaning.

Pippa wanted to strangle her little sister. "By his . . ." she prompted.

Olivia lowered her voice to a whisper. "His expertise."

"Elaborate."

"Well, he has a very clever tongue."

Pippa's brow furrowed. "*Tongue?*"

At her shocked reply, Olivia pulled up straight. "Oh. You and Castleton haven't kissed."

Pippa frowned. What on earth did a man do with his

tongue in such a situation? The tongue was an organ designed for eating and speaking. How did it play into kissing? Though, logically, mouths touching would make for tongues being rather near each other . . . but the idea was unsettling, honestly.

" . . . I suppose I shouldn't be surprised, of course," Olivia went on.

Wait.

Pippa looked to her sister. "What?"

Olivia waved that rubied hand again. "I mean, it is *Castleton.*"

"There's nothing wrong with Castleton," Pippa defended. "He's a kind, good man." Even as she said the words, she knew what Olivia meant. What Mr. Cross had meant the day before, when he'd suggested that Castleton was a less-than-superior groom.

Castleton was a perfectly nice man, but he was not the kind who inspired kissing.

Certainly not with tongues.

Whatever that meant.

"Of course he is," Olivia said, unaware of Pippa's rioting thoughts. "He's rich, too. Which helps."

"I am not marrying him because he's rich."

Olivia's attention snapped to Pippa. "Why *are* you marrying him?"

The question was not outrageous. "Because I have agreed to."

"That's not what I mean, and you know it."

Pippa did know it, and there were any number of reasons why she was marrying him. All the things she'd told Olivia and Mr. Cross were true. The earl was good and kind and liked dogs. He appreciated Pippa's intelligence and was willing to allow her full access to his estate and its inner workings. He might not be intelligent or terribly quick or very amusing, but he was better than most.

No, he was not what most women would deem a catch—

not a viscount destined for prime minister like Olivia's fiancé, and not a self-made marquess with a gaming hell and a wicked reputation like Penelope's Bourne—but neither was he old like Victoria's husband or absent like Valerie's.

And he'd asked her.

She hesitated at the thought.

That, as well.

Philippa Marbury was odd, and Lord Castleton didn't seem to mind.

But she didn't want to say that aloud. Not to Olivia—the most ideal bride that ever there was, on the cusp of a love match with one of the most powerful men in Britain. So, instead, she said, "Perhaps he's an excellent kisser."

Olivia's expression mirrored Pippa's feelings on the matter. "Perhaps," she said.

Not that Pippa would test the outlandish theory.

She couldn't test it. She'd agreed to Mr. Cross's wager. She'd promised.

A vision flashed, dice rolling across green baize, the warm touch of strong fingers, serious grey eyes, and a deep, powerful voice, insisting, *You shall refrain from propositioning other men.*

Pippa Marbury did not renege.

But this was something of an emergency, was it not? Olivia was kissing Tottenham, after all. No doubt kissing one's fiancé was not within the bounds of the wager.

Was it?

Except she didn't want to kiss her fiancé.

Pippa's gaze fell to the rosebush on which she'd been so focused prior to her sister's arrival . . . the lovely scientific discovery that paled in comparison to the information Olivia had just shared.

It was irrelevant that she did not wish to proposition Castleton.

And it was irrelevant that it was another man, altogether, whom she wished to proposition—especially so, considering the fact that he'd tossed her out of his club with utter disinterest.

As for the tightness she felt in her chest, Pippa was certain that it was not in response to the memory of that tall, fascinating man, but instead, normal bridal nervousness.

All brides were anxious.

"Twelve days cannot pass quickly enough!" Olivia pronounced, bored with their conversation and oblivious to Pippa's thoughts.

All brides were anxious, it seemed, but Olivia.

"Twenty-eight hours." Digger Knight lazily checked his pocket watch before grinning smugly. "I confess, my blunt was on fewer than twelve."

"I like to keep you guessing." Cross shrugged out of his greatcoat and folded himself into an uncomfortable wooden chair on the far side of Knight's massive desk. He tossed a pointed look over his shoulder at the henchman who had guarded his journey to Digger's private offices. "Close the door."

The pockmarked man closed the door.

"You are on the wrong side of it."

The man sneered.

Knight laughed. "Leave us." When they were finally alone, he said, "What can I say, my men are protective of me."

Cross leaned back in the small chair, folding one leg over the other, refusing to allow the furniture to accomplish its goal—intimidation. "Your men are protective of their cut."

Knight did not disagree. "Loyalty at any price."

"A fine rule for a guttersnipe."

Knight tilted his head. "You're sayin' your men aren't loyal to the Angel for the money?"

"The Angel offers them more than financial security."

"You, Bourne, and Chase never could resist a poor, ruined soul," Knight scoffed, standing. "I always thought that particular job best left to the vicar. Gin?"

"I know better than to drink anything you serve."

Knight hesitated in pouring his glass. "You think I'd poison you?"

"I don't pretend to know what you'd do to me if given the chance."

Knight smiled. "I've got plans for you alive, my boy."

Cross did not like the knowledge in the words, the smug implication that he was on the wrong side of the table here— that he was about to be pulled into a high-risk game to which he did not know the rules. He took a moment to have a good look at the inside of Knight's office.

He'd been here before, the last time six years earlier, and the rooms had not changed. They were still pristine and uncluttered, devoid of anything that might reveal their owner or his private life. On one side of the small room, heavy ledgers—insurance, Knight called them—were stacked carefully. Cross knew better than anyone what they contained: the financial history of every man who had ever played the tables at Knight's eponymous gaming hell.

Cross knew, not only because a similar set of ledgers sat on the floor of his own offices, but also because he'd seen them that night, six years before, when Digger had thrown open one enormous book, his ham-fisted henchmen showing Cross the proof of his transgressions before they'd beaten him almost to death.

He hadn't fought them.

In fact, he'd prayed for their success.

Knight had stopped them before they could finish their job and ordered Cross stripped of his money and thrown from the hell.

But not before setting Cross on a new path.

The older man had leaned in, ignoring Cross's bruised

face and his bloody clothes and broken ribs and fingers. *You think I don't see what you're doing? How you're playing me? I won't kill you. It's not your time.*

Cross's eyes had been swollen nearly shut, but he'd watched as Knight leaned in, all anger. *But I won't let you fleece me again,* the older man had said. *The way you feel right now . . . this is my insurance. You come back, it will get worse. Do yourself a favor and stay away before I have no choice but to destroy you.*

He'd already been destroyed, but he'd stayed away nonetheless.

Until today.

"Why am I here?"

Knight returned to his chair and tossed back a swig of clear alcohol. With a wince, he said, "Your brother-in-law owes me ten thousand pounds."

Years of practice kept Cross from revealing his shock. Ten thousand pounds was an exorbitant sum. More than most men would make in a lifetime. More than most peers would make in a year. In two. And definitely more than Baron Dunblade could ever repay. He'd already parceled off every bit of free land from the barony, and he had an income of two thousand pounds a year.

Two thousand, four hundred and thirty-five pounds, last year.

It wasn't much, but it was enough to keep a roof over Dunblade's wife's and children's heads. Enough to send his son to school, eventually. Enough to provide an illusion of respectability that allowed for the baron and baroness to receive coveted invitations from the rest of the *ton*.

Cross had made sure of it.

"How is that possible?"

Knight leaned back in his chair, rolling the crystal tumbler in his hands. "The man likes the tables. Who am I to stop him?"

Cross resisted the urge to reach across the table and grab the older man by the neck. "Ten thousand pounds is more than liking the tables, Digger. How did it happen?"

"It seems the man was given a line of credit he could not back."

"He has never in his life had that kind of money."

Knight's tone turned innocent and grating. "He assured me he was good for it. I can't be held responsible for the fact that the man lied." He met Cross's eyes, knowledge glittering there. "Some people can't help it. You taught me that."

The words were meant to sting—to recall that long-ago night when Cross, barely out of university, bright-eyed and cocksure, had played the tables at Knight's and won. Over and over, he'd mastered *vingt-et-un*—unable to do anything but win.

He'd gone from hell to hell for months, playing one night here, two there, convincing every onlooker that he was simply lucky.

Every onlooker but Digger. "So this is your revenge? Six years in the making?"

Knight sighed. "Nonsense. I'm long past it. I never believed in revenge served cold. Always liked my meals hot. Better for the digestion."

"Then clear the debt."

Knight laughed, his fingers spreading wide over his mahogany desk. "We're not *that* even, Cross. The debt stands. Dunblade's a fool, but it doesn't change the fact that I'm owed. It's business, I'm sure you'll agree." He paused for a long moment, then, "It's a pity he's a peer. Debtor's prison might be better than what I have in store for him."

Cross did not pretend to misunderstand. He ran a hell himself, after all, and knew better than anyone what secret punishments could be meted out to peers who thought themselves immune to debt. He leaned forward. "I can bring this place to rubble. We've half the peerage in our membership."

Knight leaned forward as well. "I don't need half the peerage, boy. I have your sister."

Lavinia.

The only reason he was here.

A memory flashed, Lavinia, young and fresh-faced, laughing back at him as she pulled ahead on her favorite chestnut mare along the Devonshire cliffs. She was youngest by seven years, spoiled rotten and afraid of nothing. It was no surprise that she had come to face Knight. Lavinia had never been the kind to stay quiet—even when it was best for everyone.

She'd married Dunblade the year after Baine had died and Cross had left home; he'd read about the marriage in the papers, a fast courtship followed by an even faster wedding—via special license to skirt the issue of the family's state of mourning. No doubt their father had wanted the marriage done quickly, to ensure that *someone* would marry his daughter.

Cross met Knight's brilliant blue gaze. "She is not a part of this."

"Oh, but she is. It is interesting how ladies manage to get themselves into trouble, isn't it? No matter how hard one tries to keep her at bay, if a lady has it in mind to meddle, meddle she will," Knight said, opening an ornate ebony box on his desk and extracting a cheroot and tapping the long brown cylinder, once, twice on the desk before lighting it. After a long pull on the cigarette, he said, "And you have two on your hands. Let's talk about my new acquaintance. The lady from yesterday. Who is she?"

"She is no one of consequence." Cross caught the misstep instantly. He should have ignored the question. Should have brushed past it. But his too-quick answer revealed more than it hid.

Knight tilted his head to one side, curious. "It seems that she is very much of consequence."

Dammit. This was no place, no time for Philippa Marbury

with her enormous blue eyes and her too-logical mind and
her strange, tempting quirks. He pushed back the thoughts.

He would not have her here.

"I came to discuss my sister."

Knight allowed the change in topic. Too easily, perhaps.
"Your sister has character, I will say that."

The room was warm and far too small, and Cross resisted
the urge to shift in his seat. "What do you want?"

"It isn't about what I want. It's about what your sister has
offered. She's been very gracious. It appears the young lady
will do anything to ensure that her children are safe from
scandal."

"Lavinia's children will remain untouched by scandal."
The words were firm and unwavering. Cross would move the
Earth to ensure their truth.

"Are you sure?" Knight asked, leaning back in his chair.
"It seems they are rather close to quite devastating scandals.
Poverty. A father with a penchant for gambling away their
inheritance. A broken mother. Add all that to their uncle—
who turned from family and society and never looked back,
and . . ." The sentence lingered, completion unnecessary.

It wasn't true.

Not all of it.

He'd never turned from them.

Cross narrowed his gaze. "You've lost your accent, Digger."

One side of Knight's mouth kicked up. "No need to use
it with old friends." Knight took a long pull on the cheroot.
"But back to those lucky young boys. Their mother is a
strong one. She's offered to repay me. Pity she doesn't have
any money."

It did not take a brilliant mind to hear the insinuation. To
understand the foulness in the words. A lesser man would
have allowed rage to come without seeing all the pieces in
play, but Cross was not a lesser man.

He did not simply hear the threat. He heard the offer.

"You will not speak to my sister again."

Knight dipped his head. "Do you really believe you are in a position to make such a pronouncement?"

Cross stood, transferring his coat to the crook of one arm. "I will pay the debts. Double them. I'll send the draft around tomorrow. And you will steer clear of my family."

He turned to leave.

Knight spoke from his place. "No."

Cross stopped, looking over his shoulder, allowing emotion into his tone for the first time. "That is the second time you have refused me in as many days, Digger. I do not like it."

"I'm afraid the debt cannot be repaid so easily."

Digger Knight had not made his name as one of the most hardened gamers in London by playing by the rules. Indeed, it was Knight's penchant for rule-breaking that had saved Cross's hide all those years ago. He'd enjoyed the way Cross's mind had worked. He'd forced him to reveal how he counted the deck, how he calculated the next card, how he knew when and how much to bet.

How Cross always won.

At the tables, at least.

He turned back to his nemesis. "What, then?"

Digger laughed, a full-throated, heaving-bellied guffaw that had Cross gritting his teeth. "What a remarkable moment . . . the great Cross, willing to give me whatever I want. How very . . . responsible of you." There was no surprise in the tone, only smug satisfaction.

And that's when Cross realized that it had never been about Dunblade. Knight wanted something more, and he'd used the only thing Cross held dear to get it.

"You waste my time. What do you want?"

"It's simple, really," Knight said. "I want you to make my daughter a countess."

If he'd been asked to guess the price Knight would place on his sister's reputation and the safety of her children, Cross would have said there was nothing that could surprise him. He'd have been prepared for an offer to become part-owner in the Angel, for a request for the Angel's floor boss or bouncers to come work for Knight's, or for Cross himself to take up post at Digger's hell.

Cross would have expected extortion—a doubling of the debt, a tripling of it, enough to level a financial blow. He would even have imagined some proposal of joint partnership between the clubs; Knight loathed the way The Fallen Angel had catapulted to aristocratic success in a matter of months after opening, while Knight's remained a mediocre, second-rate hell that collected the peers rejected by the Angel's rigorous standards of membership.

But never, ever would he have imagined this request.

So he did the only thing one could do in this situation. He laughed. "Are we listing the things we would like? If so, I should like a gold-plated flying apparatus."

"And I would find a way to give it to you if you held in your hands one of the few things I hold dear." Knight stamped out his cheroot.

"I was not aware that you held Meghan dear."

Knight's gaze snapped to Cross's. "How do you know her name?"

A hit.

Cross considered what he knew of Knight's only child, the information he'd learned from the files kept locked away in the inner safe of the Angel. The ones that held the secrets of their potential enemies—politicians, criminals, clergy with a love of fire and brimstone, and competitors.

The information was as clear as if Knight's file were spread on the desk between them.

Name: Meghan Margaret Knight, b. 3 July 1812.

"I know quite a bit about young Meghan." He paused. "Or should I call her Maggie?"

Knight collected himself. "I never cared for it."

"No, I don't imagine you did, what with the way it oozes Irish." Cross draped his coat over the back of the chair, enjoying the small amount of control he had gained. "Meghan Margaret Knight. I'm surprised you allowed it."

Knight looked away. "I let her mother name her."

"Mary Katharine."

Mary Katharine O'Brien, Irish, b. 1796, m. Knight— February 1812.

"I should have known you would have information on them." He scowled. "Chase is a bastard. One day, I'm going to give him the pounding he deserves."

Cross folded his arms at the reference to his partner, and founder of The Fallen Angel. "I guarantee that will never happen."

Knight met his eyes. "I suppose I should be grateful. After all, you know about the girl already. It will be like marrying an old friend."

Residence: Bedfordshire; small cottage on the High Street.

Knight sends £200, 4th of every month; does not visit and has not seen the girl since mother and child were sent away, October 1813.

Girl raised with a governess, speaks mediocre French.

Attended Mrs. Coldphell's Finishing School for Girls— day student.

"Since when do you give a fig about your daughter?"

Knight shrugged. "Since she's old enough to be worth something."

There was one more line, written in Chase's bold, black scrawl.

NB: Girl required to write to Knight weekly. Letter posts Tuesday.
He does not reply.

"Ever the doting father," Cross said, wryly. "You think to buy yourself a title?"

"It's how the game is played these days, isn't it? The aristocracy isn't what it once was. Lord knows fewer and fewer have any money with the good work of you and me. Six days from now, Meghan arrives. You'll marry her. She gets the title, and my grandson will be Earl Harlow."

Earl Harlow.

It had been years since he'd heard it spoken aloud.

Temple—the fourth owner in the Angel—had said it once on the day Cross's father had died, and Cross had attacked his unbeatable partner, not letting up until the massive man had been knocked off his feet. Now, Cross held back the fury that surged at the name with a smirk. "If your daughter marries me, she gets a filthy title—covered in ash and soot. It will gain you no respect. She shan't be invited into society."

"The Angel will get you your invitations."

"I have to want them, first."

"You'll want them."

"I assure you, I will not," Cross promised.

"You haven't a choice. *I* want them. You marry my daughter. I forgive your brother-in-law's debts."

"Your price is too high. There are other ways to end this."

"Such a difficult choice you leave me with. Which do you think would be worse for the children, the scandal I can bring to their name? The quiet punishment I can call upon their father some night when he least expects it? Prostitution for their mother? With all that red hair, I assure you, there are some who would pay handsomely to take her to bed—with or without the limp."

And, like that, the rage came. Cross lunged across the

desk, pulling Knight from his chair. "I will destroy you if you touch her."

"Not before I destroy them." The words were choked from Knight, but their truth was enough to set Cross back. Knight sensed the change. "Isn't it time you keep someone in your family safe?"

The words rocketed through him, an echo of the hundreds of times he'd thought them himself. He hated Knight for them.

But he hated himself more.

"I hold all the cards," Knight repeated, and this time, there was no smugness in the tone.

Only truth.

Chapter Five

"Inquiry reveals that the human tongue is not one muscle, but rather eight unique muscles, half of which are anchored to bone—the glossus muscles—and half of which are integral to the shape and function of the larger organ.

While this additional research has cast an impressive light on an area of human anatomy of which I had been previously unaware, I remain unclear on the value of the muscle in question in activities unrelated to eating and articulation.

I may have to ask Olivia to elaborate. Solution not ideal."

The Scientific Journal of Lady Philippa Marbury
March 24, 1831; twelve days prior to her wedding

"I want him punished."

Cross watched as Temple leaned low over the billiards table at the center of the owner's suite of The Fallen Angel and took a clear shot, the white cue knocking into its red sister and rebounding against the rail to hit a third, spotted ball.

"Are you certain? Vengeance has never been in your baili-wick. Particularly not with Knight." Bourne stepped forward and considered the playing field. "Damn your luck, Temple."

"At least give me billiards," Temple replied. "It's the only game in which I've a chance of taking you both." He stepped back and leaned one hip against a nearby chair, returning his attention to Cross. "There are ways of disappearing him."

"Leave it to you to suggest killing the man," Bourne said, taking his own shot, missing the second ball by an impres-sive margin, and swearing roundly.

"It's quick. And final." Temple shrugged one massive shoulder.

"If anyone outside of this room heard you say that, they'd believe the stories about you," Cross said.

"They believe the stories about me already. All right, no killing. Why not just pay the debt?"

"It's not an option."

"Probably for the best. Dunblade would just run up more and we'd be back where we started in a month." Bourne turned for the sideboard, where Chase kept the best scotch in the club. "Drink?"

Cross shook his head.

"Then what?" Temple asked.

"He wants his daughter married."

"To you?"

Cross did not reply.

Temple whistled long and low. "Brilliant."

Cross's gaze flew to Temple's. "Marriage to me is not even close to brilliant."

"Why not?" Bourne interjected, "You're an earl, rich as Croesus, and—even better—in the family business. Gaming-hell royalty."

"One of you should marry her, then."

Temple smirked, accepting a tumbler of scotch from Bourne. "We both know Digger Knight would no more let me near his daughter than fly. It's you, Cross. Bourne is married, my reputation is forever ruined, and Chase is . . . well . . . Chase. Add to it the fact that you're the only one of us he respects, and you're the perfect choice."

He was no such thing. "He's misjudged me."

"He's not the first," Bourne said. "But I'll admit that if he had my sister in his clutches, I'd consider doing his bidding. Digger Knight is ruthless. He'll get what he wants any way he can."

Cross turned away from the words, ignoring the thread of guilt they brought with them. After all, Bourne's sister-in-law had been in Knight's clutches a day earlier. Tall, slim Pippa caught in Knight's strong arms, pressed against his side as he whispered God knew what in her ear. The image made him furious.

Bourne's sister. Then his own.

He set his cue aside and paced the length of the dark room until he reached the far wall, where a mosaic of stained glass overlooked the main floor of the casino. The window was the centerpiece of The Fallen Angel; it depicted the fall of Lucifer in glorious detail—the great blond angel tumbled from Heaven to the floor of the hell, six times the size of the average man, useless wings spread out behind him, chain around one ankle, glittering jeweled crown clasped in his massive hand.

The window was a warning to the men below—a reminder of their place, of how close they were to their own fall. It was a manifestation of the temptation of sin and the luxury of vice.

But for the owners of the Angel, the window was something else.

It was proof that those banished into exile could become rulers in their own right, with power to rival those they'd once served.

Cross had spent the last six years of his life proving that he was more than a reckless boy cast from society, that he was more than his title. More than the circumstances of his birth. More than the circumstances of his brother's death. More than what came after.

And he would be damned if he would let Digger Knight resurrect that boy.

Not when Cross had worked so hard to keep him at bay.

Not when he had sacrificed so much.

His gaze flickered over the men on the floor of the hell. A handful at the hazard tables, another few playing ecarte. The roulette wheel spun in a whir of color, a fortune laid out across the betting field. He was too far away to see where the ball fell or to hear the call of the croupier, but he saw the disappointment on the faces of the men at the table as they felt the sting of loss. He saw, too, the way hope rallied, leading them into temptation, urging them to place another wager on a new number . . . or perhaps the same one . . . for certainly luck was theirs tonight.

Little did they know.

Cross watched a round of *vingt-et-un* directly below, the cards close enough to see. Eight, three, ten, five. Queen, two, six, six.

The deck was high.

The dealer laid the next cards.

King. *Over.*

Jack. *Over.*

There was no such thing as luck.

His decision made, he turned back to his partners. "I won't let him ruin my sister."

Bourne nodded once, understanding. "And you won't let Temple kill him. So . . . what? Marry the daughter?"

Cross shook his head. "He threatens mine; I threaten his."

Temple's brows shot up. "The girl?"

"He doesn't care an ounce for the girl," Cross said. "I mean the club."

Bourne propped one arm on the end of his cue. "Knight's." He shook his head. "You'll never convince his membership to leave him. Not without inviting them to join us."

"Which won't happen," Temple said.

"I don't need them all to leave him for good," Cross said, several steps ahead. "I need them to leave him for one night. I need to prove that his kingdom exists only because of our benevolence. That if we had the mind to do so, we could destroy him." He turned back to the floor of the club. "She arrives in six days. I need the upper hand before then."

I need control.

"Six days?" Temple repeated, grinning when Cross nodded. "Six days makes it March the twenty-ninth."

Bourne whistled. "There's the upper hand."

"Pandemonium." The word hovered in the dark room, a solution that could not have been better devised if the devil himself had done it.

Pandemonium—held every year on the twenty-ninth of March—was the one night of the year when the Angel opened its doors to nonmembers. An invitation provided its bearer with access to the casino floor from sundown to sunup. With one, a man could steep himself in sin and vice and experience the clandestine, legendary world that was The Fallen Angel.

Each member of the club received three invitations to Pandemonium—small, square cards so coveted that they were worth thousands of pounds to men desperate to join the club's ranks. Desperate to prove their worth to the owners of the Angel. Certain that if they wagered enough, they might leave with a permanent membership.

They rarely did.

Most often, they left with pockets thousands of pounds lighter and a tale with which to regale their friends who had not been so lucky to receive an invitation.

Cross met Temple's gaze. "Every man who gambles regularly at Knight's is desperate for access to the Angel."

Bourne nodded once. "It's a good plan. One night without his biggest gamers will prove we can take them whenever we like."

"There are how many . . . thirty of them?"

"Fifty, more like," Bourne said.

Cross returned his attention to the floor of the club, his mind racing to formulate a plan, to set the gears in motion. He would save his family.

This time.

"You'll need someone on the inside to identify the men."

"I have her," he said, watching the wagers below.

"Of course," Temple said, admiration in his tone. "Your women."

"They aren't mine." He made sure of it. Not one of them had ever come close to being his.

"Irrelevant," Bourne said. "They adore you."

"They adore what I can do for them."

Temple's tone turned wry. "I'll bet they do."

"What of your sister?" Bourne asked. "The only way the threat works is if she stays away from him. Dunblade as well."

Cross watched the men below, absently calculating their bets—how much they usually wagered, how much the take was when their hand was lost. How much was risked when they won. "I shall speak with her."

There was a long silence that he did not misunderstand. The idea that he might speak to his sister—to any member of his family—was a surprise. Ignoring his partners' shock, Cross turned to meet Bourne's gaze. "Why are there so few members here tonight?"

"The Marbury betrothal ball," Bourne said, his words punctuated by the crack of ivory on ivory. "I understand my mother-in-law has invited the entire peerage. I'm surprised the two of you did not receive invitations."

Temple laughed. "Lady Needham would run for her smelling salts were I to darken her doorstep."

"That does not say much. The lady runs for her smelling salts more often than most."

The Marbury betrothal ball. *Pippa Marbury's betrothal ball.*

Guilt flared again. Perhaps he should tell Bourne everything.

Don't tell Bourne, please. The lady's plea echoed through him, and he gritted his teeth. "Lady Philippa is still for Castleton?" Cross asked, feeling like an idiot, certain that Bourne would see through the query, would recognize his curiosity. Would question it.

"She's been given every opportunity to end it," Bourne said. "The girl is too honorable, she'll be bored with him in a fortnight."

Less than that.

"You should stop it. Hell, *Needham* should stop it," Cross said. Lord knew the Marquess of Needham and Dolby had stopped engagements before. He'd nearly ruined all five of his daughters' chances for proper marriages by ending a legendary engagement years ago.

"It's my fault, dammit. I should have put an end to it before it even began," Bourne said bitterly, no small amount of regret in his words. "I've asked her to end it—Penelope, too. We've both told her we'd protect her. Hell, I'd find her a proper groom tonight if I thought it would help. But Pippa doesn't want it stopped."

I shall do it because I have agreed to, and I do not care for dishonesty. He heard the words, saw her serious blue gaze as she defended her choice to marry Castleton—a man so far beneath her in intellect, it was impossible to believe the impending marriage was not a farce.

Nevertheless, the lady had made a promise, and she intended to keep it.

And that, alone, made her remarkable.

Unaware of Cross's thoughts, Bourne straightened and adjusted his coat sleeves with a wicked swear. "It is too late now. She's at her betrothal ball in front of all the *ton* as we speak. I must go. Penelope will have my head if I do not appear."

"Your wife has you right where she wants you," Temple said dryly, the carom balls clacking together as he spoke.

Bourne did not rise to the bait. "She does indeed. And someday, if you are lucky, you will take the same pleasure I do in the location." He turned to leave, heading for his other life—a newly returned aristocrat.

Cross stopped him. "Most of the peerage is there?"

Bourne turned back. "Is there someone specific you seek?"

"Dunblade."

Understanding flared in Bourne's brown eyes. "I imagine he will attend. With his baroness."

"Perhaps I will pay Dolby House a visit."

Bourne raised a brow. "I do enjoy operating beneath my father-in-law's notice."

Cross nodded.

It was time he see his sister. Seven years had been too long.

*H*alf of London was in the ballroom below.

Pippa peered down from her hiding place in the upper colonnade of the Dolby House ballroom, pressed flat against one massive marble column, stroking the head of her spaniel, Trotula, as she watched the swirling silks and satins waltz across the mahogany floor. She pushed back a heavy drape of velvet curtain, watching her mother greet an endless stream of guests at this—what might be the Marchioness of Needham and Dolby's greatest achievement.

It was not every day, after all, that mothers of five daughters have the opportunity to announce the marriage of her final offspring. Her final *two* offspring. The marchioness was fairly weak from glee.

Sadly, not weak enough to forgo a double betrothal ball large enough to accommodate an army. "Just a selection of dear friends," Lady Needham had said last week, when Pippa had questioned the sheer volume of replies that had arrived piled high on a silver tray one afternoon, threatening to slide off the charger and onto the footman's shiny black boot.

Dear friends, Philippa recalled wryly, her gaze scanning the crowd. She'd have sworn she'd never even met the greater share of people in the room below.

Not that she did not understand her mother's excitement. After all, this day—when all five of the Marbury girls were officially and publicly matched—was a long time coming, and not without its hesitations. But finally, finally, the marchioness was to have her due.

Weddings were nothing if not for mothers, were they not?

Or, if not weddings, at least betrothal balls.

That went doubly so when the betrothal ball was to celebrate *two* daughters.

Pippa's gaze slid from her mother's flushed face and effusive movements to settle on the youngest Marbury sister, holding a court of her own on the opposite end of the ballroom, in a crush of well-wishers, smiling wide, one bejeweled hand on the arm of her tall, handsome fiancé.

Olivia was the prettiest and most ebullient of the quintet, she had seemed to get all the best bits from the rest of the family. Was she utterly self-involved and filled with more than her fair allotment of confidence? Certainly. But it was difficult to judge the traits harshly, as Olivia had never once met a person she could not win.

Including the man who was predicted to soon become one of the most powerful in Britain, for if there were two things a politician's wife required, they were a bold smile and a desire to win—things Olivia had in spades.

Indeed, all of London was abuzz with the news of the

couple's impending marriage, Pippa rather thought that no one downstairs would even notice she was gone.

"I thought I might find you here."

Pippa let the curtain drop and spun to face her eldest sister, the recently minted Marchioness of Bourne. "Shouldn't you be at the ball?"

Penelope leaned down to pay Trotula some attention, smiling when the hound groaned and leaned into the caress. "I could ask you the same thing. After all, now that I'm married off, Mother is far more interested in you than she is me."

"Mother doesn't know what she's missing," Pippa replied. "You're the one married to the legendary scoundrel."

Penelope grinned. "I am, aren't I?"

Pippa laughed. "So proud of yourself." She turned back to the ball, scanning the crowd below. "Where is Bourne? I don't see him."

"Something kept him at the club."

The club.

The words echoed through her, a reminder of two days earlier. Of Mr. Cross.

Mr. Cross, who would have been as out of place in the world below as Pippa felt. Mr. Cross, with whom she had wagered. To whom she had lost.

She cleared her throat, and Penelope mistook the sound. "He swore he'd be here," she defended her husband. "Late, but here."

"What happens at the club at this hour?" Pippa could not keep herself from asking.

"I—wouldn't know."

Pippa grinned. "Liar. If your hesitation had not revealed the untruth, your red face would have."

Chagrin replaced embarrassment. "Ladies are not supposed to know about such things."

Pippa blinked. "Nonsense. Ladies who are married to casino owners may certainly know such things."

Penelope's brows rose. "Our mother would disagree."

"Our mother is not my barometer for how women should and should not behave. The woman lunges for her smelling salts every thirty minutes." She pushed back the curtain to reveal the marchioness far below, deep in conversation with Lady Beaufetheringstone—one of the *ton*'s greatest gossips. As if on cue, Lady Needham released an excited squeak that carried high into the rafters.

Pippa looked to Penelope knowingly. "Now, tell me what happens at the club."

"Gaming."

"I know *that*, Penny. What else?"

Penelope lowered her voice. "There are women."

Pippa's brows went up. "Prostitutes?" She supposed there would be. After all, in all the texts she'd read, she'd come to discover that men enjoyed the company of women—and rarely their wives.

"Pippa!" Penny sounded scandalized.

"What?"

"You shouldn't even know that word."

"Why on earth not? The word is in the Bible, for heaven's sake."

"It is not."

Pippa thought for a long moment before leaning back against the colonnade. "I think it is, you know. If it isn't, it should be. The profession is not a new one."

She paused.

Prostitutes would have eons of institutional knowledge to address her concerns. To answer her questions.

Have you asked your sisters? The echo of Mr. Cross's words from the previous afternoon had Pippa turning to her eldest sister. What if she *did* ask Penny?

"May I ask a question?"

Penelope raised a brow. "I doubt I could stop you."

"I'm concerned about some of the . . . logistics. Of marriage."

Penelope's gaze grew sharp. "Logistics?"

Pippa waved one hand in the air. "The . . . personal bits."

Penelope went red. "Ah."

"Olivia told me about tongues."

The eldest Marbury's brows rose. "What does she know about them?"

"More than I think either of us imagined," Pippa replied, "but I couldn't ask her to elaborate—I couldn't bear taking lessons from my youngest sister. You, on the other hand . . ."

There was a pause as the words sank in, and Penelope's eyes went wide. "Surely you don't expect me to school you!"

"Just on a few critical issues," Pippa said urgently.

"For example?"

"Well, tongues, for one."

Penelope put her hands over her ears. "No more! I don't want to think of Olivia and Tottenham doing . . ." She trailed off.

Pippa wanted to shake her. "Doing *what*?"

"Doing any of it!"

"But don't you see? How can I be prepared for all this if I don't understand it? Bulls in Coldharbor are not enough!"

Penelope gave a little laugh. "Bulls in Coldharbor?"

Pippa went red. "I've seen . . ."

"You think it's like that?"

"Well, I wouldn't if someone would tell me . . . I mean, are men's . . . are their . . ." She waved a hand in a specific direction. "Are they so *large*?"

Penelope clapped a hand over her mouth to stem her laughter, and Pippa found herself growing irritated. "I am happy I'm giving you such a laugh."

Penny shook her head. "I'm—" She giggled again, and Pippa cut her a look. "I'm sorry! It's just . . . no. *No.* They have little in common with the bull in Coldharbor." There was a pause. "And thank God for that."

"Is it . . . frightening?"

And, like that, Penelope's gaze filled with doe-eyed sentimentality. "Not at all," she whispered, all treacle, and while the honest answer was comforting, Pippa nevertheless resisted the urge to roll her eyes.

"And, like that, I've lost you."

Penelope smiled. "You're curious, Pippa. I understand. But it will all become clear."

Pippa did not like the idea of relying on the promise of clarity. She wanted it *now*.

Damn Mr. Cross and his idiot wager.

Damn herself for taking it.

Penelope was still speaking, voice all soft and saccharine. "And if you're lucky, you shall discover . . ." She sighed. "Well, you shall enjoy it quite a bit, I hope." She shook her head, coming out of her dream, and laughed again. "Stop thinking about bulls."

Pippa scowled. "How was I to know?"

"You've a library full of anatomy texts!" Penny whispered.

"Well, I question the scale of the illustrations in several of those texts!" Pippa whispered back.

Penny started to say something and thought better of it, changing tack. "Conversations with you always take the strangest turns. Dangerous ones. We should go downstairs."

Sisters were useless. Pippa would be better off talking to one of the prostitutes.

The prostitutes.

She adjusted her spectacles. "Back to the ladies, Penny. Are they prostitutes?"

Penny sighed and looked to the ceiling. "Not in so many words."

"It is only one word," Pippa pointed out.

"Well, suffice to say, they come with the gentlemen, but they are certainly not ladies."

Fascinating.

Pippa wondered if Mr. Cross associated with the ladies in question. She wondered if they lay with him on that strange, small pallet in his cluttered, curious office. At the thought, something flared heavy and full in her chest. She considered the feeling, not quite nausea, not quite breathlessness.

Not quite pleasant.

Before she could assess the sensation further, Penelope continued. "At any rate, no matter what is happening at the club this evening, Bourne is decidedly *not* consorting with prostitutes."

Pippa couldn't imagine her brother-in-law doing anything of the sort. Indeed, she couldn't imagine her brother-in-law doing much but dote on his wife these days. Theirs was a curious relationship—one of the rare marriages built on something more than a sound match.

In fact, most rational people would agree that there was absolutely nothing about Penelope and Bourne that would make for a sound match.

And somehow, they'd made just that.

Another curiosity.

Some might call it love, no doubt. And perhaps it was, but Pippa had never given much credence to the sentiment— with so few love matches in society, they were rather like mythological figures. Minotaurs. Or unicorns. Or Pegasuses.

Pegasii?

Neither, presumably, as there was only one Pegasus, but, as with love matches, one never knew.

"Pippa?" Penelope prodded.

Pippa snapped back to the conversation. What had they been discussing? *Bourne.* "Well, I don't know why he *would* come," Pippa pointed out. "No one expects him to stand on ceremony for society."

"I expect him to do so," Penelope said simply, as if that were all that mattered.

And apparently, it was. "Really, Penny. Leave the poor man alone."

"Poor man," Penny scoffed. "Bourne gets everything he wants, whenever he wants it."

"It's not as though he doesn't pay a price," Pippa retorted.

"He must love you fiercely if he is coming. If I could avoid tonight, I would."

"You are doing an excellent job of it as it is, and you *cannot* avoid tonight."

Penny was right, of course. Half of London was below, and at least one of them was waiting for her to show her face.

Her future husband.

It was not difficult to find him among the throngs of people. Even dressed in the same handsome black frock coat and trousers that the rest of the peerage preferred, the Earl of Castleton seemed to stand out, something about him less graceful than a normal aristocrat.

He was at one side of the ballroom, leaning low as his mother whispered in his ear. Pippa had never noticed it before, but the ear in question also stood out at a rather unfortunate angle.

"You could still beg off," Penelope said quietly. "No one would blame you."

"The ball?"

"The marriage."

Pippa did not reply. She could. She could say any number of things ranging from amusing to acerbic, and Penny would never judge her for them. Indeed, it would very likely make her sister happy to hear that Pippa had an opinion one way or another about her betrothed.

But Pippa had committed herself to the earl, and she would not be disloyal. He did not deserve it. He was a nice man, with a kind heart. And that was more than could be said about most.

Dishonesty by omission remains dishonest.

The words echoed through her, a memory of two days earlier, of the man who had questioned her commitment to truth.

The world is full of liars. Liars and cheats.

It wasn't true, of course. Pippa wasn't a liar. Pippa didn't cheat.

Trotula sighed and leaned against her mistress's thigh. Pippa idly stroked the dog's ears. "I made a promise."

"I know you did, Pippa. But sometimes promises . . ." Penelope trailed off.

Pippa watched Castleton for a long moment. "I dislike balls."

"I know."

"And ballrooms."

"Yes."

"He's kind, Penny. And he asked."

Penelope's gaze turned soft. "It's fine for you to wish for more than that, you know."

She didn't. *Did she?*

Pippa fidgeted inside her tightly laced corset. "And ball *gowns*."

Penelope allowed the change in topic. "It is a nice gown, nonetheless."

Pippa's gown—selected with near-fanatical excitement by Lady Needham—was a beautiful pale green gauze over white satin. Cut low and off the shoulder, the gown followed her shape through the bodice and waist before flaring into lush, full skirts that rustled when she moved. On anyone else, it would look lovely.

But on her . . . the gown made her look thinner, longer, more reedy. "It makes me look like the *Ardea cinerea*."

Penelope blinked.

"A heron."

"Nonsense. You are beautiful."

Pippa ran her palms over the perfectly worked fabric. "Then I think it's best I stay here and keep that illusion intact."

Penelope chuckled. "You are postponing the inevitable."

It was the truth.

And because it was the truth, Pippa allowed her sister to lead them down the narrow stairs to the back entrance of the ballroom, where they released Trotula onto the Dolby

House grounds before inserting themselves, unnoticed, into the throngs of well-wishers, as though they'd been present for the entire time.

Her future mother-in-law found them within moments. "Philippa, my dear!" she effused, waving a fan of peacock feathers madly about her face. "Your mother said it would be just a little *fête*! And what a *fête* it is! A *fête* to *fête* my young Robert and his soon-to-be-bride!"

Pippa smiled. "And do not forget Lady Tottenham's young James and *his* soon-to-be-bride."

For a moment, it seemed that Countess of Castleton did not follow. Pippa waited. Understanding dawned, and her future mother-in-law laughed, loud and high-pitched. "Oh, of course! Your sister is *lovely*! As are *you*! Isn't she, Robert?" She swatted the earl on his arm. "Isn't she lovely!"

He leapt to agree. "She is! Er—you are, Lady Philippa! You are! Lovely!"

Pippa smiled. "Thank you."

Her mother bore down upon them, the Marchioness of Needham and Dolby eager to compete for the most-excited-mother award. "Lady Castleton! Are they not the most handsome of couples!"

"So *very* handsome!" Lady Castleton agreed, maneuvering her son to stand close to Pippa. "You simply must dance! *Everyone* is *desperate* to see you dance!"

Pippa was virtually certain that there were only two people in the room with any interest whatsoever in watching them dance. In fact, anyone who had ever seen Pippa dance knew not to expect much in the way of grace or skill, and her experience with Castleton indicated similar failings on his part. But, unfortunately, the two in question were mothers. And unavoidable.

And, dancing would limit the number of exclamations in her proximity by a good amount.

She smiled up at her fiancé. "It seems we are required to dance, my lord."

"Right! Right!" Castleton leapt to attention, clicking his heels together and giving her a small bow. "Would you afford me the very great honor of a dance, my lady?"

Pippa resisted the urge to laugh at the formality of the question and instead took his hand and allowed him to lead her into the dance.

It was a disaster.

They all but stumbled across the floor, creating a devastating spectacle of themselves. When they were together, they trod on each other's toes and tripped over each other's feet—at one point, he actually clutched her to him, having lost his balance. And when they were apart, they tripped over their own feet.

When he was not counting his steps to keep time with the orchestra, Castleton kept up conversation by fairly bellowing across the dance floor.

The couples nearby did their best not to stare, but Pippa had to admit, it was near impossible when Castleton announced from ten feet away on the opposite side of the line, "Oh! I nearly forgot to tell you! I've a new bitch!"

He was discussing his dogs, of course—a topic in which they had a shared interest—but Pippa imagined it was something of a shock to Louisa Holbrooke when Castleton hurled the announcement right over her perfectly coiffed head.

Pippa could not help it. She began to snicker, drawing a strange look from her own partner. She lifted a hand to hide her twitching lips when Castleton added, "She's a beauty! Brindled fur! Brown and yellow . . . yellow like yours!"

Eyes around them went wide at the comparison of her blond hair to the golden fur of Castleton's most recent four-legged acquisition. And that's when the snicker became a laugh. It was, after all, the strangest—and loudest—conversation she'd ever had while dancing.

She laughed through the final steps of the quadrille, her shoulders shaking as she dipped into the curtsy ladies were required to make. If there was one thing she would not miss upon her marriage, it was dancing.

She rose, and Castleton came instantly to her side, shepherding her to one end of the room, where they stood in awkward silence for a long moment. She watched the other attendees fall gracefully into the party, keenly aware of Castleton beside her. *Robert.*

How many times had she heard Penny refer to her husband as Michael in that tone of utter devotion?

Pippa turned to look up at Castleton. She could not imagine ever calling him Robert.

"Would you like some lemonade?" He broke their silence.

She shook her head, returning her gaze to the room. "No, thank you."

"I should have waited to tell you about the dog until we were through dancing," he said, drawing her attention once more. Color rose on his cheeks.

She did not like the idea that he was embarrassed. He did not deserve it. "No!" she protested, grateful for the return of the topic. It was easy to talk about dogs. "She sounds lovely. What do you call her?"

He smiled, bright and honest. He did that a lot. It was another good quality. "I thought perhaps you would have an idea."

The words set her back. It would never occur to her to ask Castleton for his opinion on such a thing. She'd simply name the hound and announce her as part of the family. Her surprise must have shown on her face, because he added, "After all, we are to be married. She will be our hound."

Our hound.

The hound was Castleton's ruby ring. A living, breathing chromium-filled crystal.

Suddenly, it all seemed very serious.

They were to be married. They were to have a hound. And she was to name it.

A hound was much more than betrothal balls and trousseaus and wedding plans—all things that seemed utterly inconsequential when it came right down to it.

A hound made the future real.

A hound meant a home, and seasons passing and visits from neighbors and Sunday masses and harvest festivals. A hound meant a family. Children. *His children.*

She looked up into the kind, smiling eyes of her fiancé. He was waiting, eager for her to speak.

"I—" She stopped, not knowing what to say. "I haven't any good ideas."

He chuckled. "Well, she doesn't know the difference. You are welcome to think about it." He leaned low, one blond lock falling over his brow. "You should meet her first. Perhaps that would help."

She forced a smile. "Perhaps it would."

Perhaps it would make her want to marry him more.

She liked dogs. They had that in common.

The thought reminded her of her conversation with Mr. Cross, during which she'd told him the same as proof of her compatibility with the earl. He'd scoffed at her, and she'd ignored it.

It was all they'd said of the earl . . . until Mr. Cross had refused her request and sent her home, with a comment that echoed through her now, as she stood awkwardly beside her future husband. *I suggest you query another. Perhaps your fiancé?*

Perhaps she *should* query her fiancé. Surely he knew more than he revealed about the . . . intricacies of marriage. It did not matter that he'd never once given her even the slightest suggestion that he cared a bit for those intricacies.

Gentlemen knew about them. Far more than ladies did.

That this was a horrendously unequal truth was not the point, currently.

She peered up at Castleton, who was not looking at her.

Instead, he appeared to be looking anywhere *but* her. She took the moment to consider her next step. He was close, after all—close enough to touch. Perhaps she ought to touch him.

He looked down at her, surprise flaring in his warm brown gaze when he discovered her notice. He smiled.

It was now or never.

She reached out and touched him, letting her silk-clad fingers slide over his kid-clad hand. His smile did not waver. Instead, he lifted his other arm and patted her hand twice, as he might do a hound's head. It was the least carnal touch she could imagine. Not at all reminiscent of the wedding vows. Indeed, it indicated that he had no trouble with the bit about not entering into marriage like a brute beast.

She extricated her hand.

"All right?" he asked, already returning his attention to the room at large.

It did not take a woman of great experience to know that her touch had had no effect on him. Which she supposed was only fair, as his touch was absent an effect on her.

A lady laughed nearby, and Pippa turned toward the sound, light and airy and false. It was the kind of laugh she'd never perfected—her laughs were always too loud, or came at the wrong time, or not at all.

"I think I would like some lemonade, if the offer remains," she said.

He jolted to attention at the words, "I shall fetch it for you!"

She smiled. "That would be lovely."

He pointed to the floor. "I shall return!"

"Excellent."

And then he was gone, pushing through the crowd with an eagerness that one might associate with something more exciting than lemonade.

Pippa planned to wait, but it was something of a bore, and with the pressing heat of the room and the hundreds of people, it might take Castleton a quarter of an hour to return, and waiting alone, rather publicly, felt strange. So instead, she slipped away to a darker, quieter edge of the room where she could stand back and observe the crowd.

People appeared to be having a lovely time. Olivia was holding court on the far end of the room, she and Tottenham surrounded by a throng of people who wanted the ear of the next prime minister. Pippa's mother and Lady Castleton had collected Tottenham's mother and a clutch of doyennes who were no doubt engaged in a round of scathing gossip.

As she scanned the crowd, her attention was drawn to an alcove directly across from her, where a tall, dark-haired gentleman leaned too close to his companion, lips nearly touching her ear in a manner that spoke clearly of a clandestine assignation. The couple appeared to care not a bit for their public locale, and were no doubt causing tongues to wag throughout the ballroom.

Not that such a thing was out of the ordinary for those two.

Pippa smiled. Bourne had arrived and, as ever, had eyes only for her sister.

Few understood how Penny had landed the cold, aloof, immovable Bourne—Pippa rarely saw the marquess smile or show any emotion whatsoever outside of his interactions with his doting wife—but there was no doubt that he had been landed, and was utterly smitten.

Penny swore it was love, and that was the bit that Pippa did not understand. She never liked the idea of love matches— there was too much about them that could not be explained. Too much that was ethereal. Pippa did not believe in ethereal. She believed in factual.

She watched as her proper sister placed her hands on her husband's chest and pushed him away, laughing and blushing like a newly out debutante. He caught her close once more, pressing a kiss to her temple before she pulled away and dove back into the crowd. Bourne followed, as if on a string.

Pippa shook her head at the strange, unlikely sight.

Love, if it were a thing, was an odd thing, indeed.

A draft of cold air rustled her skirts, and she turned to find that a set of great double doors behind her had been opened—no doubt to combat the stifling heat in the room—and one had blown wide. She moved to close it, leaning out onto the great stone balcony to reach the door's handle.

That's when she heard it.

"You need me."

"I need no such thing. I have taken care of myself without you for some time."

Pippa paused. Someone was out there. *Two* someones.

"I can fix this. I can help. Just give me time. Six days."

"Since when are you interested in helping?"

Pippa's hand closed on the edge of the glass-paneled door, and she willed herself to close it. To pretend she had heard nothing. To return to the ball.

She did not move.

"I've always wanted to help." The man's voice was soft and urgent. Pippa stepped out onto the balcony.

"You certainly haven't showed it." The lady's voice was steel. Angry and unwavering. "In fact, you have never helped. You have only hindered."

"You're in trouble."

"It is not the first time."

A hesitation. When the man spoke, his whispered words were clipped and filled with concern. "What else?"

She laughed quietly, but there was no humor in the sound—only bitterness. "Nothing you can repair now."

"You shouldn't have married him."

"I didn't have a choice. You didn't leave me with one."

Pippa's eyes went wide. She'd stumbled into a lover's quarrel. Well, not current lovers by the sound of it . . . past lovers. The question was, who where the lovers in question?

"I should have stopped it," he whispered.

"Well, you didn't," she shot back.

Pippa pressed against a great stone column that provided a lovely shadow in which to hide, and edged her head to one side, holding her breath, unable to resist her attempt to discover their identity.

The balcony was empty.

She poked her head out from behind the column.

Totally empty.

Where were they?

"I can repair the damage. But you must stay away from him. Far away. He mustn't have access to you."

In the gardens below.

Pippa moved quietly toward the stone balustrade, curiosity piqued in the extreme.

"Oh, I am to believe you now? Suddenly, you are willing to keep me safe?"

Pippa winced. The lady's tone was scathing. The gentleman in question—who was no gentleman at all, if Pippa had to guess—had most definitely wronged her in the past. She increased her pace, nearly to the edge, almost able to peer over the side of the balcony and identify the mysterious ex-lovers below.

"Lavinia . . ." he began softly, pleading, and excitement coursed through Pippa. *A name!*

That's when she kicked the flowerpot.

They might not have heard the little scrape that came as she made contact with the great, footed beast of a thing . . . if only she hadn't cried out in pain. It did not matter that her hand immediately flew to cover her mouth, turning her very loud "Oh!" into a very garbled "Oof."

But the instant silence from below was enough to prove that they'd heard her quite clearly.

"I shouldn't be here," the lady whispered, and Pippa heard a rustle of skirts fading away.

There was a long moment of silence, during which she

remained still as stone, biting her lip against the throbbing pain in her foot before he finally spoke, cursing in the darkness. "Goddammit."

Pippa crouched low, feeling for her toes, and muttered, "You no doubt deserved that," before realizing that taunting an unidentified man in the darkened gardens of her ancestral home was not a sound idea.

"I beg your pardon?" he asked quietly, no longer whispering.

She should return to the ball. Instead, she said, "It does not sound as though you have been very kind to the lady."

Silence. "I haven't been."

"Well then, you deserve her desertion." She squeezed her smallest toe and hissed in pain. "Likely more than that."

"You hurt yourself."

She was distracted by the pain, or she wouldn't have responded. "I stubbed my toe."

"Punishment for eavesdropping?"

"No doubt."

"That will teach you."

She smiled. "I hardly think so."

She couldn't be sure, but she was almost positive that he chuckled. "You had best be certain that your partners do not tread upon your toes when you return."

A vision of Castleton flashed. "I am afraid it is very likely that at least one of them will do just that." She paused. "It seems you gravely wronged the lady. How?"

He was quiet for so long that she thought he might have left. "I was not there for her when she needed me."

"Ah," she said.

"Ah?" he asked.

"One need not read romantic novels as frequently as my sister does to understand what happened."

"You don't read romantic novels, of course."

"Not often," Pippa said.

"I imagine you read books on more important things."

"I do, as a matter of fact," she said, proudly.

"Tomes on physics and horticulture." Pippa's eyes went wide. "Those are the purview of Lady Philippa Marbury."

She shot to her feet and peered over the edge of the balcony, into the pit of darkness below. She couldn't see anything. She heard the swipe of wool as his arms shifted, or perhaps his legs. He was right there. Directly beneath her.

She moved without thinking, reaching for him, arms extending toward him as she whispered, "Who are you?"

Even through the silk of her gloves, his hair was soft—like thick sable. She let her fingers sink into the strands until they rested on his scalp, the heat of it a stark contrast against the cold March air.

It was gone before she could revel in it, replaced by one large, strong hand, no more than a shadow in the yawning blackness, capturing both of hers with ease.

She gasped and tugged.

He did not let go.

What had she been thinking?

Her spectacles were slipping, and she stilled, afraid they would topple off her nose if she moved too much.

"You should know better than to reach into the darkness, Pippa," he said softly, the sound of her name familiar on his lips. "You never know what you might find."

"Release me," she whispered, risking movement to look over her shoulder to the still-open door to the ballroom. "Someone will see."

"Isn't that what you want?" His fingers tangled with hers, the heat of his grasp nearly unbearable. How was he so warm in the cold?

She shook her head, feeling the wire frames of her glasses slip more. "No."

"Are you certain?" His grip shifted, and suddenly, it was she holding him, not the other way around.

She forced herself to release him. "Yes." She put both hands safely on the stone railing, straightening, but not before her glasses dropped into the darkness. She reached for them, knocking them off course with her fingertips, sending them shooting through the night. "My spectacles!"

He disappeared, the only sign of him the whisper of fabric as he moved away from her. And she didn't know how, but she could feel the loss of him. The top of his head came into view, a few inches of blurred, burnt orange gleaming in the candlelight loosed from the ballroom.

Recognition surged on a tide of excitement. *Mr. Cross.*

She pointed toward him. "Do not move."

She was already heading for the far end of the balcony, where a long staircase led down to the gardens.

He met her at the base of the stone steps, the dim light from the house casting his face into wicked shadows. Extending her spectacles to her, he said, "Return to the ballroom."

She snatched the glasses and put them on, his face becoming clear and angled once more. "No."

"We agreed you would relinquish your quest for ruination."

She took a deep breath. "Then you should not have encouraged me."

"Encouraged you to eavesdrop and hobble yourself?"

She tested her weight on the foot, wincing at the pinch of pain in the toe. "I think at the worst it is a minor phalangeal fracture. It will heal. I've done it before."

"Broken your toe."

She nodded. "It's just the smallest toe. A horse once stepped on the same toe on the opposite side. Needless to say, ladies' footwear does not provide much in the way of protection from those so far better shod than we."

"I suppose anatomy is another one of your specialties?"

"It is."

"I am impressed."

She was not certain he was telling the truth. "In my experience, 'impressed' is not the usual reaction to my knowledge of human anatomy."

"No?"

She was grateful for the dim light, as she could not seem to stop speaking. "Most people find it odd."

"I am not most people."

The response set her back. "I suppose you're not." She paused, thinking of the conversation she'd overheard. She ignored the thread of discomfort that came with the memory. "Who is Lavinia?"

"Go back to your ball, Pippa." He turned away from her and started along the edge of the house.

She could not let him leave. She might have promised not to approach him, but he was in her gardens. She followed.

He stopped and turned back. "Have you learned the parts of the ear?"

She smiled, welcoming his interest. "Of course. The exterior portion is called the *pinna*. Some refer to it as the *auricle*, but I prefer the *pinna*, because it's Latin for feather, and I've always rather liked the image. The inner ear is made up of an impressive collection of bones and tissue, beginning with—"

"Amazing." He cut her off. "You seem to know so much about the organ in question, and yet you fail so miserably at using it. I could have sworn I told you to return to your ball."

He turned away again. She followed.

"My hearing is fine, Mr. Cross. As is my free will."

"You are difficult."

"Not usually."

"Turning over a new leaf?" He did not slow.

"Do you make it a practice to force the ladies of your acquaintance to run to keep up with you?"

He stopped, and she nearly ran into him. "Only those whom I would like to lose."

She smiled. "You came to *my* location, Mr. Cross. Do not forget that."

He looked to the sky, then back at her, and she wished that she could see his eyes. "The terms of our wager were clear;

you are not to be ruined. If you remain here, with me, you will be missed, and sought. And if you are discovered, you will be ruined. Return. Immediately."

There was something very compelling about this man—about the way he seemed so calm, so controlled. And she had never in her life wanted to do something less than leave him. "No one will miss me."

"Not even Castleton?"

She hesitated, something akin to guilt flaring. The earl was likely waiting for her, lemonade warming in hand.

Mr. Cross seemed to read her mind. "He is missing you."

Perhaps it was the darkness. Or perhaps it was the pain in her foot. Or perhaps it was the way the quick back-and-forth of their conversation made her feel as though she had finally found someone with a mind that worked the way hers did. She would never know why she blurted out, "He wants me to name his hound."

There was a long moment of silence during which she thought he might laugh.

Please don't laugh.

He didn't laugh. "You are marrying the man. It is a rather innocuous request in the grand scheme of things."

He did not understand. "It's not innocuous."

"Is there something wrong with it?"

"The dog?"

"Yes."

"No, I think she's probably quite a nice dog." She lifted her hands, then dropped them. "It just seems so . . . So . . ."

"Final."

He *did* understand. "Precisely."

"It is final. You're marrying him. You're going to have to name his children. One would think the dog would be the easy bit."

"Yes, well, it seems the dog is the much harder bit." She took a deep breath. "Have you ever considered marriage?"

"No." The reply was quick and honest.

"Why not?"

"It is not for me."

"You seem sure of that."

"I am."

"How do you know?"

He did not reply, saved from having to by the arrival of Trotula, who came careening around the corner of the house with a happy, excited *woof.* "Yours?" he asked.

She nodded as the spaniel barreled to a stop at their feet, and Cross crouched low to pet the dog, who sighed and leaned into the caress.

"She likes that," Pippa said.

"Name?"

"Trotula."

One side of his mouth kicked up in a small, knowing smile. "Like Trotula de Salerno? The Italian doctor?"

Of course he would know she'd named the dog for a scientist. Of course he would guess. "Doctoress."

He shook his head. "That's a terrible name. Perhaps you shouldn't name Castleton's dog after all."

"It is not! Trotula de Salerno is an excellent namesake!"

"No. I shall allow you 'excellent example for young women' or 'excellent scientific hero,' but I will not allow you 'excellent namesake.'" He paused, scratching the spaniel's ear. "Poor beast," he said, and Pippa warmed to the kindness in his tone. "She's mistreated you abominably."

Trotula turned over onto her back, displaying her underside with an alarming lack of shame. He scratched her there, and Pippa was transfixed by his strong, handsome hands—the way they worked in her fur. After a long moment of observation, she said, "I'd rather stay outside. With you."

His hand stilled on the dog's stomach. "What happened to your aversion to dishonesty?"

Her brows snapped together. "It remains."

"You are attempting to escape your betrothal ball with another man. I would say that's the very portrait of dishonesty."

"Not another man."

He stiffened. "I beg your pardon?"

She hurried to rephrase. "That is, you are another man, of course, but you aren't a real man. I mean, you are not a threat to Castleton. You are safe." She trailed off . . . suddenly feeling not at all safe.

"And the fact that you've asked me to assist you in any number of activities that might destroy your reputation and summarily end your engagement?"

"It still doesn't make you a man," she said quickly. Too quickly. Quickly enough to have to take it back. "I mean. Well. You know what I mean. Not in the way *you* mean."

He exhaled on a low laugh and stood. "First you offer to pay me for sex, then you throw my masculinity into question. A lesser man would take those words to heart."

Her eyes went wide. She'd never meant to imply . . . "I didn't . . ." She trailed off.

He stepped toward her, close enough for her to feel his heat. His voice turned low and quiet. "A lesser man would attempt to prove you wrong."

She swallowed. He was intimidatingly tall when he was so close. So much taller than any other man of her acquaintance. "I—"

"Tell me, Lady Philippa." He raised a hand, one finger lingering at the indentation of her upper lip, a hairsbreadth from touching her. "In your study of anatomy, did you ever learn the name of the place between the nose and the lip?"

Her lips parted, and she resisted the urge to lean toward him, to force him to touch her. She answered on a whisper. "The philtrum."

He smiled. "Clever girl. It is Latin. Do you know its meaning?"

"No."

"It means love potion. The Romans believed it was the most erotic place on the body. They called it Cupid's bow, because of the way it shapes the upper lip." As he spoke, he ran his finger along the curve of her lip, a temptation more than a touch, barely there. His voice grew softer, deeper. "They believed it was the mark of the god of love."

She inhaled, low and shallow. "I did not know that."

He leaned down, closer, his hand falling away. "I'd be willing to wager that there are any number of things about the human body that you do not know, my little expert. All things that I would happily teach you."

He was so close . . . his words more breath than sound, the feel of them against her ear, then her cheek, sending a riot of sensation through her.

This is what it should feel like with Castleton. The thought came from nowhere. She pushed it aside, promised to deal with it later.

But for now . . . "I would like to learn," she said.

"So honest." He smiled, the curve of his lips—his philtrum—so close, and as dangerous as the weapon for which it was named. "This is your first lesson."

She wanted him to teach her everything.

"Do not tempt the lion," he said, the words brushing across her lips, parting them with their touch. "For he most certainly will bite."

Dear God. She welcomed it.

He straightened, stepping back and adjusting the cuffs of his coat casually, utterly unmoved by the moment. "Go back to your ball and your betrothed, Pippa."

He turned away, and she sucked in a long breath, feeling as though she had been without oxygen for a damaging length of time.

She watched him as he disappeared into the darkness, willing him back.

Failing.

Chapter Six

*H*ours later, long after the last gamer had left the Angel, Cross sat at his desk, attempting to calculate the evening's take for the third time. And failing for the third time.

Failing, because he could not eradicate the vision of blond, bespectacled Philippa Marbury charging down the rear steps of Dolby House toward him. Indeed, every time he attempted to carry a digit from one column to the next, he imagined her fingers threading through his hair or her lips curving beneath his hand, and he lost the number.

Cross did not lose numbers. Much of his adult life had been spent in punishment for being unable to lose numbers.

He bowed over the book again.

He'd added three lines of the column before the pendula on his desk caught his attention, and he remembered her soft touch setting the drops in motion. Temptation flared, and he imagined that same touch setting other things in motion. Like the fastenings on his trousers.

The nib of his pen snapped against the ledger, sending a splatter of ink across the ecru page.

She thought him safe.

And with any other woman, he was. With any other woman, he was safety incarnate.

But with her . . . his control—that which he valued above all else—hung by a thread. A delicate, silken thread, soft as her hair. Her skin. Her voice in the darkness.

With a groan, he shoved his hands through his hair and pushed his chair away from the desk, tilting it back against the wall and spreading his legs wide. He had to exorcise her memory from this place. Everywhere he looked—the abacus, the globe, the damned desk—everything was sullied with her. He was almost certain that he could still smell her there, the lingering scent of sunlight and fresh linen.

Goddammit.

She'd ruined his office . . . as thoroughly as if she'd marched into the room and removed all her clothes.

And laid herself across his desk, wearing nothing but her spectacles and her little crooked smile, her skin pale and beautiful against the ebony.

He closed his eyes, the vision altogether too easy to conjure. He pinned her with one hand just below her beautiful white breasts, their tips the color of her lips—fresh peaches drizzled with honey. His mouth watered; he wouldn't be able to stop himself from leaning over her, from taking one of those perfect nipples into his mouth and tasting her. He'd spend an age on those breasts, teasing her until she was writhing beneath him, savoring her until she was desperate for him to move on—begging him to move lower.

And only when she begged would he give her what they both wanted—spreading her thighs, running his hands over her soft, creamy skin, and—

A knock on the door sounded like a rifle's report. His chair slammed to the floor, punctuated by his wicked curse.

Whoever it was, Cross was going to murder him. Slowly. And with great pleasure.

"What?" he barked.

The door opened, revealing the founder of The Fallen Angel. "A fine welcome."

Cross considered leaping over the desk and strangling Chase. "I must have said it wrong. Barring the club being aflame, you are unwelcome."

Chase did not listen, instead closing the door and dropping into a large wing chair on the opposite side of the desk.

Cross scowled.

His partner shrugged. "Let's say the club is aflame."

"What do you want?"

"The book."

Gentlemen's clubs across London prided themselves on their betting books, and the Angel was no different. The massive leather-bound volume was used to catalog all wagers made on the main floor of the club. Members could record any wager—no matter how trivial—in the book, and the Angel took a percentage of the bets to make certain the parties were held to whatever bizarre stakes were established.

Chase dealt in information, and loved the book for the secrets it revealed about the club's membership. The insurance it provided.

Cross set the heavy tome on the desk.

Chase did not reach for it. "Justin tells me that you were not here for most of the evening."

"Justin needs a sound thrashing for all the information he gives you regarding our whereabouts."

"I care less about the others' whereabouts these days," Chase said, extending one arm and setting the massive globe in motion. "I'm chiefly concerned with yours."

Cross watched the globe spin, hating the realization that the last person to interact with the giant orb had been Philippa Marbury and resenting Chase's touching it. "I don't know why."

"Knight is easier to watch when I know where to find him."

Cross's brows rose. Surely he had misunderstood. "Are you suggesting that I ignore the fact that he has ruined my brother-in-law, threatened my sister's safety, and blackmailed me?"

"No. Of course not." Chase stopped the globe, one long finger on the Sahara. "And I care not a bit about whether you marry the girl or not. But I want you to be careful about the way you choose to punish Knight. He will not take kindly to half measures."

Cross met his partner's gaze. "Meaning?"

"Meaning you have one chance to do this. You establish our might wholly, or not at all."

"I have plans for wholly."

"There is a reason why his largest players do not have memberships to the Angel. They are not men we would ordinarily welcome at our tables."

"Maybe not. But respect tempts them. Power. The chance to rub elbows with those who have it, those who are titled. The chance to play the Angel."

Chase nodded, reaching for a box of cigars on a nearby table. "Where were you tonight?"

"I do not require a keeper."

"Of course you do. You think I don't already know where you were?" The words came from behind a cloud of smoke.

Irritation flared. "You did not have me followed."

Chase did not respond to the anger. "I don't trust Knight around you. The two of you have always had a . . . troublesome . . . rapport."

Cross stood, towering over the desk and his partner. "You did not have me followed."

Chase rolled the cigar between thumb and finger. "I do wish you had scotch in here."

"Get out." Cross had had enough.

Chase did not move. "I didn't have you followed. But I see now that it would have been edifying had I done."

Cross swore, brutal and barbaric.

"You have had a bad night, haven't you? Where did you go?"

"I saw my sister."

Chase's golden brows rose. "You went to Needham's ball?"

I also saw Philippa Marbury. Well, he certainly wasn't going to tell Chase *that*. Instead, he said nothing.

"I take it the meeting did not go well," Chase said.

"She wants nothing to do with me. Even when I told her I would take care of Knight, she had little to say. She didn't believe me."

Chase was quiet for a long moment, considering the situation. "Sisters are difficult. They do not always respond well to the dictates of older brothers."

"You would know that better than anyone."

"Would you like me to speak with her?"

"You think far too highly of yourself."

Chase smiled. "Ladies tend to welcome me with open arms. Even ladies like your sister."

Cross's gaze narrowed. "I don't want you near her. It's bad enough she's to deal with Digger . . . and with me."

"You wound me." Chase savored the cigar. "Will she stay away from him?"

He considered the question, and his sister's fury earlier in the evening. Lavinia had been seventeen when Baine died, when Cross left. She'd been forced into a marriage with Dunblade because he'd been willing to take her on—despite her imperfections.

Imperfections Cross had caused.

Imperfections that should have been overlooked—would have been if she'd been able to escape their mother's sorrow and their father's wrath. If she hadn't been forced to survive on her own, with no one to help her.

Without a brother to keep her safe.

No wonder she did not believe him when he told her he would repair the damage Knight and her husband had done. Anger and frustration and not a small amount of self-loathing flared. "I don't know what she'll do. But I know Knight won't do anything to jeopardize his daughter's marriage."

"We should have ruined him years ago." When Cross did not reply, Chase added, "You've always had too soft a spot for him."

Cross lifted one shoulder in a small shrug. "Without him . . ."

White teeth flashed. "You wouldn't have us."

Cross laughed at that. "When put that way, perhaps I shouldn't hesitate in ruining him."

Chase savored a long puff on the cigar, thinking before saying, "You have to keep up the ruse until you're ready to take him out. To protect Lavinia." Cross nodded. "Temple said you're planning to use the ladies? You realize you'll need me to get the ladies."

Cross raised a brow. "I don't think that will be necessary."

"Are you sure? They like me a great deal."

"I am sure."

Chase nodded once. "I wonder what the daughter is like."

"She's Knight's progeny, so I'm guessing either a raving bitch or a poor soul."

"She's also a woman, so those are the two most likely options, of course." A pause. "Perhaps you should marry her. It did wonders for Bourne."

"I am not Bourne."

"No. You're not." Chase sat up, spinning the globe once more and looking around the room. "It is a wonder you can find anything in here. I've half a mind to have the girls come in and clean up."

"Try it."

"Not worth your wrath." Chase tamped out the cigar and stood, coming nearer and tapping one finger on the enormous betting book. "It's late, and I am for home, but before I go, I thought perhaps you'd like to make a wager."

"I don't wager in the book. You know that."

One of Chase's golden brows rose. "Are you certain you don't want to make an exception for this one? You've excellent odds."

Unease settled in Cross's chest, and he folded his arms, leaning back in his chair to level his partner with a cool look. "What is it?"

"Lady Philippa Marbury," Chase said.

Unease turned to dread. *Chase knew.* It was not a surprise. Not really. Chase always knew everything. Still, Cross was not required to admit it. "Who?"

Chase cut him a look. "Is this how it is to be then? You're going to pretend not to know to what I am referring?"

"No pretending about it," Cross made a show of leaning back in his chair. "I haven't any idea what you're on about."

"Justin let her in, Cross. Pointed her in the direction of your office. And then he told me about it."

Goddammit. "Justin is a gossiping female."

"Having one or two of them around can be rather helpful, I find. Now, about the girl."

Cross scowled, his mood turning from dark to deadly. "What of her?"

"What did she want here?"

"It's none of your concern."

"But it might be Bourne's concern, so I ask nonetheless."

If he had my sister in his clutches, I'd consider doing his bidding.

Bourne's words echoed through Cross on a tide of guilt.

"What she wanted is irrelevant. But it's worth mentioning that Knight saw her."

A casual observer would not have seen the slight stiffening of Chase's spine. "Did he recognize her?"

"No." *Thank God.*

Chase heard the hesitation in the word. "However?"

"She intrigued him."

"I'm not surprised. Lady Philippa is an intriguing sort."

"That's a mild way of putting it." He did not like the understanding that flashed in his partner's eyes at the words.

"You haven't told Bourne?"

For the life of him, Cross didn't know why. Bourne was widely considered one of the coldest, hardest men in London. If he thought for one moment that Pippa was in danger, Bourne would destroy the threat with his bare hands.

But Cross had promised to keep her secrets.

The world is full of liars.

The words whispered through him. There was no reason to keep his promise to the lady. He should tell Bourne. Tell him, and be through with it.

And yet . . .

He thought of her earlier in the evening, smiling happily at her hound, the expression on her face sending a thread of warmth through him even now. He liked to watch her smile. He liked to watch her do just about anything.

He liked her.

Shit.

"I took care of it."

Chase was quiet for a long moment before repeating, "You did."

Cross resisted the urge to look away. "The girl came to me."

"I remain unclear on those particulars."

"You needn't know everything."

One side of Chase's mouth lifted in a wry smile. "And yet, I so often do."

"Not this."

Chase considered him for a long moment, a battle of will. "No. It seems not."

"You'll refrain from telling Bourne?"

"Unless he requires telling," Chase said, leaning back in the chair. "And besides, telling Bourne won't help my end of the wager."

He shouldn't care.

But the echo of Pippa's soft touch and her strange words had clearly made him as mad as she was. "What are the terms?"

Chase grinned, all white teeth. "One hundred pounds says she's the woman who breaks you of your curse."

His curse.

It took everything he had not to react to the words. To the taunt in them.

One golden brow rose. "Not willing to take it?"

"I don't wager in the book," Cross repeated, the words coming out like gravel.

Chase smirked, but said nothing, instead standing, limbs unfolding with an uncanny grace. "Pity. I thought for sure that would make me a quick hundred."

"I did not know you were short on blunt."

"I'm not. But I do like to win."

Cross didn't reply as his partner left, the sound of the large mahogany door closing softly the only sign that Chase had been there at all.

Only then did Cross release the long breath he'd been holding.

He should have taken the wager.

Chase might know more than most about the secrets of London's elite, but there was one fact that was beyond doubt.

Cross would not touch Philippa Marbury again.

He couldn't.

"Pippa, it's time to try your dress."

The Marchioness of Needham and Dolby's words—part excitement, part scolding—drew Pippa's attention from where she'd been watching the mass of bodies weaving in and out of the shops on Bond Street. While Pippa liked the window of Madame Hebert's shop very much—it afforded a rather spectacular view of the rest of the London aristocracy going about their daily business—she did not particularly care for dressmakers. They, like dancing, were not her preferred way of spending time.

But wedding dresses required modistes. As did trousseaus.

And so, here she was, at what would most certainly be the longest trip to the dressmaker in the history of dress shopping.

"Philippa!" She snapped her attention from the group of men across the street at the entrance to Boucher & Babcock's Tobacconist and toward her mother's sharp, excited cry from the inner fitting room of the shop. "Come see your sister!"

With a sigh, Pippa turned from the window and pushed her way through the curtains, feeling as though she were steeled for battle. The velvet drapes hadn't returned to their place when she came up short, taking in Olivia, petite and perfect on a raised platform at the center of the room, in what had to be the most beautiful wedding dress ever made.

"Olivia," Pippa said quietly, shaking her head. "You are . . ."

"Gorgeous!" the marchioness exclaimed, clapping her hands together in maternal glee.

Olivia fluffed the skirts of the lovely ivory lace and grinned. "Absolutely stunning, aren't I?"

"Stunning," Pippa agreed. It was the truth after all. But she could not resist adding, "And so modest."

"Oh, tosh," Olivia said, turning to look more carefully in the mirror. "If you cannot tell the truth in Hebert's back room, where can you? Dressmaker's shops are for gossip and honesty."

The seamstress—widely acknowledged as the best in Britain—removed a pin from between her lips and pinned the bodice of the gown before winking at Pippa from her position behind Olivia's shoulder. "I could not agree more."

Olivia was unable to take her eyes off her reflection in one of the score of mirrors placed around the room. "Yes. It's perfect."

It was, of course. Not that Olivia needed a dress to make her beautiful. The youngest, prettiest Marbury sister could wear a length of feed sack fetched from the Needham Manor stables and still look more beautiful than most women on their very best days. No, there was little doubt that two weeks hence, when Olivia and Viscount Tottenham stood in St. George's in front of all of London society, she would be a stunning bride—the talk of the *ton*.

Pippa would no doubt pale in comparison as she played her part in the double wedding.

"Lady Philippa, Alys is ready for you." The dressmaker pulled her from her thoughts with a wave of one long arm, adorned with a scarlet pincushion, in the direction of a young assistant standing near a tall screen on one end of the room, a mass of lace and silk in her hands.

Pippa's wedding gown.

Something turned deep within, and she hesitated.

"Go on, Pippa. Put it on." Olivia looked down at the dressmaker. "It's very different, I hope. I wouldn't like us to be thought to wear the same dress."

Pippa had no doubt that, even if the dresses were an exact copy, there would be no mistaking the two brides on the fast-approaching day.

Where the four older Marbury daughters had been landed with flat, ashy blond hair, skin either too ruddy (Victoria and Valerie) or too pale (Pippa and Penelope), and bodies either too plump (Penelope and Victoria) or too lean (Pippa and Valerie), Olivia was perfect. Her hair was a lush, sparkling gold that shimmered in the sunlight, her skin was clear and pink, and her shape—the ideal combination of curved and trim. She had a body that was made for French fashion, and Madame Hebert had designed her a dress to prove it.

Pippa doubted the dressmaker—best in London or no—could do the same for her.

The gown was over her head then, the sound of fabric rustling in her ears chasing away her thoughts as the young seamstress tightened and fastened, buttoned and tied. Pippa fidgeted through the process, keenly aware of the harsh lace edging against her skin, of the way the stays threatened to suffocate.

She had not yet seen herself in it, but the dress was remarkably uncomfortable.

When Alys had completed her work, she waved Pippa out into the main room, and for one small moment, Pippa wondered what would happen if, instead of emerging to the critical gaze of her sister and mother and the finest dressmaker this side of the English Channel, she fled into the rear of the shop and out the back door.

Perhaps then she and Castleton could forgo the entire wedding and simply get to the marriage bit. That was, after all, the important part of it all, wasn't it?

"This shall be the wedding of the season!" Lady Needham crowed from beyond the screen.

Well . . . perhaps marriage was not the most important part for mothers.

"Of course it shall," Olivia agreed. "Didn't I tell you that, Penny-disaster or no, I would marry well?"

"You did, my darling. You always achieve that which you set your mind to."

Lucky Olivia.

"My lady?" The young seamstress looked confused. Pippa gathered that it was not every day that a bride was so hesitant to show off her wedding gown.

She stepped around the screen. "Well? Here I am."

"Oh!" Lady Needham nearly toppled from her place on a lavishly appointed divan, tea sloshing from her cup as she bounced up and down on the sapphire fabric. "Oh! What a fine countess you shall make!"

Pippa looked past her mother to Olivia, who was already back to watching the half dozen young seamstresses on their knees, pinning the hem of her gown, lifting flounces and moving ribbons. "Very nice, Pippa." She paused. "Not as nice as mine, of course . . ."

Some things did not change. Thankfully. "Of course not."

Madame Hebert was already helping Pippa up onto her own raised platform, pins lodged firmly between the dress-maker's teeth as she cast a disparaging gaze along the bodice of the gown. Pippa turned to look at herself in a large mirror, and the Frenchwoman immediately stepped into her line of vision. "Not yet."

The seamstresses worked in silence as Pippa ran the tips of her fingers over the bodice of the gown, tracing the curves of lace and the stretches of silk. "Silk comes from caterpillars," she said, the information a comfort in the odd moment. "Well, not precisely caterpillars—the cocoons of the silkworm." When no one replied, she looked down at her hands, and added, "The *Bombyx mori* pupates, and before it can emerge as a moth—we get silk."

There was silence for long moments, and Pippa looked up to discover everyone in the room staring at her as though she had sprouted a second head. Olivia was the first to reply. "You are so *odd*."

"Who can think of *worms* at a time like this?" the mar-chioness chimed in. "Worms have nothing to do with wed-dings!"

Pippa thought it was rather a perfect time to think of worms. Hardworking worms that had left the life they'd known—and all its comforts—and spun cocoons, prepar-ing for a life they did not understand and could not imagine, only to be stopped halfway through the process and turned into a wedding gown.

She did not imagine that her mother would care for that description, however, and so she said nothing as the woman began to pin, and the bodice of the gown grew tighter and tighter. After several long moments, Pippa coughed. "It's rather constricting."

Madame Hebert did not seem to hear her, instead pinching a quarter of an inch of fabric at Pippa's waist and pinning it tight.

"Are you sure—?"

Pippa tried again before the modiste cut her a look. "I am sure."

No doubt.

And then the dressmaker stepped away and Pippa had a clear line to the looking glass, where she faced her future self. The dress was beautiful, fitted simply to her small bust and long waist without making her look like any kind of long-legged bird.

No, she looked every inch a bride.

The dress seemed to be growing tighter by the moment. Was such a thing possible?

"What do you think?" the dressmaker asked, watching her carefully in the mirror.

Pippa opened her mouth to respond, not knowing what was to come.

"She adores it, of course!" The marchioness's words came on a squeal. "They both adore them! It shall be the wedding of the season! The wedding of the *century*!"

Pippa met the modiste's curious chocolate gaze. "And the century has barely begun."

The Frenchwoman's eyes smiled for the briefest of instants before Olivia sighed happily. "It shall indeed. And Tottenham shan't be able to resist me in this dress. No man could."

"Olivia!" the marchioness said from her place. "That is entirely unladylike."

"Why? That is the goal, is it not? To tempt one's husband?"

"One does not *tempt* one's husband!" the marchioness insisted.

Olivia's smile turned mischievous. "You must have tempted yours once or twice, Mother."

"Oh!" Lady Needham collapsed back against the settee.

Madame Hebert turned away from the conversation, waving two girls over to work on Pippa's hem.

Olivia winked at Pippa. "Five times, at least."

Pippa could not resist. "Four. Victoria and Valerie are twins."

"Enough! I cannot abide it!" The marchioness was up and through the curtains to the front of the shop, leaving her daughters to their laughter.

"That you might some day be wife to the prime minister worries me not a small amount," Pippa said.

Olivia smiled. "Tottenham enjoys it. He says the European leaders will all appreciate my increased character."

Pippa laughed, happy for the distraction from the unsettling view of the bride in the looking glass. "Increased character? That is a kind way of putting it."

Olivia nodded, waving the dressmaker over. "Madame," she said, quietly, "now that our mother is gone, perhaps we could discuss the particulars of tempting one's husband?"

Pippa's brows rose. "Olivia!"

Olivia waved away the scolding and pressed on. "The trousseaus my mother ordered . . . they're filled with cotton and linen night rails, aren't they?"

Madame Hebert's lips twisted in a wry smile. "I would have to pull the orders, but knowing the preferences of the marchioness, there is little designed to tempt in the collections."

Olivia smiled her sweetest, brightest smile. The one that could win any man or woman in creation. The one that made her the favorite Marbury girl Britain-wide. "But there could be?"

"*Oui.* The bedchamber is my specialty."

Olivia nodded once. "Excellent. We both require your very best in that area." She waved a hand at Pippa. "Pippa most of all."

That set her back. "What does that mean?"

"Only that Castleton seems the type to require guideposts

along the way." Olivia looked to the seamstress, and added, "I don't suppose guideposts are an option?"

The Frenchwoman laughed. "I make certain they find their way."

Guideposts. Pippa recalled her hand on Castleton's the prior evening. The way he'd smiled down at her, and she'd felt not a twinge of temptation. Not a hint of the knowledge that she sought.

Perhaps Pippa required guideposts.

How was one to know?

"I'm not worried," Olivia said, her eyes flashing with a knowledge beyond her years, rubied hand tracing the edge of her gown. "Tottenham has no difficulty finding his way." Pippa felt her jaw go lax. The words called to mind thoughts of much more than kissing. Olivia looked at her and laughed. "You needn't look so shocked."

"You've—?" She lowered her voice to a bare whisper. "More than the kissing? With the tongues?"

Olivia smiled and nodded. "Last night. There was still kissing, though. And a lovely amount of tongue. In intriguing locations." Pippa thought perhaps her eyes would roll from her head. "You did not have a similar experience, I gather?"

No!

"How? *Where*?"

"Well, there's the answer to *my* question," Olivia said dryly, inspecting one long lace sleeve. "I should think the ordinary way. As for when and where, you'd be surprised by how resourceful an intelligent, eager gentleman can be."

Little Olivia, the youngest Marbury. Deflowered.

Which made Pippa the only Marbury to remain . . . flowered.

Olivia lowered her voice, and added, "I hope for your sake that Castleton discovers his resourcefulness. It's a *very* rewarding experience."

Pippa shook her head. "You—" She didn't know what to say.

Olivia gave her a look of surprise. "Really, Pippa. It's perfectly normal for betrothed couples to . . . experiment. Everyone does it."

She pushed her glasses higher on her nose. "*Everyone?*"

"All right, apparently not *everyone.*"

Olivia turned back to the seamstress to discuss the line of her dress, or the cut of the fabric, or something equally inane, unaware of the thoughts rioting in Pippa's head.

Experiment.

The word echoed through her, a reminder of her encounter with Mr. Cross. She had planned to gain a semblance of understanding prior to marriage, knowing that her interactions with her husband would be rudimentary at best.

But she'd never once imagined that Olivia would . . . that Lord Tottenham and Olivia would . . . had . . . had knowledge of each other. In the biblical sense.

Castleton had never even tried to *kiss* her. Not in two years of dancing around the edge of courtship. Not in a month of official courtship. Not even last night, at their betrothal ball, after she'd touched him. He'd had plenty of opportunity to ferret her away as they'd stood to one side of the room in stilted silence.

But he hadn't.

And she hadn't thought it at all uncommon.

Until now.

Now, when she required experimentation more than ever.

And she'd wagered away her opportunity for it. Utterly.

I will refrain from asking any other men to assist in my research.

The wager rang in her ears as though she'd spoken the words aloud, there and then. She'd wagered and lost. She'd given her word. But now, as her heart and mind raced, she found herself desperate for a solution. It was one thing, after all, for her not to have the experience she wished on her wedding night; it was another entirely for her not to have the experience she was expected to have.

She was to be married altogether too quickly. She caught her own gaze in the mirror. *She was wearing her wedding gown, for heaven's sake.*

There was so little time. Research was imperative. With, or without him.

Perhaps she ought to ask Olivia.

Her gaze slid to her sister's perfect pink smile—filled with knowledge that Pippa hadn't before seen but could absolutely now identify.

She needed to act. Immediately.

And like that, the solution was clear.

She had to get to the Angel.

With that keen awareness rocketing through her, Pippa stared at her younger sister, beautiful in her own wedding gown, and announced, the words, not entirely false. "I am unwell."

Olivia snapped her attention back to Pippa. "What do you mean you are unwell?"

Pippa shook her head and put a hand to her stomach. "I am feeling quite . . . unwell." She considered the girls at her feet, working furiously, ants charging a discarded sweet at a picnic.

"But what of your gown?" Olivia shook her head.

"It's lovely. And fine. But I must remove it." The girls looked up in unison. "Now."

She had research to conduct. Pressing research.

She looked to Madame Hebert. "I cannot stay. I shall have to come back. What with how unwell I feel."

The Frenchwoman watched her carefully for a long moment. "Of course."

Olivia looked horrified. "Well, whatever you feel, I don't wish to catch it."

Pippa descended from the platform, hurrying for the changing screen. "No. I wouldn't like for that. For you to feel . . ."

Madame Hebert filled in the rest. "Unwell?"

Pippa supposed that the repetition of the word might be odd. "Sick," she blurted out.

Olivia's pert nose wrinkled. "For heaven's sake, Pippa. Go home. But take a hack. Mother and I will need the carriage to carry all our parcels."

She did not wait to be told twice. "Yes. I think I shall do just that."

Of course, she didn't.

Instead, she restored her clothing to normal, assured her mother that she would be thoroughly safe to make her way home, and left the dress shop, her destination clear and unequivocal.

Head down, cloak tight around her, Pippa headed right down Bond and across Piccadilly, where she and her maid entered a hack together on one side, and Pippa slid across the seat, pulled up the hood of her cloak and whispered a plea for secrecy before exiting, alone, directly through the door on the opposite side.

She slipped, unnoticed, down a narrow alleyway that ran behind St. James's and counted the buildings from the rear—one, two, three—before stopping before a heavy steel door and giving it a good, firm rap.

No one answered.

She redoubled her efforts. Banging on the steel with the flat of her palm, making an utter racket.

If she were found—

There were a hundred ways to finish that question. Best not to dwell on them.

She knocked again, harder. Faster.

And then, after what seemed like an age, a hidden slot slid open at the center of the great steel door, and black eyes met hers, irritation quickly giving way to surprised recognition.

"What in hell?" The voice was muffled by the steel.

"I am Lady Philippa Marbury," she announced, but the words were lost in the sound of the slot closing, several locks being thrown on the opposite side of the door, and the scrape of steel on stone.

The door opened, revealing a great, yawning blackness and the largest, most dangerous-looking man she'd ever seen, tall and broad with a scar at his lip and a nose that appeared to have been broken more than once.

A thread of uncertainty coiled through her as she opened her mouth to speak. "I am . . ."

"I know who you are," he said curtly. "Get in here."

"I don't—" she started, then stopped. "Who are you?"

He reached out, one massive hand grasping her arm and pulling her into the club. "Did it not occur to you that someone might see you out there?" he said, poking his head out the door and looking first one way, then the other, down the alley before, satisfied that she had not been seen, closing the door, throwing the locks and turning away from her, pushing through another set of curtains and into a beautifully appointed hallway before bellowing, "What in hell do we pay doormen for? Why isn't there anyone manning the goddamned door?"

She called out from her place in the entryway. "There doesn't seem to be anyone manning most of your doors at this time of day."

The enormous man turned back to her, curiosity in his gaze. "And, how would you know that?"

"I've been here before," she said, simply.

He shook his head, smiling wryly. "Does Bourne know that Penelope is giving her sister tours?"

"Oh, you misunderstand. I haven't come here with Penelope. I was here with Mr. Cross."

That set the large man back. "Cross," he said, and Pippa noticed the shift in his tone. Disbelief. Maybe something else.

She nodded. "Yes."

His black brows rose. "Cross," he repeated. "And you."

Her brow furrowed. "Yes. Well, not regularly, but I did have good reason to call on him earlier in the week."

"Did you."

The words were not a question, but she answered nonetheless. "Yes." She hesitated, then added, "Though it might be best if you not tell him I am here today."

His gaze turned knowing. "Might it."

Too knowing.

She extended her hand. "I'm afraid you have the better of me, sir. I've not made the pleasure of your acquaintance."

He gave her proffered hand a long look before meeting her gaze once more, as though giving her the chance to change her mind. "I am Temple."

The Duke of Lamont.

The murderer.

She stepped back, her hand falling involuntarily at the thought before she could stop it. "Oh."

His lips twisted in a wry smile. "Now you're wishing you hadn't come here after all."

Her mind raced. He wouldn't hurt her. He was Bourne's partner. He was Mr. Cross's partner. It was the middle of the day. People were not killed in Mayfair in the middle of the day.

And for all she'd heard about this dark, dangerous man, there wasn't a single stitch of proof that he'd done that which he was purported to have done.

She extended her hand once more. "I am Philippa Marbury."

One black brow arched, but he took her hand firmly. "Brave girl."

"There's no proof that you're what they say."

"Gossip is damning enough."

She shook her head. "I am a scientist. Hypotheses are useless without evidence."

One side of his mouth twitched. "Would that the rest of England were as thorough." He released her hand and held back the curtain, allowing her entry into the hallway, lushly appointed with wall coverings of silk and velvet that Pippa could not resist reaching out to touch.

"Bourne isn't here," he said.

She smiled. "I know. He's in Surrey with my sister. I am not here for him."

He hesitated in his long strides, and she took a moment to marvel at the way such a large man—one who was clearly no stranger to violence and brutality—could move with such grace, shifting his weight to stay his forward movement.

And then he was moving again, as though he'd never paused. "And not for Cross, either?"

"No. He doesn't enjoy my company."

The words were out before she could stop them, and Temple caught her gaze. "He said that?"

She shrugged, adjusting her spectacles. "Not in so many words, but he made it clear he wasn't interested in assisting me with my project, so . . ."

"Which project?" he prodded.

My ruination. She couldn't say *that.*

"A piece of research with which I had hoped he would . . . aid me."

Temple flashed her a smile. "And what about me? I could aid you."

She considered the offer for a long moment. No doubt, this man could answer all of her questions. And then some.

But he wasn't Cross.

She resisted the thought and the discomfort that came with it, instead focusing on the duke who turned to face her, absently opening one of what seemed like an endless string of closed doors and stepping aside to let Pippa into a large room, at the center of which stood two tables, covered in green baize.

"No, thank you. I promised Mr. Cross I wouldn't . . ." She trailed off.

"Wouldn't what?" he prompted.

"Wouldn't ask another man."

His eyes went wide briefly. "Now that sounds like fascinating research."

She ignored the words, turning to face him, hands clasped tightly as he closed the door behind them and pocketed the key. "But he didn't say anything about women."

He stilled. "I beg your pardon?"

She took a deep breath. "I require an audience with one of your ladies."

"My ladies?"

She waved one hand in the air, absently. "Your, in the plural. Your ladies." When he did not reply, she blurted out her clarification. "Your prostitutes."

He was quiet for a long moment, and Pippa wondered if, perhaps, she had not spoken.

And then he laughed, big and booming.

And she wondered if she'd made a serious mistake.

Chapter Seven

*"In order to produce quality silk, the silk maker
(NB: sericulturist) ensures a careful diet of
mulberry leaves for his worms, taking care that no
odd foodstuffs (or even odors) come into contact
with the creatures. Once they have eaten their fill,
the worms pupate, spinning their cocoons and,
when several days have passed, the sericulturist
thwarts their incubation and halts the emergence of
the moth mining the cocoons for silk.*

*I have no intention of allowing this to happen to me.
Thank goodness for* ~~loopholes~~ *logical thinking."*

**The Scientific Journal of Lady Philippa Marbury
March 25, 1831; eleven days prior to her wedding**

Temple's laughter echoed through the small, locked
room. "Your Grace?" she prompted.

His laugh stopped, as quickly as it had started. He did
not respond, instead moving past her to the bookcase that
dominated the far end of the room. He inspected the books
for a long moment.

He was sending her home. Likely looking for a book to

keep strange, scientific Philippa Marbury occupied until he could notify someone of her presence. "I don't need a book," she said, "I'm perfectly capable of entertaining myself." He didn't reply. "Please don't tell Bourne. Or my father."

He slid a red leather-bound volume from a high shelf. "Tell them what?"

The question was forgotten as the wall moved, swinging inward to reveal a yawning, black space.

Pippa gasped and came closer to inspect it. "I've never . . ." She reached for the bookcase, peering down what seemed to be an endless corridor. She looked to him, unable to keep the smile from her face. "It's a secret passageway."

Temple smiled. "It is." He handed her a candle and replaced the book, waving her into the mysterious space. But not before she saw the volume that unlocked this impressive secret.

Paradise Lost.

Pippa stepped into the blackness.

Indeed.

Temple led the way down the hallway, and Pippa's heart pounded, her excitement growing exponentially as they moved deeper into the passage. There were no doors that she could see, and the wall curved in what seemed like an enormous circle. "What is on the other side of this wall?"

Temple did not hesitate. "Nothing of import."

"Oh, yes. I believe that."

He laughed. "Perhaps Cross will show you someday. Or Lady Bourne."

Her brows shot up. "Penelope knows?" It was hard to imagine her proper sister exploring a secret passageway in a notorious men's club. But then, Penelope was married to one of the owners. "I suppose she does." It was unfortunate that she could not ask Penelope her questions without rousing suspicion.

Not suspicion. Utter panic.

Not that panic was necessary. After all, if Penelope could know the secrets of the club, why not Pippa?

Because Pippa did not have a protector here.

Not really.

After what seemed like an eternity, Temple stopped and placed his hand flat on the exterior wall of the corridor. Like magic, a door opened as if from nowhere.

He let her into an alcove off the main floor of the Angel, closing the door behind them with a soft click. She turned to inspect the wall, running her fingers along the textured silk. It was only because she knew there was one that she found the seam. She turned wide eyes on her companion. "That is remarkable."

He didn't immediately reply, instead staring blankly at the wall for a long moment, as though seeing it for the first time and understanding that the rest of the world did not include secret passageways and curved walls and mysterious men. When realization struck, he smiled. "It is, rather, isn't it?"

"Who designed them?"

He grinned, white teeth flashing in the dim space. "Cross."

Her hand went back to the invisible seam in the wall. *Of course he had.*

"Temple!"

The bellow surprised her, but Temple seemed prepared for it, stepping through the curtains at the entrance to the alcove. He revealed himself to the room at large . . . and a stream of excited French. The enormous man raised his hands as if in surrender and made his way across the casino floor, out of sight. Pippa poked her head out to watch.

There was a woman at the far end of the room, cheeks red, hair asunder, wearing a black apron and . . . was that a fish in her hand? Either way, she was cursing like a sailor. A French sailor.

She switched to English. "That imbecile Irvington sent word that he is bringing a collection of his imbecile friends for dinner. And he thinks to tell me how to prepare his fish! I cooked for Charles the Second! He should get down on his knees and thank God himself that I am willing to cook for Idiot Irvington the First!"

Pippa was fairly certain that he was not the first Irvington to be an idiot. Nor the first to be insensitive. Nor unpleasant.

"Now Didier—" Temple began in perfect French, his voice low and smooth, as though he were speaking to some kind of untamed animal.

And perhaps he was. "You will send word to that cretin and tell him that if he does not want to eat the fish the way I wish to cook it, he may find another fish . . . and another chef . . . and another club!" The last fairly shook the rafters of the massive room.

Not a dozen feet from where the strange woman stood, the door to Mr. Cross's office flew open. "What in hell is going on?"

Pippa's breath caught as the man emerged, tall and lanky and unshaven. He was in his shirtsleeves, cuffs rolled up, and her gaze flew to those long, lean forearms, where muscle curved and rippled over bone. Her mouth went dry. She'd never thought of the forearm as being particularly interesting, but then it was not every day that she saw such a fine specimen.

Yes. It was the anatomy in which she was interested. The bones.

Radius. Ulna.

That did help, to think of the bones.

The cook waved her fish. "Irvington thinks to criticize my sauce! The imbecile would not know a proper sauce if he had a quart of it in his pocket!"

Mr. Cross rolled his eyes. "Didier . . . return to your kitchen and cook your fish. Irvington will eat what we tell him to eat."

The chef opened her mouth.

"He will eat what we serve him and shan't know any better."

"The man has the palate of a goat," the cook grumbled.

Temple grinned, hands outstretched. "Well, for all our sakes, I hope you do not serve him *poisson en papier maché*."

The cook smiled at that. As did Pippa. "I don't like him."

"Neither do I, but he and his friends like to lose, so we keep him nonetheless."

The fight seemed to go out of the cook. "Very well," she said, wielding the fish in one hand. "I will cook him fish."

"Perhaps not that exact fish," Cross said, wryly.

Pippa laughed, forgetting herself, forgetting that sound carried—quick and loud across a cavernous room. His grey eyes snapped to her location. She pulled her head back into the alcove, pressing her back to the wall, heart pounding.

"Now Cross," she heard Temple cajole from his place on the casino floor.

There was no reply. Pippa strained to hear what happened next, edging closer to the exit, eager for any indication that he'd seen her, that he'd noticed her.

Silence.

For what seemed like an eternity.

Finally, unable to resist, she peered carefully around the side of the enclosure.

To find Mr. Cross standing not six inches away, arms folded over his chest, waiting for her.

She started at his nearness, and said the first thing that came. "Hello."

One ginger brow rose. "Hello."

She stepped out to face him, hands clasped tightly in front of her. The cook and Temple were turned toward them, curiosity in their stares. As though this confrontation were somehow stranger than a Frenchwoman brandishing a trout on the floor of a casino.

Well, it wasn't.

Pippa knew that with utter certainty.

She met Mr. Cross's cool, grey gaze, and waited for him to say something else.

He did not.

Fine. She could wait. She'd waited before.

Except, after what seemed like a quarter of an hour, she could no longer bear it. "I suppose you are wondering how it is that I came to be here."

"You are becoming quite a lurker, Lady Philippa."

She straightened. "I do not lurk."

"No? My office? Your balcony? Now here . . . in my club . . . in a dark alcove? I would call it lurking."

"The balcony was mine," she couldn't help but point out. "If anyone was lurking, it was you."

"Mmm." He narrowed his gaze. "Perhaps you would like to explain your current location?"

"I was nearby," she explained. "Nearby the club. Not the alcove. Though I suppose one might say that nearby to one is the same as to the other. But I presume the conceptual proximity for each is relative. In your mind. At least."

Temple snorted from his place a good distance away.

"You would do well to leave us," Cross said to his partner, not taking his gaze from Pippa. "Before I punish you for letting her in."

"What was I to do, leave her in the alleyway banging on our door, until someone found her?" Temple's tone was light and teasing. Out of place. "Besides, she's not here for you."

Cross's grey eyes darkened at the words, and Pippa's heart began to pound. He was angry. She stepped away from him, unable to stop herself, back into the alcove. He followed, pressing her back, letting the curtains fall behind them, cloaking them in darkness. They were feet from others—who knew they were here, and yet her pulse began to race as he spoke, his voice went dark and threatening. "Why are you here?"

She lifted her chin. "It's not—" She cleared her throat. "It's not your concern."

There was a pause, a hitch in his breathing, as though she'd surprised him. "Did we, or did we not, make a wager?"

"We did."

He reached out, placing one hand on the wall behind her head, that forearm, clad only in shirtsleeves, more than a little distracting. "And am I wrong in recalling that it involved your commitment to stay away from men who are not your fiancé?"

She did not care for his tone. "You are not wrong."

He leaned in, so close. Her eyes fell to the open collar of his shirt, where he should have been wearing a cravat but wasn't. She was irrationally drawn to the triangle of skin there, dusted with hair. She wanted to touch it.

"Explain to me, then, what in hell you are doing with Temple?" His anger pulled her back to the moment at hand. She could hear it in his voice, low and unsettling.

She tried to get her bearings—nearly impossible in this dark space with him so very close. "He let me in."

"If you even dream of reneging on our wager, I will send God, Bourne, and your father to keep you in check. In that order."

"I should not be surprised that you believe you have some control over the Almighty," she retorted.

He looked like he might like to murder someone.

"Cross." From beyond the curtain, Temple came to her aid.

Rescued. Pippa released the breath she had not known she had been holding.

Cross turned his head but did not move from where he crowded her. "Leave us."

Temple yanked the curtains back, letting light into the small space. "I don't think that's a good idea. The lady is not here for you."

Cross was across the alcove in seconds. "She sure as hell isn't here for you."

A jolt of excitement threaded through her at the words. As

though he were defending her. As though he were willing to fight for her.

How fascinating. She caught her breath at the way he moved, quick and economical. They were inches from each other now—Cross tall and lean, all corded muscle and tension, Temple a few inches shorter, but wider by half . . . and smirking.

"No. She's not," Temple said. "She's here for something else."

Cross looked back to her, over his shoulder, grey eyes flashing.

"I only have eleven days," she said, ready to explain her purpose. Surely he'd understand, she was in a critical situation.

Temple interjected, "Perhaps you'd like to give her escort?"

At the light words, Cross's eyes went blank, and she had the instant and irrational desire to reach out to him, as though he could bring back his emotion. Not that she wanted to. Emotion was not her goal.

Knowledge was.

But she couldn't have, anyway, as he had already turned away, pushing past Temple and making his way to his office.

She followed, as though on a lead. "Is that all?"

When he arrived at the door to his office, he turned back to her. "You are not my concern."

A sharp pulse of something akin to pain threaded through her at the words. She rubbed absently at her chest. "You are correct. I am not."

He ignored the last. "I will not be your keeper. Indeed, I've more important matters at hand."

He opened the door to his office, not attempting to conceal the woman inside.

The beautiful, raven-haired woman with dark eyes and red lips and a smile that seemed like a scandal in itself. Pippa took a step back, her gaze riveted to the other woman as she replayed the events of the last few minutes in her head—his unshaven jaw and wrinkled shirtsleeves, the way he'd opened the door with irritation, as though the cook had interrupted something very important.

He'd been inside his office with this woman, this woman who smiled as though he were the only man in the world. As though she were the only woman.

As though they were tasked with repopulation.

Pippa swallowed. "I see."

He smirked. "I'm sure you do."

She took another step back as he closed the door.

"I've never seen you treat a woman so," Sally Tasser said, pulling her legs up beneath her in the large wing chair to allow Cross room to pace.

Cross ignored the words and the pang of guilt that came with them. "Where were we?"

Why was she here? How had she twisted their wager— one afternoon together—into a welcome for her to invade his space anytime she liked?

The prostitute raised raven brows in silent disbelief and consulted her notes. "I've thirteen girls, all working on the list." She paused. "Who is she?"

She is temptation incarnate. Sent to destroy him.

"Can they be trusted?"

And what the hell was she doing with Temple?

"They know you deliver on promises." Another pause. "At least, promises made to whores."

He spun to face her. "What does that mean?"

"Only that you've never been anything but a gentleman to my women. And yet this afternoon you appear to have gravely mistreated a lady."

He resisted the truth in the words. "And since when have you had sympathy for aristocrats?"

"Since that one looked as though you'd kicked her dog."

The reference to Pippa's dog reminded Cross of their conversation the night prior—of Castleton's request—of her hesitation to name his hound. Of the way her lips curved around the words as she attempted to explain her reticence.

Of the way the entire conversation made him want to steal her away and convince her that marriage to Castleton was absolutely wrong for her.

He did not tell Sally any of that, of course. Instead he said, "I want the fifty biggest gamers in the hell. No one can be missed."

The woman leveled him with a frank look. "You'll get them. When have I ever failed you?"

"Never. But there is always time to begin."

"What's he got on you?"

Cross shook his head. "It doesn't matter."

She smiled, small and nearly humorless. "I assume you've something to do with the way he's crowing with pride about marrying his girl off to an earl."

Cross gave her his darkest look. "I'm not marrying the daughter."

"So you think. She'll be here in five days, and when she gets here, he'll stop at nothing to get you married." When he did not reply, she added, "You don't believe it? This is *Knight*."

"I am not marrying the girl," he repeated.

Sally watched him for a long moment before saying, "I shall work the floor that night. If a single deep pocket comes through the door, I'll slip him an invitation to Pandemonium myself." She inclined her head toward the door. "Now tell me about the girl."

He forced himself to sit, and to deliberately misunderstand the question. "I've never met Meghan. Ask Knight about her."

She smiled wryly. "Really, Cross? This silly game?"

He resisted the urge to shove his hands through his hair, instead leaning back in his chair, all control. Pippa Marbury was more than any decent man could handle. *And he was far from decent.* "She's someone who should not have come here."

He should have barred her from entry.

She laughed. "You did not have to tell me that. Yet come here she did."

"She has a taste for adventure."

"Well, she's sniffing round the wrong tree if she wants that."

He didn't reply, knowing better.

"You're trying to keep her away from you?"

God, yes. He didn't want her here. He didn't want her touching his things, leaving her mark, tempting him. Didn't want her threatening his sanctuary. Didn't want her tainting this dark place with her light. "I'm trying to keep her away in general."

She leaned forward. "She's not your lover."

"Of course not."

One of her black brows rose. "There's no of course about it. Perhaps there would have been if I hadn't seen her face."

"I may well owe the girl an apology, but that doesn't make her anything close to my lover."

Sally smiled at that. "Don't you see, Cross? It's because you feel you owe her an apology that makes her closer to your lover than any of the rest of us." She paused for a long moment before adding, "And even if you didn't feel that way, the girl's face would have been enough."

"She came to request my assistance in a matter." A ridiculous matter, but Sally need not know that.

"She may *request* your assistance in one matter," the prostitute said with a soft, knowing laugh, "but she *wants* your assistance with something else entirely."

Cross's gaze narrowed. "I don't know what you're talking about."

"Sex," she said, plainly, as though she were talking to a child. A child wise beyond his years. "The woman saw what I am. She knows what I do. And she was jealous."

Cross met her dark eyes, seeing only Pippa's large, shocked blue ones, made massive by the lenses of her spectacles. "There's no reason for her to be jealous."

"Sadly, that is true." Sally's mouth pursed in a perfect moue, and she leaned back in the chair. "But she doesn't know that."

Frustration coursed through him. "I mean, she wasn't jealous."

Sally smiled. "Of course she was. She wants you."

"No. She wants my assistance with some"—he hesitated on the word—"research."

Sally laughed, long and loud. "I've no doubt she does."

Cross turned away, reaching blindly for a file he did not need. "We are finished."

Sally sighed and stood, approaching the desk. "Just tell me, does she know?"

He closed his eyes, frustrated. "Does she know what?"

"Does she know that she'll never have you?"

"She's marrying a lord in just over a week." *And even if she weren't, she's legions too good for me.*

"Engagements are made to be broken."

"I forget how cynical you can be."

"It's a hazard of the occupation." She moved to the door, turning back before she opened it. "You should tell her. Before the poor thing becomes sick with unrequited love."

He did not reply.

After a long moment, she said, "I'll see you tomorrow with your list."

"Thank you."

She nodded once and opened the door, turning to leave before she looked back, a smile playing over her too-red lips. "Shall I allow your next appointment in?"

He knew before he looked what he would find when Sally stepped out of the doorway.

Philippa Marbury was seated on a high croupier's stool, not five feet away, nibbling at the edge of a sandwich.

He did not mean to stand, but he stood anyway, coming around his desk as though he were chased. "Did someone *feed* you?"

Of course someone had fed her. Didier, no doubt, who had a soft spot for any soiled dove who found her way to the kitchens of the Angel.

But Philippa Marbury was no soiled dove.

Yet.

And she wouldn't be if he had anything to say about it.

"Your chef was kind enough to make me a plate while I waited." Pippa stood, extending the plate in question to him. "It's quite delicious. Would you like some?"

Yes. God, yes, he wanted some.

"No. Why would she *feed* you?"

"I'm pupating."

He looked to the ceiling, desperate for patience. "How many different ways do I have to tell you that I'm not interested in helping you emerge from this particular cocoon?"

Her jaw went slack. "You referenced metamorphosis."

The woman was driving him mad. "You referenced it first. Now, did I or did I not tell you to go home?"

She smiled, a lovely, wide grin that he should not have liked so very much. "In point of fact, you did not tell me to go home. Indeed, you quite washed your hands of me."

He considered shaking the maddening woman. "Then tell me why it is that you remain here, waiting for me?"

She tilted her head as though he were a strange specimen under glass at the Royal Entomological Society. "Oh, you misunderstand. I am not waiting for you."

What in hell? Of course she was waiting for him.

Except she wasn't. She stood, thrust her plate—along with her half-eaten sandwich—into his hands and directed her full attention to Sally. "I'm waiting for *you*."

Sally cut him a quick look, clearly unsure of how to proceed.

Pippa did not seem to notice that she'd thrown them all

off, instead stepping forward and extending her hand in greeting. "I am Lady Philippa Marbury."

Goddammit.

He would have given half his fortune to take back the instant when Pippa told Sally her name. One never knew when the madam might rethink her allegiance, and knowledge made for heady power.

For now, however, Sally pushed her surprise away and took Pippa's hand, dipping into a quick curtsy. "Sally Tasser."

"It's lovely to meet you, Miss Tasser," Pippa said, as though she were meeting a new debutante at tea rather than one of London's most accomplished whores in a gaming hell. "I wonder if you have a few moments to answer some questions?"

Sally looked supremely entertained. "I believe I do have some time, my lady."

Pippa shook her head. "Oh, no. There's no need to stand on ceremony. You must call me Pippa."

Over his decaying corpse.

"There is absolutely every reason to stand on ceremony," he stepped in, turning to Sally. "You will under no circumstances call the lady anything but just that. *Lady.*"

Pippa's brows snapped together. "I beg your pardon, Mr. Cross, but in this conversation, you are superfluous."

He gave her his most frightening stare. "I assure you, I am anything but that."

"Am I right in understanding that you have neither the time nor the inclination to speak to me at this particular moment?"

She had backed him into a corner. "Yes."

She smiled. "There it is, then. As I find myself with both, I believe I shall begin my research now. Without you." She turned her back on him. "Now, Miss Tasser. Am I right in my estimation that you are, indeed, a prostitute?"

The word slipped from her lips as though she said it a dozen times a day. "Dear God." He shot Sally a look. "Do not answer."

"Whyever not?" Pippa smiled at Sally. "There's no shame in it."

Even Sally's brows rose at that.

Surely this was not happening.

Pippa pressed on. "There isn't. In fact, I've done the research, and the word is in the Bible. Leviticus. And, honestly, if something is in a holy text, I think it's more than reasonable for one to repeat it in polite company."

"I'm not exactly polite company," Sally pointed out, brilliantly, Cross thought.

Pippa smiled. "Never mind that . . . you're the perfect company for my purposes. Now, I can only assume that your career is just what I imagine, as you are very beautiful and seem to know precisely how to look at a man and make it seem as though you are very much in love with him. You fairly smolder."

Cross had to stop this. Now. "And how do you know that she is not simply in love with me?"

That was not the way he'd intended to stop it. At all. Dammit.

She looked over her shoulder at him, then back at Sally. "*Are* you in love with him?"

Sally turned her very best smolder on Pippa, who chuckled, and said, "I didn't think so. That's the one. It's very good."

Sally met his gaze over Pippa's shoulder, laughter in her eyes. "Thank you, my lady."

Well. At least she'd used the honorific.

"May I speak plainly?" Pippa asked, as though she had not been speaking plainly for the last four days. For her entire life.

"Please," Sally said.

The moment was getting away from him. Something had to be done.

"No," he interrupted, inserting himself between the two women. "No one is speaking plainly. Certainly not to Sally."

"I'm happy to speak to the lady, Cross," Sally said, and he did not miss the dry humor in her tone.

"I've no doubt of that," he said. "And yet, you won't. As you have somewhere to be. Right now."

"Nonsense," Pippa protested, edging him out of the way with a firm elbow at his side. Actually, physically moving him. "Miss Tasser has already said she has time for me." She blinked up at him from behind thick lenses. "You are dismissed, Mr. Cross."

Sally barked her laughter.

Pippa returned her attention to the prostitute, taking the woman's arm and walking her away from Cross, toward the main entrance of the club. She was going to exit the casino, onto St. James's in the middle of the day, on the arm of a prostitute. "I wonder if you might be willing to teach me how you do it."

"It?" He hadn't meant to say it aloud.

Pippa ignored him, but answered the question. "To smolder. You see, I am to be married in eleven days. Slightly less than that now, and I need to—"

"Catch your husband?" Sally asked.

Pippa nodded. "In a sense. I also require your obvious knowledge in other matters of . . . marriage."

"What kind of matters?"

"Those relating to procreation. I find that what I thought I knew about the mechanics of the act are—well, unlikely."

"Unlikely, how?"

"To be honest, I thought it was similar to animal husbandry."

Sally's tone turned dry. "Sometimes, my lady, I'm afraid it isn't that different."

Pippa paused, considering the words. "Is that so?"

"Men are uncomplicated, generally," Sally said, all too sage. "They're beasts when they want to be."

"Brute ones!"

"Ah, so you understand."

Pippa tilted her head to one side. "I've read about them."

Sally nodded. "Erotic texts?"

"The Book of Common Prayer. But perhaps you have an erotic text you could recommend?"

And there it was—the end of his tether.

"Did you not lose a wager with me that prohibited precisely this kind of interaction?" The words were harsh and unkind. Not that he cared. He turned to Sally. "Leave now, Sally."

Pippa raised her chin in what he was coming to think of as her most frustrating stance. "I promised no questioning other *men*. There was nothing in the wager relating to women."

He opened his mouth to reply. Closed it.

She nodded once, filled with self-satisfaction, and returned her attention to Sally. "Miss Tasser, I assume from what I witnessed that you are clearly skilled . . . at least, Mr. Cross seems to believe so."

Was she out of her mind?

"Cross and I have, unfortunately, never . . . done business," Sally said.

Pippa's mouth fell into a perfect *O*. "I see," she said, when she clearly didn't. "You must be discreet of course. I appreciated that. And I would be happy to pay you for the instruction," she added. "Would you be willing to visit me at my home?"

He had been wrong; *there* was the end of his tether.

She would learn nothing from Sally. Nor from Temple. Nor from Castleton, dammit—it didn't matter that he was her fiancé.

Cross didn't want anyone touching her.

Not if he couldn't.

He reached for Pippa, taking her by the arm, pulling her away from Sally, away from whatever scandalous path she had been considering taking. He ignored her gasp of outrage and the way his fingers fairly rejoiced at their contact. "Sally, it is time for you to go." He turned back to Pippa. "And you. Into my office, before someone discovers you here."

"The club is closed. Who would discover me?"

"Your brother-in-law, perhaps?"

Pippa remained unmoved. "Bourne and Penelope are fishing today. They left for Falconwell this morning. Back tomorrow."

"To fish." If he had an eternity to try, he could not imagine Bourne lakeside, fishing.

"Yes. They've fished together for much of their life. I don't see why it's such a surprise."

Sally shook her head. "Tragic when a rogue of Bourne's caliber goes soft."

Pippa met her gaze. "I suppose it is for most . . . but my sister seems happy with the results."

"No doubt she is. Bourne has always been able to keep a lady happy."

Pippa considered the words for a long moment. "Do you mean to say you have . . . with Bourne?"

"She means no such thing." He gave Sally a pointed look. "Out."

The prostitute tilted her head, a wicked gleam in her eye. "I'm afraid I can't leave, Cross. Not without giving the lady the information she requests."

Pippa seemed to forget her question about Bourne. Thank heaven. "It's very kind of you to come to my defense."

Sally Tasser had spent too long on the streets for kindness. The prostitute did nothing that would not advance her cause. The only reason she was willing to cross Knight was because the Angel offered to pay her triple the amount she received from her current benefactor.

Cross made sure she understood his thoughts with nothing more than a look.

"Sally is leaving, Lady Philippa." The words came out more harshly than he'd intended. But a man could only be pushed so far.

For a moment, he thought both women would fight him. And then, Sally smiled, tilting her head and turning her coyest smile on him. "Well, someone should answer the lady's questions."

Pippa nodded. "It's true. I will not leave without it."

The words were out before he could stop them. "I shall answer them."

Sally looked immensely pleased.

Shit.

There was nothing he wanted to do less than to answer the questions Philippa Marbury had collected in preparation for her lessons from a prostitute.

Pippa's gaze narrowed. "I don't know."

"Cross is highly skilled," Sally said, extracting herself from Pippa's grasp, fairly purring the rest. "He knows all your answers, I'm sure."

Pippa cut him a doubtful look that made him want to prove the prostitute right this very moment.

Sally noticed the exchange and turned a bright, knowing smile on him. "Isn't that right, Cross? I'm certain you don't need my help. Aren't you?"

"I'm certain." He felt as uncertain as Pippa looked.

"Excellent. I shall see you tomorrow, as planned, then."

He nodded once.

She turned to Pippa. "It was wonderful meeting you, Lady Philippa. I hope we have the chance to meet again."

Not if he had anything to say about it.

Once Sally had disappeared through a dark passageway to a rear entrance to the club, he rounded on Philippa. "What would possess you to lie in wait for a prostitute inside a casino?"

There was a long silence, and Cross wondered if she might not reply, which wouldn't be terrible, as he had had more than enough of her insanity.

But she did reply, eyes wide, voice strong, advancing on him, stalking him across the floor of the casino. "You don't seem to understand my predicament, Mr. Cross. I have eleven days before I have to take vows before God and man relating to half a dozen things of which I have no knowledge. You and the rest of Christendom—including my sisters, apparently—would have no trouble at all with such an act, but I *do* have difficulty with it. How am I to take vows that I don't understand? How am I to marry without knowing all of it? How am I to vow to be a sound wife to Castleton and a mother to his children when I lack the rudimentary understanding of the acts in question?"

She paused, adding as an aside, "Well, I do have the experience from the bull in Coldharbour, but . . . it's not entirely relevant understanding, as Penelope and you have both pointed out. Can't you see? I only have eleven days. And I *need every one of them.*"

He backed into the hazard table, and she kept coming. "I need them. I need the knowledge they can give me. The understanding they can afford. I need every bit of information I can glean—if not from you, then from Miss Tasser. Or others. I have promised to be a wife and mother. And I have a great deal of research to do on the subject."

She was breathing heavily when she stopped, eyes bright, cheeks flushed, and the skin of her pale breasts straining against the edge of her rose-colored gown. He was transfixed by her, by her passionate concern and her commitment to her ridiculous solution—as though understanding the mechanics of sex would change everything. Would make the next eleven days easy, and the next eleven years even easier. Of course, it wouldn't.

Knowledge wasn't enough.

He knew that better than anyone.

"You can't know everything, Pippa."

"I can know more than I do," she retorted.

He smiled at that, and she took a step back, staring up at him, then down at her widespread hands. There was something so vulnerable about her. Something he did not like.

When she returned her unblinking gaze to his and said, "I am going to be a wife," he had the wicked urge to ferret her into one of the club's secret rooms and keep her there.

Possibly forever.

A wife. He hated the idea of her as a wife. As Castleton's wife. As anyone's.

"And a mother."

A vision flashed, Pippa surrounded by children. Beaming, bespectacled children, each fascinated with some aspect of the world, listening carefully as she explained the science of the Earth and the heavens to them.

She would be a remarkable mother.

No. He wouldn't think on that. He didn't like to consider it.

"Most wives don't frequent prostitutes to develop their skills. And you have time for maternal research."

"She seemed as good a research partner as any, considering you've already cut my pool of possibilities in half. After all, you have not been helping. Is she your paramour?"

He ignored the question. "Prostitutes seemed a reasonable next step in your plan?"

"Interestingly enough, they didn't until last night. But when Penelope suggested that there might be prostitutes here—"

"*Lady Bourne* knows about your ridiculous plans and hasn't tied you to a chair?" Bourne's wife or no, the lady deserved a sound thrashing for allowing her unmarried, unprotected sister to gallivant through London's darker corners without purchase.

"No. She simply answered a few questions about the Angel."

About him? He wouldn't ask. He did not wish to know.

"What kind of questions?"

She sighed. "The kind that ended with me knowing that there might be a prostitute or two here. Is she very skilled?"

The question was so forthright, his head spun. She did not need to know that Sally Tasser was perhaps the most skilled workingwoman this side of Montmartre.

"What do you want to know?"

She blinked up at him with those big blue eyes and said, as though it were a perfectly reasonable thing to say, "Everything."

For one long, lush moment, he was lost to the vision of just what *everything* might entail. To the way her body might fit to his, the way she might taste, soft and sweet on his tongue, to the wicked, wonderful things she might allow him to do to her. To the lessons for which she did not even know she was asking.

He wanted to show her everything.

And he wanted to begin now.

"Do you think that Miss Tasser would be willing to provide a lesson of sorts?"

It was becoming difficult to breathe. "No."

Pippa tilted her head. "Are you certain? As I said, I would be willing to pay her."

The idea of Pippa Marbury paying to learn Sally Tasser's trade made Cross want to destroy someone. First Bourne, for allowing his sister-in-law to run untethered throughout London, and then the Marquess of Needham and Dolby, for raising a young woman who was completely lacking in sense, and then Castleton, for not keeping his fiancée properly occupied in the weeks leading up to their wedding.

Unaware of the direction of his rioting thoughts, she said, "Lord Castleton has never attempted to compromise me."

The man was either idiot or saint.

If Cross were Castleton, he'd have had her a dozen different ways the moment she'd agreed to be his wife. In darkened hallways and dim alcoves, in long, stop-and-start carriage rides through the crush of midday traffic, and outside, quickly, against a strong, sturdy tree, with none but nature to hear her cries of pleasure.

To hear their *mutual* cries of pleasure.

But he was not Castleton.

He was Cross.

And this was thoroughly, completely wrong.

He took a step back, his thoughts making him guilty—making him look around the dim casino floor in sudden fear that someone might see them. Might hear them.

Why was it that she was always where ladies should never be?

"Last night, I attempted to indicate to him that I was happy for him to touch me. Kiss me, even."

He hated the earl with a wicked, visceral intensity.

She was still talking. "But he didn't even seem to notice me. Granted, it was just a touch on the hand, but . . ."

Cross would pay good money for her to touch him so simply.

Her big blue eyes were trained on him again. "Do you know why he hasn't attempted to seduce me?"

"No." Again, sainthood seemed the only logical answer.

"You needn't feel that you must protect me from the truth."

"I don't." Except he did. He didn't want her to know the truth of his own thoughts. Their sordid nature.

"It's because I am odd." And then she looked up at him with those enormous blue eyes, and said, "I can't help it."

God help him, he wanted to kiss her senseless, odd or not. He wanted to kiss her senseless *because* she was odd.

"Pippa—" he said, knowing he shouldn't speak.

She cut him off. "Don't tell me it's not true. I know it is. I'm strange."

"You are."

Her brows knit together. "Well, you don't have to tell me it *is* true either."

He couldn't help it. He smiled. "It is not a bad thing."

She looked at him as though it was he—and not she—who was mad. "Of course it is."

"No. It's not."

"You're a good man."

He was nothing of the sort. And there were several key parts of his body that wanted to prove that to her. One of them in particular.

"It's fine that he is not interested in seducing me," she said, "but it cannot go on forever."

"Perhaps he is trying to be a gentleman."

She did not believe it. "That hasn't stopped Tottenham."

A thread of fire shot through him. "Tottenham has attempted to seduce you?" He'd murder him, next prime minister or not.

She looked at him as though he'd sprouted a second head. "No. Why would Tottenham seduce me?"

"You said it."

"No. I said he'd tried to seduce Olivia."

She hadn't said any such thing, but he let it go.

"Not tried to," she pressed on, "*did*. Has done." She closed her eyes. "I'm the only Marbury daughter who has not been seduced."

He could rectify this tragic wrong.

Except he couldn't.

She looked up at him. "Can you believe it?"

He did not know what to say. So he said nothing.

"You can, I see." She took a deep breath. "This is why I required your help from the beginning, Mr. Cross. I need you to show me how to do it."

Yes.

He swallowed back the word. Surely he was misunderstanding. "How to do what?"

She sighed, frustrated. "How to attract him."

"Whom?"

"Are you even listening? Castleton!" She turned away, heading for the nearest table, where a roulette wheel stood quiet in its thick oak seat. She spoke to the wheel. "I didn't know that he should be attempting to seduce me now. Before our wedding. I didn't know that was a part of it."

"It's not. He shouldn't be doing any such thing."

"Well, you've clearly never been engaged because it seems that this is precisely the kind of thing that happens between to-be-married couples. I thought I had two weeks. Apparently, I don't."

There was a roar in his ears that made it difficult to understand her, but when she turned to face him again, shoulders back, as though she were about to do battle, he knew he was done for. "My research must begin immediately."

He was being punished. That was the only explanation.

"I need someone"—she paused, then reframed the statement—"I need *you* to teach me how to be normal."

What a travesty that would be.

"Normal."

"Yes. Normal." She lifted her hands helplessly. "I realize now that my original request—for the experience of ruination?" she asked as though he might have somehow forgotten the request in question. As though he might ever forget it. He nodded, nonetheless. "Well, I realize now that it is not at all a strange request."

"It's not?"

She smiled. "No. Indeed. In fact, it seems that there are plenty of women in London who *fully* experience those things that I am interested in before their wedding night—including my sisters. That bit is between us, I hope?"

Finally, a question to which he knew the reply. "Of course."

She was already moving on. "You see, I thought I would require a certain amount of knowledge on the night in question because Lord Castleton might not have the knowledge himself. But now, I realize . . . well . . . I require it because it's ordinary."

"It's ordinary."

She tilted her head and considered him curiously. "You do a great deal of repeating me, Mr. Cross."

Because listening to her was like learning a second language. Arabic. Or Hindi.

She was still talking. "It's ordinary. After all, if Olivia has it, and Lord Tottenham is quite the gentleman, well then, many must have it, don't you think?"

"It."

"Knowledge of the inner workings of the marital . . ." She hesitated. "Process."

He took a long breath and let it out. "I'm still not certain why you need a prostitute to teach you such . . . workings."

"It's no different, really. I continue to require a research partner. Only, it seems now I require research on normalcy. I need to know how it is that ordinary females behave. I need help. Rather urgently. Since you refused, Miss Tasser will do."

She was killing him. Slowly. Painfully.

"Sally Tasser is no ordinary female."

"Well, I understand that she is a prostitute, but I assume she has all the required parts?"

He choked. "Yes."

She hesitated, and something flashed across her face. Disappointment? "You've seen them?"

"No." Truth.

"Hmm." She did not seem to believe him. "You do not frequent prostitutes?"

"I do not."

"I am not entirely certain that I support the profession."

"No?" Thank God. He would not put it past Pippa to simply pronounce a newfound desire to explore all aspects of the world's oldest profession.

"No." She shook her head. "I am concerned that the ladies are ill-treated."

"The ladies who frequent The Fallen Angel are not ill-treated."

Her brows knit together. "How do you know?"

"Because they are under my protection."

She froze. "They are?"

He was suddenly warm. "They are. We do all we can to

ensure that they are well treated and well paid while under our roof. If they are manhandled, they call for one of the security detail. They file a complaint with me. And if I discover a member is mistreating ladies beneath this roof, his membership is revoked."

She paused for a long moment, considering the words, and finally said, "I have a passion for horticulture."

He wasn't certain how plants had anything to do with prostitutes, but he knew better than to interrupt.

She continued, the words quick and forthright, as though they entirely made sense. "I've made a rather remarkable discovery recently," she said, and his attention lingered on the breathlessness of the words. On the way her mouth curved in a small, private smile. She was proud of herself, and he found—even before she admitted her finding—that he was proud of her. Odd, that. "It is possible to take a piece of one rosebush and affix it to another. And when the process is completed properly . . . say, a white piece on a red bush . . . an entirely new rose grows . . ." She paused, and the rest of the words rushed out, as though she were almost afraid of them. "A pink one."

Cross did not know much about horticulture, but he knew enough about scientific study to know that the finding would be groundbreaking. "How did you—"

She raised a hand to stop the question. "I'll happily show you. It's very exciting. But that's not the point."

He waited for her to arrive at the point in question.

She did. "The career . . . it is not their choice. They're not red or white anymore. They're pink. And you're why."

Somehow, it made sense that she compared the ladies of the Angel to this experiment in roses. Somehow, this woman's strange, wonderful brain worked in a way that he completely understood.

And as he considered that odd, remarkable truth, she prodded, "Aren't you?"

It was not the simplest of questions. Nor was it the easiest of answers. "It is not always their choice, no. In many cases, girls fall into it. But here, they are well treated. Well fed. Well paid. And the moment they want to stop their work, we find them other places."

Her brows rose. "Where?"

He smiled. "We are very powerful men, Pippa. Our membership has need of servants; our vendors require shopgirls. And, if not that, then there are always safe houses far from London, where girls can begin anew." After a long silence, he added, "I would never force a girl into this life."

"But some of them choose it?"

It was an incomprehensible truth for some. "The white branch."

She nodded. "Like Miss Tasser."

"Like Sally."

"Well, all the more reason for me to mine her expertise." She pushed her spectacles up the bridge of her nose. "If she chooses it, she must enjoy it to a certain extent. And there's no one else. It's not as though Castleton has offered his assistance."

As it should be.

No. Not as it should be. Of course Castleton should be offering his assistance. He should be doing much more than that.

The thought made Cross more murderous.

She pursed her lips. "Do you think I ought to ask him? Perhaps that's how these things are done?"

No! "Yes."

She blushed, tempting him. "I'm not sure I could."

"But you can ask me?"

She blinked up at him. "You are different. You are not the kind of man one marries. It's easier to . . . well . . . engage in a candid discussion of my research with you." She smiled. "You are a man of science, after all."

There it was, again. That certainty that he would keep her safe.

That he was in control. Always.

You should tell her.

Sally's words echoed through him, mocking and correct.

He should tell her. But it wasn't precisely the kind of thing one told a young, beautiful woman standing by and begging for lessons in ruination.

At least, not an *ordinary* young woman in such a situation.

But Philippa Marbury was nothing close to ordinary.

Telling her the truth would push her away. And that would be best. For all involved.

Especially him.

Pippa shook her head. "He'll say no. Don't you see? There's no one. No one but Miss Tasser."

She was wrong, of course.

"There is me," he said, the words out before he knew they were coming. Her eyes went wide, and she met his gaze.

There was a beat as she heard the words. Their meaning. "You," she said.

He smiled. "Now it is you repeating me."

She matched his smile, and he felt the expression deep in his gut. "So I am."

Perhaps he could do this.

Lord knew he owed it to her, owed it to her for allowing her into the clutches of Knight and Sally and Temple and God knew whoever else she'd met while inside the casino. He owed it to Bourne to keep her safe.

Excuses.

He paused at the thought. Perhaps they were excuses. Perhaps he just wanted a reason to be near her. To talk to her, this bizarre, brilliant woman who threw him off axis every chance she got.

It would be torture, yes.

But Lord knew he deserved torture.

He had to move. Away from her.

He crossed to a hazard table, lifting a pair of dice and testing their weight in his hand. She followed without prompting, moving past him in a cloud of softness scented with fresh linens. How was it that she smelled like sunshine and fresh air even here in darkness? Surrounded by sin and vice?

She had to leave. She was too much temptation for him to bear.

Unaware of his thoughts, she turned her open, fresh face up to him. "I have a number of questions. For example, Madame Hebert has committed to making me nightclothes that she swears will tempt Castleton into seducing me. Can nightclothes do the trick?"

The words were an assault, consuming him with the idea of blond, lithe Pippa in a silk-and-lace creation designed to send men completely over the edge. Something with a devastating number of ribbons, each one in a perfect little bow that, when untied, revealed a patch of soft, warm skin—a luxurious, unbearable present.

A present worthy of the wrapping.

"I don't think they will be enough," she said, distracted.

He was certain they would be too much.

"And what of Miss Tasser's smolder? Can you teach me to do that? It seems like it will help. With the tempting."

He didn't look at her. He couldn't. But he also couldn't stop himself from saying, "You don't need to smolder."

She paused. "I don't?"

"No. You are tempting in a different way."

"I am?"

You should tell her.

Before she tempted him anymore.

But he couldn't.

He met her gaze. "You are."

Her eyes were wide as saucers behind those maddening spectacles. "I am?"

He smiled. "You are repeating me again."

She was quiet for a moment. "You won't change your mind, will you?"

"No." The idea of her finding another was altogether unacceptable.

Not when it could be him. Not when he could show her pleasure that would shatter her innocence and thoroughly, completely ruin her. He wanted to give her everything for which she asked.

And more.

Like that, the decision was made. "No. I shan't renege."

She let out a long breath, and the sound slid through him in the quiet room, making him wonder what else would tempt that little exhalation.

"I should have known that. Gentlemen do not renege."

"In this case, neither do scoundrels."

"I don't understand."

"The rules of gentlemen insist that honor keep them from reneging, even during a bad bet," he explained, tempted to smooth the furrow on her brow, resisting it. "The rules of scoundrels insist one only wager if one can win."

"Which—" She hesitated. "Which are you?"

He could give her the knowledge without giving in to his own desires. Without relinquishing his own commitments. Without relinquishing his own control.

He stepped forward, crowding her. "Which do you think?"

She stepped back. "A gentleman."

Without touching her.

Because he knew, without a doubt, that after six years of celibacy, if he touched Philippa Marbury, he would not survive it.

Scoundrel.

"Tomorrow. Nine o'clock."

Chapter Eight

*"Astronomy has never been my forte, but I find
myself considering the scope of the universe today.
If our Sun is one of millions of stars, who is to say
that Galileo was not right? That there is not another
Earth far away on the edge of another Galaxy?
And who is to say there is not another Philippa
Marbury, ten days before her wedding, waiting for
her knowledge to expand?*

*It's irrelevant, of course. Even if there were a
duplicate Earth in some far-off corner of the
universe, I'm still to be married in ten days.*

And so is the other Pippa."

The Scientific Journal of Lady Philippa Marbury
March 26, 1831; ten days prior to her wedding

The next evening, Pippa sat on a small bench perched
just outside a collection of cherry trees in the Dolby House
gardens, cloak wrapped tightly about her, Trotula at her feet,
stargazing.

Or, at least, attempting to stargaze.

She'd been outside for more than an hour, having finally
given up on feigning illness and escaping the house once

supper had been officially served, preferring outside to inside, even on this cold March night.

She was too excited.

Tonight, she would learn about seduction.

From *Cross*.

She took a deep breath and released it, then another, hoping they would calm her racing thoughts. They did not. They were clouded with visions of Mr. Cross, of the way he looked as he glowered at her across the floor of his gaming hell, the way he smiled at her in the darkness, the way he crowded her in his office.

It wasn't him, of course. She would feel this way if anyone had promised her the lesson he'd promised.

Liar.

She exhaled long and loud.

The breathing was not helping.

She looked over her shoulder at the dim light trickling down from the Dolby House dining room. Yes, it was best that she spend the time leading up to their meeting alone in the cold rather than going mad at a meal with her parents and Olivia, who would no doubt be discussing the particulars of "The Wedding" at that exact moment.

A vision flashed from the previous afternoon, Olivia resplendent in her wedding gown, glowing with the excitement of prenuptial bliss, Pippa's reflection in the mirror behind, smaller and dimmer in the wake of her younger, more luminous sister.

The Wedding would be remarkable. One for the ages. Or, at least the gossips.

It would be just what the Marchioness of Needham and Dolby had always dreamed—an enormous, formal ceremony designed to showcase the pomp and circumstance befitting the Marbury daughters' birth. It would erase the memory of the two previous weddings of the generation: Victoria and Valerie's double wedding to uninspiring mates, performed hastily in the wake of Penelope's scandalous, broken engagement, and, more recently, Penelope's wedding, performed by special license in the village chapel near the Needham country estate the day after Bourne had returned from wherever it was he'd gone for a decade.

Of course, they all knew where Bourne had gone.

He'd gone to The Fallen Angel.

With Mr. Cross.

Fascinating, unnerving Mr. Cross, who was beginning to unsettle her even when she was not near him. She took a deep breath and closed her eyes, assessing the change that came over her when she was in proximity—either mental or physical—to the tall, ginger-haired man who had begrudgingly agreed to assist her in her quest.

Her heart seemed to race, her breath coming more shallowly. More quickly.

Her muscles tensed and her nerves seemed to hover at attention.

She grew warm . . . or was that cold?

Either way, they were all signs of heightened awareness. Symptoms of excitement. Or nervousness. Or fear.

She was being overly dramatic. There was nothing to fear from this man—he was a man of science. In utter control at all times.

The perfect research associate.

Nothing more.

It did not matter that the research in question was somewhat unorthodox. It was research nonetheless.

She took another breath and withdrew the watch from her reticule, holding it up to read its face in the dim light seeping through the windows of the ground-floor sitting room.

"It's nine o'clock." The words were soft, rising out of the darkness, and Trotula leapt to her feet to greet the newcomer, giving Pippa a chance to address the thundering of her heart. Later, she would wonder at the fact that she was breathless, but not startled, instead something different. Something more.

In the moment, however, there was only one thing she could think.

He had come.

She smiled, watching him crouch to greet her hound. "You are very punctual."

His task completed, he rose and sat next to her, close enough to unsettle, far enough away to avoid contact. Out of the corner of her eye, she realized how long his thighs were—nearly half again the length of her own, pulling the wool of his trousers tight along lean muscle and bone. She should not be considering his thighs.

Femurs.

"And yet, you are waiting for me."

She turned to him to find him watching the sky, face shadowed in the darkness, leaning back on the bench as though they had been sitting there all night, as though they might sit there still, all night. She followed his gaze. "I've been here for more than an hour."

"In the cold?"

"It's the best time for stargazing, don't you think? Cold nights are always so much clearer."

"There's a reason for that."

She turned to face him. "Is there?"

He did not look to her. "There are fewer stars in the winter sky. How is your toe?"

"Right as rain. You are an astronomer as well as a mathematician?"

He turned to face her, finally, half his face cast into shadowy light from the manor beyond. "You are a horticulturalist as well as an anatomist?"

She smiled. "We are surprising, aren't we?"

His lips twitched. "We are."

A long moment stretched out between them before he turned away again, returning his attention to the sky. "What were you looking at?"

She pointed to a bright star. "Polaris."

He shook his head, and pointed to another part of the sky. "That's Polaris. You were looking at Vega."

She chuckled. "Ah. No wonder I was finding it unimpressive."

He leaned back and stretched his long legs out. "It's the fifth brightest star in the sky."

She laughed. "You forget I am one of five sisters. In my world, fifth brightest is last. She looked up. "With apologies to the star in question, of course."

"And are you often last?"

She shrugged. "Sometimes. It is not a pleasant ranking."

"I assure you, Pippa. You are rarely last."

He had not moved except to turn his head and look at her, the angles of his face hard and unforgiving in the darkness, sending a shiver of something unfamiliar through her. "Be careful what you say. I shall have to tell Penny that you find her lacking."

He turned a surprised look on her. "I didn't say that."

"She's the only one of my sisters whom you've met. If I am not last, then in your mind, she must trail behind."

One side of his mouth kicked up. "In that case, let's not recount this conversation to anyone else."

"I can agree to that." She returned her attention to the sky. "Tell me about this magnificent, fifth-best star."

When he spoke, she could hear the laughter in his deep voice, and she resisted the urge to look at him. "Vega belongs to the constellation Lyra, so named because Ptolemy believed it looked like Orpheus's lyre."

She couldn't resist teasing him, "You're an expert in the classics, as well, I gather?"

"You mean you are not?" he retorted, drawing a laugh from her before adding, "Orpheus is one of my favorites."

She looked to him. "Why?"

His gaze was locked on the night sky. "He made a terrible mistake and paid dearly for it."

With the words, everything grew more serious. "Eurydice," she whispered. She knew the story of Orpheus and his wife, whom he loved more than anything and lost to the Underworld.

He was quiet for a long moment, and she thought he might not speak. When he did, the words were flat and emotionless. "He convinced Hades to let her go, to return her to the living. All he had to do was lead her out without looking back into Hell."

"But he couldn't," Pippa said, mind racing.

"He grew greedy and looked back. He lost her forever." He paused, then repeated, "A terrible mistake."

And there was something there in his tone, something that Pippa might not have noticed at another time, in another man. Loss. Sorrow. Memory flashed—the whispered conversation in this very garden.

You shouldn't have married him.

I didn't have a choice. You didn't leave me with one.

I should have stopped it.

The woman in the garden . . . she was his Eurydice.

Something unpleasant flared in her chest at the thought, and Pippa couldn't resist reaching out to touch him, to settle her hand on his arm. He jerked at the touch, pulling away as though she'd burned him.

They sat in silence for a long moment. Until she couldn't stop herself from saying, "You made a mistake."

He slid his gaze to her fleetingly, then stood. "It's time to go. Your lesson awaits."

Except she did not want to go anymore. She wanted to stay. "You lost your love." He did not look to her, but she could not have looked away if a team of oxen had driven through the gardens of Dolby House in that moment. "The woman in the gardens. Lavinia," she said, hating that she could not simply keep quiet. *Don't ask, Pippa. Don't.* "You . . . love her?"

The word was strange on her tongue.

It should not surprise her that he had a paramour, after

all, there were few men in London with the kind of reputation that Mr. Cross had as both a man and a lover. But she confessed, he did not seem the kind of man who would be drawn to more serious emotions—to something like love. He was, after all, a man of science. As she was a woman of science. And she certainly did not expect for love to ever make an appearance in her own mind.

And yet, in this strange moment, she found she was desperate to hear his answer. And there, in the desperation, she discovered that she was hoping that his answer would be no. That there was no unrequited love lurking deep in his breast.

Or requited love, for that matter.

She started at the thought.

Well.

That was unexpected.

His lips twisted at the question, as he turned his face from the light and into the darkness. But he did not speak. "Curiosity is a dangerous thing, Lady Philippa."

She rose to face him, keenly aware of how much taller he was than she, keenly aware of *him*. "I find I cannot help myself."

"I have noticed that."

"I only ask because I am intrigued by the idea of your loving someone." *Stop it, Pippa. This is not the path down which intelligent young ladies tread.* She changed tack. "Not you, that is. Anyone. Loving someone."

"You have opposition to love?"

"Not opposition so much as skepticism. I make it a practice not to believe in things I cannot see."

She'd surprised him. "You are no ordinary female."

"We have established that. It is why you are here, if you recall."

"So it is." He crossed his long arms over his chest, and added, "So you wish to tempt your husband, whom you do not expect to love."

"Precisely." When he did not immediately respond, she

added, "If it helps, I do not think he expects to love me, either."

"A sound English marriage."

She considered the words. "I suppose it is, isn't it? It's certainly like any of the marriages to which I am close."

His brows rose. "You doubt the fact that Bourne cares deeply for your sister?"

"No. But that's the only one." She paused, considering. "Maybe Olivia and Tottenham, too. But my other sisters married for much the same reason as I shall."

"Which is?"

She lifted one shoulder in a little shrug. "It is what we are expected to do." She met his gaze, unable to read it in the darkness. "I suppose that doesn't make sense to you, seeing as you are not an aristocrat."

One side of his mouth kicked up. "What does being an aristocrat have to do with it?"

She pushed her spectacles up on her nose. "You may not know this, but aristocrats have a great many rules with which to contend. Marriages are about wealth and station and propriety and position. We cannot simply marry whomever we wish. Well, ladies can't at least." She thought for a moment. "Gentlemen can weather more scandal, but so many of them simply flop over and allow themselves to be dragged into uninspired marriages anyway. Why do you think that is?"

"I wouldn't like to guess."

"It is amazing what power men have and how poorly they use it. Don't you think?"

"And if you had the same powers?"

"I don't."

"But if you did?"

And because he seemed genuinely intrigued, she said, "I would have gone to university. I would join the Royal Horticultural Society. Or maybe the Royal Astronomical Society—then I would know the difference between Polaris and Vega."

He laughed.

She continued, enjoying the way she could be free with him. "I would marry someone I liked." She paused, instantly regretting the way the words sounded on her tongue. "I mean—I don't dislike Castleton, he is a nice man. Very kind. It's just . . ." She trailed off, feeling disloyal.

"I understand."

And for a moment, she thought he might.

"But all that is silly, you see? Natterings of an odd young lady. I was born into certain rules, and I must follow them. Which is why I think it is likely easier for those who live outside of society."

"There you are, seeing in black and white again."

"Are you saying it's not easier for you?"

"I am saying that we all have our crosses to bear."

There was something in the words—an unexpected bitterness that made her hesitate before she said, "I suppose you speak from experience?"

"I do."

Her mind spun with the possibilities. He'd said once that he did not think on marriage. That it was not for him. Perhaps at one time, it had been. Had he wanted to marry? Had he been refused? Because of his name, or his reputation, or his career? Title or no, he was an impressive specimen of man—clever and wealthy and powerful and rather handsome when one considered all factors.

What lady would refuse him?

The mystery lady in the garden had.

"Well, either way, I am happy that you are not a peer."

"If I were?"

You would be like none I have ever met. She smiled. "I would never have asked you to be my research associate. I have compiled a list, by the way. Of my questions."

"I expected nothing less. But you don't think it would make everything easier if I were a peer? No skulking about in gaming hells."

She smiled. "I rather like skulking about in gaming hells."

"Perhaps." He stepped closer, blocking out the light from the house. "But perhaps it is also because when you complete your research, you can walk away and forget it ever happened."

"I would never forget it," she said, the truth coming quick and free. Pippa flushed at the words, grateful for the shadows that kept the color from him.

But she wouldn't forget this. In fact, she had no doubt that she would harken back to this night when she was Lady Castleton, rattling around in her country estate with nothing but her hothouse and her dogs to keep her company.

And she certainly would not forget *him*.

They were quiet for a long moment, and she wondered if she'd said too much. Finally, he said, "I brought you something." He extended a brown-paper-wrapped package toward her.

Her breath quickened—a strange response to a small box, no doubt—and she took the parcel, pushing away Trotula's inquisitive wet nose and quickly unwrapping it to discover a domino mask on a bed of fine paper. She lifted the wide swath of black silk, heart pounding.

She looked up at him, unable to read his gaze in the darkness. "Thank you."

He nodded once. "You will need it." He turned away from her then, moving quickly across the gardens.

Trotula followed.

Pippa did not wish to be left behind. She hurried to keep up with man and beast.

"Are we . . . we are going somewhere public?"

"Of a sort."

"I thought . . ." She hesitated. "That is, I was under the impression that the instruction would be in private." She lifted her reticule. "I cannot ask you about the specifics in *public*."

He turned back, and she nearly plowed into him. "Tonight is not about specifics. It is about temptation."

The word slid through her, and Pippa wondered, fleetingly, if it was possible that language was somehow made more powerful in the absence of light. It was a silly question, of course. Obviously, the senses were heightened when one was removed. She couldn't see him, so she heard him all the more.

It had nothing to do with the word itself.

Temptation.

He began walking once more, adding, "To understand how to tempt a man, you must first understand temptation yourself."

She followed, hurrying to catch up. "I understand temptation."

He slid her a look.

"I do!"

"What tempts you?" They had arrived at a black carriage, and Mr. Cross reached up to open the door and lower the stepping block. The spaniel leapt into the carriage happily, surprising them both into laughter.

She snapped her fingers. "Trotula, out."

With a sad sigh, the dog did as she was bid.

Pippa pointed to the house. "Go home."

The hound sat.

Pippa pointed again. "Home."

The hound refused to move.

Cross smirked. "She's somewhat unbiddable."

"Not usually."

"Perhaps it's me."

She cut him a look. "Perhaps so."

"I shouldn't be surprised. You're rather unbiddable around me as well."

She feigned shock. "Sirrah, are you comparing me to a hound?"

He smiled, flashing eyes and white teeth causing a strange little flutter to take up residence in her stomach. "Maybe."

Then, "Now. Let's return to the task at hand. What tempts you, Pippa?"

"I—" She hesitated. "I care a great deal for meringue."

He laughed, the sound bigger and bolder than she expected.

"It's true."

"No doubt you do. But you may have meringue anytime you like." He stood back and indicated that she should enter the carriage.

She ignored the silent command, eager to make her point. "Not so. If the cook has not made it, I cannot eat it."

A smile played on his lips. "Ever-practical Pippa. If you want it, you can find it. That's my point. Surely, somewhere in London, someone will take pity upon you and satisfy your craving for meringue."

Her brow furrowed. "Therefore, I am not tempted by it?"

"No. You desire it. But that's not the same thing. Desire is easy. It's as simple as you wish to have meringue, and meringue is procured." He waved a hand toward the interior of the carriage but did not offer to help her up. "In."

She ascended another step before turning back. The additional height brought them eye to eye. "I don't understand. What is temptation, then?"

"Temptation . . ." He hesitated, and she found herself leaning forward, eager for this curious, unsettling lesson. "Temptation turns you. It makes you into something you never dreamed, it presses you to give up everything you ever loved, it calls you to sell your soul for one, fleeting moment."

The words were low and dark and full of truth, and they hovered in the silence for a long moment, an undeniable invitation. He was close, protecting her from toppling off the block, the heat of him wrapping around her despite the cold. "It makes you ache," he whispered, and she watched the curve of his lips in the darkness. "You'll make any promise, swear any oath. For one . . . perfect . . . unsoiled taste."

Oh, my.

Pippa exhaled, long and reedy, nerves screaming, thoughts muddled. She closed her eyes, swallowed, forced herself back, away from him and the way he . . . *tempted her.*

Why was he so calm and cool and utterly in control?

Why was he not riddled with similar . . . feelings?

He was a very frustrating man.

She sighed. "That must be a tremendous meringue."

A beat followed the silly, stupid words . . . words she wished she could take back. *How ridiculous.* And then he chuckled, teeth flashing in the darkness. "Indeed," he said, the words thicker and more gravelly than before.

Before Pippa could wonder at the sound, he added, "Trotula, go home."

The dog turned and went as he returned his attention to Pippa, and said, "Get in."

She did. Without question.

The alley behind the Angel looked different at night. More ominous.

It did not help that he punctuated the slowing of the carriage with, "It is time for the mask," before he opened the door and leapt down from the conveyance without aid of step or servant.

She did not hesitate to do his bidding, extracting the slip of fabric and lifting it to her face, filled with excitement—she'd never had cause to mask her identity before.

The mask promised equal parts excitement and edification.

Her first foray incognito. Her first moment as more than just the oddest Marbury sister.

In the mask, she imagined herself not odd, but mysterious. Not only scientific, but also scandalous. She would be a veritable Circe in the making.

But now, as she attempted to affix the mask to her head,

she realized that imagination was not reality. And that masks were not made for spectacles.

On the first attempt, she tied the ribbons too loosely, and the mask gaped and slipped, sliding down over the lenses of the glasses, blocking her view and threatening to fall past her nose and to the floor of the carriage if she moved too quickly.

On the second try, she tied the ribbons with a much firmer hand, wincing as she captured a few stray hairs in the messy knot. The result was not much better, the mask now forced the spectacles against her eyes, warping the thin gold rims until the nose and earpieces dug into her skin, and making her feel decidedly *un*-Circe-like.

Committed to soldiering on, she slid across the seat to exit to the carriage, where Mr. Cross stood waiting for her. She would not allow a little thing like poor eyesight to ruin the evening. The mask perched haphazardly on her spectacles, she stepped blindly from the carriage, her slipper finding the top step by some miracle other than peripheral vision.

Not so, the second step.

Pippa stumbled, emitting a loud squeak and throwing her arms wide to somehow regain her balance. She failed, toppling to the left, directly into Mr. Cross, who caught her to his chest with a soft grunt.

His warm, firm chest.

With his long, capable arms.

He sucked in a breath, clutching her tightly and for a moment—not even a moment, barely an instant—the length of her was pressed to the length of him, and she was looking directly into his eyes. Well, not precisely *directly*, as the dratted mask had of course shifted during the journey, and she was left with a fraction of her usual visibility.

But had she full use of her faculties, she was certain she would discover him laughing. And there it was again, embarrassment, hot and unavoidable in the instant before he set her down.

Once on terra firma, Pippa lifted one hand from where it had been desperately clutching his wool coat and attempted to right the mask. She succeeded in upsetting both it and her spectacles, which tumbled from their perch.

He caught the frames in midair.

She looked from the spectacles to his face, its angles stark in the light from the exterior of the carriage. "This was not how I expected the evening to proceed."

He was not laughing, she would give him that. Instead, he seemed to consider her carefully for a long moment before he stepped back and removed a handkerchief from his pocket. "Nor I, I assure you," he said, cleaning the glasses carefully before returning them to her.

She put them on quickly and huffed a little sigh. "I cannot wear the mask. It will not fit." She hated the pout in her voice. She sounded like Olivia.

She wrinkled her nose and met his gaze.

He did not speak, instead reaching out to straighten the glasses on her nose without touching her. They hovered there, in silence, for a long moment before he said, softly, "I should have thought of that."

She shook her head. "I'm sure you've never had such a problem before . . ." A vision of Sally Tasser flashed, the beautiful, perfectly sighted woman who would have no difficulty whatsoever wearing a mask and achieving flawless mystery.

The only thing Pippa achieved flawlessly was peculiarity.

And suddenly, she was keenly aware that this world, this night, this *experience* was not for her. It was a mistake. Orpheus looking back into Hell.

"I should not be here," she said, meeting his gaze, expecting to see satisfaction there—relief that she had finally given up.

But she did not see relief. Instead, she saw something else. Something firm and unyielding. "We shall just have to be careful in a different way." He started for the club, the expectation that she should follow clear.

As they approached the great steel door that marked the rear entrance to the hell, a second carriage came trundling down the alleyway, stopping several yards from the conveyance in which they had arrived. A servant stepped down as the carriage door swung open from within on a collection of feminine laughter.

Pippa stopped at the sound, turning toward it.

Mr. Cross swore, low and wicked and grabbed her by the hand before she could resist, spinning her back against the outer wall of the club and blocking her from view with his looming frame.

She tried to move, and he pressed her to the wall, preventing her from seeing the women who had descended from the carriage and were now giggling and chattering as they made their way to the wall. She craned her neck to see them, curiosity making her careless, but he predicted her movements and shifted closer, crowding her back, making it impossible for her to see anything.

Anything but him.

He was so very tall. She'd never known anyone as tall as him. And when he was so close, it was difficult to think of anything but him. Him, and his warmth, the way his unbuttoned coat fell open around them, bringing her closer to a man in shirtsleeves than she'd ever been before.

Her thoughts were interrupted by another burst of laughter, followed by a hushing sound. "Look!" a woman said loudly. "We're disturbing the lovers!"

"Someone couldn't wait until she was inside!" Another feminine voice said.

"Who is it?" a third whispered.

Pippa's eyes went wide, and she spoke to his chest. "Who are they?"

"None you need worry about." He crowded closer, grimacing as he lifted one hand and placed it flat on the wall above her head, obscuring her face with his long arm and the lapel of his coat.

She was a hairsbreadth from his chest, and she couldn't stop herself from inhaling, the scent of clean, fresh sandalwood wrapping around her. Her hands, hanging limp at her sides, itched to touch him. She clenched her fists and looked up at him, meeting his dark eyes.

"I can't see her," one of the ladies said, "but I'd know that man anywhere. It's Cross." She raised the volume of her voice. "Isn't it, Cross?"

A thread of heat coursed through Pippa at the woman's familiarity, at the laughter in her tone—as though she knew precisely what it was like to be here, pressed between the stone wall of London's most legendary gaming hell and her proud, brilliant owner.

"Go inside, ladies," he said at full volume, without looking away from Pippa. "You're missing the fight."

"It looks like there's just as much to watch outside, tonight!" one retorted, drawing a chorus of appreciative laughter from the others.

Cross shifted, dropping his head, and Pippa realized how it would appear to the onlookers—as though he was about to kiss her. "Now, ladies," he said, his voice low and filled with promise, "I don't gawk at your evening entertainments."

"You're welcome to anytime you like, darling."

"I'll remember that," he said, the words lazy and luxurious. "But I'm occupied this evening."

"Lucky girl!"

Pippa gritted her teeth as a knock sounded on the steel door, and the ladies were admitted to the club.

Leaving them alone in the alleyway once more, in the closest thing she'd ever had to an embrace.

She waited for him to move, to unwrap himself from her.

Except he didn't.

No, he remained just as he was, pressed close, lips at her ear. "They think you lucky."

Her heart was pounding like mad. She was sure he could hear it. "I thought you didn't believe in luck."

"I don't."

Her voice was shaking. "If you did, would you call this lucky?"

"I would call this torture."

It was at that moment, the words a breath against the sensitive skin beneath her ear, that she realized that he wasn't touching her. He was so close . . . but even now, pushing her back against the stone façade of this massive building, he was careful not to touch her.

She sighed.

Apparently she was the only female in Christendom whom he had resolved not to touch.

Fleetingly, she wondered what would happen if she were to take matters into her own hands. She turned her head toward him, and he pulled back—not far, but far enough to ensure distance between them. Now they were face-to-face, their lips barely apart, at once millimeter and mile from each other.

A millimeter for him, for all he had to do was close the non-space and she was his. A mile for her, for she knew he would not do it . . . and she could not bring herself to kiss him. Even though, in that moment, there was nothing she wanted to do more.

But he did not wish the same.

This was an evening for intellectual pursuits. Not physical ones.

No matter how much she might wish differently.

So she did the only thing she could do. She took a deep breath, and said, "Cross?"

There was an immense, yawning pause as they both realized she'd dropped the Mister, but somehow, here, in a dark London alleyway, the title seemed too gentlemanly for this tall, wicked man.

"Yes, Pippa?"

"Can we go inside now?"

Chapter Nine

"Hazard is a problematic game—one that appears one way and plays another. For example, one casts two dice, thinking the roll will sum between one and twelve, but a roll of one is completely impossible . . . and rolls of two and twelve nearly so. Why then, when the fallacies of the game are so obvious, does it call so loudly to gamers?

There may be geometry to this game of chance— but there is sacredness to it as well.

It occurs that the sacrosanct rarely makes scientific sense."

The Scientific Journal of Lady Philippa Marbury
March 27, 1831; nine days prior to her wedding

There was nothing in the wide world that Cross would have refused her in that moment.

Not when she had spent the last hour tempting him with her big blue eyes and her quick mind and that lovely, lithe body that made him desperate to touch her. When the women had come, he'd thought of nothing but protecting her from discovery, shielding her with his body and hating himself for ever even considering bringing her here to this dark, filthy place that she did not deserve.

That did not deserve her.

As he did not deserve her.

He should tell Bourne everything and let his partner beat him to within an inch of his life for ever even thinking of ruining Philippa Marbury. For even dreaming of being this close to her. Of being tempted by her.

For she was the greatest lesson in temptation there ever was.

When she'd toppled from the carriage straight into his arms, he'd thought he was done for, her lithe lines and soft curves pressed against him, making him ache. He'd been sure that moment was the ultimate test . . . the hardest thing he'd ever have to do, setting her on her feet and stepping back from the precipice.

Reminding himself that she was not for him.

That she never would be.

But that had been easy compared to minutes later when, pressed between him and the stone façade of the club, she'd turned and spoken to him, her breath fanning his jaw, making his mouth dry and his cock hard. *That* had been the most difficult thing he'd ever done.

He'd come close to kissing her and putting them both out of their misery.

God help him, for a moment, he thought she would take the decision out of his hands and take matters into her own.

And he'd wanted it.

He wanted it still.

Instead, she'd asked him to continue this madness—to bring her inside the hell and give her the lesson he'd promised. To teach her about temptation.

She thought him safe. Scientific. Without danger.

She was mad.

He should pack her back into that carriage and see her home, without a second thought. He should keep her far from this place filled with peers who would find immense entertainment in her presence here, and in the gossip her presence would fuel.

There were rules on this side of the hell, of course—the ladies allowed membership were expressly forbidden to reveal the secrets to which they were exposed. And as women with secrets of their own who craved their time at the club, they were careful to follow those rules.

But it would not change the threat to Pippa.

And he would not have it.

"I shouldn't take you inside," he replied, the words lingering between them.

"You promised."

"I lied."

She shook her head. "I don't care for liars."

She was teasing him. He heard the soft laughter in the words. But whether there or not, he also heard the truth in them. And he wanted her to care for him.

The thought came like a blow, and he straightened instantly, suddenly eager to be away from her.

It was not her.

It couldn't be.

It was the special circumstance of her. It was that she was the first woman he'd allowed this close, this frequently, in six years. It was that she smelled of light and spring, and that her skin was impossibly soft, and the way her pretty pink lips curved when she smiled, and that she was smart and strange and everything that he'd missed about women.

It was not her.

It was everything. With Knight and Lavinia and the rest of his world crashing down around him, the last thing he needed was Pippa Marbury in his club. In his life. Causing trouble. Taking over his thoughts.

The madness would go away the moment he was rid of her.

He had to be rid of her. Tonight.

He ignored the thread of irritation that coursed through him at the thought and rapped on the steel door.

"That's a different rhythm than the one the ladies used."

Of course, she would notice that. She noticed everything, with her great blue eyes.

"I am not the ladies." He heard the terseness in his tone, refused to regret it as the door opened.

She did not seem to notice it. "Everyone has a different knock?" She followed him into the entryway, where Asriel sat in his usual place, reading by the dim light of a wall sconce.

The doorman cast his black gaze over first Cross, then Pippa. "She's not a member."

"She's with me," Cross said.

"A member of what?" Pippa asked.

Asriel returned to his book, ignoring them both. Pippa tilted to see the book in Asriel's hand. Her head snapped up, eyes meeting his in disbelief. "*Pride and Prejudice*?"

He snapped the book shut and looked at Cross. "She's still not a member."

Cross cut him a look. "We are lucky, then, that I am an owner."

Asriel seemed not to care much either way.

Pippa, however, appeared not to be able to help herself. "Perhaps we should start again? We were not properly introduced. I am—"

Asriel cut her off. "Cross."

"I confess, I am happy to see that she is just as maddening for others as she is for me." He paused. "Vallombrosa?"

If Asriel thought anything of the request, he did not show it. "Empty. Everyone is at the fight. If you don't want her seen without a mask, I would stay clear of it."

As though Cross would not have thought of that himself.

"That's the second time someone has mentioned a fight," Pippa interjected. "What does that mean?"

Asriel was quiet for a long moment. "It means there is a fight."

Her brows rose. "You are not the most forthcoming of gentlemen, are you?"

"No."

"You're ruining my fun," she said.

"That is not uncommon."

Cross resisted the urge to laugh. Pippa would not be the first to attempt to engage Asriel in conversation, and he was willing to wager that she also would not be the first to succeed.

She tried, nonetheless, with a wide, friendly smile. "I do hope we shall meet again. Perhaps we could have a reading club of sorts. I've read that one." She leaned in. "Have you reached the part where Mr. Darcy proposes?"

Asriel narrowed his gaze on Cross. "She did that on purpose."

Pippa shook her head. "Oh, I did not ruin it. Elizabeth refuses." She paused. "I suppose I *did* ruin *that*. Apologies."

"I find I like your sister much more."

Pippa nodded, all seriousness. "That is not uncommon."

At the repetition of Asriel's words, Cross did laugh, and when he tried to hold it back, it came out in a strangled mess—one Asriel correctly identified with a scowl. Cross took his cue, pushing aside the heavy velvet curtain and taking care that they would not be seen before leading Pippa down the long, narrow passageway to Vallombrosa, one of a handful of hazard rooms on the ladies' side of the club.

She entered ahead of him, turning slowly once inside, taking in the small, lavishly appointed chamber designed for private games. "This building is remarkable," she said, reaching up to unbutton her cloak. "Truly. Every time I come, there is a new piece available for exploration."

She removed her cloak, revealing a simple green walking dress—entirely ordinary, one might even say uninteresting in comparison to the silk and organza creations that the rest of the women who frequented this side of the club wore on a regular basis. The neckline was high, the sleeves long, and the skirts heavy—a combination that should have cooled Cross's response to their interaction in the alleyway—but Pippa could have been wearing a lace negligee for how the vision of her in that plain frock impacted him.

It did too good a job hiding her.

He wanted it off.

Immediately.

He cleared his throat and took her cloak, draping it over the back of the chaise. "It is designed to make you feel that way. Visitors are left wondering what they might have missed."

"So they are tempted to return?" The question was rhetorical. She was learning. "Is that the goal for tonight? To tempt me with your pretty rooms and your secret passageways?"

He was not sure what the goal for tonight was anymore. All the clear thoughts he'd had, the perfectly controlled plans for her lesson, they'd been muddled by her presence.

She turned away from him, moving to inspect an oil painting that took up a large section of one wall. It depicted four young men playing a dice game on a cobblestone street by the light of a pub. "Speaking of secret passageways," she asked, "I'm very impressed by your architectural skill."

"Temple talks too much."

She smiled. "Do all the rooms have them?"

"Most of them. We like to have means for escape." The place where her jaw met her neck cast the most intriguing shadow. Cross wondered at the feel of the skin there. Silk or satin?

"Why?"

He focused on the question. "There are many who would like to see us destroyed. It is a benefit to be able to move about without risk of discovery."

She turned to face him, eyes wide. "Is that not what the man reading *Pride and Prejudice* is for?"

"In part."

"People get past him?"

"It is not unheard of. I once awoke to a woman in my office. I assure you, she had not been invited. And only yesterday, I found her on the floor of the casino."

She smiled at the reference. "She sounds like a special case."

Indeed.

"I do not care for the idea that you might have to flee from some nefarious character."

He resisted the thrum of pleasure that coursed through him at the idea that she might care for him at all. "Do not concern yourself. I rarely flee."

He moved past her, rounding the table to put distance and mahogany between them. She stayed where she was. "Does this room have one?"

"Maybe."

She looked around, eyes narrowed, carefully considering each stretch of wall. "And if it did, where would it lead?"

He ignored the question, reaching for the dice on the hazard table, lifting them, testing their weight. "Would you like to ask questions about the architecture? Or would you like your lesson?"

Her gaze did not waver. "Both."

The answer did not surprise him. Philippa Marbury was a woman so intrigued by knowledge that she would find it tempting on a variety of topics—not simply sex. Unfortunately, her innate curiosity was one of the most tempting things he'd ever experienced.

His goal for the evening returned.

She had to lose.

If she lost, he could regain his sanity.

Reclaim his control.

That alone was worth it.

He tossed the dice in her direction. "Both it is."

Her eyes lit as though he'd just offered her jewels. "Who were the women outside?"

He shook his head. "It's not that easy, Pippa. The lesson

is about temptation. You want to know more . . . you have to win it."

"Fine."

"And you have to wager."

She nodded once. "I have five pounds in my reticule."

He smirked. "Five pounds will not do. It is not enough for the lesson for which you ask."

"What, then? I have nothing else of value."

You have your clothing. It took everything in his power not to say the words. "I would like to buy back your time."

Confusion furrowed her brow. "My time?"

He nodded. "If you win, I tell you what you wish to know. If you lose, you lose time for this insane research project. There are what, eleven days left before you marry?"

There were ten. He had deliberately miscalculated.

She corrected him, then shook her head firmly. "We have an agreement."

Perhaps, but he had all the power. At least, in her mind. "Then I suppose there is no lesson."

"You said you wouldn't renege. You promised."

"And as I said before, my lady, scoundrels lie." Not always because of their nature, he was realizing. Sometimes they lied to preserve their sanity. He moved for the door. "I shall send someone with a hooded cloak to escort you from the club and return you home."

He was at the door, hand to handle, when she said, "Wait."

He steeled his countenance and turned back. "Yes?"

"The only way I get my lesson is to wager?"

"Think of it as double the research. Lessons in gaming are an adventure many women would not pass up."

"It's not an adventure. It's research. How many times must I tell you?"

"Call it whatever you like, Pippa. Either way, it's something you desire."

She looked to the hazard table, longing in her gaze, and he knew he'd won. "I want the gaming."

"This is it, Pippa."

She met his gaze. "My first lesson in temptation."

Clever girl. "All or nothing."

She nodded. "All."

Clever, doomed girl.

He moved back to the table and handed her a pair of ivory dice. "On the first roll at the Angel, a seven or eleven wins. Roll a two or three, and lose."

Her brows rose. "Only a two or three? How did I lose on a nine during our first meeting?"

He couldn't stop his smirk. "You offered better odds; I took them."

"I suppose I should know better, gaming with a scoundrel."

He tilted his head toward her. "I imagine you've learned the lesson since."

She met his gaze, eyes large behind her spectacles. "I'm not so sure."

The honest words went straight through him, bringing desire and something even more base with them. Before he could reply, she was casting the dice.

"Nine," she said. "My lucky number?"

"Already an inveterate gamer." He collected the dice and handed them back to her. "The play is simple. Roll a nine again, and you win. Roll a seven, and you lose."

"I thought a seven was a win."

"Only on the first roll. Now you've established that your main is nine."

She shook her head. "I don't care for those rules. You know as well as I that the odds of rolling a seven are better than of doing the same with any other number."

"Care for them or not, those are the rules to which you agreed when you chose hazard."

"I didn't chose it," she grumbled, even as she tested the dice in her palm. She wasn't leaving.

He leaned against the table. "Now you see why gambling is a very poor idea, indeed."

She cut him a look. "I think it is much more likely that I see why you are a very rich man, indeed."

He smiled. "No one forced you into the game."

Her brows rose. "You did just that!"

"Nonsense. I gave you something to risk. Without it, there is no reward."

She looked to the table skeptically. "I am fairly certain that there will be no reward anyway."

"One never knows. Some espouse the benefits of Lady Luck."

One of her golden brows rose. "A lady, is she?"

"It has to do with her being so very changeable."

"I take no small amount of offense to that. I am in no way changeable. When I make a promise, I keep it."

She tossed the dice, and a memory flashed of their first meeting.

I dislike dishonesty.

"Two and four," she announced. "Six. What now?"

He lifted the dice and passed them to her again. "You roll again."

"I have not won?"

"If it is any consolation, you have not lost, either."

She rolled three more times, a ten, twelve, and eight, before wrinkling her nose and saying, "Why, precisely, does this make men do silly, untenable things?"

He laughed. "At the Angel, onlookers can bet on anything related to the game. The outcome of the individual roll, whether any one throw will be higher or lower than the last, the precise combination of pips on the die. When someone at the table is winning on every toss, the game becomes very exciting."

"If you insist," she said, sounding utterly disbelieving as she threw the dice again, rolling a six and three. "Oh!" she cried out. "A nine! I won! You see? Luck is on my side."

She was smiling, cheeks flushed with the thrill of the win. "And now you see why men enjoy the games so well."

She laughed and clapped her hands together. "I suppose I do! And now, I receive the answer to a question!"

"You do," he agreed, hoping she'd keep her queries to the club.

"Who were the women outside?"

He reached for the dice. "Members."

"Of the Angel?" she fairly squeaked, reaching out to accept the ivory weights. "I thought it was a men's club?"

"It is more than it seems. This is not, technically, the Angel."

Her brow furrowed. "What is it?"

"That is another question." He nodded to her hand. "The games are more complicated upstairs, but for the purposes of our game, we shall keep with the same. You win with a nine."

She tossed again. Six and three.

"I win again!" She crowed, smile widening into a full-on grin. He could not help matching it as he shook his head and retrieved the dice. "What is it?"

"It does not have a name. We refer to it as the Other Side. It is for ladies."

"Which ladies?"

He handed her the dice.

She rolled a five, then a ten, then a nine. "Huzzah!" she cried, meeting his surprised gaze. "You didn't think I would win again."

"I confess, I did not."

She smiled. "Which ladies?"

He shook his head. "I can't answer that. Suffice to say, ladies who wish to remain anonymous. And have their own adventures."

She nodded. "Why should men have access to the wide world and women . . . not?"

"Precisely."

She paused, then blurted, "Will there be pain?"

He nearly choked.

She mistook the sound for misunderstanding, apparently. "I mean, I know there will likely be pain for me. But will it hurt him as well?"

No. No, he will find pleasure like he's never known.

Just as you would if I had anything to do with it.

He held back the words. "No."

Relief shone in her eyes. "Good." She paused. "I was concerned that it might be possible to perform incorrectly."

Cross shook his head once, firmly. "I think you won't find it difficult to learn."

Pippa smiled at that. "Anatomy helps."

He did not want to think about her understanding of anatomy in this context. He did not want to imagine how she would use her simple, direct words to guide her husband, to learn with him. Cross closed his eyes against the vision of those words, of that knowledge on her lips. "Castleton may be a fool, but he's not an idiot. You needn't worry about his not understanding the mechanics of the situation."

"You shouldn't call him that."

"Why not? He isn't *my* betrothed." Cross lifted the dice, offered them to her. When she reached to take them, he couldn't stop himself from closing his palm around her fingers—holding her still. He couldn't stop himself from saying, softly, "Pippa."

Her gaze locked instantly with his. "Yes?"

"If he hurts you . . ." He paused, hating the way her eyes went wide at the words.

"Yes?"

If he hurts you, leave him.

If he hurts you, I'll kill him.

"If he hurts you . . . he's doing it wrong." It was all he could say. He released her hand. "Roll again."

Four and three.

"Oh," she said, crestfallen. "I lost."

"One less day of your research. That makes nine days."

Her eyes went wide. "An entire *day*? For *one* poor roll?"

"Now you know what it feels like to lose as well as win," he said. "Which is more powerful? The risk? Or reward?"

She thought for a long moment. "I'm beginning to see it."

"What is that?"

"Why men do this. Why they stay. Why they lose."

"Why?"

She met his eyes. "Because the winning feels wonderful."

He closed his eyes at the words, at the way they tempted him to show her how much more wonderful he could make her feel than those cold dice. "Do you wish to continue?"

Say no, he urged her. *Pack up and return home, Pippa. This place, this game, this moment . . . none of it is for you.*

As she thought, she worried her lower lip between her teeth, and the movement transfixed him, so much so that when he finally released the slightly swollen flesh, and said, "I do," he had forgotten his question.

When he did not immediately offer up the dice, she extended her hand. "I would like to roll again, if you don't mind."

He did mind. But he relinquished the ivory cubes and she tossed them across the baize with gusto.

"Eight days." She scowled at the four and three at the far end of the table.

"Again," she said.

He handed her the dice.

She rolled.

"Seven days."

She turned a narrow gaze on him. "Something is wrong with the dice."

He collected the ivory cubes and offered them to her, palm up. "Temptation is not always a good thing."

"It is when one is preparing to tempt one's spouse."

He'd almost forgotten her goal. God, he didn't want to teach her to tempt another man. *He wanted to teach her to tempt him.*

He wanted to teach her to let him tempt her.

She took the dice. "Once more."

He raised a brow. "If we had sixpence for every time those words were spoken beneath this roof, we would be rich men."

She rolled an eight, and met his gaze. "You *are* rich men."

He grinned, passing her the ivory blocks once more. "Richer."

She rolled once—*eleven*—twice—*four*—a third time. "Ah-ha!" she celebrated. "Six and three! Again!" She turned to him, something familiar in her eyes—the heady thrill of the win. He'd seen it countless times in the gaze of countless gamers, and it never failed to satisfy him. That look meant one, unassailable truth: that the gamer in question was in for the night. But now, with Pippa, it failed to satisfy. Instead, it made him ache with desire.

Desire to see the same thrill far from a gaming table, as she won something else entirely.

As she won him.

She reached for her reticule. "I have been keeping a log of my research questions." *Of course she had.* God knew what extravagant queries Lady Philippa Marbury had in the name of research. She opened the book, worried her lower lip as she considered the considerable amount of text there, and Cross knew, with the keen understanding of one who had been around a number of enormous wagers in his time, that she was about to ask something outrageous.

He turned away from her and the table, walking to a small sideboard and extracting a bottle of Chase's finest whiskey, blessedly stored there for trials just such as this one. Pouring himself two fingers of the amber liquid, he looked over his shoulder to find her watching him carefully, paper in hand. "Would you like a drink?"

She shook her head instantly. "No, thank you. I couldn't."

His lips twisted in a wry smile. "Ladies don't drink whiskey, do they?"

She shook her head, matching his smile with her own. "The irony of this situation is not lost on me, I assure you."

He toasted her and drank the entire glass in one great swallow, enjoying the burn of the alcohol down his throat—embracing its distraction. "Your question?"

She did not answer for a moment, and he forced himself to look in her direction, where he found her gaze trained on the crystal tumbler he clutched in his hand. He set it on the sideboard with a thud, and the soft sound pulled her from her reverie. She dipped her head, focusing on the small book in her hands.

Because she was not looking at him, it gave him leave to watch the pink wash over her cheeks as she framed the question that was sure to destroy his sanity.

God, he loved to watch her blush.

"I suppose I shall start at the beginning. It appears that I'm utterly lacking in knowledge of the basics. I mean, I understand dogs and horses and such, but humans . . . well, they're different. And so . . ." She paused, then rushed forward, the words pouring out of her. "I wonder if you could explain the use of the tongue."

The words were a blow, one of Temple's strong, unpulled punches, and—just as it happened inside the ropes—it took a moment for the ringing in Cross's ears to subside.

When it did, she had grown impatient, adding softly, "I understand it has its uses in kissing. And other things, too, if Olivia is to be believed—which she isn't all the time. But I don't know what to do with it, and if he were to kiss me . . ."

If he were to kiss her, Cross would take great pleasure in destroying him.

It took every ounce of his strength to keep from leaping over the table, lifting her in his arms, pressing her back against the wall, and ravishing her. He opened his mouth to speak, not knowing what would come, but knowing, without a doubt, that if she said one more perfectly reasonable, rational, insane thing, he would not be able to resist her.

Before either of them could speak, there was a knock at the door, and he was saved.

Or perhaps ruined.

Either way, *Pippa* was saved.

They both looked to the door, surprised and confused by the sound for an instant before he was moving to open it, using his tall frame to block the view into the room.

Chase stood on the other side of the door.

"What is it?" Cross snapped. Smirking, Chase attempted to see past him into the room. Cross narrowed the gap between door and jamb. "Chase," he warned.

There was no mistaking the smug laughter in Chase's brown eyes. "Hiding something?"

"What do you want?"

"You have a visitor."

"I am otherwise occupied."

"Intriguing." Chase attempted another look into the room, and Cross could not help the low, unintelligible threat that came at the movement. "Did you just growl? How primitive."

Cross did not rise to his friend's bait. "Tell someone to handle it. Handle it yourself."

"As the *it* in this scenario is your . . . Lavinia, I am not certain you would like me handling it."

Lavinia.

Surely he'd misunderstood. "Lavinia?"

"She is here."

She couldn't be. She wouldn't risk herself. She wouldn't risk her children. Fury flared, hot and quick. "Are we simply allowing entry to every woman in London these days?"

Chase was still attempting to see inside the room. "Some of us are more to blame for the recent rash of peeresses than others. She is in your office."

Cross swore, harsh and soft.

"Shame on you. In front of a lady, no less."

He closed the door on Chase's smug face, turning to Pippa. What a disaster.

She and his sister, under the same, scandalous roof, and it was his fault.

Goddammit.

He was losing control of the situation, and he did not care for it.

She had edged closer, her curiosity making her brave, and she was only a few feet from him. Two minutes earlier, and he would have closed the distance and kissed her senseless.

But Chase's intrusion was best for both of them, clearly.

Perhaps he could will it to be true.

He had to deal with his sister.

Now.

"I shall be back."

Her eyes went wide. "You're leaving me?"

"Not for long."

She took a step toward him. "But you didn't answer my question."

Thank God for that.

He took a step back, reaching for the handle of the door. "I will be back," he repeated. "You're safe here." He opened the door a crack, knowing that there was little he could do. Lavinia could not be left alone in the casino.

Not that Pippa was entirely trustworthy. Indeed, this lady could wreak no small amount of havoc if she were left to her own devices here, on the Other Side.

For a moment, he hovered between staying and going, finally meeting her big blue eyes and saying in his most commanding tone, "Stay."

Lord, deliver him from women.

*D*id he think her a hound?

Pippa circled the hazard table, absently collecting the dice and rotating them over and over in the palm of her hand.

She hadn't heard much, but she'd heard Cross say her name.

Felt the keen disappointment that came—altogether irrationally—with the syllables on his tongue.

He'd left her, for another woman. For Lavinia. The woman from the gardens.

With nothing more than a masterful, "Stay."

And he hadn't even answered her question.

She hesitated, turning to face one long edge of the table, placing her hands on the finely carved mahogany bumper that kept the dice from rolling right off the table and clattering to the floor. She tossed the dice that she had been clutching in frustration, not watching as they knocked against the wood and tumbled to a stop.

The man would learn quickly that she was in no way houndlike.

Leaning over the table, she stared long and hard at the hazard field, mind racing, the green baize, with its white and red markings, blurring as she considered her next course of action. For she certainly was not going to stand by and wait in this tiny, constricting chamber as all manner of excitements occurred in the club beyond.

Not while he scurried off to do whatever it was scoundrels did with women for whom they pined.

And he certainly pined for this Lavinia person.

He'd pined enough that he'd met her clandestinely, at Pippa's betrothal ball. He'd pined enough that he chased after her today. And he clearly pined enough that honoring his commitment to Pippa was easily forgotten in Lavinia's presence.

Suddenly, her chest felt quite tight.

Pippa coughed, standing straight, her gaze falling on the closed door to the little room where he'd left her. She lifted one hand to her chest, running her fingers along the bare skin above the edge of the wool bodice, attempting to ease the discomfort.

She took a deep breath, the thought of Cross's rushing through the gaming hell and into the welcoming arms of his lady—who had clearly realized he was a man worthy of forgiving—overwhelming all others.

She was likely beautiful, petite, and perfectly curved. No doubt, she was one of those ladies who knew precisely what to say in any situation and never ever found herself saying the wrong thing or asking an inappropriate question.

Pippa would wager that his Lavinia could not name a single bone in the human body.

No wonder Cross adored her.

The tightness in her chest became an ache, and Pippa's hand stilled.

Oh, dear. It was not physiological. It was *emotional*.

Panic flared. *No*.

She leaned back over the table, closing her eyes tightly and sucking in a long breath. No. She wouldn't allow emotion into the scenario. She was here in the interest of discovery. In the name of research.

That was all.

She opened her eyes, searched for a point of focus, and found the dice she'd tossed earlier.

Six and three.

Her gaze narrowed on the winning toss.

Six and three.

Suspicion flared. She collected the dice. Rolled again. *Six and three.*

Inspected them carefully. Rolled again. *Six and three.*

Just one die. *Three.*

Three.

Three.

Her eyes went wide as understanding came. The die was weighted. The *dice were* weighted.

She hadn't won.

He'd *let her* win.

He'd been directing the game all along.

There's no such thing as luck.

He'd lied to her.

He'd been working the game, no doubt with losing dice, too . . . planning to fleece her of all her research plans, planning to take from her these last weeks of freedom before she was Countess Castleton. He'd stolen from her!

Worse, he'd stolen from her and left her to meet another woman.

She stood straight, scowled at the door where she'd seen him last.

"Well," she said aloud to the empty room, "that won't do."

And she headed for the door, putting all her strength into the movement when she reached for the door handle, and found the door locked.

A little sound escaped her, a cross between shock and indignation, as Pippa tried the door again, certain that she was mistaken. Sure that there was no possible way that he had locked her in a room in a gaming hell.

After cheating her.

No possible way.

After several attempts, Pippa was confident of two things: First, he had indeed locked her in a room in a gaming hell after cheating her. And second, he was clearly mad.

Crouching low, she peered through the keyhole into the hallway beyond. She waited a few moments, uncertain of what precisely she was waiting for, but waiting nonetheless. When no one appeared or passed through the corridor on the other side of the door, she stood, pacing away from the door and back again, confronting the wide oak.

She had only one course of action. She had to pick the lock. Not that she'd ever done such a thing before, but she'd read about the practice in articles and novels and, honestly, if small children could accomplish the task, how difficult could it be?

Reaching up, she removed a hairpin and crouched low once more, jamming the little strip of metal into the lock and wiggling it about. Nothing happened. After what seemed like an eternity of attempting the impossible, growing more and more infuriated at her situation and the man who had caused it, Pippa sat down with a huff of frustration and returned the hairpin to its rightful place.

Apparently, there were a number of small children in London who were significantly more accomplished than she. She cast an eye at the enormous painting she'd noticed before. No doubt the young men in the oil would have no trouble at all with the lock. No doubt, they would have a half dozen ways of escaping this small room.

Like a secret passageway.

The thought had her on her feet in seconds, one hand against the silk wall coverings, tracing the edge of the small room in search of a secret door. It took her several minutes to check every inch of wall, from one side of the painting to the other, finding nothing out of the ordinary. There was no secret passage. Not unless it was into the painting itself.

She eyed the painting.

Unless.

Grabbing one side of the massive frame, she pulled, and the painting swung out into the room, revealing a wide, dark corridor.

"Triumph!" she crowed to the room at large before lifting a candelabrum from the nearby table and stepping into the corridor, pulling the wide door closed behind her with a thud.

She couldn't help her self-satisfied smile. Cross would be shocked indeed when he unlocked her cage and discovered her gone.

And he would deserve it, the rogue.

As for Pippa, she would be wherever this passageway led.

Chapter Ten

I have studied a great many species of flora and fauna over the years, and if there is one truth to be found, it is this: Whether hounds or humans, siblings almost always display more heterogeneity than they do homogeneity. One need only look at Olivia and me to see the proof.

Parents are the red rosebush . . . offspring the white branch.

The Scientific Journal of Lady Philippa Marbury March 28, 1831; eight days prior to her wedding

"I came to tell you to leave us alone."

Cross stood just inside the closed, locked door to his office, beyond which two hundred of Britain's most powerful men wagered. On the way there, he'd considered a half dozen things he might say to his sister, all variations on the theme of "What in hell would possess you to come here?"

But he did not have the opportunity to say any of them. His sister spoke the instant the lock clicked, as though she had nothing in the world about which to worry but that single calm, clear sentence.

"Lavinia—" he began, but she cut him off, her serious brown gaze unwavering.

"I am not here to discuss it," she said, the words like steel. "I came from Knight's, and he refused to see me. Because of you."

Ire flared. "As well it should be. You should never have gone to him. And if he knows what's best for him, he'll never see you again."

She looked tired—pale and thin and uncomfortable, with dark circles beneath her eyes and hollow cheeks, as though she had not slept or eaten in days. But it had been more than days that had made her this way—that had stolen the bright-eyed, happy seventeen-year-old girl and left behind this stoic twenty-four-year-old woman who seemed years older and decades wiser.

Too wise. She did not back down. "This is none of your concern."

"Of course it is my concern. You're my sister."

"You think that the pronouncement of the words makes them true?"

He moved toward her, hesitating when she pressed back, clasping the edge of his desk as though she could gain strength from the great slab of ebony. "There is no making about it. They are true."

Her lips twisted in a bitter, humorless smile. "How simple you make it seem. As though you have done nothing wrong. As though we are all expected to forget that you deserted us. As though we are expected to pretend that all is well, and nothing has changed. As though we are to slaughter the fatted calf and welcome you back into our lives—our prodigal son."

The words stung, even as Cross reminded himself that Lavinia had been so young when Baine had died. Seventeen and barely out, she'd been too focused on her own pain and her own tragedy to see the truth of what had happened. To see that Cross had had no choice but to leave the family.

To see that he'd been pushed out.

To see that they would have never forgiven him. That, in their eyes, he would never have been good enough, strong enough, *Baine* enough.

Not only in their eyes. His as well.

He did not correct her—did not tell her. Instead, he let the words sting. Because he deserved them. Still.

He always would.

When he did not reply, his sister added, "I have come to tell you that whatever arrangement you have made, whatever deals you have struck with Mr. Knight—I don't want them. I want you to rescind them. I shall take responsibility for my family."

The words made him angry. "*You* should not have to take responsibility. You have a husband. This is his purpose. His role. It is he who should be protecting his children's futures. His wife's reputation."

Her brown eyes flashed. "That is none of your concern."

"It is if you require protecting, and he cannot provide it."

"Now you play the expert in familial protection? The perfect older brother? Now, after seven years of desertion? After seven years of invisibility? Where were you when they married me to Dunblade to begin with?"

He'd been counting cards in some casino, trying to pretend he did not know where his sister was. What she was doing. Who she was marrying. *Why.* Ironically, that casino had likely been Knight's. "Lavinia," he tried to explain, "so much happened when Baine died. So much you don't know."

She narrowed her gaze on him. "You still think me a little girl. You think I don't know? You think I don't remember that night? Need I remind you that I was there? Not you. Me. I am the one who carries the scars. The memory of it. I carry it with me *every day.* And somehow, it is you who has taken ownership of the evening."

She shifted, and he noticed the flash of discomfort on her face as she leaned into her finely wrought cane. He moved to a nearby chair, lifting a stack of books from its seat. "Please. Sit."

She stiffened, and when she spoke, the words were like ice. "I am quite able to stand. I may be lame, but I am not crippled."

Goddammit. Could he do nothing right? "I never meant—Of course you are able to stand. I simply thought you would be more comfortable—"

"I don't require you to make me comfortable or to make my life easier. I require you to stay out of my life. I came to tell you that. And to tell you that I will not allow you to involve yourself with Knight on my behalf."

Anger flared, and frustration. "I am afraid the decision is out of your hands. I will not allow you to sacrifice yourself to Knight. Not when I can help it."

"It's not your place to step in."

"It is precisely my place. Like it or not, this is my world, and you are my sister." He paused, hesitating on the next words, not wanting to say them, but knowing he owed them to her. "Knight came after you to get to me."

Her brows snapped together. "I beg your pardon?"

He hated himself in that moment, almost as much as he hated the look in her eyes, suspicion and disbelief. "He wants me, Lavinia. Not you. Not Dunblade. He knew that threatening you would be the fastest way to get what he wants from me."

"Why would he think that?" she scoffed. "You've never given a moment's thought to us."

The words stung. "That's not true."

She shifted again, and he couldn't stop himself from looking to her cane again, from wishing he could see her leg. He knew how it pained her; he paid her doctors handsomely to keep him apprised of the seven-year-old injury.

He looked up at her. "Lavinia," he began. "Please. Sit. We will discuss this."

She did not sit. "We suffer because of you?"

It did not matter that they suffered because her husband was weak-willed. If Cross were not Cross . . . if he did not have a past with Knight . . . they would be safe. "He threatens you to access me. To take from me what he wants. Stay away from him. I will make this go away. I need four days."

"What does he want?"

My title. My name. Your children's inheritance. "It does not matter."

"Of course it does."

"No. It does not matter because he will not get it. And he will not get you, either."

Something flared in her brown eyes, something close to loathing, and she laughed without humor. "I suppose I should not be surprised. After all, my pain has always been the result of your actions, hasn't it? Why should now be any different?"

Silence stretched between them, the words hovering in the room, their weight familiar and unbearable, echoing the cold accusations of his father that night, seven years ago. *It should have been you.*

And the keening wails of his mother. *If only it had been you.*

And of Lavinia's cries of pain as the surgeons did what they could to set bone and clean wounds, and rid her young, frail body of the fever that had raged, threatening her young life.

Threatening Cross's sanity.

He wanted to tell her the truth, that he'd been consumed with guilt that night, and fear the nights after, that he'd wished over and over, again and again, for years, that it had been him in that carriage. That it had been Baine at home—strong, steady, competent Baine, who never would have left them. Who never would have let her marry Dunblade.

That it had been Cross who had died—so he never would have failed them.

But the words wouldn't come.

Instead he said, "I will repair the damage. He will never bother you again."

That laugh again, hurt and hateful, with more experience than it should hold. "Please, don't. You are too good at causing damage to have any skill at repairing it." She added, "I don't want you in my life. I will deal with him."

"He won't see you," he said. "That is part of our bargain."

"How dare you negotiate with him on my behalf?"

He shook his head and spoke the truth, tired of holding it back. "He came to me, Lavinia. And as much as you would like to believe otherwise, I couldn't let him hurt you. I will never let him hurt you."

The words might have had an impact, but he would never know, because at that precise moment, as they faded into the air around him, there was a loud *thump* from the opposite side of the large painting that hung on one wall of his office, and a dreadful knowledge settled deep and unpleasant in his gut. He knew what was on the other side of that painting, knew where it led.

Knew, too, with utter certainty, who was standing mere inches away from his office.

Lifting a hand to keep his sister from saying any more, he rounded his desk and grasped one edge of the massive gilt frame, giving the enormous oil painting a heavy yank, opening the secret entrance and revealing a wide-eyed Philippa Marbury, who tumbled out of the passageway beyond, barely catching herself on a nearby table before straightening and facing the occupants of the room.

She did not miss a beat, righting her spectacles and moving past him, into the office, to say, "Hello, Lady Dunblade," before turning a cool blue gaze on him, triumphantly setting a pair of ivory dice on the edge of his great black desk, and adding, "You, sir, are a liar and a cheat. And I will not be ordered about like a prize hound."

There was a moment of collective stunned silence, during which Lavinia's jaw dropped and Cross wondered how precisely his calm, collected life had gone spiraling so completely out of control.

*H*is Lavinia was Lavinia, Baroness Dunblade. A *lady*.

It was fascinating how simply society rendered invisible those who had suffered unfortunate circumstances. Lady Dunblade might require a cane to aid in her unavoidable limp, but now, as she stood on one side of Mr. Cross's cluttered office, Pippa wondered how the lady could escape notice. Injury aside, she was tall and beautiful, with lovely red hair and brown eyes that Pippa could not help but admire.

Apparently, she was not the only one to admire those eyes. Apparently, Mr. Cross thought they were worthy of admiration as well. Pippa shouldn't be surprised. After all, Mr. Cross was a notorious rogue—even if he'd never even hinted at any kind of roguish behavior with Pippa—and Lady Dunblade so often went beyond notice, that she could easily come and go from The Fallen Angel without causing scandal.

But scandal she was, apparently, as she was here, standing in Cross's office, straight and proud, like a Grecian queen.

And why shouldn't she stand proud? She'd apparently caught the attention of one of the most powerful men in London.

Pippa would be quite proud herself if she had done the same.

She resisted the thought and the thread of newly, unpleasantly, defined emotion that coursed through her with it, and turned to close the door to the secret passageway. She should have guessed that he had chosen a room with a passage leading to his office—he was not the kind of man who relied on coincidence.

And he was likely not the kind of man to be happy that she'd just tumbled through the wall and into his office . . .

and if what she had overheard was to be believed . . . into a very private conversation.

I will never let him hurt you.

Even through the wall, she'd heard the fierceness in his tone. The commitment. Even through the wall, she'd felt the words like a blow. He clearly cared for the lady. Cared for her enough to leave Pippa in a locked room and go to her.

She shouldn't be upset. After all, theirs was a partnership, not a relationship.

This was no time for jealousy. No place for it. There was no jealousy in science.

Except, apparently, there was.

She shouldn't be jealous. She should be angry. He'd defiled their agreement by cheating her with weighted dice and wicked lies. Yes. In fact, that was why she had come here furious, was it not? If she was upset, it should be for that reason, and nothing else.

Certainly not because he'd left her to come for this lady.

She should not be upset about that at all.

And yet, that seemed to be precisely the reason for her upset.

Curious, that.

Once the passageway was closed, she spun back to face Mr. Cross and Lady Dunblade. Taking in the fury on his face and the shock on hers, Pippa said the first thing that came to mind. "I am sorry to interrupt."

There was a beat, as they heard the words, before they both spoke.

"We are through," said the lady, shoulders squaring as she seemed to remember where she was, backing toward the door. "I am leaving."

"What in hell are you doing inside that passageway? I told you not to move from that room," said Mr. Cross at the same time.

"You left me in a locked room and expected me not to attempt to escape?" Pippa said, unable to keep the frustration from her tone.

"I expect you to keep yourself safe from harm."

Her eyes went wide. "What harm could possibly come to me?"

"In a dark, secret passageway in a gaming hell? You're right. No harm indeed."

She took a step back. "Sarcasm does not become you, Mr. Cross."

He shook his head in frustration and turned to Lady Dunblade, who had reached the door. "You are not leaving."

The lady's gaze narrowed. "We are through. I have delivered my message. And I am most definitely leaving."

Pippa pressed back against the painting through which she'd come, as Cross took a step toward Lady Dunblade, the emotion in his words obvious. "Lavinia—" he started before she held up a hand and stopped him.

"No. You made this choice. You cannot change the past."

"It is not the past I wish to change, dammit. It is the future."

Lavinia turned and made for the door that led to the floor of the casino. "The future is not yours to affect."

Pippa watched them, head turning from one to the other, as though they were in a badminton match, questions rising, desperate for facts. What had happened in their past? What was happening now to threaten their future? How were they connected?

And there, seeking her answer, she discovered the anguish in his gaze.

He loved her.

She stiffened at the last, the thought unsettling and unpleasant.

Lavinia's hand settled on the door handle and Cross swore. "Goddammit, Lavinia. Half of London is out there. If you're seen, you'll be ruined."

She looked over her shoulder. "Am I not already on that path?"

What did that mean?

His gaze narrowed. "Not if I can stop it. I shall take you home."

Lavinia looked to Pippa. "And Lady Philippa?"

He turned to Pippa, surprise in his gaze, as though he'd forgotten she was there. She ignored the disappointment that flared at the thought. "I shall take you both home."

Pippa shook her head. Whatever was happening here with Lady Dunblade, it did not change Pippa's plans for the evening. Ignoring the weight in her chest at her earlier discovery—a pang that was becoming familiar—she said, "I am not interested in returning home."

At the same time, Lavinia said, "I will not go anywhere with you."

He reached for one of several pulls on the wall behind him, yanking it with more force than necessary. "I will not force you to stay, but I will not allow you to destroy yourself either. You will have an escort home."

Bitterness laced the baroness's tone. "Once more, you leave me in the hands of another."

Cross went ashen at the words; the room was suddenly too small, and Pippa was out of place. There was something so connected about these two, in the way they faced each other, neither one willing to back down. There was a similarity in them—in the way they stood tall and refused to cow.

There was no doubt they had a past. No doubt they'd known each other for years.

No doubt there had been a time they cared for each other. *Still did, perhaps.*

The thought had Pippa wishing she could crawl back into the painting and find another way out of the club. She turned to do just that, pulling once on the heavy frame, preferring that empty, locked hazard room to this.

But this time, when the painting swung open, it was to

reveal a man in the passageway. The enormous brown-skinned man seemed as surprised by Pippa as she was by him. They stared at each other for a moment before she blurted, "Excuse me. I should like to get past."

His brows furrowed and he turned a confused look on Cross, who swore wickedly and said, "She's not going anywhere."

Pippa looked back at him. "I shall be quite fine."

He met her gaze, grey eyes serious. "Where do you plan to go?"

She wasn't exactly sure. "Into the . . ." She waved into the blackness behind the large man blocking the entryway, " . . . wall," she finished.

He ignored her, his attention flickering to the man in the wall. "Take Lady Dunblade home. Be sure she is not seen."

Pippa craned her head to look up at the large man—larger than any man she'd ever met. It was difficult to imagine that he was skilled at clandestine late-night female ferreting, but Mr. Cross was a legendary rake, so this was likely not the first time he'd been asked to do just that.

"I'm not going with him," Lady Dunblade said firmly.

"You do not have a choice," Cross said, "unless you would prefer I take you."

Pippa found she did not like that idea, but remained quiet.

"How do I know I can trust him?"

Cross looked to the ceiling, then back to the lady. "You don't. But it strikes me that your choices of whom to trust or mistrust are entirely arbitrary, so why not place him in the trustworthy column?"

They stared at each other, and Pippa wondered what would happen. She would not have been surprised if Lady Dunblade had thrown open the main door to Mr. Cross's office and marched, proud and proper, out onto the floor of the casino, just to spite him.

What had he done to her?

What had she done to him?

After a long moment, Pippa could not help herself. "Lady Dunblade?"

The lady met her gaze, and Pippa wondered if she'd ever had a conversation with this woman. She didn't think so. Right now, in this moment, she was certain that if she had, she would remember this proud, brown-eyed, flame-haired warrior. "Yes?"

"Whatever it is," Pippa said, hesitating over the words, "it is not worth your reputation."

There was a beat as the words carried through the room, and for a moment, Pippa thought the baroness might not react. But she did, leaning into her cane and moving across the room to allow the massive man, still elevated inside, to help her up into the dark passageway.

Once there, Lady Dunblade turned back, meeting Pippa's gaze. "I could say the same to you," she said. "Will you join me?"

The question hovered between them, and somehow Pippa knew that her answer would impact more than her activities that evening. She knew that a *yes* would remove her from Mr. Cross's company forever. And a *no* might keep her there for far too long.

For longer than she had been planning.

She looked to him, his grey gaze locking with hers, unreadable and still so powerful—able to quicken her breath and tumble her insides. She shook her head, unable to look away. "No. I wish to stay."

He did not move.

Lady Dunblade spoke. "I do not know why you are here, Lady Philippa, but I can tell you this—whatever this man has promised you, whatever you think to gain from your acquaintance, do not count on receiving it." Pippa did not know how to respond. She did not have to. "*Your* reputation is on the line."

"I am taking care," Pippa said.

One of the baroness's ginger brows rose in disbelief, and

something flashed, familiar, there then gone before Pippa could place it. "See that you do."

The baroness disappeared into the blackness of the secret passageway, the hulking man following behind. Pippa watched them go, the light from the body-man's lantern fading around a corner before she closed the painting once more and turned back to Cross.

He was pressed to the far side of the room, back to a large bookshelf, arms folded over his chest, eyes on the floor.

He looked exhausted. His shoulders hunched, almost in defeat, and even Pippa—who never seemed to be able to properly read the emotions of those around her—understood that he had been wounded in the battle that had taken place in this room.

Unable to stop herself, she moved toward him, her skirts brushing against the massive abacus that stood to one side of the room, and the sound pulled him from his thoughts. He looked up, his grey gaze meeting hers, staying her movement.

"You should have gone with her."

She shook her head, her words catching in her throat as she replied, "You promised to help me."

"And if I said I wish to dissolve our agreement?"

She forced a smile she did not feel. "The desire is not mutual."

His eyes darkened, the only part of him that moved. "It will be."

She couldn't resist. "Who is she?"

The question broke the spell, and he looked away, rounding the edge of his desk, placing the wide ebony surface between them and fussing with the papers on the desk. "You know who she is."

She shook her head. "I know she is the Baroness Dunblade. Who is she to you?"

"It does not matter."

"On the contrary, it seems to matter quite a bit."

"It should not to you."

It was rather unsettling how much it mattered. "And yet it does." She paused, wishing he would tell her, knowing that her request was futile, and still unable to stop herself from asking, "Do you care for her very much?"

Don't tell me. I don't want to know.

Except she did. Quite desperately.

When he did not reply, she added, "I only ask because I am curious as to why her visit would move you to lock me in a hazard room for an indefinite amount of time."

He looked up. "It was not indefinite."

She came to stand on the opposite side of the desk. "No thanks to you."

"How did you find the passageway?"

"You would be surprised by what irritation does to aid one's commitment to a cause."

One side of his mouth twitched. "I assume you refer to your imprisonment?"

"And to your cheating," she added.

His gaze flickered to the dice she had placed on the edge of the desk. "Those are the winning dice."

"You think I care if the dishonesty was for win or loss? It's still cheating."

He laughed, the sound humorless. "Of course you don't care. It was for your own good."

"And the sevens?"

"Also weighted."

She nodded. "The nine I rolled on that first afternoon? The wager that sent me home, vowing not to approach any more men?"

He poured himself a glass of scotch. "Those, too."

She nodded once. "I told you I do not care for liars, Mr. Cross."

"And I told you, scoundrels lie. It was time you learned."

The man was frustrating. "If all lies are as easily recognized as your silly weighted dice, I think I shall be just fine in the world."

"I am surprised you noticed."

"Perhaps your other ladies would not have noticed an epidemic of sixes and threes," Pippa said, unable to keep the ire from the words, "but I am a scientist. I understand the laws of probability."

"My other ladies?" he pressed.

"Miss Sasser . . . Lady Dunblade . . . any others you have lying about," she said, pausing at the visual her words brought about and not particularly enjoying it. "At any rate, I am unlike them."

"You are unlike any woman I have ever known."

The words stung. "What does that mean?"

"Only that most women do not frustrate me quite so much."

"How interesting, as I have never met a man who exasperates me quite so much." She pointed to the painting. "You should not have locked me inside that room."

He drank deep and returned the tumbler to its place on the sideboard. "I assure you, you were quite safe there."

She hadn't felt unsafe, but that wasn't the point. "What if I were phobic?"

His head snapped up, his gaze instantly meeting hers. "Are you?"

"No. But I could have been." She hesitated. "What if there had been a fire?"

His gaze did not waver. "I would have fetched you."

His certainty set her back for a moment. When she recovered, she asked, "Through your miracle passageway?"

"Yes."

"And if the fire had already destroyed it?"

"I would have found a way to get to you."

"I am to believe that?"

"Yes." He sounded so certain, as though nothing would stop him.

"Why?"

"Because it is true." The words were ever so quiet in the small, enclosed space, and Pippa realized two things in that moment. First, that they had both leaned in, across the great slab of ebony—an emblem of power as strong as Charlemagne's army—until they were mere inches apart.

And second, that she believed him.

He would have come for her.

She let out a long breath, and said, "I came for you, instead."

One side of his mouth twitched into a half smile. "You didn't know where the passage would lead."

Everything about him, his eyes, his voice, the sandalwood scent of him tempted her, and she hovered on the edge of closing her eyes and leaning into the moment, into him. When she spoke, the words were barely above a whisper. "I was hopeful that it would lead to excitement."

That it would lead to you.

He pulled back sharply, as though she'd spoken the words aloud, jerking her from the moment. "In that case, I am sorry that it brought you here."

She straightened as well, turning her attention to the painting through which she had come—the painting she'd barely noticed the first two times she'd been inside this room and that now seemed to swallow the space, dwarfing one wall of the office, five feet wide and twice as tall, at once grotesque and beautiful and deeply compelling.

At the center of the oil, a woman wrapped in white linens slept on her back in a state of utter abandon, arms above her head, blond curls tumbling to the floor, loose and free. Her skin was pale and perfect, and the only source of light in the piece, so bright that it took a moment to see what lurked in the shadows of her bedchamber.

To one side, through a red velvet curtain peeked a great, black horse, with terrifying, wild eyes and a wide-open mouth filled with enormous white teeth. The beast seemed to leer at the sleeping figure, as though he could sense her dreams and was merely biding his time before he struck.

But the stallion would have to wait his turn, for seated on the woman's long torso, in the shadowy stretch between breast and thigh, was a small, ugly figure, part beast, part man. The creature seemed to stare straight out of the painting, meeting the eyes of anyone who dared look. The expression on the goblin's face was at once patient and possessive, as though he would wait for an eternity for the lady to awaken—and fight to the death to keep her.

It was the most compelling thing she'd ever seen, scandalous and sinful. She moved closer. "This piece—it is remarkable."

"You like it?" She heard the surprise in his tone.

"I don't think one *likes* it. I think one is captivated by it." She wanted to reach out and wake the woman in the painting, to warn her of what was no doubt the beginning of a terrible demise. "Where did you find it?"

"It was used to pay a debt," Cross said, closer, and she looked over her shoulder to find him at the edge of his desk, one hand on the ebony, watching her move toward the oil.

"A very large one, I imagine."

He inclined his head. "I liked the piece enough to allow the debt wiped from the books—free and clear."

She was not surprised that he had been drawn to this painting—to the wickedness in each brushstroke, to the darkness of the story it told. She turned back, drawn once more to the strange creature seated on the sleeping woman. "What is it?" she asked, reaching out to the little man, afraid to touch him.

"It's an incubus." He paused. Continued. "A nightmare. Demons were once thought to come at night and wreak havoc on those who slept. Male demons, like that one, preyed upon beautiful women."

There was something in the way he spoke, a hint of—memory?—and Pippa looked to him. "Why do you have this?"

He was no longer watching her, instead, he stared down at the desk, lifting the dice she had placed there, clutching them in his palm. "I do not care much for sleep," he said, as if it were an acceptable answer.

Why not?

She wanted to ask it, but knew, instantly, that he would not tell her. "I am not surprised, considering you spend most of your day in the shadow of this painting."

"One becomes comfortable with it."

"I rather doubt that," she said. "How often do you use the passageway?"

"I find I don't have much need of it."

She smiled. "Then I might appropriate it?"

"You do not use it well. I heard you the moment you came near."

"You did not."

"I did. You will no doubt be surprised to discover that you are not very good at sneaking, Lady Philippa."

"I've not had much cause for the activity, Mr. Cross."

One side of his mouth kicked up in an approximation of a smile. "Until recently."

"This place rather calls for it, don't you think?"

"I do, actually."

He returned the dice to the desk with a soft click, and the little white cubes captured her attention and she spoke to them. "Now, if I remember correctly, you owe me the answers to three questions. Four, if you count the one you left unanswered."

In the silence that followed the statement, she could not stop herself from lifting her gaze to his. He was waiting for her. "All the dice were weighted. I owe you nothing."

Her brows snapped together. "On the contrary, you owe me plenty. I trusted you to tell the truth."

"Your mistake, not mine."

"You are not ashamed of cheating?"

"I am ashamed of being caught."

She scowled. "You underestimated me."

"It seems I did. I will not make the mistake again. I will not have the opportunity."

She snapped her head back. "You are reneging?"

He nodded. "I am. I want you out of this place. Forever. You don't belong here."

She shook her head. "You said you wouldn't renege."

"I lied."

The unexpected words shocked her, so she said the only thing that came to mind. "No."

Surprise flared in his eyes. "No?"

She shook her head, advancing and stopping a foot from him. "No."

He lifted the dice again, and she heard the clatter of ivory on ivory as he worried them in his palm. "Upon what grounds do you refuse?"

"Upon the grounds that you owe me."

"Do you plan to run me before a judge and jury?" he asked wryly.

"I don't need to," she retorted, playing her last, most powerful card. "I only have to run you before my brother-in-law."

There was a beat as the words sank in, and his eyes widened, just barely, just enough for her to notice before he closed the distance between them, and said, "A fine idea. Let's tell Bourne everything. You think he would force me to honor our agreement?"

She refused to be cowed. "No. I think he would murder you for agreeing to it in the first place. Even more so when he discovers that it was negotiated by a lady of the evening."

Emotion flared in his serious grey gaze, irritation and . . . admiration? Whatever it was, it was gone almost instantly, extinguished like a lantern in one of his strange, dark passageways. "Well played, Lady Philippa." The words were soft as they slid over her skin.

"I rather thought so." Where had her voice gone?

He was so close. "Where would you like to begin?"

She wanted to begin where they'd left off. He could not escape now, not as they stood here, in his office . . . in a gaming hell, feet away from sin and vice and half of London sure to ruin her thoroughly if they were to find her.

And inches away from each other.

This was the risk she had vowed to take; his knowledge was the reward.

Excitement thrummed through her, promising more than she could have expected when she'd left the house this evening. "I should like to begin with kissing."

Chapter Eleven

She might have wanted to begin with kissing, but he wanted to end with her naked, spread across his desk, open to his hands and mouth and body, like a country summer.

And that was the problem.

He could not give her what she wanted. Not without taking everything he desired.

Dammit. She was too close. He took a step back, grateful for his long legs and the firm edge of his desk behind him providing stable, unmoving comfort. "I do not think Bourne would appreciate my instructing you in . . ." He trailed off, finding it difficult to say the word.

The lady did not have the same problem. "Kissing?"

He supposed he should be happy she had not asked about the other thing she seemed to have no difficulty referencing. "Yes."

She tilted her head, and he could not help but be drawn to the long cord of her neck, the soft white skin there. "I don't think he would mind, you know," she said after a long moment. "In fact, I think he would be rather happy that I asked you."

He laughed—if one could call the loud, quick *ha* of disbelief a laugh. "I think you couldn't be more wrong."

Bourne would kill him with his bare hands for touching her. Not that it wouldn't be worth it.

It would be worth it.

He knew that without question.

She shook her head. "No, I think I'm right," she said, more to herself than to him, he sensed, and there was a long moment while she pondered the question.

He'd never known a woman to think so carefully. He could watch her think for hours. For days. The ridiculous thought startled him. *Watch her think? What in hell was wrong with him?*

He didn't have time to consider the answer because something changed in her gaze, partially hidden by the glass of her spectacles when she focused on him once more. "I don't think this is about Bourne at all."

It wasn't. But she needn't know that. "Bourne is one of the many reasons why I won't tell you about it."

She looked down at her hands, clenched tightly in front of her, and when she spoke there was something he did not like in her tone. "I see."

She shook her head, and he could do nothing but look down at her pale, yellow hair, the color of cornsilk, gleaming in the candlelight.

He shouldn't ask. It didn't matter. "What do you see?"

She spoke to herself, softly, without looking up. "It never occurred to me. Of course, it should have. Desire is a part of it."

Desire. Oh yes. It was an enormous part of it.

She looked up at him, then, and he saw it. Part uncertainty, part resignation, part—damn him to hell—sadness. And everything he had, everything he was, screamed to reach out to her.

Dear God. He tried to put more space between them, but his massive desk—the one from which he'd drawn such comfort just seconds earlier—was now trapping him there, altogether too close to her as her big blue eyes grew liquid, and she said, "Tell me, Mr. Cross, do you think I might convince *him* to touch me?"

He could have managed the words if not for their intonation—for the slight, panicked emphasis on the *him,* meaning someone other than he. Meaning Castleton.

Meaning she had been hoping for *Cross* to touch her.

She was temptation. She was torture.

All he had to do was reach out and take her. No one would ever know. Just once. Just a taste, and he would send her on her way, to her husband. To her marriage.

To her life.

No.

She was untouchable. As untouchable as every other woman he'd known for the last six years. *More* untouchable.

Infinitely better.

His throat worked as he searched for words, hating that she'd rendered him speechless. If his partners could see him now, clever Cross, laid low by this bizarre, bespectacled, beautiful woman.

The words did not come, so he settled on, "Pippa . . ."

Color flooded her cheeks, a wicked, wonderful blush—the kind that a younger, reckless Cross would have read as invitation. The kind he would have accepted.

Instead, she looked back at her hands, spread them wide, not knowing how those crooked fingertips tempted him. "I'm sorry. That was thoroughly . . . It was . . . that is . . ." She sighed, her shoulders bowing with near-unbearable weight. Finally, she looked up and said, simply, "I should not have said it."

Don't ask her. You don't want to know.

Except he did. Desperately.

"What did you mean by it?"

"I would rather not tell you."

One side of his mouth kicked up. Even now, when she no

doubt wished to do so, she would not lie. "And yet I would know."

She spoke to her hands. "It's just that . . . since we met, I have been rather . . . well, fascinated by . . ."

You.

Say it, he willed, not entirely certain what he would do if she did, but willing to put himself to the test.

She took another breath. "By your bones."

Would she ever say anything expected? "My bones?"

She nodded. "Yes. Well, the muscles and tendons, too. Your forearms. Your thighs. And earlier—while I watched you drink whiskey—by your hands."

Cross had been propositioned many times in his life. He'd made a career of refusing women's requests. But he had never been complimented on his bones.

It was the strangest, sexiest confession he'd ever heard.

And he had no idea how to respond.

He didn't have to, however, as she was pressing on. "I can't seem to stop thinking about them," she said, her voice low and filled with utter misery. "I can't seem to stop thinking of touching them. Of their . . . touching me."

God help them both, neither could he.

He shouldn't ask. He *shouldn't.*

But the King himself could have stormed into the room and it wouldn't have stopped him. "Touching you where?"

Her head snapped up, fast enough to have done damage if she had been standing any nearer—if she'd been standing as near as he would like for her to be. He'd shocked her. "I beg your pardon?"

"It's a simple question, Pippa," he said, leaning back against the desk, impressed with his ability to seem calm while his heart raced and his fingers itched for her. "Where do you imagine coming into contact with my bones?"

Her mouth fell open, honeyed lips soft in their surprise, and he crossed his arms. Her gaze followed the movement, his hands clutching his biceps, the only thing keeping him from grabbing her and kissing her until they were both gasping for air.

"Your hands," she whispered.

"What about them?"

"I wonder what they might feel like on . . ." She swallowed, and the movement drew his attention to her throat, where her pulse no doubt pounded. He missed the next words on her lips—which was likely best for them both. "On my skin."

Skin. The word conjured images of pale, beautiful flesh, heated curves and soft swells, of wide expanses open to exploration. She would be sin and silk, and everywhere he touched, she would respond to him. He imagined the sounds she would make, the way she would gasp as he stroked up one leg, the way she would sigh when he ran the flat of his palm down her torso, the way she would laugh when he inevitably found a place where she was ticklish.

She was riveted by his left hand, braced against his arm, and he knew without question that if he moved it, if he reached for her, she would let him have anything he wanted. *Everything* he wanted.

He did not move it.

"Where, specifically, Pippa?"

She shouldn't tell him, of course. She should run from this room as quickly as she could . . . no doubt she would be safer on the floor of the casino than she was here, with him. But he wasn't about to tell her that.

"My hands," she started, the hands in question splaying wide. "M—my cheek . . . my neck . . ."

As she spoke, she traced the body parts she named—unbeknownst to her, he would wager—and his desire deepened with every word, with every soft touch. Her fingers trailed down the long column of her neck, across the soft, pale skin of her chest, toward the edge of her bodice, where it stilled, hovering there on the green fabric.

He wanted to reach out and rend it in two, to ease the passage of those marvelously flawed fingertips. He wanted to watch her touch every inch of her body, pretending her hands were his.

Damn that. He wanted her to use his hands.

He wanted to do the touching.

No.

"What else?" he said, moving his hand, releasing her from her trance.

She met his gaze, eyes wide, cheeks pink. "I—" She stopped. Took a breath. "I should like to touch you, as well."

And there, in the simple, unbridled confession, he discovered the last, fragile thread of his control. He was too close to her. He should move. Should place distance between them. Instead he said, "Where?"

He knew he was asking too much of her—this innocent girl who knew the human body but had no knowledge of it. But he couldn't stop himself. He couldn't have her. But he could have this.

Even if he would burn in Hell for taking it.

Hell would be a welcome respite to the torture he suffered now. Here.

"Where would you like to touch me, Pippa?" he prompted after a long silence.

She shook her head, hands spread wide, and for a moment, he thought she might give up. Go home. Disappointment flared, hot and frustrating.

And then she said, simply, "Everywhere."

The single word robbed him of strength and breath and control, leaving him shattered and raw. And desperate for her.

Desperate to show her pleasure. Some way. *Any way.*

"Come here."

He heard the roughness in his voice, the urgency, and was shocked that she was so quick to do his bidding, coming to stand mere inches from him. Her dress was a collection of layers, the topmost fastened by a thick green belt. He pointed. "Open it."

God help him, she did, as though it were the most normal

thing in the world, the edges of the gown falling open to reveal a finer green fabric beneath. "Take it off."

She shrugged out of the outermost layer, letting it pool at her feet, her breath coming faster. His, as well. "All of it."

She turned her back to him. She was saying no. Strength where he was weakness. Frustration flared, and he reached out, stopping just short of touching her, of tearing the cloth from her body and replacing it with his own.

Of course she was saying no. She was a *lady*. And he should not be near her. He was the worst kind of villain, and he should be flogged for what he had done. For what he demanded.

The heavy green wool of her dress lay on the floor at his feet, and he crouched to retrieve it, fingers brushing the fine fabric in desperation, as though it were her skin. As though it were enough.

It had to be.

He cursed himself, promising Heaven and himself that he would pack her back into this dress and send her home, but it was too late.

A layer of linen joined the heavy wool, the soft fabric brushing against his knuckles, still warm from her body. *Scorching.* His breath caught at the sensation and he froze, knowing with the keen understanding of one who had fallen before that this moment would be his destruction.

Knowing he shouldn't look up.

Knowing he couldn't stop himself.

She was clad in nothing but a corset, pantalettes, and stockings, arms crossed over her chest, cheeks flaming— the red wash an irresistible promise.

He fell to his knees.

She couldn't believe she'd done it.

Even now, as she stood in this marvelous, wicked room, cool air running across her too-warm skin, she couldn't quite believe she'd removed her clothes, simply because he'd ordered it in that dark, quiet tone that sent strange, little flutters through the pit of her stomach.

She should research those flutters.

Later.

Now, she was more interested in the man before her, on his knees, hands fisted on his long, lovely thighs, eyes roaming over her body.

"You removed your clothes," he said.

"You asked me to," she replied, pushing her spectacles up the bridge of her nose.

One side of his mouth rose in the half smile, and he ran the back of one hand across his lips, slow and languid, as though he might well devour her. "So I did."

The flutters became more pronounced.

He was staring at her knees, and she was suddenly, very aware of the condition of her stockings, a plain, cream wool, chosen for warmth rather than . . . well . . . than this. No doubt they were hideous in comparison to the silk stockings he was used to women wearing in his presence. Miss Tasser likely had stockings in a score of colors, all laced and lovely.

Pippa had always been practical about her undergarments.

She pressed her knees together and tightened her arms across her chest, uncertain, wishing he would reach out for her. When he didn't, she wondered if she somehow disappointed him—she wasn't as beautiful as the women he was no doubt used to, but she'd never thought of herself as being unpleasant-looking.

Why wouldn't he touch her?

She swallowed back the question, hating the way it whispered through her, making her cold and hot all at once, and said, "What next?"

The words came out sharper than she'd intended, but they served their purpose, bringing his attention instantly to her face. He stared at her for a long moment, and she was distracted by his eyes—more pewter than grey, with little black flecks, framed by long, auburn lashes.

As she watched, his gaze flickered to the large chair several feet to her right, then back to her, slow and languid. "Sit."

It was not what she'd expected. "Thank you, I prefer to stand."

"Do you want your lesson or not, Pippa?"

Her heart leapt at the words. "Yes."

The half smile came again, and he inclined his head toward the chair. "Then sit."

She moved. Sat as primly as possible, back straight, hands clenched tightly on her lap, legs pressed together, as though she were not alone in a casino with one of London's most notorious rogues, wearing nothing but a corset and pantalettes. And her spectacles.

She closed her eyes at the thought. *Spectacles.* There was nothing tempting about spectacles. She reached up to remove them.

"No."

She stilled, her hand halfway to her face. "But—"

"Leave them."

"They're not—" she began. *They're not smoldering. They're not seductive.*

"They're perfect." He did not move toward her, instead leaning against the heavy ebony desk, extending one long leg in front of him and raising the other knee, propping his arm on it as he watched her through heavy-lidded eyes. "Lean back."

"I'm quite comfortable," she said quickly.

One ginger brow rose. "Lean back anyway."

She retreated on the chair until she felt the soft leather back against her skin. He hadn't stopped watching her, eyes narrowed, taking in every bit of her, every movement.

"Relax," he said

She took a deep breath and exhaled, attempting to follow instructions. "It isn't easy."

The smile again. "I know." There was a long moment of silence, and he said, "You're very beautiful."

She flushed. "I'm not." He did not reply. She filled the silence with, "These underclothes are quite old. They were not meant to be . . ." She trailed off as his gaze flickered to the edge of her corset, suddenly tighter. " . . . seen."

"I'm not talking about the clothes," he said, low and dark. "I'm talking about you. All that skin you want me to touch."

She closed her eyes at the words, mortification and something much more dangerous coursing through her.

He didn't stop talking. "I'm talking about your lovely long arms and your perfectly shaped legs . . . I find I am quite jealous of those stockings for knowing the feel of you, the warmth of you." She shifted, unable to keep still beneath the onslaught of his words. "I'm talking about that corset that hugs you where you are lovely and soft . . . is it uncomfortable?"

She hesitated. "Not usually."

"And now?" She heard the knowledge in the question.

She nodded once. "It's rather—constricting."

He tutted once, and she opened her eyes, instantly meeting his, hot and focused on her. "Poor Pippa. Tell me, with your knowledge of the human body, why do you think that is?"

She swallowed, tried for a deep breath. Failed. "It's because my heart is threatening to beat out of my chest."

The smile again. "Have you overexerted yourself?"

She shook her head. "No."

"What, then?"

She was not a fool. He was pushing her. Attempting to see how far she would go. She told the truth. "I think it is you."

He closed his eyes then, hands fisting again, and pressed his head back against the side of the desk, exposing the long column of his neck and his tightly clenched jaw. Her mouth went dry at the movement, at the way the tendons there bunched and rippled, and she was quite desperate to touch him.

When he returned his gaze to hers, there was something wild in those pewter depths . . . something she was at once consumed and terrified by. "You shouldn't be so quick with the truth," he said.

"Why?"

"It gives me too much control."

"I trust you."

"You shouldn't." He leaned forward, bracing his arm against his raised knee. "You are not safe with me."

She had never once felt unsafe with him. "I don't think that's correct."

He laughed, low and dark, and the sound rippled through her, a wave of pleasure and temptation. "You have no idea what I could do to you, Philippa Marbury. The ways I could touch you. The wonders I could show you. I could ruin you without thought, sink with you into the depths of sin and not once regret it. I could lead you right into temptation and never ever look back."

The words stole her breath. She wanted it. Every bit of it. She opened her mouth to tell him so, but no sound would come.

"You see? I've shocked you."

She shook her head. "I have shocked myself." His gaze turned curious, and she added, "Because I find that I would like to experience those things."

There was a long moment of silence, in which she willed him to move, to come to her. To touch her. To show her.

"Show me," he said, the words seeming to come from her thoughts.

Startled, she said, "I—I beg your pardon?"

"Before, you told me that you wished I would touch you. Show me where."

She couldn't. But her hand was already moving, already trailing up the bones of her corset to the place where silk met skin. The edge of the stays was lower than the line of the dress had been, mere centimeters from—

"Your breasts?"

She flushed at the words. "Yes."

"Tell me how they feel."

She closed her eyes, focused on the question. On the answer. "Full. Tight."

"Do they ache?"

So much. "Yes."

"Touch them." Her eyes flew open, captured instantly by his. "Show me how you wish I would touch you."

She shook her head. "I can't."

"You can."

"But why not you? Your hands are here . . . you are here."

His gaze darkened, and a muscle leapt in his jaw. "This is all there is, Pippa. I won't touch you. I won't ruin you."

Obstinate man. She was aching and frustrated, could he not see that? "I'm ruined, whether you touch me or not."

"No. If I don't touch you, you're safe."

"And if I don't wish to be safe?"

"I'm afraid you haven't a choice." He flexed one large hand, as though it ached him. "Shall I tell you what I would do if I could touch you?"

The words were soft and dark and all irresistible temptation. "Yes, please."

"I would lift them from that prison in which you keep them, and I would worship them in the manner they deserve."

Oh, my. Her hands froze, rendered unusable by his beautiful, liquid voice.

"And then, when they'd forgotten how it felt to be caged by silk and bone, I would teach you about kissing, just as you asked." Her lips parted, and she met his gaze, filled with dark promise. "But not on your mouth—on your beautiful breasts. On the soft pale skin of them, on the places that have never seen light, that have never felt a man's touch. You would learn about the tongue, my little scientist . . . there on those pretty, aching tips."

The image he painted was graphic and groundbreaking, and she was instantly entranced by the idea of his tongue on her—too entranced to be embarrassed, her hands following his words, teasing, touching, and for a moment she could almost believe it was him touching her. Making her ache. She sighed, and he shifted, straightening, but coming no closer, damn him.

"Would you like me to tell you where else I would touch you?"

"Yes, please." The words were a whisper.

"So polite." He leaned forward. "There's no place for politeness here, my bespectacled beauty. Here, you ask and I give. You offer and I take. No please. No thank you."

She waited for him to continue, every inch of her humming with excitement, with anticipation.

"Hook one leg over the arm of that chair." Her eyes went wide at the order. She'd never in her life sat in such a way. She hesitated. He pressed on. "You asked."

So she had. She moved, opening to him, her thighs widening, the cool air of the room rushing through the slit in her pantalettes. Her cheeks burned and she moved her hands to block his view.

He was watching them, and he made a low sound of approval. "That's where my hands would be as well. Can you feel why? Can you feel the heat? The temptation?"

Her eyes were closed now. She couldn't look at him. But she nodded.

"Of course you can . . . I can almost feel it myself." The words were hypnotic, all temptation, soft and lyric and wonderful. "And tell me, my little anatomist, have you explored that particular location, before?"

Her cheeks burned.

"Don't start lying now, Pippa. We've come so far."

"Yes."

"Yes, what?"

"Yes, I've explored it before." The confession was barely

sound, but he heard it. When he groaned, she opened her eyes to find him pressed back against the desk once more. "Did I say the wrong thing?"

He shook his head, his hand rising to his mouth once more, stroking across firm lips. "Only in that you made me burn with jealousy."

Her brows furrowed. "Of whom?"

"Of you, lovely." His grey gaze flickered to the place she hid from him. "Of your perfect hands. Tell me what you found."

She couldn't. While she might know the clinical words for all the things she had touched and discovered, she could not speak them to him. She shook her head. "I cannot."

"Did you find pleasure?"

She closed her eyes, pressed her lips together.

"Did you?" he whispered, the sound loud as a gunshot in this dark, wicked room.

She shook her head. Once, so small it was barely a movement.

He exhaled, the sound long and lush in the room, as though he'd been holding his breath . . . and he moved. "What a tragedy."

Her eyes snapped open at the sound of him—of trouser against carpet as he crawled toward her, eyes narrow and filled with wicked, wonderful promise.

He was coming for her. Predator stalking prey.

And she could not wait to be caught.

She exhaled, the breath coming out on a low, shaking sigh that could have become a moan if she weren't careful and, God help her, she moved her hands, opening to his touch and sight, ready to thank God and Lucifer and anyone else who might have had a hand in this moment for finally, finally bringing him to her.

Except, he didn't touch her.

"Shall I show you how to find it, lovely?" he asked, and

she could have sworn she felt his breath against her hands, hot and tempting. "Where to find it?"

She'd never know where the courage came from—how she pushed past the embarrassment and the shame that should have been there. "Please," she fairly begged, and he did, in soft, devastating words.

She did as he told her, parting folds of fabric, then folds of a more secret kind, following his whispered instructions, answering his wicked questions.

"So pretty and pink . . . does it feel good, love?"

She whimpered her reply.

"Of course it does. I can smell the pleasure on you . . . sweet and soft and very very wet." The words brought sensation, a thundering pleasure that she'd never felt before, not even in the dark nights when she'd quietly explored on her own.

"Oh, Pippa . . ." he whispered, turning his head, breathing against the curve of her knee, but not touching—never touching. He was destroying her. "If I were there . . . if my fingers were yours, I would spread you wide and show you how much more pleasurable it can be when the experience is shared. I would use my mouth to give you your second lesson in kissing . . . I would teach you everything I know about the act."

Her eyes went wide at the raw confession, for she could see it. She could see *him,* on his knees before her, brushing her hands from her and replacing them with his beautiful, firm mouth, stroking, touching . . . *loving.* She had no reference for the act—she'd never even imagined it before now—but she knew, without question, that it would be magnificent.

"I would feast on you . . . yes . . . right there, lovely," he urged her on, rewarding the bold, little movements of her fingers with a growl of pleasure, knowing, even before she did, that she was on the edge of something stunning. "Would you like my mouth there, my sweet?"

Did that happen? Dear heaven. Yes. She wanted it.

"I would stay for hours . . ." he promised. "My tongue would show you pleasure you've never known. Over and over. Again and again until you were weak from it. Until you couldn't bear it, and you begged me to stop. Would you like that, love?"

Her body answered him, rocking against the chair and her hand, giving her everything he promised . . . and somehow none of it. She cried out for him, reaching toward him, desperate for the feel of him, for his strength and sinew.

In that moment, she was his, open and raw, racked with pleasure and somehow, still aching with desire.

Desire only he could slake.

She whispered his name, unable to keep the wonder from her voice, and her fingers grazed his hair, gleaming red silk.

He moved like lightning at the touch, rolling to his feet with a grace that defied six and a half feet of man. He crossed the office, turning his lovely lean back to her, one long arm reaching out to brace himself on a pile of ledgers stacked a dozen high in the corner of the room.

The loss of him was like a blow, stripping her of fleeting pleasure. Leaving her wanting. Empty. Unfulfilled.

His head bowed, candlelight highlighting the ginger strands she itched to touch. She did not move as his shoulders rose and fell once, twice, a third time—his breath coming as harshly as hers did.

"That's enough research for tonight," he said to the books in front of him, the words firmer, louder than any of the others he'd spoken that evening. "I promised to teach you about temptation, and I believe I've accomplished the task. Dress. I'll have someone take you home."

Chapter Twelve

*Progress has been made. It appears that there are
any number of ways in which the female anatomy
might be . . . addressed. Associate revealed more
than one of those ways last evening—to remarkable
physical result. ~~Unfortunately,~~ Interestingly, the
results also had a considerable emotional effect. A
personal effect.*

*But he still didn't touch me. That, too, had a
personal effect.*

There is no place in research for personal effects.

**The Scientific Journal of Lady Philippa Marbury
March 29, 1831; seven days prior to her wedding**

Three days later, Pippa was curled on a low settee in the
Dolby House library, failing to read an unprecedented text
relating to the cultivation of dahlias. The volume had been
delivered directly from the publisher, and a month earlier,
Pippa had been desperate for its arrival.

Unfortunately, Mr. Cross had ruined even the excitement
of a new book.

Irritating man.

How was it that one man, one moment, could bring her such pleasure and such frustration all at once? How was it that one man could simultaneously consume her and hold her at bay?

It did not seem possible and yet, he'd proven it.

With his soft words and his absent touch.

It was the touch that hurt the most. The lack of it. She'd heard the rumors about him, she'd known what she risked when she asked him to assist her in her research. She'd been prepared to fend him off and push him away and resist his charms.

She'd never once considered the possibility that he would have no interest in charming her.

Though she supposed she should have been prepared for it. After all, if Castleton wouldn't touch her, who would even dream that a man like Mr. Cross would? It was only logical that he would be more difficult to . . . entice.

Not that she should be angling to entice him at all.

Absolutely not. The only man she should even consider enticing was the Earl of Castleton. Her future husband.

Not the other, infuriating, utterly abnormal man. Oh, he looked ordinary enough. Certainly taller and more intelligent than most, but at first glance, he had the same traits that marked the rest of his species: two arms, two legs, two ears, two lips.

Lips.

It was there that things went awry.

She groaned, dropping one hand to her thigh with enough weight to attract the attention of the hound curled at her side. Trotula looked up, soulful brown eyes seeming to understand that Pippa had lost too many waking hours to thoughts about those lips.

It was abnormal. In the extreme.

Trotula sighed and returned to her nap.

"Lady Philippa?"

Pippa started at the words spoken quietly from the door to the library where Carter, the Dolby House butler, stood at the ready, an enormous package in his hands. She smiled. "You surprised me."

He came forward. "Apologies, my lady."

"Have the guests begun to arrive?" The Marchioness of Needham and Dolby was hosting a ladies' tea that afternoon, designed to gather all the women related to The Wedding. Pippa had spent an hour being primped and prodded before her maid had announced her presentable, and she'd come to the library to hide in advance of the event itself. She stood. "I suppose I must into the fray."

Carter shook his head. "Not yet, my lady. This parcel arrived for you, however. As it is marked urgent, I thought you might like it straightaway."

He extended the large box in her direction, and she took it, curiosity flaring. "Thank you."

Task accomplished, Carter retreated from the room, leaving Pippa with the parcel, which she set beside her on the settee and opened, untying string and folding back unremarkable brown paper to reveal a heavy white box, adorned with an elaborate golden *H*.

Disappointment flared. The package was not urgent. It was a part of her trousseau. Most women in London could identify this box, from Madame Hebert's modiste shop.

She sighed and opened the box to find a layer of fine gauze of the palest blue, tied with a beautiful sapphire ribbon. Beneath the ribbon was a single ecru square, stamped with a delicate female angel. She slipped the card from the square envelope and read the message in strong, black script.

Pandemonium
The Fallen Angel
Midnight

And, on the back,

> *A carriage will collect you.*
>
> *Chase*

Chase. The fourth, most mysterious partner in The Fallen Angel. From what she understood, few had ever met the man who had started the club and grown it—certainly Pippa had never had the opportunity. And she absolutely should not be accepting an invitation from an unknown man. To something called *Pandemonium*.

But she knew before she even inspected the contents of the box that she would not be able to refuse him. Or the chance to see Cross again.

Pandemonium sounded like precisely the kind of thing that would afford her all sorts of knowledge.

Heart pounding, Pippa reached for the ribbon, untying it carefully, as though it might release something living. Peeling back the gauze, she gasped at the stunningly crafted silver mask that lay on a bed of sapphire silk—no, not silk.

Dress.

She lifted the mask, startled by the weight of it, running one hand along the perfect curve of the filigree, marveling at the delicacy of the swirling, twisting design etched into its face and the thick satin ribbons marking its edges, the same sapphire as the dress below.

When she turned the mask over, inspecting its inside, and instantly understanding why the piece was so much heavier than expected. Inlaid in the back of the mask was a special ridge, lined in sapphire velvet the exact color of the gown it had arrived with, designed to house a set of spectacles.

The mask had been made specifically for her.

She smiled, running her fingers over the metalwork, admiring the frivolity of the gorgeous craftsmanship.

And practical Pippa Marbury, who had never in her life

been tempted by clothing or triviality, could not wait for night to come.

So she could drape herself in silk.

It occurred to her that her view of the fabric had changed drastically in mere moments. Thousands of *Bombyx mori* had given themselves to this dress.

They'd cocooned themselves to set Pippa free.

"Pippa!" Her mother's call came from beyond the library door, shaking Pippa from her reverie. Rescuing the wrapping from Trotula's long pink tongue, she crammed the mask back into its box and haphazardly rewrapped the parcel, moving with lightning speed to hand it off to a footman just outside the door and request that it be delivered, immediately, to her maid.

"Pippa!" Her mother called again, no doubt announcing the start of the ladies' tea set for the afternoon. The Countess of Castleton would be here, and Lady Tottenham, and Penny, and a dozen others. No doubt the Marchioness of Needham and Dolby had recited the guest list more than once, but Pippa hadn't been listening much over the past few days.

She'd been too consumed with the events of her evening with Mr. Cross over and over, recalling every word, every interaction. And realizing that she was lacking in critical areas. It should not be difficult to convince a man to touch her. Certainly not a man who was purported to have such extensive taste in females. And yet, it was difficult.

Pippa was clearly in no way able to entice anything. Or anyone. If she could have, wouldn't it have happened? Wouldn't being nearly naked in Mr. Cross's office have drawn him to her in some way? Have tempted him?

Of course it would have.

Which is why she was utterly certain she possessed not a single viable feminine wile.

Perhaps Pandemonium would change that.

Her heart raced once more.

"Pippa!" Her mother called again, closer.

And without those wiles—or at least an understanding of them—she would never be able to meet the expectations that had been set for her. As a wife. As a mother.

As a woman.

She required additional research.

But today, she was doomed to an afternoon of tea. She set the volume down and addressed her sleeping companion. "Shall we go, Trotula?"

The spaniel raised her soft, sable head instantly, tail pounding against the plush settee with satisfying thuds. Pippa smiled and stood. "I remain able to tempt you, at least."

Trotula came off the furniture with a long stretch and a wide, lolling grin.

Pippa exited the library, hound at her heels, and pushed open the wide, paneled doors to the tearoom, where her mother's guests had gathered, already cooing over Olivia.

She took a deep breath and steeled herself to enter the fray.

"Lady Philippa!"

Castleton was here.

Pippa turned to find Trotula bounding toward the earl, who crouched low to give the dog a long scratch. Trotula leaned into the caress, hind leg thumping her pleasure, and Pippa couldn't help but laugh at the picture. "Lord Castleton," she said, moving toward her fiancé. "Are you here for tea?" She hadn't detected the hint of panic that usually laced her mother's tone when eligible gentlemen were nearby.

"No!" he said, happily, cocking his head to one side as he looked up at her, his smile wide and friendly. "I was meeting with your father. Hashing out the final bits of the marriage arrangement and all that."

Most brides-to-be would not have appreciated the frank reference to the exchange of funds that came with marriage, but Pippa found the concrete items relating to the event to be calming. She nodded once. "I've some land in Derbyshire."

He nodded and came to his feet. "Needham said that. Lots of sheep."

And four thousand acres of crops, but Pippa doubted Castleton had paid her father much mind.

Silence fell, and he rocked back on his heels, craning to see into the tearoom. After a long moment, he said, "What happens at a ladies' tea?"

Pippa followed his gaze. "Ladies drink tea."

He nodded. "Capital."

Silence again. "There are usually biscuits," Pippa added.

"Good. Good. Biscuits are good." He paused. "Cakes?"

She nodded. "Sometimes."

He nodded. "Smashing."

It was excruciating.

But he was her fiancé. In one week, he would be her husband. And in no time, he'd be the father of her children. So excruciating wasn't an acceptable outcome.

He might not be the most compelling of companions, nor was he the kind of man who took an interest in her interests. But there were not many men who did take interest in anatomy. Or horticulture. Or biology. Or physics.

There was one man.

She resisted the thought. Cross might be a man of science, but he was not the kind of man one . . .

She stopped the thought before it could form, forcing her thoughts back to the matter at hand—Castleton. She must work at Castleton. At engaging him. At attracting him. Even if she'd failed before.

With another.

No. She wouldn't think of Cross. Wouldn't think of her failed interaction with him. She was a scientist, after all . . . and scientists learned from all experiments. Even failed ones.

She smiled brightly. Possibly too brightly. "My lord, would you like to see if there are any cakes left in the kitchens?"

At reference to the kitchen, Trotula's tail set off at a remarkable speed, but it took Castleton a moment to understand Pippa's question. "The kitchens! For cake! With you!"

She smiled. "Indeed."

"Pippa!" Her mother's cry came from the doorway of the tearoom, instantly replaced by a surprised, breathless, "Oh! Lord Castleton! I did not know you were here! I shall—" She hesitated, hand on the door, considering her next step.

Most mothers would never dream of allowing their daughters to hover, unaccompanied, in an empty hallway with their fiancés, but most daughters were not the offspring of the Marchioness of Needham and Dolby. Aside from Pippa's being odd and—as the rest of the family apparently knew—lacking in the basic social experience of a soon-to-be-married lady, the daughters of the house of Needham and Dolby did not receive high marks when it came to actually marrying their betrotheds. Surely the marchioness wouldn't mind a bit of scandal to ensure that her second youngest made it all the way down the aisle.

"I'll just pull this door to," Lady Needham said, offering an exaggerated smile in their direction. "Pippa, you join us when you are free, darling."

The irony was not lost on Pippa that freedom was associated with a roomful of cloying, gossiping ladies.

Once they were alone once more, Pippa returned her attention to her betrothed. "The kitchens, my lord?"

He nodded his agreement, and they were off, Trotula leading the way.

There were leftover cakes in the kitchens, easily cajoled from the cook and wrapped in cheesecloth for a walk on the Dolby House grounds. Pippa tried not to think too carefully about the direction of their walk, but she could not deny that she was deliberately avoiding the copse of cherry trees where she'd waited for Mr. Cross several evenings earlier, deciding, instead, to head for the river a quarter of a mile down the gently sloping lawns.

Trotula ran out ahead with a series of loud, happy barks,

enjoying her freedom on the uncommonly warm March day, circling back now and then to ensure that Pippa and Castleton followed. They walked in silence for several minutes— long enough for Pippa to consider her next action. When they were far enough away from the house not to be seen, she stopped, turning to face the man who would be her husband.

"My lord—" she started.

"Do you—" he said at the same time.

They both smiled. "Please," he said. "After you."

She nodded. Tried again. "My lord, it's been more than a year since you began courting me."

He tilted his head, thinking. "I suppose it has been."

"And we are to be married. In seven days."

He smiled. "That I know! My mother cannot seem to stop speaking of it."

"Women tend to enjoy weddings."

He nodded. "I've noticed. But you don't seem to be in as much of a state over it, and it's your wedding."

Except she was in a state over it. Just not the kind of state he expected. Not the kind of state anyone noticed.

Anyone except Cross. Who was no help at all.

"Lord Castleton, I think it's time you kissed me."

If a hedgehog had toddled up and bit him on the toe, she didn't think that he could have looked more surprised. There was a long silence, during which Pippa wondered if she'd made an enormous mistake. After all, if he decided she was too free with her favors, he could easily march back to the house, give back the land in Derbyshire, and bid farewell to the house of Needham and Dolby.

Would that be so bad?

Yes. Of course it would.

The answer did not matter, however, because he didn't do any of those things. Instead, he nodded happily, said, "All right then," and leaned down to kiss her.

His lips were soft and warm and dry, and they pressed

against her with not an ounce of passion, settling on hers lightly, as though he were taking care not to startle or infringe upon her. She lifted her hands to the thick wool of his topcoat, clasping his arms, wondering if, perhaps, she should be doing something differently.

They stood like that for a long moment, lips pushed against lips, noses at a rather strange angle—though she blamed her spectacles for that—hands unmoving.

Not breathing. Not feeling anything but awkward discomfort.

When they pulled apart, gasping for air and met each other's gaze, she pushed the thought away and adjusted her spectacles, straightening them on the bridge of her nose. She looked away to find Trotula, tongue lolling, tail wagging.

The dog did not seem to understand.

"Well," Pippa said.

"Well," he agreed. Then, "Shall we try again?"

She considered the offer. After all, the only way to ensure the proper outcome of an experiment was to repeat it. Perhaps they'd done it wrong the first time. She nodded. "That sounds fine."

He kissed her again. To startlingly similar effect.

This time, when they separated, Pippa was sure. There was absolutely no threat of their entering into the sacrament of marriage for reasons at all relating to carnal lust.

She supposed that should make her feel better.

They returned to the house in silence, retracing their steps through the kitchens and into the foyer beyond the tearoom, where the soft sounds of ladies' laughter trickled through the open mahogany door. Castleton offered to leave her there, at the party, but Pippa found that she was even less tempted by tea than she had been earlier in the afternoon, and instead, she escorted her fiancé to the main door of the house, where he paused in the open doorway and looked down at her seriously.

"I am looking forward to our marriage, you know."

It was the truth. "I know."

One side of his mouth kicked up in a little smile. "I don't worry about the rest. It shall come."

Should they really have to wait for it to arrive?

She nodded. "Thank you, my lord."

He bowed, straight and serious. "My lady."

She watched from the top step of the house as his carriage trundled down the drive, leaving her to reflect on their kiss. Castleton hadn't felt anything. She had seen it in his eyes—in the way they'd remained patient and kind, nothing like Cross's eyes several evenings prior. No, Cross's eyes had been storms of gunmetal, full of emotions that she couldn't read but that she would have spent a lifetime studying.

Emotions she would never have a chance to study.

The ache was back in her chest, and she lifted one hand absently to soothe it, her mind on the tall, grey-eyed man who had showed her pleasure without giving even an inch of himself.

She did not like that ache. She did not like what she thought it was coming to mean.

With a sigh, Pippa removed her spectacles to clean them and closed the main door to the house behind her, leaving Castleton and the rest of the word on the outside as she cleaned the glass.

"Lady Philippa?"

Pippa's gaze snapped to the blurred shape of a lady halfway down the grand staircase of Dolby House—a tea-party guest who had lost her way.

She raised a hand to halt the lady's movement, already heading for the stairs to meet the guest as she replaced her spectacles. With a smile she did not feel, she looked up . . . and met the gaze of Lavinia, Baroness Dunblade.

She nearly tripped on the stairs. "Lady Dunblade."

"I told myself I wouldn't come," the baroness replied. "I told myself that I would stay out of whatever it is that you have with Jasper."

Jasper?

The baroness continued, "But then I received your mother's invitation—your sister has been very kind to me since she became Marchioness of Bourne. I suppose I should not be surprised."

There was something in the words, an implication that Pippa should understand their subtext. She didn't. "Lady Dunblade . . ."

The beautiful woman shifted, leaning into her cane, and Pippa reached toward her. "Would you like to sit?"

"No." The refusal was instant and unwavering. "I am fine."

Pippa nodded once. "Very well. I'm afraid you are under the impression that I am closer to Mr. Cross than I am."

"Mr. Cross." The baroness laughed, the sound humorless. "I still have trouble believing that name."

Pippa tilted her head. "Believing it?"

Lavinia's gaze turned surprised. "He hasn't told you."

The words unsettled. Perhaps they were designed to. Either way, Pippa couldn't resist. "His name is not Mr. Cross?" Pippa was face-to-face with the baroness now, halfway up the wide, curving staircase that marked the center of Dolby House.

"I think you're the only one who uses the mister."

Cross. No need for the mister. "Just Cross then. It's not his name?"

One side of the baroness's mouth kicked up. "No. How sweet that you believed that."

Of course she'd believed it. She'd never had reason not to. He'd never given her reason not to. But the idea that he might have lied—it wasn't foreign. After all, he'd lied to her from the beginning. The dice, the wagers, the way he'd tempted her and failed to touch her . . . it was all a lie. His name would be one more. Unsurprising.

And somehow, more devastating than all the others.

Her stomach roiled. She ignored it. "What is it you wished to tell me?"

Lavinia paused, clearly surprised by the firmness in Pippa's tone. "You should be cautious of him."

A lesson Pippa had already learned.

The baroness continued. "Jasper . . . he loves women. More than he should. But when it comes time for him to follow his word . . . he fails." She hesitated, then said, "I should hate to see you ruined because you believed him."

The words were full of sorrow, and Pippa hated the way they made her feel—the tightness and discomfort they brought with them . . . with their meaning. With the knowledge that this woman had known him. Had received promises from him. Had been betrayed by him.

Things Pippa hadn't warranted.

She stiffened at the thought. She shouldn't want to be betrayed by him. She shouldn't want his promises. She shouldn't want him at all. This was science, was it not? Research. Nothing more. Certainly nothing emotional.

A memory flashed—the Earl of Castleton's lips dry and warm against hers.

Nothing emotional.

She shook her head. "There is nothing between us."

One of the baroness's auburn brows rose in a familiar gesture. "You came through a secret passageway into his office."

Pippa shook her head. "He didn't know I would find it. He never expected me there. Never wanted me there." She hesitated. "It's clear he cares deeply for you, Lady Dunblade. I believe he loves you a great deal."

Not that Pippa knew anything about love, but she recalled the sound of his voice in the darkness . . . muffled by his marvelous secret passageway, and the expression in his grey eyes when Lavinia had battled him, standing strong and firm in his office.

They were as close to love as Pippa could imagine.

That, and he wouldn't touch her.

A knot formed in her throat, and she swallowed around it, willing it away.

The baroness laughed, and Pippa hated the hollowness of the sound. "He doesn't know what love is. If he knew what was best for us, he would stay away from us."

Something tightened in Pippa's chest at the words. "That may be so," she said, "but no matter what happened in the past, it's clear you were a very important piece of it . . . a very important . . ." She hesitated. What did one call a paramour in polite company? She was certain that her mother would insist that one did *not* call a paramour in polite company. But she and Lady Dunblade were here, and there was no one else in hearing distance, so Pippa did not mince words. " . . . lover."

Lady Dunblade's blue eyes went wide. "He is not my lover."

Pippa kept on. "At any rate, it does not matter. I have no hold whatsoever on the gentleman. He was to assist me in some research. It is now complete."

The baroness interjected. "Jasper is not my lover."

Pippa waved one hand. "Perhaps not now, but at one time. Again, it's irrel—"

"Lady Philippa." Lavinia's tone was unyielding, urgent. "Dear heaven. He is not my lover." She paused, and the look on her face was a mix of panic and despair and not a small amount of horror. "He is my *brother*."

Chapter Thirteen

Cross stood in the owner's suite of The Fallen Angel, watching as half of London gambled on the floor below. The very wealthy half of London.

The floor was packed with people: women in vibrant silks and satins, their identities hidden by elaborate masks designed for this very occasion; men with thousands of pounds burning in their pockets—eager to play, and win, and savor this moment when they might outsmart the Angel.

For five years, since the first Pandemonium, men had fallen victim to the Angel's temptation and wagered everything they had on her tables, on their own luck. And every year, a subset of those men had lost. And the owners of the Angel had won.

Chase liked to say that they won because none of them had enough riding on the night to lose. Most nights, Cross knew better. They won because they could do nothing less. They'd sold their collective souls, and their gift was fleecing the gentlemen of London.

Tonight, however, Cross doubted them. Doubted their keen, unwavering ability to win.

Doubted himself.

Too much was riding on Pandemonium tonight. Too much that he couldn't control. Too much that made him desperate to win.

And desperation was not good for winning, not even when the plan was working.

He braced one hand against the stained glass, his wide, flat palm on Satan's thigh as he watched the tables below. *Vingt-et-un* and roulette, hazard and piquet, the movement of the club was a blur of tossed cards and rolled dice and turned wheels and lush green baize.

On a normal night, Cross would have been calculating winnings—one thousand from hazard, twenty-two hundred from roulette, half again from *vingt-et-un*. But tonight, he was focused on the fifty who marked his fate.

Fifty of Knight's biggest players were dispersed across the floor below—fifty men who would never have been allowed to wager at this club if not for their special invitations. Fifty men who did not deserve to play here but played nonetheless.

At Cross's will.

Sally had kept her promise, delivering the gentlemen to the floor of the Angel, and now it was the Angel's task to keep them there. The employees of the hell had their orders. If a man had a wager in one hand, he had a full glass in the other. If a gamer appeared lonely, or bored, it was not long before he would be joined by another masked reveler—someone who had been paid handsomely to ensure that all in attendance left with light spirits and lighter pockets.

The Angel was known for delivering on gamers' fantasies, and tonight . . . it would deliver well.

And Knight would know that he could not beat the Angel.

That he could not beat Cross.

The door to the suite opened and closed behind him, but Cross did not turn to face his new companion. Only a handful of people were allowed access to the owner's suite—any one of them someone whom Cross would trust with his life.

Instead, he watched the roulette table below, the spinning wheel, the ivory ball rolling along the mahogany edge, around and around as the bettors leaned in. On one end of the roulette field, a young man no more than twenty-five lifted his mask and watched the roll of the ball with wild eyes—eyes that Cross had seen countless times over the years. Ordinarily, Cross would see nothing but profit in the young man's demeanor, but tonight, for a moment, he saw more.

"Lowe," Temple said, quietly, at his shoulder, following the line of his gaze.

Cross looked to his friend. "Did you know he was one of them?"

Temple shook his head once, firmly. "I did not. I wouldn't have allowed him inside the club."

"He's not after you," Cross said. "Anyone can see that."

The ball dropped into the roulette wheel, and the young man winced, turning away from the table as though in pain. In seconds, he had collected himself and returned his attention to the field, already reaching for money to wager again.

Temple shook his head. "He can't stop himself."

"We could stop him."

"He'd just go back to Knight's. Might as well have him lose to us tonight. As long as he causes no trouble."

Cross cut Temple a look. "What trouble would he cause? We'd defend you to the death."

One of Temple's massive shoulders lifted in a great shrug. "Defend me or no, a boy who has been wronged so well is a danger indeed."

Cross returned his gaze to Christopher Lowe, now watching as the ball rolled in the roulette track once more. "Is that why you're up here? In hiding?"

Temple rolled his shoulders back into his black jacket. "No. I'm here for you."

"What about me?"

"It looks like your plan is working."

Cross pressed his hand against the cool glass, savoring the wide, smooth pane against his palm. "We shan't know until we get proof that Knight's is empty of real gamers tonight."

"It will come," Temple said before going quiet for a long moment, then adding, "I hear the daughter arrived on time, this morning."

Cross had heard the same, that Meghan Margaret Knight had been set up in a lavish town house on the edge of Mayfair. "She won't stay long. Not with us pulling Knight's strings."

Temple didn't reply. He didn't have to. Instead, he watched the gaming below. "Bourne and Penelope are here."

Cross's gaze flickered to the far end of the room, where his partner sat—unmasked—happily next to his wife, watching as she knocked firmly against the baize to request another card for her hand of *vingt-et-un*. Penelope smiled at the flop and turned to her husband, lifting her face to his for a kiss. "She's winning, as usual, I see."

There was a smile in Temple's tone. "I'm certain he fixes the games."

Cross raised a brow. "If I ever get proof of that, he and I shall have a talk."

Temple laughed. "Be careful with that judgment, friend. Someday, it will be the lady *you* wish to impress."

Cross did not find the words amusing. "There are no doubt many things that might happen," he said, scanning the floor. "But my being laid low by a lady is not one of them."

He couldn't be.

Even if he did touch them—even if they were an option—a future with a woman was not. He owed Lavinia too much. He owed *Baine* too much.

He couldn't bring either of them back . . . couldn't return them to the lives they deserved. But he could ensure that Lavinia's children got everything Baine's should have had. He could be certain that they never knew the gnawing disappointment of want.

He would leave them a kingdom. Built from sin, but a kingdom nonetheless.

A crowded hazard table erupted in cheers, drawing the attention of half a dozen others nearby. At one end of the table, smug as ever, was Duncan West, owner of three major newspapers and a half dozen scandal sheets. West was rich as Crocsus and lucky as sin. More importantly, he was on the roll, and would take everyone nearby with him.

Cross remembered that pleasure keenly—the knowledge that he would win.

It had been a long time since he'd taken such pleasure.

"I would have bothered Bourne with this," Temple said casually, as though they were anywhere but the owners' suite of the most legendary gaming hell in London, "but since he is so busy with his lady, I thought perhaps you might step in."

Cross heard the amusement in Temple's tone. "I'm a little busy for your games, Temple."

"Not my games. Chase's. I am simply the messenger."

The words sent a tremor of unease through him. With a soft curse, Cross scanned the floor of the club, looking for the founder of the Angel, who, of course, was nowhere to be seen. "I don't need Chase's games either."

Temple chuckled. "It might be too late for that."

The words had barely been spoken when Cross's gaze settled on the lone figure at the center of the casino floor below, the only person in the entire room who was not moving. Of course.

She was always on a separate course from the rest of the universe—the planet that orbited in reverse, the sun that rose in the west. And now she stood at the center of his hell, surrounded by debauchery—in its thrall. He did not have to see her face to know that.

Just as he did not have to see her unmasked to know that she was stunning. Not as stunning as she had been in that chair in his office a week earlier, bared to him, finding her pleasure, tempting him with her shape and her sounds and her scent, but stunning nonetheless.

After she'd left him that night, he'd sat on the floor of his office, staring at that chair for hours, reliving the way she'd writhed against it, straining to hear the echoes of her gorgeous sounds, and finally, finally placing his forehead to the cool leather seat with a foul curse and vowing to stay away from her.

She was too much for him to resist.

She had returned, swathed in sapphire, hair like spun silk, porcelain skin, standing at the center of his club, under threat of sin and vice and wickedness. And him. From this vantage point, he had an unparalleled view of the swell of her beautiful breasts, all lovely curves and dark, promising shadows. Enough to send a grown man to his knees.

The hand on the glass clenched in a tight fist. "What in hell is she doing here?"

"Ah," Temple said, "you've noticed our guest."

Of course he'd noticed her. Any man with eyes would notice her. She was the most fascinating thing in the room. "Don't make me ask again."

"Asriel tells me she had an invitation."

No doubt she did. No doubt Chase found this entire scenario amusing. Chase deserved a sound beating. "She is no more suited to that room than she is to fly."

"I don't know." Temple paused, considering her. "I rather like the way she looks in that room."

Cross snapped his attention to his massive partner. "Stop liking it."

Temple smirked and rocked back on his heels. "I could like it very much."

Cross resisted the urge to put a fist into the larger man's face. Fighting with Temple was futile, as he was enormous and unbeatable, but it would feel good to try. It would feel good to lose himself to the physical when he had spent so much of the last week resisting just that. Cross felt confident that he could draw blood. Or blacken an eye. "Stay away from Philippa Marbury, Temple. She's not for you."

"But she is for you?"

Yes, goddammit. He bit back the words. "She's not for any of us."

"Chase disagrees."

"She's most definitely not for Chase."

"Shall I tell Bourne she's here, then?" Cross heard the teasing in Temple's voice. The knowledge that Cross would not be able to resist action. "Penelope could take her home."

He should let it happen. Should let Bourne and Penelope handle their errant sister. Should let someone else tend to Pippa Marbury before she ruined herself and half of London besides.

A month ago, he could have. A week ago.

But now. "No."

"I didn't think so." Temple's amusement grated.

Cross cut him a look. "You deserve a sound thrashing."

One side of Temple's mouth kicked up in a wicked smirk. "You think you're the one to deliver it?"

"No, but you'll get it before long. And we shall all have a good long laugh."

Something flickered in Temple's black gaze at that. "Such promises tease, friend." He put a hand to his chest dramatically. "They tease."

Cross did not waste more words on his idiot partner. Instead, he left the room, long strides eating up the dark corridor that led to the back stairwell of the Angel, then soaring down the stairs to reach his quarry, his heart pounding, eager to find her. To capture her before someone else did.

If another touched her, he'd kill him.

He pushed out a private door, into one of the small, private antechambers on one side of the casino floor and out onto the floor, filled with laughing masked revelers. Not that he would have any trouble finding her . . . he could find her among thousands.

But he didn't have to look very hard.

She gave a little squeak as they collided, and he reached out to capture her, hands coming to her shoulders to hold her steady. A mistake. He wasn't wearing gloves, and this dress appeared to have a shocking lack of fabric. Her skin was soft and warm—so warm it fairly singed him.

And made him want to linger.

He did not release her, not even when her hands came to his chest to brace herself, her sapphire skirts swirling around them both, tangling in his legs as surely as the scent of her tangled in his mind, bright and fresh and utterly out of place in this dark, wicked world.

Instead, he pulled her back into the alcove from which he'd come, and said harshly, "Why aren't you wearing gloves?"

The question surprised them both, but she recovered first. "I don't like them. They eliminate a sense."

It was hard to imagine losing any sensation when she was about . . . consuming his. He ignored the answer and tried again. "What are you doing here?" His voice was soft in the darkness—too soft. He meant to scold her. To scare her.

"I was invited."

Nothing scared Pippa Marbury. "You shouldn't have come."

"No one can see me. I'm masked."

He reached up for the mask in question, running his fingers along the delicate curving piece, all fine metalwork and architecture. Of course, Chase would have considered her spectacles. Chase considered everything. A thread of irritation began to unfurl in Cross's chest, adding a harshness to his next words. "What would possess you to accept this invitation? Anything could happen to you here. Tonight."

"I came to see you."

The words were soft and simple and unexpected, and Cross had to pause for a moment to take them in. "To see me," he repeated, like the imbecile into which he turned whenever she was around.

She nodded once. "I am angry with you."

She didn't sound it. And that was how he knew it was true. Pippa Marbury wouldn't suffer ire the way other women would. Instead, she would develop the emotion and consider it from all angles before acting on it. And with that uncommon precision, she would take her opponent off guard as easily as if she'd launched a sneak attack in the dead of night.

"I am sorry," he said, in the interest of self-preservation.

"For what?" she asked. He paused. No woman had ever asked him that. At his lack of reply, she added, "You don't know."

Not accusation. Fact.

"I don't."

"You lied to me."

He had. "About what?"

"I take your question to mean that you've done it more than once," she said.

He couldn't see her eyes through the mask, and he wanted to tear it from her face for this conversation.

No, he didn't. He didn't want to have this conversation at all.

He wanted her to go home and get into bed and behave like a normal, aristocratic lady. He wanted her to be locked in a room until she became Lady Castleton and left London and his thoughts forever.

It appeared that he lied to himself, too.

He released her shoulders, loathing the loss of her soft skin.

"You're an earl."

The words were quiet, but the accusation in them was undeniable.

"I don't like to think on it much."

"Earl Harlow."

He resisted the urge to wince. "I like to hear it even less."

"Did you enjoy making a fool of me? Embarrassing me? All that mistering? And when I told you that if you'd been an aristocrat, I wouldn't have asked for your help? Did you laugh uproariously after I left you that night?"

After she'd left him that night, he'd been utterly destroyed and desperate to be near her again. Laughing had been the farthest thing from his mind. "No," he said, knowing he should add something else. Knowing there was more to be said. But he couldn't find it, so he repeated, "No."

"And I am to believe that?"

"It is the truth."

"Just like the fact that you are an earl."

He wasn't entirely certain why this was such a frustration for her. "Yes. I'm an earl."

She laughed, the sound devoid of humor. "Earl Harlow."

He pretended it didn't bother him, the name on her lips. "It's not as though it's a secret . . ."

"It was a secret to me," she defended.

"Half of London knows it."

"Not my half!" Now she was growing irritated.

As was he. "Your half was never meant to know. Your half never *needed* to know."

"I should have known. You should have told me."

He shouldn't feel guilty. He shouldn't feel beholden to her. He shouldn't feel so out of control. "Why? You already have an earl. What good are two?"

Where in hell had that come from?

She stiffened in the darkness, and he felt low and base and wrong. And he hated that she could make him feel that way. He wanted to see her eyes. "Remove your mask."

"No." And that's when he heard it. The sting in her voice. The edge of sorrow. "Your sister was right."

The words shocked him. "My sister?"

"She warned me off you. Told me you never followed your word . . . told me never to believe you." Her voice was low and soft, as though she wasn't speaking to him, but to herself. "I shouldn't have believed in you."

He heard the addition of the *in*. Hated it. Lashed out at her. "Why did you, then? Why did you believe in me?"

She looked up at him, seeming surprised by his words. "I thought—" she began, then stopped. Rephrased. "You saw me."

What in hell did that mean?

He didn't ask. She was already explaining. "You listened to me. You *heard* me. You didn't mind that I was odd. In fact, you seemed to enjoy it."

He did enjoy it. By God, he wanted to bask in it.

She shook her head. "I wanted to believe that someone could do all those things. Perhaps, if you did . . . then . . ."

She trailed off, but he heard the words as though she'd shouted them. *Then Castleton might.*

If he hadn't already felt like a dozen kinds of ass, he would now. "Pippa." He reached for her again, knowing he shouldn't. Knowing that this time he could not resist touching her. And he might not be able to resist claiming her.

She stepped away from him, out of his reach, returning to the present. To him. "No." Before he could act, move, take, repair, she took a deep breath, and spoke. "No. You are right, of course. I do have an earl, who is kind and good and soon to be my husband, and there is nothing about you or your past—or your present for that matter—that should be relevant to me."

She backed away, and he followed her like a dog on a lead. Hating the words she spoke—their logic and reason. She was unlike any other woman he'd ever known, and he'd never in his life wanted to understand a woman so much.

She kept talking, looking down at her hands, those imperfect fingers woven together. "I understand that there is nothing about me that is of interest to you . . . that I'm more trouble than I'm worth . . . that I should never have brought you into my experiments."

He stopped her. "They aren't experiments."

She looked up at him, eyes black in that ridiculous mask. He'd like to tear it from her, crush it beneath his boot and take a horsewhip to Chase for having it made. "Of course they are."

"No, Pippa. They aren't. They're a desire for knowledge, certainly, a need for it, even. But more than that, they're a need for understanding of this thing that you are about to do, that you have refused to stop and that terrifies you. They are a desperate ploy to stop yourself from feeling all the doubt and frustration and fear that you must be feeling. You say you want to understand what happens between men and women. Between husbands and wives. But instead of going to any number of those who know better—who know first-hand . . . you come to me. In the darkness."

She backed away, even as he stalked her. "I came to you in the middle of the day."

"It's always night inside the Angel. Always dark." He paused, loving the way her lips parted, just barely, as though she could not get enough air. Neither could he. "You came to me because you don't want it. The ordinary. The mundane. You don't want him."

She shook her head. "That's not true. I came to you because I don't understand what all the fuss is about."

"You came to me because you fear that it's not worth the fuss with him."

"I came to you because I thought you were a man I would not see again."

"Liar." The word was harsh in the small space, at once accusation and accolade.

She looked up at him, those black eyes empty. "You would know. You've lied to me from the very beginning with your weighted dice and your false promises and your *Mr. Cross*."

"I never lied, love."

"Even that is a lie!"

"I told you from the beginning that I was a scoundrel. That was my truth."

She gaped at him. "And that absolves you of your sin?"

"I've never asked for absolution." He reached for the horrid mask, pulling it from her face, regretting the movement the moment he saw those enormous blue eyes, swimming with emotion.

Not regretting it at all.

Adoring it.

Adoring *her.*

"I told you to leave me. I told you never to come near me." He leaned in, torturing them both—so close and still an unbearable distance. "But you couldn't resist. You want me to teach you the things you should learn from him. You want my experience. My sin. *My* kiss. And not his."

Her gaze was on his mouth, and he held back a groan at the hunger in those blue eyes. God, he'd never wanted anything the way he wanted her.

"You've never kissed me," she whispered.

"I've wanted to." The words were so simple, they felt like a lie. Want didn't come close to articulating the way he felt. About her touch. About her taste. About her.

Want was a speck in the universe of his desire.

She shook her head. "Another lie. You can't even touch me without pulling away as though you've been burned. You clearly aren't interested in touching me."

For someone who prided herself on her commitment to scientific observation, Philippa Marbury was utterly oblivious.

And it was time he set her straight.

But before he could, she added, "At least Castleton kissed me when I asked."

He froze. *Castleton had kissed her.*

Castleton had taken what Cross had resisted. What Cross had left.

What should have been Cross's.

Vicious jealousy flared, and six years of control snapped. He caught her to him without hesitation, lifted her in his arms, pressed her to the richly upholstered wall, and did what he should have done the first moment he met her.

He kissed her, reveling in the feel of her lips on his, of the way she softened instantly against him, as though she belonged in his arms—his and no one else's.

And she did.

She made a small, irresistible sound of surprise when he aligned his mouth to hers and claimed it for his own, swallowing the gasp and running his tongue along the full curve of her bottom lip until surprise turned to pleasure, and she sighed—giving herself to him.

And there, in that moment, he knew he would not stop until he'd had all of her. Until he'd heard every one of her little squeaks and sighs, until he'd tasted every inch of her skin, until he'd spent a lifetime learning the curves and valleys of her body and her mind.

It was the years of celibacy. After six years, any kiss would be this powerful. This earth-shattering.

Lie.

It was her.

It would always be her.

Lifting his lips from hers, he whispered, "You do burn me, Pippa. You enflame me." He pressed her into the wall, pinning her with his body so he could free his hands to explore, to cup her jaw in one hand and tilt her lips to his and gain better access. He took her mouth again, throwing himself into the fire, stroking deep, wanting to consume her, wanting to erase every memory of every other man from her mind.

He ran the edge of his teeth along her lower lip, adoring the way she sighed and lifted her arms to wrap around his neck. And then, dear God, she was kissing him back—his brilliant bluestocking—first repeating his movements, then improving on them until the student surpassed the master to tortuous, nearly unbearable effect.

She writhed against him—as eager for him as he was for her—rocking her hips into his, the rhythm promising more than she could possibly know. He broke the kiss on a groan—a low, wicked sound that rumbled around them in this small, private place.

He trailed kisses across the line of her jaw to her ear, where he whispered, "He might have kissed you, love, but his kiss is nothing like mine, is it?"

She shook her head, her reply coming on heavy gasps of breath. "No." He rewarded her honesty with a long lick along the curl of her ear, pulling the soft lobe of it in his teeth, worrying it until she sighed, "Cross."

He lifted one hand to the line of her dress and yanked the fabric down, baring one perfect, pale breast, tracing his finger around and around her nipple until it went hard and aching. He tore his gaze away to find her equally transfixed by his touch.

Watching her beautiful blue eyes, he moved, pinching the straining tip, loving the way her head tilted back resting against the wall as she sighed his name once more. He kissed her softly at the soft spot behind her jaw, tonguing the skin there. "His kiss doesn't make you cry out his name."

"No," she said, pressing her breast into his hand, asking for more. As though she had to ask. He dipped his head, taking her nipple into his mouth, sucking until she cried out, the glorious sound muffled by curtains and the din of gamers nearby, who had no idea of what happened mere feet from them.

He rewarded her unbridled response with a deep, thorough kiss, reaching down to lift her skirts, fingers tracing along silk stockings and then silken skin as they climbed higher and higher. Her fingers tangled in his hair, clutching him to her as she gasped against his lips. He returned to her ear, whispering, "Tell me, my gorgeous, honest girl, does his kiss make you want to lift your skirts and take your pleasure here? Now?"

"No," she confessed, soft and strained.

His hand moved higher, finding what he sought, downy

hair and glorious wet heat. He stroked the backs of his fingers along the seam of her, wanting her more than he'd ever wanted anything in his life. "But mine does, doesn't it?"

He slid one finger deep into her softness, and they both groaned at the pleasure of it. She was wet and wanting, and he couldn't wait to give her everything she desired. He stroked, long and lush, through the wet, wonderful core of her as he whispered in the darkness, "It makes you want to hold your skirts high as I give you everything you deserve—as I teach you about sin and sex, with half of London a hairsbreadth away."

"Yes." She gasped, and he lifted her skirts higher with one hand, working his fingers high against her, making good on his promise, one finger pressing deep into her as his thumb worked a tight circle at the hard, straining center of her pleasure.

"This isn't a lie, Pippa. This is truth. Wicked, undeniable truth."

She clutched his arm, moving against him, not knowing what to do.

But he knew. It had been six years, but he had been waiting for this moment.

For her.

"Take your skirts, darling."

She did as she was told, holding them high as he sank to his knees before her once more, as he had several nights earlier, only this time, he allowed himself access to her, to her heat and her scent and the magnificence of her body.

He lifted one of her legs, pressing a kiss to the inside of her knee, swirling his tongue against the finely spun silk there before hooking her knee over his shoulder and leaning forward to place a kiss against her beautiful mound. He stroked deep, first with one finger, then two as he blew a long stream of air over the spot where his thumb had been swirling. She sucked in a deep breath. "Cross," she whispered. "Please—"

And in that plea, he lost himself. "Yes, love," he said, inhaling her heady, glorious scent. "I'll give you everything you want. Everything you need."

He stroked into her softness again, and he wondered at the way she wept for him, not knowing what he would give her . . . what he could do to her . . . and wanting it nonetheless. "Do you feel it? The truth of it? How much you want me?"

"I want . . ." she started, then stopped.

He turned his head, nipping at the soft skin of her inner thigh, reveling in the softness there—that untouched, uncharted, silken spread. "Say it." He would give it to her. Anything in his power. Anything beyond it.

She looked down at him, blue eyes fairly glowing with desire. "I want you to want me."

He closed his eyes at that; trust Pippa to be forthright even here, even now, even as she bared herself to his eyes and mouth and hands. Trust her to strip this moment of all remaining shrouds, leaving it raw and bare and honest.

God help him, he told her the truth. He wasn't certain he could do anything but. "I do, love. I want you more than you could ever know. More than I could have ever dreamed. I want you enough for two men. For ten."

She laughed at that, the sound coming on a wicked movement of strong hips and soft stomach. "I don't require ten. Just you."

Even as he knew he would never be worthy enough for her, the words went straight to the hard, straining length of him, and he knew he would never be able to resist her—not when she asked with truth in her big blue eyes and passion on her soft, lyric voice.

He leaned in, and spoke to the heart of her. "And you shall have me."

And then he was where he had wanted to be for a week. For longer. He removed his hand from where it had been working its irresistible rhythm, retreating slowly, killing them both until she moved to seek his touch. He couldn't stop the wicked grin that spread across his face at the proof that she wanted him. "Easy."

"No." The word came out on a near desperate whine. "Now, Cross."

"So demanding," he teased, his blood running hot at her insistence. "Now, it is." And he spread her gently, revealing the core of her, willing and wet and perfect.

He kissed her then, the way he'd promised he would that night in his office, the way he'd dreamed late at night as he lay in the darkness and imagined this vision of a woman rising above him, open and available for worship.

Just as she was now, standing above him, one hand holding her sapphire skirts, the other thrust into his hair, holding him against her as he pressed his tongue into her softness, savoring her taste, making love to her with slow, languid strokes that made her sigh and writhe and push against him. She was pleasure and heat and passion—the first, fresh drink of water after years in the desert.

He found the heart of her desire, working it first slowly, then longer and faster until time faded and he was wrapped in her sound and her feel and her taste, with no desire to move or stray from her. He'd promised her hours, and he could make good on it—he could worship her from here, on his knees, for an eternity.

She lost her grip on her skirts, and her thighs trembled against him as she arched away from the wall, a wicked, wonderful offering. He took it without question, reaching up to hold her, returning his fingers to the heat of her in one long, deep thrust.

She came apart then, against his hands and his mouth, crying her pleasure beneath his tongue and teeth, and he carried her over the edge, through her passion, working her with his touch and his kiss and every bit of desire and depravity he'd resisted over the last six years . . . over longer than that. He reveled in her softness and her sounds, not wanting to leave her. Wanting the experience with her.

She called out his name, her fingers tight in his hair, and he came with her, hard and hot and unavoidable. And in that moment, his own pleasure startled from him by hers, he should have felt embarrassment or shame or something infinitely more base. But instead he felt as though he'd been waiting for that moment.

For her.

And there, in the darkness, her soft cries echoed by the roar of London's wealthiest gamers scant feet away, he caught his breath and ran his hands along her thighs, guiding her skirts back into place, and considered the startling possibility that Pippa Marbury was indeed his savior.

The thought rocketed through him as quick and unexpected as his climax, and he bowed his head, looking down at her little sapphire slippers, shocked as hell, even as he knelt at her feet and reveled in the feel of her hands in his hair.

That's how Temple found them.

He came up short just inside the door to the owner's suite, six feet of muscle going perfectly still, his scarred face a portrait of shock. "Shit," he said, backing up, propelled from the space by its intimacy. "I didn't—"

Pippa's hands moved like lightning, and Cross was naked at the loss of her touch. "Your Grace," she said, and Temple's title startled him, a reminder of all their places. Of the wrongness of her being here. "I— We—"

He needed time to think.

He needed time to understand what had just happened.

How everything had changed.

He rose. "Get out."

Pippa turned her wide gaze on him. "Me?"

No. Never her. But he couldn't bring himself to speak to her yet. He didn't know what he would say. How he would say it. She'd wrecked him, thoroughly, and he wasn't prepared for it. For her.

For the way she made him feel.

For the things she made him do.

For the future she tempted him with.

"I think he meant me, my lady," Temple cut in.

Then why was he still here?

Temple replied as though Cross had spoken the words aloud.

"Knight has arrived."

Chapter Fourteen

~~Oh, my.~~

It seems that all the discussion of brute beasts
and carnal lust addressed in the text of the wedding
vows was not just for the groom.

I have never in my life felt anything so . . .
~~Remarkable.~~
~~Magnificent.~~
~~Emotional.~~
Unscientific.

**The Scientific Journal of Lady Philippa Marbury
March 30, 1831; six days prior to her wedding**

*H*e left Pippa immediately, releasing her into Temple's
protection, even as he loathed the idea of her in his club with
another man, outside of his own protection. Outside of his
sight.

Outside of his embrace.

He wanted her home. Safe. Far from this place, and these
villains. He wanted to be with her. He paused in the process
of fastening the fall of a fresh pair of trousers, the thought
throwing him.

He wanted to be with her in his home.

Not in his cluttered office, on his inferior, makeshift bed. At his town house. Where he'd never taken a woman. Where he rarely was in residence. Where the demons never ceased to threaten.

Pippa wouldn't stand for demons.

One side of his mouth kicked up at the thought. Pippa would exorcise every one of his demons with her logical mind and her incessant questions and her impossibly sure touch. A touch he found himself rather desperate to experience once more.

He wanted her to touch him everywhere. He wanted to touch her everywhere. He wanted to explore her, and hold her, and kiss her and make her his in every imaginable way.

She wanted to understand lust? He could show it to her. There was time. She had six days before she married Castleton.

Not enough time.

Something tightened in his chest at the thought.

She was going to marry Castleton.

He sat to pull on his boots with vicious force.

I shall do it because I have agreed to, and I do not care for dishonesty.

Goddammit. She was engaged to the ordinary, uninspiring, idiot man.

Not so much an idiot now. He'd proposed to Pippa, after all. Snatched her up while the rest of England was looking the other way.

But she had come apart in *Cross's* arms. Against *his* mouth. Did that account for nothing?

There was nothing he could do. Not to stop it. She deserved her perfect wedding with her handsome—if simpleminded—earl. She deserved a man without demons. A man who would give her a home. Horses. Hounds. *Family.*

Those children flashed again, the little blond row of them, each wearing a little pair of spectacles, each smiling up at their mother. *At him.*

He pushed the vision aside and stood, straightening his jacket.

Impossible.

Philippa Marbury was not for him. Not in the long run. He could give her everything for which she asked now . . . he could teach her about her body and her desires and her needs . . . prepare her to ask for what she wanted.

To ask her husband.

He swallowed back a curse.

Six days would be enough.

He ripped open the door of his office, nearly pulling it from the hinges, and headed for the library of The Fallen Angel, where Knight waited for him. Dismissing the guard at the door, Cross took a deep breath and entered, regaining his control. Focusing on the task at hand.

Knight was livid. A muscle in his jaw twitched as he turned toward the door, hatred in his ice blue gaze.

Cross took pleasure that, tonight, at least this had gone well—at least this was in his control. A thread of uncertainty tainted victory, however; Knight had not come alone.

A young woman sat primly in one of the high-backed chairs at the center of the room, hands folded in her green woolen skirts, eyes cast downward, as though she could will herself invisible. She was pretty enough—pale skin, tight black curls, and a little red mouth that curved up in a bow even though she looked nothing close to happy.

Indeed, it was her misery that established her identity.

Letting the door to the room close behind him, Cross looked to Knight, meeting his nemesis's icy blue gaze. "Not very fatherly of you . . . touring your daughter about London's better hells in the middle of the night."

Knight did not respond to the insult, instead turning away from the sideboard where he stood, ignoring the girl entirely. "You think you've won? With one night?"

Cross folded himself into another large chair, extending his long legs and doing his best to look bored. He wanted this confrontation over and done with. He returned his gaze to Knight. "I know I have won. Your fifty largest players are right now losing at *my* tables. And with a word, I can keep them there, playing forever."

Knight gritted his teeth. "You don't want them. They're too base for your precious club. The others will never allow the likes of those scoundrels on the books at the Angel."

"The others will do what I choose. Your sorry lot is a sacrifice we will make to ensure that you understand your place. You are a product of our benevolence, Digger. You exist because we have not seen fit to take you down. Yet. It is time you realize that our club is more than yours will ever be. It is time you realize our power extends farther than yours ever could. Knight's exists solely and completely because of my goodwill. If I want you destroyed, I can do it. And I will not be tested."

Knight narrowed his gaze on him. "You've always liked to think of me as the enemy."

Cross did not waver. "There's no thinking about it."

"There was a time when I was the closest thing you had to a friend."

"I don't recall it that way."

Knight shrugged, uninterested in rehashing the past. "Have you forgotten Lavinia's debt? She still owes me. One way or another."

The sound of his sister's name on Knight's lips made Cross want to hit something, but he remained still. "I will pay the debt. You will refuse entry to Dunblade. Forever. And you will leave my sister alone. Also forever."

Knight's black brows rose, and he lifted his silver-tipped cane from the floor to inspect the finely wrought handle. "Or what?"

Cross leaned forward then, letting his anger show. "Or I take them all. Every last gamer."

Knight lifted a shoulder. "There are more where they came from."

"And I shall take them, too." He paused, then added, "Over and over, I shall strangle the coffers of Knight's until you can't afford the wax to keep your tables lit."

Admiration flashed in Digger's gaze. "You shall make me a fine son-in-law."

"I shall see you in Hell first."

Maggie Knight responded to that, head snapping up, eyes wide, a deer in the hunter's sight. "You wish me to marry *him*?" She hadn't known. Cross resisted the urge to say something to the girl—to comfort her.

"Don't let the crassness fool you." Knight barely looked at her. "He'll make you a countess."

"But I don't wish to *be* a countess."

"You wish for what I tell you to wish for."

"Wishing won't make it so, I'm afraid," Cross said, ending the conversation by standing and heading for the door. "My apologies, Miss Knight, but I shan't marry you."

She exhaled. "That is a relief."

Cross's brows rose. "It is, isn't it?"

"No one should be relieved." Digger turned to Cross. "We've known each other a long time, haven't we, Cross? Longer than you've known any of these nobs you call partners."

Cross stood. "I've a rather impressive group of gamers on the floor tonight, Digger. More than I had originally planned. I'm afraid I haven't the time for nostalgia. You'll have Dunblade's debt tomorrow. Or I take Knight's. Gamer by gamer. Brick by brick."

He reached for the door handle, already thinking of his next destination.

Of Pippa.

Of the way she smelled and tasted, of her smart mouth and flashing eyes, of her curiosity. She was somewhere in this building, likely gambling or interviewing a prostitute or doing something else scandalous, and he wanted to be near her.

Desperately. She was opium. One taste, and he couldn't stop himself.

Something had changed in the darkness earlier that evening.

False.

Something had changed earlier than that.

He found he was rather desperate to explore it.

Six days. He wouldn't waste another second of it in this room. He opened the door. Less than a week, then he would leave her. She would be his pleasure. His one taste. His one mistake.

And afterward, he would return to his life.

"I see I must sweeten the pot. Shall I add in Philippa Marbury?"

The words sent an icy chill through Cross, and he turned slowly, the open door forgotten. "What did you say?"

Knight smirked, cold knowledge in his gaze. "Ah, I've your attention now. You shouldn't have left Sally at the club. Whores are so easily convinced to turn traitor."

A pool of dread spread through Cross's gut as the other man continued. "I may not be the great genius you are purported to be, but I know my way around lightskirts. A few extra quid, and Sally told me everything I needed to know. Your plan to lure my big gamers to Pandemonium. The names of all the girls who helped you—every one of them out on the streets now, by the way—and most importantly, the name of the aristocratic lady who happened into your office while you were plotting my demise. Blond girl. Spectacles. Odd as an otter." Knight rocked back on his heels, his false accent returning. "Sounded right familiar, that one."

Cross could see it coming. A runaway carriage, too fast to stop.

"Philippa Marbury. Daughter of the Marquess of Needham and Dolby. Future Countess of Castleton. And the sisters . . . cor! One to be married to Tottenham, and the other Lady Bourne!" Knight whistled, long and low, the sound sending fury through Cross. "Impressive, that. Wouldn't like to see 'em ruined. Wager Bourne wouldn't neither.

"Terrible thing for an unmarried Lady Philippa to be discovered trottin' about in a gamin' hell. And with a pure scoundrel like yourself, no less . . . with your reputation? Why, she'd never be allowed in polite society again. No doubt the old Castleton bird won't have her baby boy marryin' her."

Cross froze at the words. At their implication.

He should have seen it coming.

A memory flashed, the older man leaning over him six years earlier, Cross nearly dead from the beating he'd taken at Knight's henchmen's hands.

Insurance.

He should have known that Knight would have had a second plan. An insurance policy. Should have known, too, that it would be Pippa.

What he had not expected was how very angry that made him.

He was at Knight's throat in three long strides, one large hand wrapping around the other man's neck and throwing him back against the sideboard, rattling glasses and sending a decanter of scotch toppling to the floor. He ignored the startled gasp from the girl on the opposite end of the room. "You'll stay away from Philippa Marbury, or I'll kill you. That's the game."

Knight caught his balance and smiled, as though they were discussing the weather and not his imminent demise. "I wouldn't worry. I shan't have time to go near her . . . what with all the excitement around my girl's wedding."

"I should kill you anyway."

Knight smirked. "But you won't. I saved your life, boy. Without me, you'd be drunk and half-mad with the pox, if any one of half a dozen hell owners hadn't dumped you in the Thames themselves. Without me, you'd be dead or living dead. You owe me even without my having your pretty plaything in my clutches. You were useless. Weak. Unworthy. And I gave you an exit."

The words sent a chill through Cross, their truth undeniable.

Knight removed a handkerchief from his pocket, dabbed at his lip, checking to see if there was blood. "You have me to thank for all this. Your entire empire. And the tragedy of it is that you're too honorable to ignore it. Instead, you owe me."

He shook his head, even as he knew the words were true. "Not this."

"Of course this," Knight scoffed. "It's time you realize that aristocrats or not, money or not, fancy French chef or not, I've been down this road before you, and I'll always know the terrain better than you. You can't beat me.

"I hear Duncan West is here. I wonder if the lady will make Wednesday's *Scandal Sheet*?" At Cross's flashing gaze, Knight pointed to Maggie, who stared back at the two of them with shock and confusion in her eyes. "You marry my girl, or I ruin yours. *That's* the game."

Your girl. The words echoed through him, part taunt, part hunger. All truth.

For much of his life, Cross had been known for his ability to see all possible outcomes of a situation. He could look at a spread of cards and predict the next flop. He could see the next punch in a bare-knuckle boxing match. He could plot a dozen moves forward on a chess board.

He wondered if Pippa played chess.

He pushed the thought aside. There would be no more thinking of Philippa Marbury. No more touching her. His fingers itched at that, desperate for more of the contact they'd been denied for so long. He'd only been able to touch her for a heartbeat.

He'd ached for her since the second he left her tonight. Since before that.

And he knew, with the keen knowledge of one who had

been so long in control of his desires, that he would ache for her for an eternity.

But he would take the ache to save her.

For once in his sorry, worthless life, he would save someone he cared for.

I should not have believed in you.

Pippa's words from earlier echoed through him, taunting him.

He would save her.

"Maggie's not a bad hand, Cross. She'll make you pretty heirs."

Cross lifted his gaze to follow Knight's meaning, meeting Maggie's eyes, recognizing the shock and disappointment there. She didn't want to marry him any more than he wanted to marry her. He leveled her with a serious look. "Your father is mad."

"I'm beginning to see that myself," she replied, and Cross thought that if the situation had been different, he'd have smiled at that.

But the situation was not different.

There was only one course of action.

He approached Knight's daughter—nineteen years old with mediocre French—dropped to one knee in front of her and said, "I'm afraid I haven't a choice."

He had lost so many. *This time, he would save one.*

The most important one.

Maggie nodded once. "It seems, my lord, that in that, at least, we have a great deal in common."

Unshed tears shimmered in her brown eyes, and Cross wished he could say something else. Something that would make her feel better about the whole situation. But the truth was, Meghan Margaret Knight believed him a coldhearted man who ran a den of iniquity and made his money on sin. She believed that he consorted with ruffians and prostitutes and scoundrels the likes of her father, and that a marriage to him—once blessed—would be the result of blackmail and coercion, and nothing remotely fonder.

Meghan Margaret Knight, who had not known him for the better part of an hour, already knew more of his truths than Philippa Marbury ever had.

So, instead of comforting her, he lifted one of her gloved hands from where it clutched the green fabric of her skirts, held it in his firm grasp, and said, "Miss Knight, would you do me the honor of becoming my wife?"

$\mathscr{P}$ippa was enjoying herself immensely.

She might have spent much of the last weeks unimpressed by the poorly lit, library-quiet main floor of The Fallen Angel, but tonight, she finally understood its appeal. By night, the club filled with light and sound and a long, languorous lick of sin that Pippa could never have imagined if she were not here, now, witnessing it.

Night breathed life into this great stone building, darkness somehow plunging the room into bright, bold light—a whirl of color and sound and thrill that Pippa drank in with heady excitement.

She stood at the center of the main floor of the club, surrounded by masked revelers: men in their dark suits, boldly colored waistcoats their nod to the evening festivities; women in their silks and satins, dresses designed to showcase skin and scandal.

Giving herself up to the movement of the crowd, Pippa allowed them to carry her from one side of the room, where she'd escaped Temple's chaperone, to the center of the revelry, past piquet and roulette and hazard, and throngs of laughing, masked beauties and their handsome counterparts. She knew better, of course—knew that each of these bodies had flaws, likely significant ones—but somehow, masked, they seemed more than the sum of their parts.

Just as, somehow, suddenly, she seemed more than the sum of hers.

But she did not fool herself into thinking that it was her mask that made her feel so powerful, so different. Nor was it the room.

No, it was the man.

Her heart raced as she recalled the clandestine events of mere moments ago, of the heady, overwhelming touch that she had not expected but that she had craved.

And the kiss.

One hand lifted of its own volition at the thought of that devastating, remarkable caress, the one she had known would be everything she'd imagined and nothing like it, all at once. She regretted the instant that her fingertips brushed her lips—hating that their touch had erased his.

Wishing she could take it back.

Wishing she could find him once more and urge him to restore the memory of his kiss.

A thread of feeling settled deep in her belly, unfurling in slow, steady time as she recalled the moment, as she imagined the softness of his hair in her fingers, of his skin against hers . . . of his lips.

Of his tongue.

The room grew warmer as she realized that even the thought of his touch, of his kiss, of *him,* made her ache. But it was the location of the ache that unsettled—a deep, secret place that she'd never realized existed.

He showed her things she'd never known about things she'd always thought she understood. And she adored it . . . even as it terrified her.

Even as it made her question everything she thought true.

She resisted the thought, her gaze rising to one large wall of the club, where the Angel's namesake fell in beautiful glass panels from Heaven to Hell, from good to evil, from sainthood to sin. It was the most beautiful window Pippa had ever seen, the work of true artisans, all reds and golds and violets, at once hideous and holy.

It was the angel himself who fascinated her, the enormous, beautiful man crashing to Earth, without the gifts he'd had for so long. In the hands of a poorer artist, the detail of him would have been less intricate, the hands and feet and face would have been shaped with glass of a single color, but this artist had cared deeply for his subject, and the swirls of darks and lights in the panels were finely crafted to depict movement, shape, and even emotion.

She could not help but stare at the face of the fall—inverted as he fell to the floor of the hell—the arch of his brow, the complex shade of his jaw, the curve of his lip. She paused there, thinking on another pair of lips, another fall. Another angel.

Cross.

Emotion flared, one she did not immediately recognize.

She let out a long breath.

She wanted him—in a way she knew she should not. In a way she knew she should want another. A man destined to be her husband. To be the father of her children.

And yet, she wanted Cross.

This angel.

Was it only desire?

Her heart began to pound—the physical manifestation of a thought she had been unprepared to face. One that overwhelmed and ached and enticed.

"It's magnificent, isn't it?"

The words were spoken close and soft, and Pippa spun toward the sound, finding a tall, lithe lady inches away, seated at a card table. She wore the most beautiful gown Pippa had ever seen, a deep, royal purple that fairly glowed against her warm, golden skin. A large topaz hung from a fine gold chain, drawing the attention of all who looked to the decadent plunge of the dress's bodice. She wore a feathered black mask, too elaborate to see most of her face, but her brown eyes glittered from their frames, and her lips, wine-dark, curved in a wide smile.

The smile was filled with unspoken promise.

The kind of promise Pippa had seen on Miss Tasser's lips one week prior.

When she did not immediately reply, the woman pointed one long, straight well-manicured finger toward the mural. "The angel."

Pippa found her voice, nerves and excitement making the words come faster than she'd planned. "It's beautiful. And very lavish. So much red glass. And violet."

The lady's smile broadened. "And the colors mean something?"

Pippa nodded. "To make red glass, they add gold dust. They do it for violet, as well."

Brown eyes went wide. "How clever of you to know that."

Pippa looked away; clever was rarely a compliment among women. "I read it once."

"It's no wonder Cross enjoys your company, Lady P."

Pippa's gaze snapped back to the woman, seeing the knowledge in her gaze. "How did you—"

The lady waved one hand. "Women talk, my lady."

Sally. Pippa wondered if she should be concerned. Probably.

The woman was still speaking, "He's a lovely promise, don't you think?"

"Promise?"

The smile deepened. "Of wickedness. If you're willing to ask."

Pippa's mind spun. How did this woman know what had happened? What they'd done? Had they been spied upon? "Cross?"

She laughed, the sound bright and friendly. "I was referring to the Angel, honestly." She indicated a chair to her left. "Do you play?"

Grateful for a change of topic, Pippa considered the field

of green baize, cards arranged in front of the woman and the four men seated to her right. She shook her head. "I don't."

"You should." She lowered her voice to a conspiratorial whisper. "It's Cross's favorite."

She might not have agreed to the game, but the moment the beautiful woman mentioned him, Pippa could not have stopped herself for anything in the world. She sat. "Perhaps I shall watch a round or two."

The lady smirked. "I suppose understanding the game is important to some."

Pippa laughed. "I don't have a great fortune to wager."

"My guess is that you have more than you think."

Pippa did not have a chance to reply, as the dealer carefully distributed two cards to the group, one facedown, the second faceup.

"The goal is twenty-one," the woman said, turning her cards—nine of hearts faceup—to face Pippa and carefully lifting a corner to reveal an eight of clubs. "Knaves, queens, and kings are worth ten," she said, raising her voice a touch to ensure that the rest of the table heard the reference.

Pippa understood the bluff instantly. "And aces?" she asked, helping her new acquaintance.

"Aces are the best in the deck. Ones or elevens. The card of second chances."

"Ah. So a good start," Pippa said, nodding sagely.

"I surrender."

One of the gentlemen at the table stood, taking half their wagers, and left the table. The mystery woman leaned in to Pippa, and said, "Well done. The man closest to us lacks skill, and the farthest lacks luck."

"And in the middle?"

The lady made a show of considering the handsome man at the center of the table. "That's Duncan West. Owns most of the London papers."

Pippa's heart began to race. If she were discovered by the newspaperman, she would be ruined. Olivia as well.

Perhaps that would not be so bad. She ignored the thought. "He's so young," she whispered, doing her best not to look at the man in question.

"Young and royal-rich. There's little he lacks. Except, it seems, a night with a good woman."

Pippa heard the desire in the lady's tone. "You, I take it?"

The woman turned to her, eyes glittering. "A woman can hope."

Pippa watched as the gentlemen at the table added cards to the stacks in front of them, quickly learning the simple rules of the game.

When it came time for her companion to wager, the woman turned her shielded gaze to Pippa, and said, "What say you, my lady? Do I hit or hold?"

Pippa considered the table. "You should take a card."

The other woman inclined her head to the dealer. "The lady suggests I hit."

Five.

Lips the color of Bordeaux pursed in a perfect moue. "Well, that's pretty. I shall stay."

The cards were revealed. Pippa's companion won. Collecting her winnings, she turned her smile on the rest of the table. "The luck of the novice, don't you think?"

Two gentlemen grumbled their congratulations, as Duncan West nodded his appreciation in their direction, his gaze fairly burning as it settled on the other woman. Pippa watched for a moment as one long, porcelain arm reached for her winnings, deliberately brushing against Mr. West's hand, lingering for a second, maybe less. Long enough for West's gaze to turn hot. He looked as though he might devour her if they were alone.

The look was familiar.

It was the look Cross gave her when they were alone.

She blushed, looking away, hoping that her new acquaintance would not notice. If she did, it was not obvious when she returned her attention to Pippa. "How did you know I should hit?"

Pippa lifted one shoulder. "A guess."

"Mere luck?"

Pippa shook her head. "Not lucky, really. The cards on the table were all high. The odds were that you would pull a low one."

There's no such thing as luck.

The other woman smiled. "You sound like Cross."

That the woman gave voice to Pippa's thoughts did not bother her. That she spoke Cross's name as though she knew him intimately did. "You have gambled with Cross?" She tried to sound casual. Failed.

The lady turned back to the dealer, indicating that he should deal another round. "Will you play this time, my lady?"

Pippa nodded absently, reaching into her reticule and retrieving a handful of coins. "Please."

Are you friends with Cross? she wanted to ask. *Has he touched you? Kissed you? Have you lain with him?* She hated her curiosity. Hated her reticence more.

The cards were dealt. Pippa looked at hers. Ace and three. She and the other woman watched as the dealer attended to the gentlemen at the end of the table for a long moment before her companion said, "I have gambled with him." The woman asked for a second card. "Hold. But you needn't worry."

"I wasn't—" Pippa stopped. "Hit."

Six made twenty.

"I shall hold, please. Worry about what?"

The cards were revealed. "Twenty wins."

The woman clapped politely as two men groaned, and Mr. West raised his glass in their direction. "The student surpasses the teacher." The woman leaned in. "Cross does not frequent women's beds."

Pippa coughed, blindsided by the flood of sensation that coursed through her at the words. She paused, trying to identify it. Relief? No. She didn't believe it. His reputation preceded him. But hope . . . it might be hope. One could not stop oneself from that errant, unflagging emotion, it seemed.

But even she knew that she should not hope. Not about this.

In fact she should do the opposite of hope. She should . . . unhope. Her winnings slid across the table toward her. "That does not keep him from inviting women to his," she said, dryly.

The woman laughed. "No, but I've never seen that happen either."

Pippa thought of Sally Tasser. "You haven't looked hard enough."

"Oh, you'd be surprised. Cross is a fair catch. And it's not just me who thinks it. A dozen I know would have happily joined him there. Most of them for free. Everyone in London wants a piece of Cross. Have for years."

Pippa stared at her winnings, counting the coins, pretending not to hear. Not to notice the ache in her chest at the thought of other women knowing him. Touching him. Kissing him.

She disliked every one of them.

Irrationally.

She did not like being irrational.

The woman was still talking. "All those long limbs and thick ginger hair. But he's too good to treat us like the rest. Not one of us has been there—you shouldn't believe anyone who tells you otherwise." Pippa's cheeks warmed, and she was grateful for the mask. Her new acquaintance seemed to notice the flush anyway. "But you *have* been there, haven't you?"

God, yes. And it was wonderful.

She shook her head, her body resisting the betrayal in the movement. The lie there. "I am engaged."

Not that it had mattered an hour earlier.

She started at the thought. At the emotion that came with it.

Guilt.

"That's not an answer." Red lips turned up, unaware of her thoughts. "And besides, engaged is not married."

It was close, though, wasn't it? It was the closest thing to marriage that there was. Her throat began to tighten.

"You don't have to admit it, but I think Cross likes you very much, my lady. After all, it is not every day one meets a woman as brilliant as he is."

She liked him, too.

She shook her head, emotion clouding thought. "I'm not as brilliant as he is."

If she were, she wouldn't have landed herself in this moment.

In this mess.

Desperately wanting a man she should not want. Whom she could not have. Not in the long run.

Not unless . . .

She stopped the thought before it could form. She'd made a promise. She would marry Castleton. She had to.

She ignored the ache in her chest at the thought.

She had made a promise.

"If I had to wager, I'd place bets on your being smarter." The woman turned back to the dealer. "Will you play another round?"

"She will not."

It was as though they'd conjured him. Pippa turned toward him—unable to stop herself, drawn to his deep voice and his sandalwood scent.

She had the unreasonable desire to toss herself into his arms and press her lips against his and beg him to take her to his office or some dark corner and finish what he'd started earlier in the evening. To make her forget everything else— all of her well-laid plans, all of her carefully constructed research, the fact that she only had six days before she married another man.

A man who was nothing like Cross.

And then she noticed his unmasked grey eyes trained on her companion, the corded muscle in his neck and jaw taut, his lips pressed into a thin, straight line.

He was angry.

"Cross." The woman laughed his name, apparently fearless. "You should join us. She counts the cards as well as you do."

His gaze narrowed. "No."

"So much for Cross and his kindness." The woman turned back to the baize, lifting a glass of champagne. "I was merely keeping the lady company."

His fists clenched. "Find other company to keep."

The woman smiled at Mr. West, dismissing them. "With pleasure."

Cross turned his grey gaze on her, and his teeth clenched. "My lady," he intoned, "the tables are no place for you."

He was angry with her as well.

And, strangely, that made Pippa angry, for certainly she had reason to be. More reason than he did. After all, *he* wasn't about to be forced into marriage with a perfectly ordinary, perfectly imperfect for him kind of person. *He* wasn't about to have his entire life thrown into disarray. In six days, *he* would remain fully ensconced in this remarkable existence, all sin and vice and money and beautiful women and food cooked by a chef with more talent than any one man deserved.

And she would be married to another.

No, if someone was going to be angry, it was going to be her.

"Nonsense," she said, pulling herself straight. "There are women at every one of the tables in this room. And if I were not meant to gamble tonight, I daresay I would not have been invited."

He leaned close, his words harsh at her ear. "You should not have been invited at all."

She hated the way the words made her feel, as though she were a small child being punished. "Why not?"

"This place is not for you."

"As a matter of fact," she said, allowing her irritation to sound, "I believe I *will* play another round."

The woman she'd been speaking to turned back at that, her jaw going lax for an instant before she caught herself and smiled wide. "Excellent."

He leaned close, his voice lowering to a whisper that only she could hear. "I will not have you here. Not now."

"I am simply playing cards," she said, hating the way his words stung, bringing tears to her eyes. She refused to look at him. Refused to risk his seeing the way he moved her.

He sighed, soft and irritated and somehow tempting, the feel of his breath against her shoulder. "Pippa," he said, the name more breath than sound. "Please."

There was something in the plea that stopped her. She turned to face him once more, searching his grey eyes, finding something there—pain. Gone so fast she was almost unsure it had been there to begin with. *Almost.*

She placed one hand on his forearm, feeling the muscles beneath his sleeve flinch at the touch, and whispered back, "Jasper."

She had no idea where the given name came from; she did not think of him as such. But for the rest of her life, she would remember the way his beautiful grey eyes went wide, then shuttered, as though she'd delivered him a powerful blow. He stepped back, out of her reach, and she couldn't stop herself from following, coming out of her chair and moving toward him, wanting to take it back—whatever it was she'd done.

For she had absolutely done something.

Something that would change everything. "Wait," she said, not caring that half of London was in earshot.

He stopped, his hands coming to her shoulders, holding her at a distance. "Go home. Your research is finished."

Pain shot through her, even as she knew that it was for the best. He had been right, of course. It wasn't research. It never had been. It had been fear and panic and frustration and nerves, but it had never been research.

And then it had been desire. Temptation. Want.

More.

And if it did not end soon, she might never be able to end it.

Except, she did not want to end it. She wanted it to remain. She wanted to talk and laugh and share with him. She wanted to learn from him. To teach him. She wanted to be with him.

She wanted the impossible.

She shook her head, refusing his request. "No."

"Yes," he said once more, the word like ice, before turning and plunging into the crowd. Leaving her. Again.

Infuriating man. God knew she'd had enough of that.

She followed him, tracking his movements above the crowd, where his marvelous hair stood out against the rest of London. Where *he* stood out against the rest of London. She pushed and elbowed and knocked and strained to catch him, and finally, she did, reaching out for his hand—adoring the fact that neither of them wore gloves, loving the way their skin came together, the way his touch brought wonderful heat in a lush, irresistible current.

He felt it, too.

She knew it because he stopped the instant they touched, turning to face her, grey eyes wild as Devonshire rain. She knew it because he whispered her name, aching and beautiful and soft enough for only her to hear.

And she knew it because his free hand rose, captured her jaw and tilted her face up to him even as he leaned down and stole her lips and breath and thought in a kiss that she would never in her lifetime forget.

The kiss was like food and drink, like sleep, like breath. She needed it with the same elemental desire, and she cared not a bit that all of London was watching. Yes, she was masked, but it did not matter. She would have stripped to her chemise for this kiss. To her skin.

Their fingers still intertwined, he wrapped their arms behind her back and pulled her to him, claiming her mouth with lips and tongue and teeth, marking her with one long, luscious kiss that went on and on until she thought she might die from the pleasure of it. Her free hand was in his hair then, tangling in the soft locks, loving their silky promise.

She was lost, claimed, fairly consumed by the intensity of the kiss, and for the first time in her life, Pippa gave herself up to emotion, pouring every bit of her desire and her passion and her fear and her need into this moment. This caress.

This man.

This man, who was everything she had never allowed herself to dream she would find.

This man, who made her believe in friendship. In partnership.

In love.

Shocked by the thought, she pulled back, breaking the kiss, loving the way his breath came harsh and heavy against her cheek as a collection of whistles and applause sounded around them.

She didn't care about the onlookers. She cared only for him. For his touch. For this moment.

She hadn't wanted to stop him—to stop it—but she hadn't a choice. She had to tell him. Immediately. And she couldn't tell him while he was kissing her, though she did hope to get back to kissing as soon as possible.

She moved to doff her mask, thinking of nothing but him. "Cross—"

He grabbed her hands, holding them tight. "You'll be ruined." He shook his head, urgency coming off him in waves. "You have to leave. Now. Before—"

He was utter confusion—pushing her away even as he held her close. She started to deny him. To tell him what she was feeling, to explain these strange, brave, new emotions. It was there, on her tongue.

I love you.

She was going to say it.

She was going to love him.

And in the wake of her confession, she would resolve the rest.

But before she could speak, a snide voice interrupted. "It seems *everyone* has been invited to Pandemonium this year. Lady Soon-to-be-a-countess, what a pleasure it is to see you again. And so scandalous now."

If the voice hadn't been familiar, the horrid nickname would have identified Digger Knight, suddenly at Pippa's shoulder. Pippa closed her mouth, turning to face Knight, who had a pretty, unmasked girl in tow, too young and prim to be one of his women.

"Mr. Knight," Pippa said, unaware of the way she moved, away from the brightly colored man and toward Cross, who stood behind her, warm and firm and *right*.

Knight smiled, an impressive number of straight white teeth in his head. "You remember me. I'm honored."

"I don't imagine you're easily forgotten," Pippa said coolly.

He ignored the quip. "You have a particular pleasure this evening, Lady Soon . . ." He trailed off, letting Pippa's mind go to the kiss, letting her cheeks flush. ". . . You shall be the first to congratulate Cross."

"Digger," Cross said, and Pippa realized that he hadn't spoken since Knight arrived. She looked to him, but he was deliberately not looking at her. "This isn't part of it."

"Considering what half of London just witnessed, Cross, I think it is," Knight said, tone dry and unmoved as he turned to face Pippa.

At the same time, Cross pinned her with his beautiful grey gaze. "Go home," Cross said urgently. "Hurry. Now."

His gaze was filled with worry—so much that Pippa was

almost willing to agree, her weight shifting, beginning the move to the exit.

Knight cut in. "Nonsense. She can't leave until she's heard your news."

Pippa turned a curious gaze on Cross. "Your news?"

He shook his head, perfectly serious, and a weight dropped in her stomach. Something was wrong. Terribly so.

She looked from him to Knight, to the despondent girl with him. "His news?"

Knight laughed, the sound loud and grating, as though he'd heard a joke that only he found amusing. "I'm afraid I can't wait for him to tell you himself. I'm too excited. I can't resist stealing his thunder."

Her gaze narrowed behind mask and spectacles, and she was grateful for the shield to keep her thoughts from showing. "I don't imagine I could stop you."

His eyes went wide. "Oh, I do like a lady with a sharp tongue." He shoved his hands into the pockets of his waistcoat and rocked back on his heels. "You see, darling, you're not the only one soon-to-be-a-countess . . . the Earl here has asked my daughter to marry him. She has, of course, agreed. I thought you might like to congratulate the pair." He indicated the couple, neither looking worthy of congratulations. "You have the honor of being the first."

Her mouth dropped open. It wasn't true, of course. It couldn't be.

She looked up at Cross, his grey eyes deliberate in their focus. On anything but her.

She'd misheard. She had to have. He wouldn't marry another. He'd told her . . . marriage was not in his cards.

But she saw the truth in his distant gaze. In the way he did not turn to her. In the way he did not speak. In the way he did not rush to deny the words—words that stung like the worst kind of accusation.

Panicked, Pippa looked to the other woman—black curls and blue eyes and porcelain skin and pretty red lips in a perfect little bow. She looked like she might cast up her accounts. Nothing like a bride.

She looks like you feel whenever you think of marrying Castleton.

She didn't need to ask, but she couldn't stop herself. "You are marrying him?"

Black ringlets bobbed.

"Oh." Pippa looked to Cross, unable to find another word. "Oh."

He did not look at her when he spoke, voice so soft she would not have heard it if she had not been watching his lips . . . those lips that had changed everything. This man who had changed everything. "Pippa . . ."

Marriage is not for me.

Another lie. One of how many?

Pain shot through her, sharp and almost unbearable, her chest tightening, making it difficult to breathe. He was marrying another.

And it *hurt*.

She lifted one hand, rubbing at the spot closest to the ache, as though she could massage it away. But as she looked from the man she loved to his future wife, she realized that this pain wouldn't be so easily assuaged.

Her whole life, she'd heard of it, laughed at it. Thought it a silly metaphor. The human heart, after all, was not made of porcelain. It was made of flesh and blood and sturdy, remarkable muscle.

But there, in that remarkable room, surrounded by a laughing, rollicking, unseeing collection of London's brightest and wickedest, Pippa's knowledge of anatomy expanded.

It seemed there was such a thing as a broken heart.

Chapter Fifteen

The human heart weighs (on average) eleven ounces and beats (approximately) one hundred thousand times per day.

In Ancient Greece, the theory was widely held that, as the most powerful and vital part of the body, the heart acted as a brain of sorts—collecting information from all other organs through the circulatory system. Aristotle included thoughts and emotions in his hypotheses relating to the aforementioned information—a fact that modern scientists find quaint in its lack of basic anatomical understanding.

There are reports that long after a person is pronounced dead and a mind and soul gone from its casing, under certain conditions, the heart might continue beating for hours. I find myself wondering if in those instances the organ might continue <u>to feel</u> as well. And, if it does, whether it feels more or less pain than mine at present time.

The Scientific Journal of Lady Philippa Marbury March 31, 1831; five days prior to her wedding

That night, Pippa did not sleep.

Instead, she lay on her bed, Trotula warm and solid against her side, staring at the play of candlelight over the pink satin canopy above, and wondering, alternately, how it was that she had so thoroughly misjudged Cross, herself, and their situation, and how it was that she'd never noticed that she loathed pink satin.

It was a horrid, feminine thing—all emotion.

A lone tear slid down her temple and into her ear, unpleasant, wet discomfort. She sniffed. There was nothing productive about emotion.

She took a deep breath.

He was marrying another.

She loved him, and he was marrying another.

As was she.

But for some reason, it was *his* impending marriage that seemed to change everything. That seemed to mean more. To represent more.

To hurt more.

Silly, pink satin. Silly canopies. They didn't serve a single useful purpose.

Trotula lifted her soft brown head as another tear escaped. The hound's wide pink tongue followed its path, and the quiet canine understanding set off a torrent of the salty things—a flood of wretched drops and hiccups that Pippa could not halt. She turned onto her side, tears obscuring the silver mask from Pandemonium where it lay on the bedside table, gleaming in the candlelight. She should never have accepted the invitation to the event. Should never have believed it would come without cost—that any of this would come without cost.

The candle's flame burned as she stared at it, whites and oranges barely wavering above a perfect blue orb. She closed her eyes, the memory of the flame bright even then, and took another deep breath, wishing the ache in her chest would go away. Wishing thoughts of him would go away. Wishing sleep would come.

Wishing she could go back to that morning, eight days earlier, when she'd decided to approach him, and stop herself.

How a week had changed everything.

Had changed her.

What a mess she had made.

Aching sadness rolled through her like a storm, cold and tight and bitterly unpleasant. She cried for who knew how long—two minutes. Maybe ten. Maybe an hour.

Long enough to feel sorry for herself. Not long enough to feel any better.

When she opened her eyes, she returned her attention to the candle, still and unmoving even as it burned unbearably bright. And then it did move, dancing and flickering in an unexpected draft.

A draft followed by a great *woof* and a thud as Trotula left the bed, tail wagging madly, and threw herself at the doors that led out to the narrow balcony just off Pippa's bedchamber. Doors once closed, now open, now framing the man Pippa loved, frozen just inside the room, tall and serious and beautifully disheveled.

As she watched, he took a deep breath and ran both hands through thick red hair, pushing it off his face, his high cheekbones and long straight nose stark and angled in the candlelight.

He was unbearably handsome. She'd never in her life longed for anything the way she longed for him. He'd promised to teach her about temptation and desire and he'd done powerfully well; her heart raced at the sight of him, at the sound of his heavy breath. And yet . . . she did not know what came next.

"You are beautiful," he said.

What came next was anything he wished.

Trotula lifted herself onto her hind legs and planted her forepaws on his torso, whining and sighing, quivering with excitement. He caught the dog with strong hands, keeping her upright and giving her all the affection for which she begged, instantly finding the soft spot on her temple that turned her to mush. She groaned and leaned into him, thoroughly smitten.

For the first time in her life, Pippa wished she did not have a pet. "She is a terrible protector."

He stilled at that, and the three remained that way for a long moment, silent. "You require protection from me?"

Yes.

She did not reply, instead saying, "Trotula, enough." The dog returned to all-paws, but did not stop staring up at her new love with her enormous, soulful gaze. Pippa could not fault her traitorous nature. "It seems she likes you."

"I have a special talent for ladies," he said in a warm, kind voice she at once loved and loathed. A vision of Sally Tasser flashed. And the prostitute at the card table that evening. And Knight's pretty daughter.

She swung her legs off the side of her bed. "So I've seen." His attention snapped immediately to her, but she changed tack. "This room is on the third floor."

Another man would have hesitated. Would not have instantly understood. "I would have climbed farther to see you." He paused. Then, "I had to see you."

The ache returned. "You could have fallen. Hurt yourself."

"Rather that than hurt you."

She looked down at her lap, hands twisted in the white linen of her nightgown, and whispered, "You once told me that if Castleton hurt me, he wasn't doing it right."

He stilled. "Yes."

She met his eyes. "You're not doing it right."

He was across the room in an instant, on his knees at the side of the bed, his hands on hers, sending rivers of excitement and heat and elation through her even as she knew she should push him away and return him, immediately, out the window through which he came, three stories be damned.

"I shouldn't be here," he whispered. "I should be anywhere but here." He bowed his head, his forehead coming to rest on their hands. "But I had to see you. I had to explain."

She shook her head. "There is nothing to explain," she said. "You are marrying another." She heard the hitch in her voice, the slight hesitation between the first and second syllables of *another*. Hated it.

Closed her eyes. Willed him gone.

Failed.

"You told me you wouldn't marry. Another lie."

It was as though she hadn't spoken. He did not deny it. "You've been crying."

She shook her head. "Not on purpose."

One side of his beautiful mouth rose in a crooked smile. "No, I don't imagine it was."

Something about the words, soft and filled with humor and something else, made her suddenly, startlingly irritated. "You made me cry," she accused.

He went serious. "I know."

"You are marrying another." She repeated the words for what seemed like the hundredth time. The millionth. As though if she said them enough, they would lose their meaning. Their sting.

He nodded. "As are you."

She'd been engaged for as long as they'd known each other. But somehow, his impending marriage was a greater betrayal. It was illogical, she knew, but logic did not appear to have a place here.

Another reason she did not like it.

"I hate that I've made you cry," he said, his fingers flexing over hers.

She stared down at the place where their hands were intertwined, loving the play of freckles over his skin, the soft down of the ginger hair there, between the first and second knuckle. Her thumb rubbed across his index finger, and she watched the strands move, stretching and bending before they snapped back to their original place, instantly forgetting her touch.

She spoke to those hairs. "When I was a child, I had a friend named Beavin." She paused, but did not look at him. He did not speak, so she continued, not entirely knowing where she was going. "He was kind and gentle, and he listened ever so well. I used to tell him secrets—things that no one else knew. Things that no one else would understand."

His grip on her hands tightened, and she met his gaze. "But Beavin understood. He explored Needham Manor with me. He helped me discover my love for science. He was there on the day that I stole a goose from the kitchens and dissected it. I blamed him for it. And he never minded."

His gaze darkened. "I find I don't care much for this perfect companion, Pippa. Where is he now?"

She shook her head. "He went away."

His brows snapped together. "Where?"

She smiled. "Wherever imaginary friends go."

He exhaled harshly, lifting one hand to her temple, pushing a mass of hair back from her face. "He was imaginary."

"I never understood why others couldn't see him," she whispered. "Penny used to humor me . . . pretend to interact with him, but she never believed in him. My mother tried to shame him away." She shrugged, then said, simply, "But he was my friend."

He smiled. "I like the idea of you and your imaginary friend dissecting a goose."

"There were a great deal of feathers."

The smile became a laugh. "I imagine there were."

"And not near as much blood as one might think," she added. "Though I did scare a maid nearly to death."

"In the name of science."

She smiled then. "In the name of science."

He leaned forward, and she knew he was about to kiss her.

Knew, too, that she couldn't allow it. She pulled back before their lips could touch, and he immediately retreated, releasing her and sitting back on his heels. "I am sorry."

She stood, placing distance between them, Trotula coming to stand sentry beside her. She let her fingers work the dog's soft ears for a long moment, unable to look at Cross. Unable to stop looking at him. "I don't know why I told you that."

He rose, but did not come closer. "About Beavin?"

She looked down at the floor. "It's silly, really. I don't even know why I thought of him. Except . . ." She trailed off.

He waited a long moment before prompting her to continue. "Except . . . ?"

"I've always been different. Never had many friends. But . . . Beavin didn't mind. He never thought I was odd. And then he disappeared. And I never met another person who seemed to understand me. I never thought I would." She paused. Gave a little shrug. "Until you."

And now you'll go away, too.

And it would hurt more than losing an imaginary friend ever could.

She wasn't sure she would be able to manage it.

"I can't help but think," she started, then stopped. Knowing she shouldn't say it. Knowing, somehow, that it would make everything harder. "I can't help but think . . . if only I'd . . ."

He knew it, too. "Don't."

But she couldn't stop it. She looked up at him. "If only I'd found you first."

The words were small and sad, and she hated them, even as they brought him to her—his hands to her face, cupping her cheeks and tilting her up to him. Even as they brought his lips to hers in a kiss that robbed her of strength and will and, eventually, thought.

His long fingers threaded through her hair, holding her still as he lifted his lips, met her gaze, and whispered her name before taking her mouth again in long, lavish strokes. Again and again, he did the same, whispering her name against her lips, her cheek, the heavy pulse at the side of her neck, punctuating the word with licks and nips and sucks that set her aflame.

If only she'd known that she might find someone like him. A match.

A love match.

They did exist. And here was the proof, in her bedchamber. In her arms. In her thoughts. *Forever.*

She closed her eyes tight at the thought, even as the tears came, and he sipped at them, whispering her name over and over, again and again. "Pippa . . . don't cry, love . . . I'm not worth it . . . I'm nothing . . ."

He was wrong, of course. He was everything.

Everything she could not have.

She pulled away at the thought, pressing her palms flat to his chest, loving the warmth of him, the strength of him. Loving him. Looking up at his wild grey eyes, she whispered, "My whole life . . . two and two has made four."

He nodded, utterly focused on her, and she loved him all over again for paying attention . . . for understanding her.

"But now . . . it's all gone wrong." She shook her head. "It doesn't make four anymore. It makes you." Heat flared in his gaze, and he reached for her again, but she pulled back. "And you're to marry another," she whispered, "and I don't understand." A fat tear escaped, expelled by fear and frustration. "I don't understand . . . and I hate it."

He brushed the tear away with his thumb, and said, achingly soft, "It's my turn to tell you a story. One I've never told another."

Her heart in her throat, she met his gaze, knowing with keen understanding that what he was about to say to her would change everything.

But she would never have dreamed he'd say what he did.

"I killed my brother."

*H*e'd never said the words aloud, but somehow, remarkably, saying them to Pippa was easier than he imagined.

Saying them to Pippa would save her.

She had to understand why they couldn't be together. She had to see why he was utterly, entirely wrong for her. Even as every ounce of him ached to claim her as his own, forever.

And the only way to show her these things was to show her the worst in him.

She stilled at the confession, her breath catching in her throat as she waited for him to go on. He almost laughed at the realization that it hadn't occurred to him that she might not immediately exit him from the room. It hadn't occurred to him that she might want more of an explanation.

That she might believe in him.

So few ever had.

But here she was, waiting for him to continue, quiet, serious, scientific Pippa, waiting for all the evidence to be laid out before drawing her conclusions.

Perfect Pippa.

His chest tightened at the thought, and he turned away from her, imagining that he could turn away from the truth. He went to the doors he'd left open, closing them softly as he considered his next words. "I killed my brother," he repeated.

Another woman would have launched into a litany of questions. Pippa simply watched him, eyes wide and stunning and unimpeded by spectacles. And it was her eyes on him, sure and without judgment, that spurred him on.

He leaned back, the cool windowpane comforting against his back. "Baine was perfect," he said. "The perfect son, the perfect heir, the perfect brother. He was full of all the honor and dignity that came with being the future Earl Harlow, and none of the crass entitlement that seemed to accompany titles in other men. He was a good brother and an even better heir."

The words came easier now. He spread his hands wide,

looking down at them. "I, on the other hand, was the perfect second son. I loved vice and loathed responsibility, I was highly skilled at spending my father's money and my own allowance, and I had a knack for counting cards. I could turn ten pounds into a thousand, and took any opportunity to do so. I had little time for friends, even less for family." He paused. "It never occurred to me I might someday regret that lack of time."

She was close enough that he could reach out and touch her if he chose, but he didn't—he didn't want her near this story, near the boy he'd once been. He shouldn't want her near the man he was now.

She watched him carefully, riveted to his story and for one, fleeting moment, he allowed himself to look at her, taking in her unbound hair and her blue eyes—full of knowledge and more understanding than he deserved.

He couldn't imagine how he'd ever imagined her ordinary or plain. She was stunning. And if her beauty weren't enough, there was her mind. She was brilliant and quick-witted, and so perfectly different than anyone he'd ever known. *Two and two made him.* On anyone else's lips it would have been gibberish, but on Pippa's it was the most seductive concept he'd ever considered.

She was everything he'd never known he wanted.

And he did want her. Enough to make him wish he were someone else. Enough to make him wish he were more. Different. Better.

Enough to make him wish that he did not have this story to tell. "It was the start of Lavinia's first season—she'd received her vouchers to Almack's, and she was ecstatic—certain that she would be pronounced the jewel of the *ton*."

"She is beautiful," Pippa said.

"At eighteen, she was unparalleled." His voice went raw as he remembered his flame-haired sister, all flirtation and winning smiles. "It was her first night at Almack's—she'd been presented at court the week prior."

He stopped, considering the next words, but Pippa cut in. "You chaperoned her."

He laughed bitterly at the thought. "I was supposed to. But there was nothing I wanted to do less than spend the evening at Almack's. I hated the idea of the place—wanted nothing to do with it."

"You were a young man. Of course you hated the idea of it."

He looked up at that, met her eyes. "I was her brother. It was my *duty*." She did not reply. Knew better. *Smart girl.* "I refused. Told Baine I wouldn't go." He trailed off, remembering that afternoon, when he'd laughed and taunted his older brother. "She wasn't my problem, after all. Would never be my concern. I was the middle child . . . the second son. The *spare* and thank God for that.

"Baine was furious—a rare event, but he'd had plans to see . . ." he trailed off. *A woman.* "There was a Greek opera singer looking for a new protector . . ."

Pippa nodded. "I see."

She didn't see. Not at all.

You'll have to see her another night, Cross had said with a laugh. *I promise, a few more hours won't alter her assets . . . or yours as a future earl.*

I don't give much credence to your promises, Baine had snapped in reply. *Did you not promise our sister your chaperone tonight?*

No one ever expects me to keep my word.

Cross could still remember the fury and disappointment in Baine's gaze. *You are right at that.*

"We argued, but I won—it mattered not a bit to me if Lavinia had her chaperone, and because it did matter to Baine, he had no choice but to take her. They went to her party. I went to Knight's."

Her jaw went slack at that. "To Knight's?"

"To Knight's, and then . . ." He hesitated over the confession . . . knowing it would change everything. Knowing he'd

never be able to take it back. Knowing she had to know—
that it would do more to save her than anything else he could
say. "And then to Baine's opera singer."

She closed her eyes at the words, and he hated himself
all over again, now, seven years later. The betrayal long
assigned to his brother now had a second owner—Pippa.
But this was the goal, was it not? To chase her away from
Knight—away from him—into the arms of her earl?

Every ounce of him protested it, but he'd spent years con-
trolling his body, and he would not stop now.

"I was in the arms of his future mistress when the carriage
threw a wheel while turning a corner." His words were firm
and without emotion. "Baine, the driver, and one footman
were killed instantly. A second footman died the following
day."

"And Lavinia," Pippa said quietly.

"Lavinia was crippled, her bright future extinguished."
His fists clenched. "I did it to her. If I'd been there . . ."

She reached for him then, her soft hands coming to his,
grasping tight. "No."

He shook his head. "I killed him, as surely as if I'd put a
gun to his head and pulled the trigger. If I'd been there, he'd
be alive."

"And you'd be dead!" she said harshly, drawing his attention to her blue gaze, swimming with unshed tears. "And
you'd be *dead*."

"Don't you see, Pippa . . . I deserved it. I was the wicked
one. The one who sinned. I was the one who gambled and
lied and cheated and thieved. He was good and she was
pure and I was neither; Hell came looking for me that night,
thinking it would find me in that carriage. And when it
found them instead, it took them."

She shook her head. "No. None of it was your fault."

God, how he wanted to believe her.

"I didn't even stop after the accident. I kept at it . . . kept
going to hells . . . kept winning. Tried to bury the sin with

more of it." He'd never told anyone this. Didn't know why he was telling her. To explain who he was, perhaps. Why he was wrong for her. "Don't you see, Pippa . . . It should have been me."

One tear slid down her cheek. "No," she whispered, throwing herself at him, letting him catch her and wrap her in his long arms, letting him lift her from the floor, press her against him and hold her there. "No," she repeated, and the anguish in the sound made him ache.

"That's what my father said. He hated me." She started to interrupt, but he stopped her. "No. He did. And after the accident—he couldn't look at me. Neither could my mother. We did not know if Lavinia would live or die—her leg had broken in three places, she was out of her mind with fever. And they wouldn't let me near her. For a week, my mother said nothing to me, and my father . . ." He hesitated, the pain of the memory burning for a moment before he continued, "My father said the same five words. Over and over. *It should have been you.*"

"Jasper," she whispered his given name in the darkness, and a part of him, long buried, responded to the sound of it. "He was grieving. He didn't mean it. He couldn't have."

He ignored the words . . . the pain in them. "They couldn't look at me, and so I left."

He met her blue eyes. Saw the understanding in them. "Where did you go?"

"The only place I could think to go." He stopped, knowing that this was the part of the story that most mattered. Considering his words.

He did not have to hide from her. She was already there. "To Knight's."

"I gambled for days. Straight. No sleep. I went from the tables on the floor of the hell to the beds above—tried to lose myself in gaming and women." He paused, hating the story. The boy he'd been. "I swore not to look back."

"Orpheus," she said.

One side of his mouth kicked up. "You're too smart for your own good."

She smiled. "It helps when I'm with you."

The words reminded him of how much he liked this woman. Of how much he shouldn't. "Orpheus in reverse. From Earth into Hell. Full of pain and sin and every kind of vice. I should not be alive now to tell the tale."

"But you are."

He nodded. "I am alive, and Baine isn't; I am well, and Lavinia suffers."

"It's not your fault." She came into his arms again, wrapping her arms about him and repeating the words to his chest. "It's not your fault."

He wanted to believe her so badly. But it wasn't true.

"But it is." He held her to him and confessed his sins to her beautiful cornsilk hair. "I killed my brother. That is the cross I bear."

She heard it . . . stilled. Looked up at him. And his brilliant Pippa understood. "The cross you bear." His lips twisted in a wry smile. "That's why you took the name. Cross."

"To remember whence I came. To recall sins past."

"I hate it."

He released her. "You shan't be around it much longer, love."

Her beautiful blue eyes grew wide and sad at the words, and it was he who hated . . . hated this night and their situation and himself. He swore, the word harsh in the candlelight. "I couldn't save them," he confessed before vowing. "But, goddammit . . . I can save *you*."

She jerked back. "Save me?"

"Knight knows who you are. He will ruin you if I don't stop him."

"Stop him how?" He met her gaze, and she knew. He could hear it in her voice. "Stop him how?"

"I marry his daughter, he keeps your secrets."

She stiffened in his arms, brows snapping together. "I don't care a fig if he tells the world my secrets."

She would care, of course. She would care when Knight planted the seed of their time together in the ear of the aristocracy. In Castleton's ear. She would care when it ruined her marriage and her future and her sisters' happiness. She would care when her parents could no longer look her in the eye. "You should care. You have a life to live. You have a family to think of. You have an earl to marry. I won't have your ruination on my head. I won't have it alongside all the rest."

She pulled herself up to her full height, caring not a bit that she was half-dressed and could likely not see very well. It didn't matter, of course. She was a queen. "I am not in need of saving. I am perfectly well without it. For a scandalous, wicked man, you are all too willing to assume the mantle of responsibility."

"You are my responsibility." Did she not see that? "You became my responsibility the moment you entered my office."

She'd been his from the start.

Her gaze narrowed. "I was not looking for a keeper."

Irritation flared. He took her shoulders in hand and made his promise. "Well, you haven't a choice. I have spent years atoning for my sins, desperate to keep from wreaking more destruction than I already have. I will not have you near it. I will not have you touched by it." The words came on a flood of desperation . . . panic that he could not deny. "Dammit, Pippa, I have to do this. Don't you see?"

"I don't." There was panic in her voice as well, in the way her fingers gripped his arms tight. "What of me? What of my responsibility? You think I will not feel the heavy weight of your marrying a woman you don't know out of some false sense of honor?"

"There is nothing false about this," he said. "This is what I can give you." He reached for her, pulled her close. Wished it was forever. "Don't you see, love? Saving you . . . it's my purpose. I have tried so hard . . ." He trailed off.

"To what?" When he did not immediately answer, she added, "Jasper?"

Perhaps it was his name on her lips that made him tell the truth . . . perhaps it was the soft question—and something he was too afraid to name—in her blue eyes . . . perhaps it was simply her presence.

But he told her. "To atone. If not for me . . . Baine would be alive, and Lavinia would be well."

"Lavinia has chosen her life," Pippa argued. "She's a husband and children . . ."

"A husband in debt to Knight. Children who must grow in the shadow of their useless father. A marriage born of my own father's fear that he'd never rid himself of his crippled daughter."

She shook her head. "That's not your sin."

"Of course it is!" he burst out, spinning away from her. "It's all mine. I've spent the last six years trying to rewrite it, but that is my past. It's my legacy. I am the contact for the girls at the Angel . . . I choose to be. I try to keep them safe. The second they want out . . . the moment they choose another life for themselves, I help them. They come to me; I get them out. I've helped dozens of them . . . found places for them, work that can be done on their feet instead of their back. Country estates where they can be safe . . . every one of them a placeholder for her."

For the sister he could not save, whose life he'd destroyed.

For the brother whose life he'd taken as surely as if he'd crashed the damn carriage himself.

"It's not your fault," she said again. "You couldn't have known."

He'd thought the words a hundred times. A million. But they never comforted. "If Baine were earl . . . he would have heirs. He would have sons. He would have the life he deserved."

"The life you deserve as well."

The words came on a vision of that life. Of those little blond, bespectacled girls and laughing boys capturing frogs in the heat of a Devonshire summer. Of their mother. *Of his wife.* "That's where you're wrong. I don't deserve it. I stole it from him. I robbed it from him while I was in the arms of his mistress."

She stilled at the words. "His mistress. That's why you didn't touch me. Didn't kiss me. Why you don't . . . with other women." *How the hell did she know that?* She answered before he could ask the question. "The lady at the card table . . . and Miss Tasser . . . they both implied that . . ."

Dammit. "Did they." It was not a question.

She pinned him with that knowing blue gaze. "Is it true?"

He could lie. He'd spent half a decade convincing London that he hadn't stopped the rakish behavior. That he'd made women his life's work. He could lie, and she'd never discover the truth.

But he did not want to lie to her. Not about this. "It's been six years."

"Since you've lain with a woman?"

He did not speak, and the truth was in the silence.

She pressed on, eyes wide. "Since you've lain with *any* woman?"

She sounded so shocked. "Any woman."

"But . . . your reputation. You're a legendary lover!"

He inclined his head. "I told you that you should not believe everything you hear in ladies' salons."

"Forgive me, but if I remember correctly, you did divest me of my clothes without the use of your hands."

The image of her in his office, draped over his chair, flashed. More welcome than he'd ever admit. He met her gaze. "Luck."

"You don't believe in it."

She was incredible. His perfect match.

"Six years without touching a woman," she said in awe.

He paused. "Until tonight."

"Until me," she breathed.

He wanted to share that breath, to touch her again. "I can't stop myself with you."

Her lips curved into a smile of utter feminine satisfaction, and Cross was instantly heavy and stiff, even as he renewed his vow not to take her. Not to lose himself in her. Not even now, when she owned him inch by unworthy inch.

"It is your punishment, then? Your penance? Celibacy?"

"Yes." On her lips, it sounded idiotic. Celibacy had no place near Philippa Marbury. Not when she was so obviously made for him.

Fifteen minutes in an alcove at the Angel had not been enough.

A lifetime would not be enough.

"I cannot. Not with you, Pippa. You're to be married."

She hesitated, then whispered, "To another."

He ached at the words. "Yes. To another."

"Just as you are."

"Yes." *His ultimate penance.*

She lifted one hand, settling the soft palm on his cheek and he could not resist capturing it with his own hand, holding her touch there. Savoring it. "Jasper." His given name whispered through him, and he loved it on her lips. Wanted to hear it over and over again, forever. If he were another man, he might have a chance to.

But he had to leave her.

She was not his to touch.

"Jasper," she whispered again, coming up on her bare toes, wrapping her other hand around his neck, pressing her beautiful body against him, nothing but a scrap of linen between his hands and her soft, lovely skin.

He shouldn't.

Every inch of him ached for her—the product of too long

a time without her followed by too brief a time with her. He wanted to lift her and throw her onto her bed and take her . . . just once.

It would never be enough.

"If you really want to save me . . ." she whispered, her lips disastrously close.

"I do," he confessed. "God help me . . . I can't bear the thought of you hurt."

"But you have hurt me. You hurt me even now." Her voice was low and soft, with a thread of irresistible wickedness he did not expect.

His hands came around her waist, adoring the heat of her through her night rail. "Tell me how to stop it," he said . . . knowing the answer.

"Want me," she said.

"I do." He had wanted her since the moment he met her. Since before. "I want every inch of you . . . I want your mind and body and soul." He hesitated, the words an ache in the room. "I have never wanted anything like you."

Her fingers slid into his hair, tangling in the strands. "Touch me."

He couldn't deny her. He couldn't resist looking back.

One glance. One night.

It was all he could have. It was more than he had ever deserved.

One night, and he'd leave her to her perfect, ideal world.

One night, and he would return to his Hell.

"I won't ruin your life, Pippa. I won't let you be destroyed."

She pressed her lips to his, her soft skin making him mad, and whispered so quietly he almost didn't hear it. "I love you."

The words rocketed through him, and he couldn't stop himself from lifting her into his arms and giving them both what they wanted. What would change everything and nothing at the same time. He lifted her against him, adoring the way she followed his lead, pressing herself to him, running her mouth across his jaw, setting him on fire.

She shouldn't love him.

He wasn't worth it.

Wasn't worth *her*.

"You are a remarkable man," she said, lips at his ear. "I cannot help it."

One night would destroy him.

But there was no resisting her. Her brilliant mind. Her beautiful face.

There never had been.

Chapter Sixteen

He hadn't touched a woman in six years. Had resisted them . . . until her.

Until now.

Until this moment, when he lifted her from her feet and carried her to the bed where she'd slept for her entire life, and lay her down, following her down with his heady, heavy weight, pinning her beneath him with long limbs and corded strength and the promise of a pleasure she had never known.

Eight days prior, she'd stood in his office and asked him to teach her about ruination; here, finally, was the lesson for which she had not known she'd asked. The one for which she was utterly, completely desperate.

He kissed her, entirely different than the one that shattered her thought and breath earlier in the evening, but equally devastating. This one was slow and lavish, a claiming of lips and tongue that had her clinging to him, instantly addicted to the pleasure that only he could give.

She sighed her satisfaction, and he captured the sound with another long, lush mating of lips and tongues before lifting his head and meeting her gaze in the candlelight. "You are the most incredible woman I've ever known," he whispered. "You make me want to teach you every wicked, depraved thing I've ever done . . . ever dreamed."

The words were pleasure and heat—threading through her fast and furious until she had to close her eyes at the sensation. He brushed his lips across one of her cheeks, leaning down to her ear. "Would you like that?"

She sighed her agreement, and said, "The room is spinning."

His lips curved at her earlobe. "I thought I was the only one who noticed."

She turned to face him. "What causes it?"

"My little scientist . . . if you have time to wonder about that, I am not doing my job well enough."

And then she didn't care if the room spun because the globe was off its axis, because his lips were on hers, and his hands were stroking up her legs, carrying the linen of her nightgown with them, and she wanted nothing more than to touch him in every place she could.

One long hand slid beneath the night rail, palming her bottom as he lifted his weight from her, before stroking fingers curved along her hip and urged her thighs apart.

When he settled between them, his hard heat pressing against her pulsing core, she thought she might die of the pleasure. She writhed against him, desperate to be closer to him, thinking of nothing but touching him, getting as close to him as she could.

He tore his lips from hers, gasping her name. Rocking against her once, twice, sending thick arcs of pleasure through her. He stilled above her, and she opened her eyes, instantly drawn to his beautiful grey gaze. He pressed his forehead to hers. "Shh, darling. I shall give you everything you wish . . . but you must be quiet . . . if your father hears . . . you shall be ruined."

"I don't care," she whispered, rocking up against him again. And it was true. Ruination was worth it. She would be free of Castleton and could spend the rest of her life here, with Cross. In his den of sin. In his arms. Anywhere he liked.

He would never allow it.

The practical little voice whispered through her, and she pushed it away. Anything was possible now, tonight, with him. Tomorrow, she would face the rest of her life. But tonight . . . tonight was hers. Tonight was *theirs*.

Tonight, there was no room for practical.

"Show me everything. Everything that you know. Everything that you like. Everything that you desire."

He closed his eyes, a wash of something that could have been pleasure or pain chasing over his face, and she pushed herself up on her elbows, pressing against him, loving the feel of her breasts against his warm chest, loving the way her thighs cradled his lean hips and the heavy, hard, thickness of him was seated against the part of her that ached so much for him.

She rocked against him there, testing the way they fit, and he hissed at the movement, his eyes opening to narrow slits, grey gleaming pewter in the candlelight. "You will pay for that."

She smiled. "You cannot fault me for experimentation."

He laughed softly. "I cannot. After all, without that particular penchant, I would not have you here. Now." He kissed her again, quick and intense. When they were both gasping for breath, he lifted his head again, and said, "How else can I help you with your research, my lady?"

She took a long moment, her gaze running over his beautiful face. *Stay with me,* she wanted to say. *Let me stay with you.*

But she knew better. Instead, she lifted her hands to his chest, pushing the lapels of his coat to the side and pressing her palms flat against his waistcoat. "I believe my research would be well served if you were nude."

He raised a ginger brow and did not move. "Do you?"

She raised a brow in retort, and he smirked, rolling off her and shucking his coat, waistcoat, and shirt before returning to the bed. "Does this help?"

"In point of fact, good sir," she said, letting one hand fall to the smooth skin of his torso, loving the way he stiffened at the touch, "it does. But you are not nude."

He pressed a kiss to her neck, letting his teeth scrape along delicate skin until she shivered and sighed. "Neither are you."

"You never indicated a wish for me to be."

He lifted his head and met her gaze. "Make no mistake, my lady. I wish you nude every moment of every day."

Her eyes went wide. "That would make teas and balls awkward."

His white teeth flashed, and she loved him more with the wicked smile. "No teas. No balls. Only this."

His hand rose to punctuate the sentiment, carrying the linen of her night rail with it, sending it sailing across the room, landing on Trotula, who gave a startled snort. They both looked to the hound, and Pippa laughed. "Perhaps I should send her away?"

He met her gaze, grey eyes filled with amusement, his smile sending a thread of pleasure through her as pure and unbridled as any before. "Perhaps that would be best."

Distracted by her task, she led the dog to the door, opening it just enough to shoo the beast through it. Closing the door, she turned back to him, taking in the long, muscled length of him on the bed, staring at her.

Waiting for her.

Perfection.

He was perfect, and she was bare before him, bathed in candlelight. She was instantly embarrassed—somehow more embarrassed than she had been that night in his office, when she'd touched herself under his careful guidance. At least then she'd been wearing a corset. Stockings.

Tonight, she wore nothing. She was all flaws, each one highlighted by his perfection. He watched her for a long moment before extending one muscled arm, palm up, an irresistible invitation.

She went to him without hesitation, and he rolled to his back, pulling her over his lovely, lean chest, staring up at her intently.

She covered her breasts in a wave of nerves and trepidation. "When you look at me like that . . . it's too much."

He did not look away. "How do I look at you?"

"I don't know what it is . . . but I feel as though you can see into me. As though, if you could, you would consume me."

"It's want, love. Desire like nothing I've never experienced. I'm fairly shaking with it. Come here." The demand was impossible to resist, carrying with it the promise of pleasure beyond her dreams. She went.

When she was close enough to touch, he lifted one hand, stroking his fingers along hers where they hid her breasts from view. "I tremble with need for you, Pippa. Please, love, let me see you."

The request was raw and wretched, and she couldn't deny him, slowly moving her hands to settle them on his chest, fingers splayed wide across the crisp auburn hair that dusted his skin. She was distracted by that hair, the play of it over muscle—the way it narrowed to a lovely dark line across his flat stomach.

He lay still as she touched him, his muscles firm and perfect. "You're so beautiful," she whispered, fingers stroking down his arms to his wrists.

His gaze narrowed on her. "I am happy you approve, my lady."

She smiled. "Oh I do, my lord. You are a remarkable specimen." White teeth flashed again as she gained her courage, retracing her touch, over his forearms, marveling in the feel of him, reciting from memory, "*flexor digitorum superficialis, flexor capri radialis . . .*" along his upper arms, "*biceps brachii, tricipitis brachii . . .*" over his shoulders, loving the way the muscles tensed and flexed beneath her touch, "*deltoideus . . .*" and down his chest, "*subscapularis . . . pectoralis major . . .*"

She stilled, brushing her fingers over the curve of that muscle, the landscape of him . . . the valleys of his body. He sucked in a breath as her fingers ran over the flat discs of his nipples, arching up to her touch, and she stilled, reveling in her power. He enjoyed her touch. He wanted it. She repeated the stroke, this time with her thumbs.

He hissed his pleasure, one wide hand falling to the inside of her knee, sending a river of heat through her. "Don't stop now, love. This is the most effective seduction I've ever experienced." He traced along the top of her knee. "Tell me . . . what is this?"

She took a deep breath. "The *vastus medialis.*"

"Mmm." Fingers moved, higher. "And here?"

She shivered. "*Rectus femoris.*"

They slid to inside her thigh. "Clever girl . . . and here?"

"*Adductor longus . . .*"

And higher.

"*Gracilis . . .*"

She moved, breathless, spreading her legs to afford him better access, and he rewarded her, moving higher, barely stroking. "And here, love? What's this?"

She shook her head, desperate for more. Struggled with words. "That's not a muscle."

He increased the touch, barely. Enough to drive her utterly mad. "No?"

"No." She sighed.

The touch moved away, leaving an ache in its wake. "I see."

She grabbed his hand in one hand. "Don't stop."

He laughed, the sound low and wicked, and levered himself up, taking her mouth in one of those long, maddening kisses, sucking and licking and claiming until she had lost herself in him . . . against him. And only then, when she was pressed against him once more, panting and nearly wild with heavy, tingling desire, did he give her the touch she craved.

He stroked against her pulsing flesh, soft, then firm, swirling and stroking and giving her precisely what she wanted. She gasped against his lips. "Jasper," and he rewarded the soft cry, his thumb working a tight circle at the place where pleasure pooled.

It was coming again, that secret, sinful ecstasy that he'd showed her before . . . and she wanted it in his arms, against his warmth. With him.

With him.

"No." She clasped his hand, staying his movements. "No . . . not without you."

His gaze softened on her. "Lovely Pippa . . . I want you more than you can ever know . . . but I can't take you. I can't ruin you. I won't."

Frustration flared at the words. "I don't care. I want it."

He shook his head, his hand in that dark, devastating place. "You won't want it. Not tomorrow. Not when you realize what you've done."

She levered herself over him again, pressing a soft kiss to the high curve of his chest, adoring the feel of his groan beneath the caress. "I won't regret it. I want it," she whispered to the hair there. "If we cannot have . . ." *each other.* She did not say it. "I want *tonight*." She lifted her head, aching with desire and need and the worst kind of love. "Please . . ." she begged him, her hands slipping down that trail of hair to the waist of his trousers. "Please, Jasper."

He closed his eyes, the corded muscles in his neck stretching and tensing. "Pippa. I am trying to do right. To be honorable."

The words came on a wave of understanding. He had once accused her of living in black and white, of thinking that everything was truth or lie. But in this moment, she understood grey. She saw that his right was so very wrong. That his honor would bring no comfort to either of them.

Tomorrow, he could have honor.

Tomorrow, everything could return to right and wrong. Up and down. Truth and lie.

But tonight, everything was different.

She leaned down, pressing her bare breasts to his bare chest, taking his lips in a long kiss—one she'd learned from him—refusing to let him pull away. Refusing to release him to the specter of his honor, she said, "*This* is right, Jasper. One night with you. My first night . . . my only night. Please."

His hand came to her breast, and she sensed the conflict raging in him—loved him all the more for it. "You will regret it. You and your distaste for dishonesty."

She wouldn't. She knew it with unwavering certainty. "I will never regret this. I will never regret you." It was only then that it occurred to her that it was true. That for the rest of her life, married to Castleton or ruined spinster, this night would be the greatest of her life. This moment would be one she savored forever.

And she would not let it go.

"It's your first night, as well . . . your first night in six years." His eyes darkened, and she saw the promise of pleasure in them. The way it tempted him. "Let it be me, Jasper. Let it be mine. Please."

His thumb moved, stroking over the tip of her breast, sending a thread of pleasure through her, straight to the place where his hand lay—an unbearable temptation. She gasped, and he kissed her once, thoroughly, before pulling away. "I have tried to resist you from the beginning. I have failed each time."

"Don't succeed now." She whispered the plea. "I couldn't bear it."

"I never had a chance," he replied, turning her in his arms, spreading her thighs wide and pulling her over him until she straddled his waist, her bare bottom pressed against the hard evidence of his arousal beneath his low-slung trousers. He reached up with one strong hand . . . one of those hands she'd loved for what seemed like an eternity . . . and pulled her down, ravishing her with his kiss—long and lush, making her ache everywhere—her breasts, her thighs, that soft place between them.

She rocked against him, and he tore his mouth from hers with a hiss, throwing his head back to reveal the long cords of his neck, straining with pleasure. When he returned his gaze to hers, it was heavy with pleasure. "I am going to ruin you, Pippa. I shall show you pleasure you've never known, the kind you've never dreamed. Over and over and over until you beg me never to stop."

The words rioted through the dark, deep parts of her . . . the ones that ached for him. "I am already there," she said. "Don't stop."

He smiled, his hands coming to her breasts, rolling their tips between his fingers until they were hard and aching. "I wouldn't dream of it." He pulled her to his mouth, taking her with lips and tongue and teeth until she was beside herself with sensation.

The human body was a glorious thing indeed. "Jasper . . ." she whispered, fascination and pleasure and desire packed into his name, and he released her from his grasp with one long, lovely suck, replacing his mouth with one finger, circling the straining tip with torturous slowness.

"You get so hard here . . . aching for me. For my mouth."

Two could play this game. She rocked against him. "You, too, get hard, my lord."

He pressed up against her once, twice, until she sighed her pleasure. "You make me hard, my little scientist."

She could not resist. "I should like to inspect that fascinating occurrence, if I might."

He took her hands in his, moving them to the fall of his trousers. "Far be it from me to impede your research."

Her fingers played over the hard ridge of him, and she found herself quite desperate to see him. To feel him. To be with him in every way she could. But the protocol of this particular situation escaped her. Tracing one button, she met his wild eyes. "May I . . . ?"

He exhaled on a laugh, "I wish you would."

And she did, unbuttoning his trousers as quickly as she could—ever too slowly—revealing him, hard and long and— "Oh, my," she whispered, unable to stop herself from spreading the fabric and reaching for him, stroking the long, firm length of him until he groaned softly and she paused, uncertain, looking up at him. "Is it . . ."

"It's incredible," he whispered, his hands joining hers, showing her how to touch him. She watched the play of fingers on flesh, loving the soft steel of him. "The first time I met you . . . in my office . . ." he panted the words as she fisted the length of him. "I wanted your fingers on me. I couldn't stop looking at them. I was obsessed with them."

She met his gaze, reading the desire in his eyes. "They're crooked."

He kissed her, wild and wicked. "They're perfect. I've never felt anything so close to heaven." One of his hands moved, settling at the core of her, fingers sliding deep with shocking ease. "Except this." His thumb moved, finding that wonderful spot. "This is closer to Heaven." Circling over and over, again and again. "This might *be* Heaven."

She lifted to afford him greater access, to allow his fingers to stroke deep, and she agreed, her breath coming faster, pleasure rocketing through her on wave after wave of sensation until she lost her strength, and her hands fell away from him, bracing against his chest as she gave herself up to it.

"You're so beautiful," he told her, "so soft and slick and utterly perfect."

She couldn't stop the cries he pulled from her, the movements of her hips, the way she pressed against him, begging him for the pleasure he'd shown her before . . . the pleasure he'd taught her to find and claim. He slid a second finger into the core of her, and she arched back, adoring the sensation.

"So tight. So wet," he said, the wicked words making her

more wanton, more desperate. "I want to be inside you when you come."

And when she heard the words, the wicked, strange vocabulary she'd never before heard, she realized she wanted it, too. Looking down at him, she said, "Please . . ."

His eyes narrowed to slits. "Please, what, love?"

She should have been embarrassed, but she wanted him too much. "Please . . . take me."

He swore, harsh and soft. "I cannot wait another moment."

She thought he would roll her beneath him and made to move off him, to accommodate the change in position, but he stayed the movement, lifting her above him. Confused, she met his eyes. "Shouldn't we be—"

"No."

She might be inexperienced, but she knew the mechanics of the act. She placed her hands flat on his chest, feeling his heartbeat rioting beneath the touch. "Are you sure? I've never read anything about—that is, as I understand it, I should be beneath—"

"Which one of us has done this before?" Fingers stroked deep, underscoring his skill, and she sighed, bones turning to jelly at the long, lush movement.

When it ceased, leaving her empty and wanting, logic returned. "Well, it's been a bit of time for you," she pointed out.

He huffed a little laugh, the sound soft and strained and wonderful. "Trust me, my brilliant lady." He rocked his hips—the tip of him easing into her, sending a thread of nearly unbearable pleasure through her. "I recall the basics."

And then he slid into her with slow, thorough control, and she thought she might die from the hard heat of him, from the feel of him stretching and filling her, the sensation part pain, part strangeness, and, somehow, all pleasure. Her eyes went wide as he allowed her to sink to the hilt of him, and he froze, staring up at her, worry in his gaze. His hands flew to her hips. "Pippa? Does it hurt, love? Shall we stop?"

She would kill him if he stopped. This was the most astounding thing she'd ever experienced. All the fear and questions and concerns she'd had about this act, this moment . . . they were unfounded. She understood it now, the sighs and blushes and knowing smiles she'd seen in her sisters, in women across London. And she wanted it all . . . every bit of it. "Don't you dare stop," she whispered. "It is remarkable."

She lifted, testing the feel of him inside her, and he let out a harsh, broken curse. "It is, isn't it?" he agreed, adding, "You're remarkable." His hands guided her, lifting her, letting her slide up and back along his hard, hot length. "God, Pippa . . . it feels . . . you feel . . ." He lifted her again, and they both groaned as she slid back to the hilt, the pain gone now, chased away by untenable pleasure. "Is this all right, love?"

She loved him all over again for checking on her comfort, on her pleasure. She lifted herself, experimenting, repeating the movement on her own, her hands settling to his chest as she rode him. "Yes . . . it's perfect," she said with reverence. "It's glorious." She rocked against him, meeting his eyes before his attention slid down her body, his hands and eyes following the movements she couldn't help but make.

He guided her, whispering as she found her stride, "That's it, love . . . do nothing that doesn't feel right. That doesn't make you ache and want and need. Take your pleasure, gorgeous girl . . ." The whispered encouragement was punctuated by the hot stroke of his hands over her body—exploring the curves of her breasts and belly, the soft secrets of her thighs and that place between them where he was changing everything. Where *she* was changing everything. Where he had relinquished power and control and given her the chance to find her own pleasure.

He was devastatingly seductive in the way he talked to her, in the way he watched her, eyes narrow, hands stroking in time to her rhythm—a rhythm that quickly brought them both to the edge. She couldn't stop the words from coming again, even as she knew she shouldn't speak them. "I love you," she whispered, looking down at him, feeling euphoric and royal and like she'd never felt before.

Feeling like she was finally, finally correct.

Even as she did the least correct thing she'd ever done in her life.

He was moving beneath her then, plunging up as she came down around him, loving the feel of him against her, beneath her, inside her . . . rocking hard and fast against him as he returned his fingers to that place between her thighs, where he seemed to know just how to touch her, how to claim her, how to destroy her. His thumb moved in quick, firm circles as she chased her pleasure—and his. "That's it, love . . . take it for yourself . . . take it for me."

"I want it," she said, the honest desire hot and unbridled. "I want it for you."

"I know." He leaned up, sucked the peak of one breast into his mouth, worrying it with his teeth, and the sensation was all she could take—surprise and passion crashed over her, and she fell apart in his arms, her body trembling with the intensity of the moment. She put her hands to his shoulders, her eyes locked with his, blue against grey.

"I love you," she said, the words tumbling out of her again.

The confession seemed to unlock the last vestige of his control—he clasped her hips to his, thrusting and arcing against her, taking her mind and body once more in a storm of passion. "Pippa," he cried out, and the sound of her name hot and ragged on his lips was enough to send her over the edge once more, instantly, headfirst into an ocean of pleasure. He was there with her this time, strong and sure.

Perfection.

She fell to his chest, and he wrapped his arms around her, holding her close. "Pippa," he whispered at her temple, his heart beating rapidly beneath her ear. "Philippa."

The reverence in his tone made her ache, and she felt him pull away from her even as he remained inside her, closer than anyone had ever been. More important than anyone had ever been.

She loved him.

And he was to marry another.

Because of her.

She couldn't allow it. There had to be a better way. A solution that made them both happy. She closed her eyes, loving the feel of his warm chest against her cheek, and for one, fleeting moment, she imagined what it would be like to experience happiness with him. To be his wife. His woman. His partner.

His love.

It was no longer a myth, that mysterious emotion—no longer in doubt. It was real, and it held a power that Pippa had never imagined. One she could not deny.

He was whispering at her hairline, the words more breath than sound. "You are so remarkable. I could lie here forever, with you in my arms, the rest of the world distant. I ache for you, love . . . even now. I imagine I will ache for you forever."

She lifted her head, meeting his pewter gaze. "You don't have to."

He looked away. "I do. You're my great work, Pippa. You're the one I can save. I can ensure your happiness. And I shall. And it shall be enough."

She hated the words. "Enough for whom?"

Something flashed in his eyes. Pain? Regret? "Enough for us both."

It wouldn't be, though. Not for her. She knew that without question. "No," she whispered. "No it shan't."

He stroked one hand down her bare back, sending a shiver of awareness through her. "It shall have to be."

"You don't have to marry her," she said, softly, hearing the plea in the words. Loathing it.

"But I do, lovely," he said, the words soft and firm. "You'll be destroyed if I don't. And I won't have that."

"I don't care. You could marry me. If I am able to choose the earl whom I marry, then—"

"No." He tried to cut her off. She pressed on.

"—I choose you," she said, her voice breaking on the words.

He held her close, kissing at her temple, whispering her name again before saying, "No you don't. You don't choose me."

Except she did. "Why not?"

"Because you choose Castleton."

It was somehow truth and lie, all at once. "Just as you choose Knight's daughter?"

Even as you lie here with me?

His hands stilled on her skin. "Yes."

"But you don't know her."

"No."

"You don't love her."

"No."

Do you love me?

She couldn't ask him. Couldn't bear the answer.

But he seemed to hear the question anyway, hand coming to her jaw, lifting her to meet his gaze . . . his lips.

Yes, she imagined he meant.

He rolled her to her back on the bed, keeping them joined as he settled between her thighs and made love to her mind and soul and body with everything he had, moving in her with quiet certainty, holding her gaze with undeniable intensity. Kissing the swell of her breasts and the column of her neck and worrying the soft lobe of one ear, whispering her name in a long, lovely litany.

There was nothing brute about this. Nothing beastly.

Instead, it was slow and seductive and he moved for what seemed like hours, days, an eternity, learning her, touching and exploring, kissing and stroking. And as pleasure washed over her in lush waves, rocketing through her until she could no longer hold it, he captured her cries with his lips, finding his own release, deep and thorough and magnificent before speaking again, whispering her name again and again, until she no longer heard the word and instead heard only the meaning.

The farewell.

They lay together for long minutes, until their breath was steady again, and the world returned, unable to be refused or ignored, coming with the dawn in great red streaks across the black sky beyond the window.

He pressed a kiss to her hair. "You should sleep."

She turned away from time and its march, curling into his heat. "I don't want to sleep. I don't want it to end. I don't want you to go. Ever."

He did not reply, instead wrapping her tight in his arms, holding her until she could no longer feel the place where she ended and he began, where he exhaled and she inhaled.

"I don't want to sleep," she repeated, the threat of slumber all around her. "Don't let me go to sleep. One night isn't enough."

"Shh, love," he said, stroking one wide hand down her back. "I'm here. I'll keep you safe."

Tell me you love me, she willed silently, knowing he wouldn't, but desperately wishing for it anyway.

Wishing that, even if she couldn't have him, she might have his heart.

Have his heart. As though he could pluck the organ from inside his chest and hand it to her for safekeeping.

Of course, he couldn't.

Even if it felt as though she'd done that very thing herself.

Even as she knew it wasn't safe with him.

It couldn't be.

He waited a long while before he spoke again, until she was asleep. "One night is all there is."

When she woke, he was gone.

Chapter Seventeen

There are times for experiments that make for blinding, unexpected outcomes, and there are times for those that are directed by the hand of the scientist.

~~Cross Jasper~~ A great man once told me that there is no such thing as chance. Having come around to his way of thinking, I find that I am no longer willing to leave my work to chance.

Nor my life.

The Scientific Journal of Lady Philippa Marbury
April 2, 1831; three days prior to her wedding

Pippa and Trotula walked the mile to Castleton's handsome town house on Berkeley Square two days later, as though it were an entirely ordinary occurrence for a woman to arrive on the steps of her fiancé's home with none but a dog as a chaperone.

She ignored the curious glances cast in her direction outside the house just as she ignored the surprise on the butler's face when he opened the door and Trotula rushed into the foyer, uninvited, even as Pippa announced herself. Within moments, she and the hound were ensconced in a lovely yellow receiving room.

Moving to the windows, Pippa looked out over the square, considering the proper façades surrounding the perfectly landscaped green, and imagining her life here as the Countess of Castleton. Every one of the houses was occupied by one of the most important members of the aristocracy— Lady Jersey lived next door, for heaven's sake.

Pippa couldn't imagine the patroness of Almack's finding time or inclination to either visit her new neighbor or support Pippa's odd interests. There was no room for anatomy or horticulture in this massive, manicured home.

Viscountess Tottenham rode by, proud as ever, head high from the thrill of being the mother of one of the most powerful men in Britain, future prime minister who was three days from marrying Olivia, the favorite of the Marbury daughters.

It occurred to Pippa that this room, bright and filled with lavish furnishings, on the most extravagant square in London, was the ideal home for Olivia, and that was lucky, as her sister would soon live this life. Happily.

But there was nothing about this place that made it the ideal home for Pippa.

Nothing about its master that made him the ideal husband for Pippa.

Nothing at all to recommend her to this place.

There was no Cross here.

No, Cross appeared to live in a cluttered office on the main floor of a gaming hell, surrounded by papers and strange turmoil, globes and abacuses and threatening oil paintings and more books than she'd ever known one man to have in a single room. There was barely room to move in Cross's quarters, and still she somehow felt more comfortable there than here . . .

She'd happily live there with him.

The dog sat and sighed, drawing Pippa's attention. She stroked behind the hound's ear and received a gentle wag for her troubles.

She imagined Trotula would live there with him, too.

Except they were not invited.

He'd disappeared from her bed on the night of Pandemonium, after claiming her body and soul and ensuring that she loved him quite desperately. For two days, she'd waited for him to return; for two nights, she'd lain in bed, starting at every noise, sure he'd scale the house once more and come to her. Sure he wouldn't leave her.

Sure he'd change his mind.

He hadn't.

Instead, he'd left her to think on her own future. Her own choices. Her own heart.

He'd left her to come to the clear, undeniable realization that she was not the one who required saving.

"Two lovely ladies!" Castleton's happy utterance interrupted Pippa's thoughts, and she turned toward her handsome, smiling fiancé as Trotula hurried to him, low to the ground, eager for stroking.

It was difficult to spend any time at all with Castleton without smiling oneself. He was a kind man, and good. Fairly handsome, very wealthy, and titled. An aristocratic mother's dream. Indeed, there were few things more for which a young woman could ask.

Except for love.

And suddenly, that strange, elusive, indefinable word meant everything. So much more than all the rest.

How had she become such a ninny? She, who had never believed in the emotion . . . who had always thought that the ethereal was less valuable, less *real* than the factual . . . who had always ignored the sentiment—how was it that she stood here, now, in the receiving room of what was to have been her future home, with the man who was to have been her future husband, thinking of love?

Cross had changed her.

Without even trying.

"My lord," she said, making her way across the room to greet him herself. "I am sorry to come without notice."

He looked up at her from where he was crouched with Trotula. "No need for notice," he said. "After all, in less than a week, it will be your home, and I won't have any notice at all!" He paused. "Though, I suppose this is notice . . . betrothal!"

There it was, her cue.

She had considered any number of ways to begin this particular conversation. The gentle, the diplomatic, the evasive. But as she was Philippa Marbury, she settled for the honest.

"My lord, I cannot marry you."

His hands did not stop as they worked their way through Trotula's fur, and for a moment, she thought he might not have heard her. After several long seconds, he stood, and rocked back on his heels, putting his hands in the pockets of his waistcoat.

They stood like that for what seemed like an age, Pippa refusing to hide from him, this kind man who had offered for her even when he could have had better. More normal. This good man who had courted her even when she was the oddest woman in London. "I'm sorry," she added.

"You do not think we make a good match," he said.

"I think we would have made a very good match," she replied. "But everything has gone pear-shaped."

His brows rose. "Pear-shaped?"

She took a deep breath. "I thought I could . . ." She paused. "I thought I would . . ."

I thought I could simply research marriage. Investigate pleasure. I thought I would not suffer the repercussions.

"Do you require additional time? To consider it? We needn't have the wedding so soon."

She'd had more than a year. She'd considered Castleton from every angle. She'd planned her life with him. She'd been ready for it. And in one week . . . one day . . . one minute, it seemed . . . everything had changed.

She shook her head. "I do not require additional time."

He nodded. "I understand."

She was willing to wager that he didn't understand at all.

He continued. "I think we could learn to love each other. I think I could learn to love you."

It was a kind thing to say. He was a good man.

Before, it had been enough. He had been enough. More than. He'd been willing to be her partner, to let her live the life she desired. To give her marriage. Children. Security. All the things a young woman in 1831 required.

Before.

Before she'd decided that she required more.

She met his warm brown gaze. "Unfortunately, I cannot learn to love you." His eyes widened, and she realized that she had hurt him with her careless words. She rushed to repair it. "No . . . I don't mean it in such a way. It's that . . ."

She did not know what to say. How to repair it.

She stopped, hating the feeling, the way the entire male of the species seemed to make her feel in recent days.

And she told the truth. Again. "I'm sorry, my lord," and she was. "But the vows . . . I can't speak them. Not to you."

His brows rose. "The vows?"

The silly ceremony. The one that had started it all. "Obedience and servitude, honor, sickness, and health . . . all that, I feel I could do."

Understanding flared in his brown eyes. "I'm amenable to all those." A small smile played across his lips. "I gather it is the love bit that is the problem?"

"Forsaking all others," she said. She could not forsake all others. She wasn't sure she could ever forsake the only other who mattered. She took a deep breath around the tightness in her chest. "My lord, I am afraid that I have fallen in love—quite accidentally and not at all happily. With another."

His face softened. "I see," he said. "Well, that does change things."

"It does," she agreed before she changed her mind. "Except, it doesn't, really. He . . ." She paused. *He is marrying another.* ". . . The feeling is not reciprocated."

Castleton's brow furrowed. "How is that possible?"

"You should not be so quick to defend me, you know. After all, I just ended our engagement. You're required to dislike me immensely now."

"But I don't dislike you. And I shan't. Such is the risk we take in this modern world." He paused, stroking Trotula, who leaned against his leg. "If only marriage were still arranged at birth."

She smiled. "We mourn the past."

"I would have liked a medieval keep," he said happily, "and I think you would have made an excellent lady of the castle. Surrounded by hounds. Riding out with a sword on your belt."

She laughed at the ridiculous image. "Thank you, my lord, though I wonder if the best ladies of the castle were as blind as I."

He waved to a nearby settee. "Would you like to sit? Shall I have something brought from the kitchens?" He paused, obviously considering what one offered one's ex-fiancée in such a situation. "Tea? Lemonade?"

She sat. "No, thank you."

He looked across the room to a crystal decanter. "Scotch?"

She followed his gaze. "I don't think ladies drink scotch before eleven o'clock."

"I shan't tell anyone." He hesitated. "In fact, I might join you."

"By all means, my lord . . . I wouldn't dream of preventing you from having a proper drink."

He did, pouring a finger of amber liquid into a glass and coming to sit beside her. "Our mothers will be beside themselves when they hear."

She nodded, realizing that this was the first time they'd conversed about anything serious. Anything other than dogs and weather and country estates. "Mine more than yours, I should think."

"You'll be ruined," he said.

She nodded. "I had considered that."

It had never mattered to her very much, reputation. For one who was often described as odd and strange, having little in common with others her age or gender, reputation never seemed worth much. It did not buy her friends, or invitations, or respect.

So now, it was not paramount.

"Lady Philippa," he began after a long moment of silence, "if you've . . . *er* . . . that is . . . if you have need of . . . *a-hem*."

She watched him carefully, noting his reddening face as he stumbled over the words. "My lord?" she asked after it seemed as though he might not say more.

He cleared his throat. Tried again. "If you are in a difficult spot," he blurted out, waving one hand in the general direction of her stomach.

Oh, dear. "I am not."

She supposed she might be, but that was a bridge she would cross at a later time if necessary. Without Castleton.

He looked immensely relieved. "I am happy to hear that." Then, after a moment during which they both resumed calm, he added, "I would marry you, anyway, you know."

She met his gaze, surprised. "You would?"

He nodded. "I would."

She couldn't stop herself. "Why?"

"Most people think I'm an idiot."

She did not pretend to misunderstand. "Most people are idiots themselves," she said, feeling suddenly very protective of this man who should have tossed her out of the house with glee but instead, offered her a drink and a chat.

He tilted his head. "Most people think you're odd."

She smiled. "On that, most people are right."

"You know, I used to think they were. You're brilliant and have a passion for animals and strange flowers, and you were always more interested in the crops that rotated on my estate than in the trappings of my town house. I'd never met a woman like you. But, even as I knew you were smarter than I, even as I knew that *you* knew that you were smarter than I . . . you never showed it. You've never given me any reason to believe you thought me simple. You always went out of your way to remind me of the things we had in common. We both prefer the country. We both enjoy animals." He shrugged one shoulder. "I was happy to think that you would one day be my wife."

"I don't think you simple," she said, wanting him to know that. Wanting him to understand that this mess she was making had nothing to do with him. He was not lacking. "I think you will make someone a very happy match."

"But not you," he said, simply.

She shook her head. "Not me."

There was a time when you might have. It was true. She'd been happy to live out her days in country idyll, talking of crop rotation and animal husbandry and consulting the men and women who lived on Castleton land.

There was a time when I would have been content with you.

"If you change your mind . . ." he said. "If you wake up on Sunday morning and wish for marriage . . . I shall be ready," he finished, so generous. So deserving of love.

She nodded once, seriously. "Thank you, my lord."

He cleared his throat. "What next?"

The question had rattled through her during every waking moment of every day since the morning Cross had left her, sleeping, in her bed after making it impossible for her to marry Castleton. After making it impossible to do anything but care for him . . . more than she'd ever cared for anyone. *What next?*

What happened now?

She'd approached the problem in the same way she'd forever approached every part of her life. She'd considered it from all angles, posited answers, hypothesized outcomes. And, eventually, come to a conclusion—the only one that had any chance of resulting in the outcome she desired. For which she ached.

So this morning, she'd risen early, dressed, and come to Berkeley Square. She'd knocked, met her fiancé—who seemed to be more intelligent than anyone in Britain gave him credit for—and broken her engagement.

And what came next would be the most important experiment of her life.

"I admit, I am happy that you asked." She took a deep breath, met Castleton's gaze, and answered his question. "You see, I require your assistance for what comes next."

Two hours later, Pippa and Trotula were waiting at the rear entrance to The Fallen Angel, for someone to open the door.

When no one responded to her several knocks on the great steel slab, Pippa grew impatient and moved to the entrance to the club kitchens. Knocking there produced a result—a red-faced boy who was at once elated to see a dog at the door and perplexed by the presence of the hound's mistress.

"Didier!" he called out, "'ere's a lady at the door! A real one! And a dog!"

"I am tired of the jokes you play on me, Henri," came a familiar booming voice from outside Pippa's view. "Now come back here before the béchamel is destroyed by your laziness."

"But Didier!" he called, not taking his gaze from Pippa. "*'Tis* a lady! The one who comes for Cross!"

Pippa's jaw dropped at the identification. How did this boy know about her meetings with Jasper? Before she could ask, the French cook had pushed the boy from view and faced Pippa with a wide smile. "Back for another of my sandwiches?"

Pippa smiled. "No one answered the rear door of the club."

Didier stepped back, letting Pippa into the sweltering kitchens. "That's because the doormen are all bothering me." She cast a skeptical glance at Trotula. "The hound may enter, but I won't have her near my food."

Pippa stepped inside, directing the dog to a corner and registering the stares from a motley collection of servants and workers gathered around the great table at the center of the Angel's kitchens. Uncertain and not a small amount uncomfortable, she gave a little curtsy, sending all their brows to the sky. "I am Lady Philippa Marbury."

The doorman she'd met the evening she'd come with Cross stood, hulking and overwhelming. "We know who you are."

She nodded. "Excellent. Then you won't mind telling His Grace that I am here." There was a pause, confusion flaring on several faces before she clarified. "I believe you call him Temple."

The boy who'd answered the door was the first to speak. "But yer Cross's lady," he said, as if that was all there was to say.

Cross's lady. The words warmed her.

Even if they weren't true.

"Today, I've need of Temple."

And Temple would help her get the rest.

*W*hen they arrived home that night, Pippa and Trotula had covered a wide swath of London, and both mistress and hound were exhausted.

Ignoring her mother's admonitions that *countesses did not leave the house with only their hounds to keep them com-*

pany, and that Pippa *would be devastated if she awoke on her wedding day with a cold*, and that *she simply must eat something*, she forwent the family meal and made her way to her bed, crawling between crisp linen sheets she fancied smelled of the man she'd thought of all day. All week. For what seemed like forever. She should have slept, but instead she played her plan over and over in her mind. The moving pieces, the variables—both fixed and unfixed—the process, the participants.

Stroking Trotula's head, Pippa lay in her bed, thinking of Jasper Arlesey, Earl Harlow. Of all the things she'd ever heard about this strange, elusive peer. She knew that he did not take his seat in Parliament. She knew that he did not frequent balls or dinners or even the theater. In fact, it seemed he did nothing that brought him into contact with society . . . nothing except running London's most exclusive gaming hell.

And she knew that he was being an utter cabbagehead, about to toss his life away in a mad belief that he was saving her.

But most importantly, she knew that he was wrong. It was not she who required saving.

It was he.

And she was just the woman to do it.

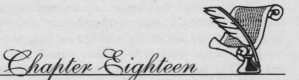

Chapter Eighteen

The time for observation is through.
It is now time for action.

The Scientific Journal of Lady Philippa Marbury
April 3, 1831; one day prior to her wedding

She was to be married tomorrow.

To another man.

And instead of being at Dolby House, in her bedchamber, in her arms—giving them both a final taste of mutual pleasure—he was here, in one of London's darkest corners, now lit in brilliant celebration of his own impending marriage.

Knight had not been able to resist glorying in paternal triumph. Cross was to marry Meghan Margaret Knight and gaming hell royalty would soon be born; if that did not call for a night of sin and debauchery, nothing would.

A group of men at a nearby hazard table cried out their excitement, as the roll turned in their favor, and Cross turned to watch as the little ivory dice were raked up and returned to the head of the field, where Viscount Densmore kissed the cubes and threw them down the table again. *Three. Four.*

The entire table groaned their disappointment at the loss,

and Cross took perverse pleasure in the sound. No one should be happy tonight if he could not be. No one should have pleasure if he could not take it.

It had been four days since he'd touched happiness— fleetingly. Four days since he'd brushed against pleasure, all soft skin and breathless words. Four days since he'd had Pippa in one perfect, devastating night. Four days that had stretched like an eternity, every moment taunting him, tempting him to go to her. To steal her away and keep her from scathing words and judging eyes.

He had twenty-five thousand acres in Devonshire where no one ever needed to see them, where she and Trotula could roam. He would build her a house for her scientific research. He'd give her everything she needed. Everything she desired. And he'd roam with them, he and their passel of children as, in his experience, rustication tended to facilitate breeding.

He'd do everything he could to keep her happy.

It wouldn't be enough.

It would never be enough. He would never be enough for her, just as he hadn't been enough for Baine or Lavinia. She deserved better.

A wicked ache settled in his chest at the thought.

Castleton wasn't better. He wouldn't challenge her. He wouldn't tempt her.

He wouldn't love her.

Nearby, Christopher Lowe leaned over at the roulette wheel and barked his triumph as the little white ball seated itself into a red square on the spinning surface.

Cross hissed his displeasure. Roulette was the worst kind of game—entirely chance, never worth the wager, even when resulting in a win. It was a game for idiots. He turned to watch the score of men patting Lowe on the back and placing their blunt on the table. "The wheel's hot now!" one called.

Cross turned away in irritation.

The whole world—every game designed to tempt and take—was designed for idiots.

"Cross."

He spun on Sally Tasser, standing several feet away. "I should kill you for what you did," he growled. "If you were a man, I would."

She'd sold him out to Knight, forced him into a marriage he didn't want. Into a life he would never have taken. In this world where they lived and breathed power and sin, pleasure and punishment, betrayal was always a possibility. Losses happened.

But Sally's actions had not simply punished him; they'd threatened Pippa.

And that, he would never forgive.

Fury raged as he advanced on the prostitute, unsettling her, pushing her back through the throngs of revelers, between card tables and dice fields until they were at the side of the room, dingier and less welcoming than the main floor of the Angel. "Tell me, what was my future worth to you? A few quid? A new gown? A string of paste? After all I've done for you? For your girls? And you repay me with this. By threatening the one thing I hold dear?"

She shook her head, brown eyes flashing. "It's so easy for you to judge me, isn't it?" she spat.

"You threatened *mine*," he thundered, wanting to put his fist through a wall. In six years, he had never felt so out of control. So unhinged. The idea of Pippa in danger made him shake with fear and anger and a half dozen terrifyingly powerful emotions.

What would he do when she was married?

Sally saved him from having to answer the question. "You with your perfect life and your piles of money and never having to get on your knees to earn your next meal and stay on them to thank some stranger for the coin . . . If you'd failed—"

"If I'd failed, I'd have kept you safe."

"Safe," she scoffed. "You'd have sent me off to the country to live out my days—an old mare put to pasture? That may be safe, but it's not satisfaction."

"Many think otherwise."

"Well, not me," she said. "If you'd failed, and Knight had discovered my role in your plans, he'd have pushed me out, and I'd be working the streets." She paused. "I've a good life, Cross, and I protected it. You would have done the same."

Except he hadn't. Protecting his life would have meant throwing Pippa to Knight and refusing his request. Refusing to take on Maggie.

But Pippa had come first.

She always would.

"If you think on it, I've done you a favor. You get yourself a wife. And an heir. You shan't regret it."

The wrong wife. The wrong heir.

"I shall regret every minute of it," he said.

"Cross—" Sally began. "I am sorry, you know. For the lady."

He stilled.

"Lady Philippa was kind to me. Kinder than any aristocratic female ever has been. And I knew the moment I told Knight about her that I'd regret it."

"You are not fit to speak her name." She was better than this place, and all of them combined.

"Likely not. But it's not your choice."

"It should be."

Sally gave a little smile. "Do not doubt for one moment that what's done was done for her. Not you."

Meaning Pippa would be happier without him—that Pippa deserved more than what he could give her.

Truth.

"Attention!" Knight's great, booming voice distracted them both, and they turned to find the man, scarlet-banded hat askew, high atop a hazard table at the center of the floor of the casino. "Attention!" he called again, banging his silver-tipped walking stick heavily on the worn baize, stopping the lively music and drunken chatter. "I've somethin' te say, ye disrespectful gits!"

Knight grinned as the room tittered its laughter, and Cross gritted his teeth, knowing what was to come.

"I'm still angry at most of ye for taking yer time at the Angel's tables fer that poncy party they call Pandemonium—drinkin' yer tea and eatin' yer cakes with a collection of nobs who don't know an ace from their arse. But I find myself in a forgivin' humor tonight, pets—in part because, well"—he turned his twinkling gaze to Cross—"at least one of those gents is about to be family!"

The announcement was met with a raucous, near-deafening cheer, as all heads turned toward Cross, who did not cheer. Did not smile. Did not move.

Knight raised a brow and reached out a hand to his future son-in-law. "Cross! Join me for a word or two!"

The cheer again, grating on every nerve, making Cross wish violence on every man here. He folded his arms across his chest and shook his head, unmoving, and Knight's gaze darkened. "Aww . . . he doesn't want to steal my roll! Don't worry, my boy. The *pips* . . ." He paused, letting the word fall between them. "They are in my favor these days!"

And with that single syllable, evocative of the woman who consumed his thoughts, Knight made it impossible for Cross to refuse the request. He moved across the room with deliberate calm, despite the desire to pull Knight from the table and tear him limb from limb, and climbed up to join the man who had outplayed him. Finally.

Knight clapped him on the back, and Cross spoke, sotto voce, "Tomorrow, she marries. And you lose that bit of control."

Knight spoke through wide, smiling teeth. "Nonsense. I can ruin her marriage and her children's reputation, with one well-placed word." He turned back to the room, a king speaking to his subjects. "And now, the beautiful lady who has captured his heart! The banns will be read tomorrow, and in three weeks' time, my girl will be his!"

Maggie was lifted up onto the table, and Cross had to give the young woman credit—no decent father would allow his daughter anywhere near this place. No man would allow a woman for whom he cared here. But this woman, clad in mauve and resignation, stood straight and still, without fidgeting, without blushing.

She looked to him, honesty in her gaze. "My lord." She curtsied, looking as graceful and proper as one could standing atop a hazard field.

He inclined his head, reminding himself that she was a pawn in this game. That it was Maggie who would lose the most. She would gain a title and wealth beyond imagining, but she would never have a husband who loved her.

Her husband would always love another.

"She's a helluva treat, Cross!" someone called from the crowd.

"I'd like to get my hands on those legs!" A man reached for her slipper, grazing the toe before she gasped and pulled away, pressing back against Cross.

He might not wish to marry her, but she didn't deserve this.

He pressed a boot down on the man's wrist, just hard enough to trap the hand to the table. "Touch her and lose it."

Knight laughed. "You see how he's already protectin' her? Can't keep his hands off her, that Cross! They'll make me handsome grandsons! I wager the Viscount Baine arrives before the year is out!"

The sound of Baine's name on Knight's lips sent a wave of heat through Cross. "I've twenty quid says he's already on the way!" came a booming retort from the crowd.

Laughter and excited cheers rose up from the floor of the hell, punctuated by a loud, "Kiss 'er!"

"Aye, give the girl a good one, Cross!"

Knight laughed. "I haven't any problem with it!"

"Of course you don't, you bastard," Cross hissed beneath the drunken cheers of agreement. "She's a future countess, and your daughter, and you want her ruined in a gaming hell?"

"She's my daughter and *your* future countess," Knight replied over the cries of agreement. "I think a kiss in a gaming hell is to be expected. And I'm nothing if not a fine host; she's not getting off this table until they get what they want."

Maggie's cheeks had turned red, and she peered up at Cross through sooty black lashes. "My lord," she whispered, "please. Let us have done with it, shall we?"

He took pity on the girl. "I'm sorry this must be here."

But Maggie pitied him as well. "I am sorry it is with me," she said, all sympathy.

She did not deserve him, either.

He huffed a little, humorless laugh. "It seems I am destined to disappoint women."

She did not reply, and he leaned down to kiss her, briefly, but the caress was enough to impress the crowd, who did not notice that it was devoid of emotion.

Lie. There was emotion. Guilt. Self-loathing. Betrayal. A dark, devastating sense of wrong. She was not Pippa. She was not his. She never would be.

Maggie would live in the shadow of his brilliant, bespectacled love, a prisoner of his desire to do what was right for one woman even as he destroyed the prospects of another.

Goddammit.

"And now"—Knight rapped his walking stick on the table once more, the blows returning Cross back to the present—"get back to losing money!"

Even that received a cheer on this night of nights, when whiskey flowed freely and the tables called, and the whole of Knight's membership celebrated their leader's great triumph.

Cross stood for a long moment on that table, waiting for Maggie and Knight to descend, looking over the casino floor as Knight's pockmarked second hand drew him away to the back office for some matter of business.

Cross was happy to be rid of his father-in-law, and took calm pleasure in the way the roulette wheel was already spinning, the cards already flying across the baize, dice already rolling down tables; Knight commanded a casino the way Wellington had commanded a battalion—there was money to be made, and it would be done with speed and efficiency.

It was the *vingt-et-un* table that caught his eye first, five seated across from the dealer, each with an ace or a face card up, the dealer staring at a two. The game went fast; not one man hit. On the flop, every player had twenty or higher.

A near mathematical impossibility.

The thought was chased away by a cheer to his left, where a hazard table celebrated a successful roll, the dice in mid-pass down the table toward the roller. Cross watched the next toss. *Six. Three.* "Nine again!" the croupier called.

His heart began to pound.

He came down from the table, distracted by the game, unable to keep himself from watching the next cast. *Six. Three.* "Huzzah!" those watching the game cried.

"What luck!" called the gamer in possession of the dice, turning to face his growing crowd, his face shielded from Cross. "I've never been so lucky!"

"Who is it?" a voice asked at his shoulder.

"If you can believe it," came the response, "it's Castleton."

"Lucky bastard!" Disbelief.

"Well, he's to marry tomorrow . . . so he deserves one night of bachelorhood to tide him over, don't you think?"

Castleton.

Married tomorrow.

For a moment, Cross forgot the thread of uncertainty that had drawn him to the game, distracted by the reminder that

Pippa was to marry tomorrow. This man, who stood at a hazard table.

Six. Three.

Winning.

Something was off.

He raised his head, scanning the crowd, his attention called to the door to the back rooms, where a great, hulking man towered above the rest of the room.

His brows knit together.

What in hell was Temple doing here?

"Two hundred and fifty quid on number twenty-three!" Christopher Lowe made an exorbitant bet at the roulette wheel to Cross's right, and Cross could not help but turn to watch as the ball rolled in the track, around and around until it landed in a red groove.

Twenty-three.

The entire table cheered; Lowe had risked a fortune, and won nearly nine thousand pounds.

Lowe, who had never won a single thing in his life.

"What did I say?" the young man crowed. "I'm lucky tonight, lads!"

There's no such thing as luck.

Something was off.

He pushed through the crowd, each person with whom he came into contact more and more elated with the breathlessness of winning, with the excitement of the flop of the ace, the roll of the hard six, the spin of the wheel, which seemed to be stuck on red . . . everyone ignoring him as he passed among their masses until they finally parted and he had a clear view of Temple, several yards away.

The massive partner of The Fallen Angel was not alone. At his side stood a reedy younger man in an evening suit that hung a touch too large on his shoulders. The man wore a cap pulled low over his brow, making it impossible for Cross to see his face . . . there was something familiar about the way he carried himself. Something unsettling.

It was only when the stranger turned to speak in the ear of one of Knight's girls, passing her a little pouch, that Cross saw the glint of gold at his temple.

Spectacles.

At *her* temple.

Philippa.

She turned to him, as though he'd said her name aloud, and smiled an enormous, brilliant smile—one that made his blood pound and his heart ache. How had he ever even imagined that she was a man? She looked scandalous and beautiful and absolutely devastating, and he was suddenly quite desperate to get to her. To touch her. To kiss her. To keep her safe.

Not that it made him want to murder her any less.

He reached for her instinctively, and Temple stepped in, placing enormous hands on Cross's chest, and said, "Not now. If you touch her, everyone will guess."

Cross didn't care. He wanted her safe. But Temple was as strong as he was right. After a long moment, he said, "I shall want my time in the ring with you for this."

Temple smirked. "With pleasure. But if she pulls it off, my guess is that you'll be thanking me for it."

Cross's brows snapped together. "Pulls it off?" He turned to Pippa. "What have you done?"

She smiled as though they were at tea. Or Ascot. Or walking in the park. Entirely calm, utterly sure of herself and her actions. "Don't you see, you silly man? I'm saving you."

The cheers from the gamers around them were impossible to ignore at that point, the thrill of winning was deafening. He didn't need to look to see what she'd done. "You fixed the tables?"

"Nonsense." Pippa grinned. "With what I know of Digger Knight, I would wager everything you have that these tables were already fixed. I *un*fixed them."

She was mad. And he loved it. His brows rose. "Everything *I* have?"

She shrugged. "I haven't very much, myself."

She was wrong, of course. She had more than she knew. More than he'd dreamed.

And if she asked, he'd let her wager with everything he owned.

God, he wanted her.

He looked around them, registering the flushed, excited faces of the gamers nearby, not one of them interested in the trio standing to the side. No one who was not playing was worth the attention. Not when so many were winning so much.

She was running the tables at one of the most successful casinos in London. He turned back to her. "How did you . . ."

She smiled. "You taught me about weighted dice, Jasper."

He warmed at the name. "I didn't teach you about stacked decks."

She feigned insult. "My lord, your lack of confidence in my intelligence wounds me. You think I could not work out the workings of deck stacking myself?"

He ignored the jest. Knight would kill them when he discovered this. "And roulette?"

She smiled. "Magnets have remarkable uses."

She was too smart for her own good. He turned to Temple. "You allowed this?"

Temple shrugged one shoulder. "The lady can be very . . . determined."

Lord knew that was true.

"She knew what she wanted," the enormous man added, "and we all wanted it as well."

"Temple was very gracious. As was Miss Tasser," Pippa added.

Cross's mind was spinning. *Miss Tasser.* Sally had helped.

Do not doubt for one moment that what's done was done for her. Not you.

This is what Sally had meant. The run on Knight's, not Cross's, engagement.

Pippa's insane plan.

But they hadn't considered everything. They hadn't considered what would happen when she was discovered. When Knight returned to the floor and understood what they'd done.

"You have to leave here. Before Knight discovers it and everything goes wild. Before he discovers *you*. You'll be destroyed, and everything I worked for will be—" He was growing panicked by the idea that she might be hurt. That Knight might react with wicked intent.

"I am not leaving." She shook her head. "I have to see this through to the end!"

"There is no end, Pippa." He reached for her again, desperate to touch her, and Temple stopped him once more. Cross stopped. Collected himself. "Dammit. Knight is the best in the business."

"Not better than you," she said.

"Yes, better than me," he corrected her. "There's nothing he cares about more than this place. Than its success. And all I care about—" He trailed off, knowing he shouldn't say it. Knowing he couldn't stop himself. "All I care about is you, you madwoman."

She smiled, her beautiful blue eyes softening behind her spectacles. "Don't you see, Jasper? You're all I care about as well."

He shouldn't like the words. Shouldn't ache for them. But he did, of course.

She moved toward him, and he would have opened his arms and taken her to bed then and there if Temple hadn't stepped in, looking anywhere but at them. "Can't you two have your private moments in private? Without me near?"

The words served as a reminder of where they were. Of the danger she was in. He turned to face the room, searching for Knight, finding him, fury in his gaze as he watched the floor, sensing with the keen understanding of a man who had done this for his entire life that something was wrong. That there was too much glee on the floor. Too much winning.

His gaze settled on Cross's over the crowd, and knowledge flared in the older man's eyes. He turned and gave instructions to his pit boss, who took off at a run—likely for fresh dice and decks—before Knight started toward them, determination in every step. Cross faced Pippa. "You must go," he said. "You cannot be caught. You're to marry tomorrow. I shall take care of this."

She shook her head. "Absolutely not. This is my plan—crafted for you. For Lavinia. To ensure that Knight can never do his damage again. I shall finish it."

Ire rose. "Pippa, this is bigger than anything you can imagine. You did not plan for an exit. Knight is not worried. He knows that he will restore the tables to working order tonight, and all these people will stay and gamble back their winnings. Gamers do not stop at the top of their streak."

She smiled. "You think I do not know that? Need I remind you that I learned about temptation from a very skilled teacher?"

Now was not the time to think of their lessons. He resisted the flash of skin and sighed at the words. "I think you could not have prepared for it. I think that, short of burning this place to the ground, there is no amount of coordinated planning that could convince five hundred gaming addicts to leave their winning tables." He turned back to Knight, registering the old man's movement. Closer. "And I think I'm through with this conversation. You will return home with Temple, and you will marry tomorrow, and you will live the life you deserve."

"I don't want it," she said.

"You don't have a choice," he replied. "This is the last thing I will give you. And it is the only thing I will ever ask of you."

She shook her head. "You don't know what you're asking!"

"I know exactly what I'm asking."

I'm asking you to walk away before I find I can no longer bear to be without you.

He feared it might be too late, as it was.

"Leave, Pippa." The words were a plea, coming on a wave of panic he did not care for. This woman had shattered his control, and he hated it. *Lie.* "I shall fix this."

She shook her head. "You once promised that when we wagered at my tables, we would play by my rules."

He wanted to shake her. "These are not your tables!"

She smiled. "But they are my rules, nonetheless." She turned to Temple. "Your Grace? Would you do the honors?"

Temple lifted a finger to his thrice-broken nose and brushed the tip. From a hazard table nearby, a loud, innocent voice piped up, "My word! That's a great deal of winnings!" Castleton. Stupid, simple Castleton was in on the plan . . . had they all gone mad?

Cross looked to Temple, who smirked and shrugged one shoulder. "The lady made the arrangements."

"The lady deserves a sound thrashing."

Pippa wasn't watching him. "You don't mean that."

He didn't, but that was beside the point.

Castleton was chattering again. "I hear that Knight doesn't usually keep much cash on hand, though. I hope he's enough to cash me out!"

There was a pause at the table as his words sunk in, then a mad dash for each man to collect his notes and winnings and rush to the cash cages. Within seconds, the shouts echoed through the room.

"Knight can't cover the wins!"

"Cash out now, before it's too late!"

"Don't be left with blank notes!"

"You'll lose everything if you don't hurry!"

And like that, the tables were empty . . . they were all headed to the cash cages, where two startled bankers hesitated, not knowing how to proceed.

She'd thought of an exit. He should have expected it, of course. Should have known that Philippa Marbury would wage war like she did everything else . . . brilliantly. Eyes wide, he looked first to Pippa, then to Temple, who smirked, folded his arms, and said nothing.

It was remarkable.

She'd done it.

She was remarkable.

Cross caught Knight's gaze, wide with shock before it slid to Pippa and narrowed in recognition, then fury.

But the club owner could not act on that anger . . . as he was too close to losing everything he'd built. He took to a tabletop once more, calling out affably, "Gents! Gents! This is Knight's! We ain't no haphazard organization! We're well able to pay our debts! Get back to the tables! Play some more!"

His big grin was sinfully tempting.

There was a pause as the sheep turned to their shepherd, and for one moment, Cross thought the desire to win would run the tables.

Until Castleton saved them all, the earl's clear, disarming voice rising above the crowd once more. "I'd just as soon have this money now, Knight . . . then I know you're good for it!"

And the press toward the cages began anew, men shouting and pushing until it was close to a riot.

Knight wouldn't be able to cover these winnings. They'd paupered him.

Pippa had paupered him.

Because she loved Cross.

Because she cared for his future.

His future, which was bleak indeed without her.

He could not linger on the thought, however, as they were jostled by a wall of gamers pressing toward the cages furiously, desperate for their money. Pippa was carried several feet by the wave of bodies. He reached for her, trying to catch her hand and pull her back, her fingers slipping through his as she fell, swallowed up by the furious crowd.

"Pippa!" he yelled, tossing himself into the fray, pulling men from the place where he had last seen her, tossing them aside until he found her, curled into a ball, hands around her head, a heavy boot connecting with her stomach.

He roared his anger, grasping her unwitting attacker by the collar and planting his fist in the man's face once, twice, before Temple caught up with him. "Let me have him," Temple said. "You see to your lady."

Your lady.

She was his.

Would ever be.

He turned the man over to Temple without a second glance, crouching to uncover Pippa's face, where one lens of her spectacles had been smashed and a wicked red streak had already bloomed high on one cheek. Suppressing his rage, he stroked his fingers carefully across the place where she'd clearly received a blow. "Can you move?"

She nodded, shaky, and he lifted her in his arms—not caring that he was revealing her as something more than a strange, thin man in an ill-fitting suit—protecting her.

She pressed her face to his neck. "My hat—"

It had been lost in the fray, and her blond hair was loose around her shoulders. "Too late for it now," he said, desperate for escape.

But there was nowhere to go. Everywhere he looked were angry throngs of gamblers, desperate for their winnings, frustration and greed and his and Temple's attacks turning them into a terrifying, raging horde.

Moving as quickly as he could, he crouched and pushed Pippa beneath the hazard table where Castleton had started it all, taking a boot to the ribs with a wince before climbing into the space with her, covering her with his body and wrapping his arms about her head to keep her from errant blows.

"Temple—" she said, struggling beneath him.

"Will be fine," he assured her, adoring the way that she cared for his friend. "He's a professional fighter—he shall love every minute of this. At least until I have a moment to tear him limb from limb for allowing you to carry out this utterly insane scheme." He stroked her hair back. "Let me look."

"It was not insane!" she protested, turning her wound toward him, one hand coming up to test the swelling at her eye. "Ow."

He ran his fingers over the red welt once more, hating the way she winced. "Gorgeous girl . . ." he whispered, removing her glasses and pressing a kiss to her temple, the corner of her lips, the soft skin at the side of her neck. She was safe. He let out a ragged breath, and said, "I should thrash you."

"Why me?" she said, eyes wide.

He shot a look at thundering boots beyond the table. "You started a riot."

"Not on purpose," she defended, turning to look. "I hypothesized that they would *leave*, not stampede."

At another time, when he was less worried for her safety, he would have smiled at the words. Not now. "Well, your hypothesis was incorrect."

"I see that now." She paused. "And technically, *you* started the riot."

"I thought you were—" He stopped, a chill racing through him. "Pippa, if anything had happened to you . . . You could have been killed," he thundered, his muscles trembling under the strain of his worry and his desire to do something—to return to the fray and fight until the fear was gone, until she was safe.

"I was with Temple," she whispered.

"Temple isn't enough. Temple cannot keep you safe," he said into her hair, letting himself feel gratitude that he'd found her before all this happened, before Knight or half a dozen other nefarious characters discovered her. "Temple doesn't love you," he said.

She stilled beneath him, raising one hand to his cheek. "And you do?"

He wouldn't say it. Shouldn't even think it. It would only make things worse. Worse than being trapped in the middle of a riot, alone, beneath a hazard table for God knew how long with the most irresistible woman in Britain. In Europe. On Earth.

Yes. Yes, I love you. Yes, I want you.

"You are a troublesome woman."

When he opened his eyes, she was beaming at him. "I always have been."

Before he could reply, Maggie fell to her knees several yards away, pushed over by what looked like another battalion of gamblers. She caught herself on her hands and Pippa gasped, and Cross hesitated, knowing he should go to the other woman and protect her, but not wanting to leave Pippa here. "She'll be trampled!" she cried, and Cross had just started to move when another came to Maggie's aid, strong arms sheltering her as the gentleman helped her to safety beneath a nearby table.

It was Castleton.

Cross raised a brow. "It looks as though your fiancé is more than any of us imagined."

Pippa smiled at the other man, sending Cross's gut twisting unpleasantly. "He's a good man."

I'm better.

How he wanted to say it, but it was false.

He wasn't better, and now Castleton was proving it with his heroics.

She would be safe with him.

Pippa turned blue eyes on him. "You kissed her."

"I did."

Her gaze narrowed. "I did not care for that."

"I had to."

She nodded. "I know. But I still did not care for it." And with that, she reached up and kissed him, pressing her soft, pink lips to his, stroking her tongue across his firm bottom lip until he groaned and tilted his head and took control of the caress. One last moment. One last kiss. One last taste of Pippa before he lived out the rest of his days without her.

She pulled away when they were both breathless. "I love you, Jasper," she whispered against his lips, and the words were weapons against his coiled, steeled strength.

"Don't," he whispered. "I'm not for you. My life, my history, my world . . . none of it is for you. Loving me will only get you ruined."

He should have known better than to believe that his impassioned plea would change anything. Instead, his perfect Pippa rolled her eyes, and said, "You idiot man. I'm already ruined. You ruined me for all others that morning in your office. I'm not marrying Castleton; I'm going to marry you."

Yes. Every ounce of him wanted to scream assent.

Every ounce but the shred of decency he found hidden deep in his core. "For a woman with legendary sense, you seem to be struggling not a small amount to come to it. Can you not see that I would make you a terrible husband? Worse than Castleton ever would."

"I don't care," she said, firm and full of those convictions he'd come to adore. "I love you."

He closed his eyes at the words, at the way they rocketed through him, all honesty and promise. And perfection.

"No you don't," he said again, even as a part of him longed to pull her into his arms and reciprocate again and again, over and over, forever. He'd live here, under this hazard table, if he could guarantee she would live here with him.

But look at what he'd done to her.

She was here. In a gaming hell—a lower hell, designed for people and things far more base than anything she'd ever dreamed. He hated that she was here, only slightly less than he hated himself for being the reason she was here. She'd run the tables on one of the longest-standing gaming hells in the city, as though she were born a cheat and a swindler.

And he loved her more for it.

But he'd turned her into this, and she would come to hate it. Hate him for it. And one day she'd realize it, and he would be too far gone in love with her to suffer it. "This is the most dishonest thing you've ever done," he said. "Orchestrating a run on a casino; stealing from a man; causing a riot, for God's sake. You once told me that you did not approve of dishonesty . . . Look at what I've turned you into. Look at how I've ruined you."

"You've done nothing of the sort. You've proven to me that black and white are not the only two options. You've made me realize that there is more than honest and dishonest, than lies and truth. What he's done . . . stealing your life, blackmailing you, forcing you into a future you do not want . . . all that is dishonest. What is honest is that I love you. And that I will do anything to keep you from being forced into a life you will hate. I would do it again and again and again without an ounce of regret. Without a moment of it."

"You don't mean that."

"Stop telling me what I mean!" she said, strong as steel, her hands on his chest. "Stop telling me what is best for me. What will make me happy . . . I know what will make me happy—you. And you come with this life . . . this fascinating, magnificent life. And it will make me happy, Jasper. It will make me happy because it is yours."

"Two weeks ago, you wouldn't have said that. You wouldn't have dreamed of running the tables of a casino. Of falsifying wins. Of ruining a man."

"Two weeks ago I was a different woman," she said. "So simple!"

He'd never once thought her simple.

"And you were a different man," she added.

Truth. She'd made him infinitely better. But he remained infinitely worse than what she deserved. She deserved better than him. So much better.

"No," he lied, wishing he could be away from her. Wishing he were not pressed against her, desperate for her. "I am the same, Pippa. I haven't changed."

Her eyes went wide at the words—at the blow in them— and before he could apologize, he saw the change in them. The way she believed him. His lie. The biggest he'd ever told.

After a long moment, she spoke, the words catching in her throat. "Stealing your life. Forcing you into a future you do not want, that's what I've done, isn't it? That's what I have done to you. What I would be doing if I forced you to marry me? I'm no worse than Knight."

He wanted to tell her the truth—that she'd not stolen his life, but made it infinitely better. That she hadn't forced him into anything except falling for her, a beautiful, brilliant lady. But he knew better. Knew that she deserved someone with more to offer than a gaming hell and a tarnished title. She deserved someone who was right and honorable and who would give her everything she ever wanted. Everything she would ever need.

Everything but love.

No one would ever love her the way he loved her. No one would ever celebrate her the way he celebrated her. No one would ever honor her the way he honored her.

He honored her.

And because of that, he did what he knew was right, instead of the thing he wanted desperately to do.

Instead of grabbing her to him, tossing her over his shoulder, and marching away with her forever . . . he gave her back the life she deserved.

"That's what you've done," he said, the words bitter on his tongue. "I told you once that marriage was not for me. That love was not for me. I don't want it."

Her face fell, and he hated himself for hurting her even as he reminded himself that she was his great work. That this would save her. That this would give her the life she deserved.

It would be the one thing he could be proud of.

Even if it hurt like hell.

"Castleton will marry you tomorrow," he said, perhaps to her . . . perhaps to himself. "He will protect you." His gaze flickered to the earl, trapped beneath a nearby table with Maggie, arms wrapped around her head. "He protected you tonight, did he not?"

She opened her mouth to say something, then stopped and shook her head, sadness in her blue eyes. "I don't want him," she whispered. "I want you."

The confession was raw and ragged and, for a moment, he thought it might wreck him with desire and longing and love. But he had spent six years mastering his desires, six years that served him well as he shook his head and drove the knife home, uncertain of whose heart he pierced.

I love you so much, Pippa.

So very much.

But I am not worthy of you.

You deserve so much more. So much better.

"I am not an option."

She was quiet for a long moment, and tears welled in her beautiful blue eyes—tears that did not fall. Tears she would not let fall.

And then she said precisely what he'd hoped she'd say.

What he'd hoped she wouldn't say.

"So be it."

Chapter Nineteen

Discovery:
Logic does not always rule the day.

The Scientific Journal of Lady Philippa Marbury
April 4, 1831; the morning of her wedding

ᴄross stood at the window of the owners' suite at the Angel the next morning, watching as the maids below extinguished candles across the floor of the casino, casting hell into darkness. He often watched this work, enjoying the organized process, the way the great chandeliers were lowered to the floor, the flames extinguished, and the wax replaced in preparation for the evening's revelry.

There was order to it. Dark followed light inside the hell even as light followed dark in the world beyond. Fundamental truths.

He placed one wide palm against the stained glass, swirling the scotch in the crystal tumbler in his hand. He'd poured the drink an hour earlier, after he'd smuggled Pippa from Knight's and left her in Temple's care, trusting his friend to return her home.

Knowing he would never be able to do the same.

He pressed his forehead to the cool glass, staring down

into the pit, watching as Justin stacked dice in neat rows along the edge of one hazard table.

She'd saved him that evening, a veritable Boadicea, with her sharp mind and her weighted dice—his weighted dice, he imagined—and her stacked decks and magnetic roulette wheel. As though it were a simple piece of scientific research, she'd controlled the pit of Knight's with the ease and comfort of a lifelong gamer.

And she'd done it for him.

She loved him.

Not nearly as much as he loved her, he imagined.

He closed his eyes, and a knock came at the door of the suite. He turned toward the already opening door. Chase stood in the shadowy space, and while Cross couldn't see his partner's eyes, he could sense the censure in them.

"You're an idiot."

He leaned back against the window. "It seems that way. What time is it?"

"Half eight."

She was to marry in less than two hours. Tightness swelled in his chest.

"Temple is returned."

Cross moved toward Chase, unable to stop himself. "Is she—"

"Preparing for a wedding to the wrong groom, I would imagine."

Cross turned away. "She is best with Castleton."

"That's shit, and you know it." When Cross did not reply, Chase continued, "But it's irrelevant. What's relevant is that Lady Philippa earned us a new casino tonight."

There was nothing at all relevant about the casino. Cross cared not a bit about it. Or about the exorbitant sum he'd paid for it. "I had to get her out of there. She could have been hurt. Or worse."

"And so you bought Knight's debts." Chase raised a brow.

"Three hundred thousand pounds seems like a great deal of money to spend on a lower hell . . . and a woman."

He'd have paid five times that. Ten times. "It won't be a lower hell for long. Not in our hands."

"We could always give it to Lady Philippa as a wedding gift," Chase said, casually. "She appears to have a knack for running tables."

The words stung with memory, and Cross turned away, back to the floor of the hell. "That's precisely why she's best with Castleton. I turned her into something dark. Something she will regret."

"The lady does not strike me as one who makes decisions without considering their consequences."

Cross wished Chase would leave him in peace. He tossed back the scotch, finally. "She is precisely that kind of lady."

"And you do not think you would make her happy?"

Her words, spoken over the din of the riot the night before, echoed in his ears. *I know what will make me happy—you.*

It couldn't be true.

He'd never in his life made someone happy.

He'd only ever been a disappointment.

"No."

There was a long pause, long enough for Cross to wonder if Chase had left. When he turned to look, it was to find the founder of the Angel seated in a low chair nearby. "That's why you're an idiot."

"Who's an idiot?" Temple had arrived. *Excellent.*

"Cross," Chase said, cheerfully.

"Damn right he is. After last night, I'm half in love with Pippa myself."

He spun on the other man. "She's Lady Philippa to you, and I'll break any part of you that touches her."

Temple rocked back on his heels. "If you feel that strongly about it, Cross, it strikes me that you *are* an idiot."

"Is she well?"

"She'll be sporting a purple eye . . . not exactly the most fitting of accessories for a bride."

She'd still be beautiful. "I don't mean the eye. I mean . . ." *What did he mean?*

"You mean, did she weep and wail the whole way home?" *Oh God. Had she?* He felt ill.

Temple took pity on him. "No. As a matter of fact, she was grave as granite. Didn't speak at all."

He couldn't have known it, but that was the worst thing Temple could have said. The idea of inquisitive, chatty Pippa without words made Cross ache. "Not at all?" he asked.

Temple met his gaze. "Not a word."

He'd hurt her.

She'd begged him to stay. To love her. To be with her. And he'd refused, knowing he was not for her. Knowing someone else would make her happy. That she would heal. She had to. "She'll heal," he said quietly, as though saying it aloud could make it true.

She would heal, and she would be happy.

And that would be enough for him.

Wouldn't it?

Chase broke the silence. "She may heal . . . but will you?"

Cross snapped his head up, met first Chase's gaze, then Temple's.

And, for the first time in an eternity, he told the truth. "No."

He'd actually thought he could resist her pull. He thought back to that first morning in his office, when they'd discussed the coupled pendula, the steel drops moving away from, then toward each other, ever drawn together.

He wanted her. Forever.

He was already headed for the door.

Chase and Temple watched as Cross left the room, desperation propelling him toward the woman he loved before it was too late.

Chase poured two tumblers of scotch and passed one crystal glass to Temple. "To love?"

Temple considered the door for a long moment, and drank without speaking.

"No toast?"

"Not to love," Temple said wryly. "Women may be warm and welcome . . . but they're not to be trusted."

"Now that you've said it, you know what that means." Temple raised a black row as Chase toasted him with a grin. "You're next."

Cross covered half of London that morning, having left the Angel and gone straight to Dolby House, thinking he could catch Pippa before she left for the ceremony.

Before she made the biggest mistake of his life.

When he'd arrived there, a very stern butler pronounced that the entire family was *not at home.* Not, *celebrating the marriage of the young ladies of the house.* Not even, *at church.* Simply, not at home.

If Cross hadn't been so terrified that he'd missed her, he would have laughed at the ridiculous moment—utterly aristocratic in its understatement. Instead, he'd returned to his curricle with a single goal. Get to the church. Immediately.

Immediately on London mornings was easier spoken than done, and by the time he turned down Piccadilly into what appeared to be a never-ending throng of traffic, he'd had enough. Did no one in this entire town understand that the woman he loved was marrying another?

And so, he did what any self-respecting gentleman would do: he left the damned carriage in the middle of the street and took off at a dead run.

Thank heavens for bipedal locomotion.

Moments later, he turned the corner to the final peal of church bells, signifying the call to service at St. George's.

He tore toward the church, stopping traffic with height and determination, and very likely the fact that few ever raced through Mayfair.

Few ever had anywhere so very important to be.

Few ever had anyone so very important to love.

He climbed the stone steps to the church door two at a time, suddenly quite desperate to be quick about it, in case he missed the bit where he was to *now speak, else hereafter forever hold his peace.*

Not that he would forever hold his peace if he were too late.

Indeed, he wasn't leaving this church until he could forever hold Philippa Marbury—soon to be Philippa Arlesey, Countess Harlow if he had anything to do with it.

His hand came to the steel handle, and with a deep breath, he tugged open the door, unlocking the low drone of a minister.

The wedding had begun.

"Dammit," he said, muscles tensing, ready to carry him straight down the aisle and into Pippa's arms, damn Castleton, damn the congregation, damn the minister if any of them thought to stop him.

"You shouldn't curse in church."

He froze at the words, which came from behind him.

She was several feet away, by one of the great stone columns that marked the exterior gallery of the church.

Not inside.

Not at the altar.

Not marrying Castleton.

The door closed once more, leaving them in the cold, grey quiet, and he couldn't stop himself. He reached out and pulled her to him, lifting her from the ground, holding her close enough to feel the heat of her through a half dozen layers of clothing, close enough to revel in her smell and her shape and the way she gave herself up to him whenever he touched her. And there, on the steps of St. George's, in full view of God and London, he kissed her, loving her little sighs and the flexing of her fingers as she threaded them through his hair and forgot that the entire city could see them.

He broke the kiss before it consumed them both and pulled away, cupping her face in his hands. "I love you." She sucked in a breath at the words, and he ran his thumb gently across the wicked bruise that encircled one of her enormous blue eyes. "My God," he whispered, consumed by emotion, before he repeated, "I love you so much."

She shook her head, tears welling. "You never said it."

"I'm an idiot."

"You are, rather."

He gave a little laugh and kissed her again, softly, lingering on her lips, wishing they were anywhere but here, in about the most public place in Mayfair. "I never believed I was worthy," he said, placing a finger over her lips when she started to speak—to correct him. "I never believed I was worthy of my family . . . of my sister . . . of happiness. And then you came along and made me realize that I am utterly, completely unworthy of you."

She grabbed his finger, pulled it away. "You're wrong."

He smiled. "I'm not. There are a hundred men—many of whom are inside that church right now—who deserve you more. But I don't care. I'm a greedy bastard, and I want you for myself. I can't imagine a life without you and your unsettling logic and your beautiful mind and your terribly named hound."

She smiled at that, and he could breathe again, thinking for a moment that he might win her. That he might succeed. The thought pushed him on. "And I don't care that I'm unworthy of you. Which probably makes me the worst kind of man . . . precisely the kind of man whom you should not marry. But I vow here and now that I will do everything I can to make myself worthy of you. Of your honesty and your kindness and your love."

He paused, and she did not speak . . . staring up at him, eyes enormous behind her spectacles.

His salvation. His hope. His love.

"I need you, Pippa . . ." he said, the words soft and ragged. "I need you to be my Orpheus. I need you to lead me out of Hell."

The tears in her eyes spilled over then, and she threw herself into his embrace. He wrapped her tight in his arms and she whispered in his ear, "Don't you see? I need you, as well. Two weeks, I've struggled under the weight of what you do to me . . . what you make me feel. How you own me, body and soul." She pulled back, meeting his gaze. "I need you, Cross or Jasper or Harlow or whoever you are. I need you to love me."

And he would. Forever.

He kissed her again, filling the caress with everything he felt, with everything he believed, with everything he vowed. When it ended, they were both breathing heavily, and he pressed his forehead to hers once more. "You did not marry him."

"I told you; I couldn't." She paused, then, "What were you going to do?"

He wrapped her in his arms again, caring only for being near her. For keeping her close. "Whatever it took."

"You would have stopped Olivia's wedding?" She sounded shocked.

"Do you think she would have forgiven me?"

She smiled. "Absolutely not."

"Do you think *you* would have forgiven me?"

"Absolutely. But I'd already stopped the wedding." She grimaced toward the door. "There shall be wicked gossip when everyone realizes it . . . but at least Olivia will be a viscountess by then."

He'd repair it. He'd make Tottenham prime minister and Olivia the most powerful woman in England.

And he'd make Pippa a countess for the ages.

"You wouldn't have married him," he said, rocked by gratitude to whatever higher power had brought her to him. Had kept her from marrying the wrong man.

"I told you once that I do not care for dishonesty," she said. "And there is nothing more dishonest, I find, than pledging to love one man when I have given my heart entirely to another."

She loved him.

"It seems impossible," he whispered, "that you might love me."

She came up on her toes and pressed a kiss to the point of his chin. No one had ever kissed him there. No one had ever loved him as she did. "How strange," she said, "as it seems quite impossible that I might *not* love you."

They kissed again, long and lush, until his options were end the caress or throw her down onto the great stone steps of Mayfair's parish church and have his way with her. With regret, he chose the first option, breaking the kiss.

Her eyes remained closed for a long moment, and he stared down at this beautiful, brilliant woman who was to be his forever, quiet satisfaction like he'd never known spreading warm and welcome through him.

"I love you, Philippa Marbury," he whispered.

She sighed and smiled and opened her eyes. "Do you know, I've always heard people say they heard bells ringing when they were very very happy . . . but I've always thought it an aural impossibility. And yet . . . now . . ."

He nodded, loving her thoroughly, his strange, scientific beauty. "I hear them, too." And he kissed her.

The smartest couple in London did hear bells—a happy, cacophonous symphony celebrating the end of the marriage ceremony uniting the new Viscount and Viscountess Tottenham . . . a ceremony both Pippa and Cross seemed to have forgotten.

They were forced to remember, however, when the doors to the church opened, and half the aristocracy poured out into the grey April morning, desperate and finally, *finally* able to gossip about the most important part of the double wedding—one missing bride—only to discover the lady in question was not missing at all. Indeed, she was right outside the church. In the arms of a man to whom she was not affianced.

Ignoring the collective gasp of their audience, Cross kissed the tip of her nose and rectified the situation. Jasper Arlesey, Earl Harlow lowered himself to one knee and—in front of all the world—proposed to his brilliant, bespectacled bluestocking.

Epilogue

If my work has taught me anything, it is this: While a great many curiosities can be explained using thorough scientific research and sound logic, there are a handful of them that resist such easy hypothesis. These mysteries tend to be the most human. The most important.
  Chief among them is love.
  That said, there remain scientific truths . . .

The Scientific Journal of Lady Philippa Marbury
August 10, 1831; four months after her wedding

Cross woke in a lavishly appointed bed, in the town house that had been inhabited by generations of Earls Harlow, already reaching for his wife.

Coming up with nothing but a wide expanse of crisp white linen, he did not hesitate in rolling to his feet, pulling on the silk robe she had gifted him on their wedding night and going in search of her.

He did not have far to travel; when they had taken up residence in the town house, Philippa had summarily chased away the demons that had lurked in its darkest corners, reminding him again and again that he was worthy of her, of their love, of this place, of this *life*.

As part of her exorcism, she'd turned the suite of rooms that had once belonged to Baine into a small indoor garden—a lush, green Eden hidden away in the family's quarters, smelling of soil and sunshine and life.

She was hunched low over her worktable when he entered the room, still wearing her own night rail, hair arranged in a haphazard pile atop her head, surrounded by pink roses. He approached quietly, moving to the sound of pen on paper, noticed only by Trotula, who stood guard over her mistress, long pink tongue lolling happily from the side of her mouth.

He snaked one long arm around his wife's waist and pulled her to him, loving the way her squeak of surprise turned to a sigh when he set his lips to the soft skin of her neck.

"Good morning," she whispered, one hand reaching up, her fingers threading into his hair.

God, he loved her touch. His tongue rewarded it with a little swirl at the place where neck met shoulder, and he smiled against the heat of her, reveling in the fact that her pulse raced for him. Only for him. "Good morning to you, Countess." He looked over her shoulder to the journal on the table, and the pile of correspondence nearby. "You're at work early."

She turned in his arms, lifting her lips to his for a proper kiss, which he was more than happy to give her. After several long, heady caresses, she pulled away with a smile. "I couldn't sleep."

He lifted her to sit on the workbench, sliding one hand along the side of her body, loving the shape of her, luxuriating in the feel of her—in the barely believable fact that she was his. Pressing his forehead to hers, he said, "You know I am always willing to help you with that problem if you care to remain abed."

She laughed, the sound warm and welcome. "Or out of bed, I've noticed."

"I simply attempt to be the best possible research associate," he said, reaching for the hem of her nightgown and sliding one hand around her soft, slim ankle. "What are you working on?"

For a moment, she seemed to have forgotten, and he loved that he had the power to befuddle her quick mind. Loved, too, that instead of thinking too much about the answer to his question, she kissed him. Thoroughly. Until he couldn't think either.

Which was why, when she lifted her head from the kiss, and said, "The roses!" it took him a moment to follow.

She twisted to reach for a discarded piece of paper on the table. "The Royal Horticultural Society has considered my research, and to their knowledge, no one has ever cultivated a new species of rose before. They invite me to attend the meeting of the Society next month to present my work. And they ask that," she read, "I inform them of the name I have selected for the rose at my earliest possible convenience."

She grinned up at him, and he was filled with admiration and pride. "I am in no way surprised, my beautiful scientist. Indeed, I would have expected nothing less." He paused, then added, "But are they aware that you're quite terrible at naming things?" He looked to Trotula, who lay in the shade of a large potted fern.

Pippa laughed. "It's not true!" She followed his gaze to the dog.

"It's most definitely true. Castleton's hound was never so lucky than the day Meghan Knight named her." The evening Pippa ran the tables at Knight's had begun a whirlwind courtship of the Earl of Castleton and his new bride; Knight had earned himself a title even as he'd lost his club.

"Trotula, he maligns you," Pippa said, and the hound's tail set to instant wagging.

Cross looked to the dog. "She could have named you anything. Daisy. Or Antoinette. Or Chrysanthemum."

Pippa cut him a look. "Chrysanthemum?"

He raised a brow. "It's better than Trotula."

"It is not." They smiled, loving each other. Loving the way they matched. "At any rate, I've already named the rose. I thought I'd call it the *Baine*."

He caught his breath at the quiet certainty in the words, at the way she stripped him bare and gave him the most simple, perfect gift she could. "Pippa," he said, shaking his head, "I don't know . . . love . . . I don't know what to say."

She smiled. "You needn't say anything; I think it a fitting memorial to your brother."

It was suddenly difficult to swallow. "I agree."

"And an excellent legacy for our son."

And then it was difficult to breathe. "Our—son?"

She smiled, her hand coming to his, moving it to the soft, perfect swell of her belly. "It could be a daughter . . ." she said, as though they were discussing the weather, "but I like to think he's a son. A handsome, ginger-haired son."

He stared at the spot where he touched her, his hand seeming to belong to another. To two others. It wasn't possible that this was his . . . that she was his . . . that this life was his. He met her gaze. "You're certain?"

She smiled. "There are scientific truths, my lord. One of which is that all that research that we have conducted has a very specific outcome." She leaned in and whispered at his ear, "That is not to say that I have concluded this line of inquiry."

His attention returned to her. "I am happy to hear that."

She hooked her ankle around his thigh, pulling him toward her, and lifting her lips to his. They kissed for a long moment, separating only when they were both breathless. "Are you happy?"

He took her face in his hands and told her the truth. "I have never in my life been happier. I feel as though I've had the greatest run of good luck there ever was."

"I thought you didn't believe in luck?"

He shook his head, "Even *I* am not this good at running

the table." His fingers were at her ankles then, trailing up the soft skin of her calves as she opened to the caress. "Speaking of tables, what do you think will happen if you lie back on this one?"

She chuckled. "I imagine that I shan't finish my letter to the Royal Horticultural Society anytime soon."

"I wouldn't dare disagree," he teased, worrying the lobe of one ear. "You are, after all, one of the great scientific minds of our day."

"It is a complex field of research . . ." She sighed as his fingers trailed higher, along the skin of her inner thighs. " . . . but ever so rewarding."

He kissed her again, long and lush and deep, pushing the linen nightdress high on her thighs and pressing between them, close to her. She gasped as he rocked against her, her hands coming to the sash of his robe, pushing the fabric wide, and finally *finally* touching him.

He let out a long, shuddering breath and met her beautiful blue eyes. "Your touch still devastates me, you know."

She smiled, trailing her hands down his torso, the movement a delicious promise. "Do not worry, my lord, you have years to become accustomed to it. It is entirely possible that someday, you shall take it entirely for granted."

"That will never happen." He captured one hand in his, lifting her perfect fingers to his lips and kissing their tips before laying her back on the table. "But if you like, I am happy to continue to research the theory."

She laughed, her fingers threading through his hair. "In the name of science, of course."

He shook his head. "Hang science," he said, grey eyes flashing with passion and promise and something much much more. "This is for love."

Author's Note

I have done my best to ensure that the science referenced in the book is accurate to scientific knowledge of the pre-Victorians, with one notable exception—Pippa's roses. The first hybrid rose is widely thought to be *La France*, a beautiful pink bloom cultivated from a red rose bush in 1867 by Frenchman Jean-Baptiste Guillot. With apologies to M. Guillot, Pippa is well ahead of her horticultural time; the *Baine* is strikingly similar to *La France*.

If the fall of Knight's seems familiar, it's because Pippa's plan is inspired by a much more modern casino heist—the one in *Ocean's Thirteen*. I would be remiss if I did not thank Danny Ocean, who inspired the Angel and her fallen owners, and the men who brought him (and his crew) to life in both 1960 and 2001, including Lewis Milestone, Frank Sinatra, Stephen Soderbergh, and George Clooney. I like to think that Pippa would have made a great twelfth to the original eleven.

Others I would want as cohorts in a casino heist include Carrie Feron, my brilliant editor (who could easily mastermind the whole thing), the fabulous Tessa Woodward, and the rest of the Avon Books team, including Pam Spengler-

Jaffee, Meredith Burks, Jessie Edwards, Seale Ballenger, Tom Egner, Gail Dubov, Shawn Nicholls, Carla Parker, Brian Grogan, and Sara Schwager. Add to it my agent, Alyssa Eisner-Henkin, and I've got a Cracker Jack team who wouldn't rest until we were safe on an island somewhere, drinking fruity drinks, safe from capture.

Thanks to Sabrina Darby, Sophie Jordan, and Carrie Ryan for early reads, hundreds of texts, hours of phone calls, excellent wine and unwavering friendship. Thanks to Scott Falagan for goose anatomy, to Dr. Dan Medel for long talks about medical history, and to Meghan Tierney for letting me borrow Beavin.

To my family—who try their very best not to get annoyed when I go underground for months at a time to write—thank you for always forgiving my absence. You're my proof that Cross is wrong; there is such a thing as luck.

Eric, thanks for sharing me with Brad and George for all that "research." They've got nothing on you.

And to you, lovely reader, thank you for loving my scoundrels as much as I do; I hope you'll join me for Temple's book, *No Good Duke Goes Unpunished*, later this year.

*G*ive in to your Impulses!

These unforgettable stories only take a second to buy and give you hours of reading pleasure!

Go to ***www.AvonImpulse.com*** and see what we have to offer.

Available wherever e-books are sold.

AVONIMPULSE